JUSTICE DENIED

The United States vs. the People

By Howell Woltz

PROLOGUE

N A S S A U ,   B A H A M A S -
E a r l y   2 0 0 6

Life could not have been on better or more secure footing. Sterling Group, the financial organization my wife and I had worked so hard to build was producing a steady stream of revenue, and two major powerhouses of the industry; UBS's private-banking division out of Geneva and John Deuss's group out of Bermuda had tried to buy us in the past year.

Sitting at my desk, surrounded by accolades from presidents and governors, and other 'evidence' of a life well-lived, I could see a cruise ship being pulled into the harbor through the cut between the Financial Centre and the Straw Market.

Watching the ship and harbor made me think of my own new boat, which had just arrived and cleared Bahamian Customs. The Captive, named after our main business those days, which was establishing private insurance companies for groups of professionals, was going on its maiden voyage that weekend.

I'd invited some friends living in southern France to come over and join us for its first day at sea, and they were arriving that afternoon.

This was to be my last year in the business. Our lease of the ground floor of the British American House was up the following year in August. My wife and I had set that as our date of retirement. We'd already sold our ownership in the bank I'd founded, Sterling Bank Limited in St. Lucia, and had decided to accept an offer for the remaining companies in the Sterling Group.

I was finishing up my Ph.D. in comparative government studies at McHari Institute in Nassau, and planned to write, spend time on The Captive, and enjoy the fruits of a life of hard work with my wife and children.

The next week would be spent in New York celebrating with a dear friend who had retired from the Chicago Mercantile Exchange and was being honored as one of the greatest traders of all time. After that, we had planned a week's vacation at our farm in North Carolina with the family, and then return to Nassau, to wind down operations and hand over the reins to the new owners.

Yes, life was pretty good. In fact, it was like a dream, I suppose.

CHAPTER 1

THE FEDERAL BUREAU
OF INVESTIGATION

April 18th, 2006 7:45 AM Middle District of North Carolina

It was a soggy, foggy morning which was to be wasted in Charlotte, North Carolina over in the Western District meeting with the FBI and a couple of assistant U.S. Attorneys on a suspicious activity report I'd filed on some North Carolina folks, years before, including one of their own kind --- the Honorable Samuel T. Currin, the former U.S. Attorney of Eastern North Carolina --- and two of his clients, the now-famous spammers, Jeremy Jaynes and Bryan Kos.

I'd known Sam since 1971, back when he worked for Senator Jesse Helms, and later as a judge and Chairman of the Republican Party. He'd made a lot of enemies in those days, and it smelled like a politically motivated attack, but I had no way of knowing. All that my report had said was that they would not give us "source of funds" information.

We played by the rules, and the financial authorities where we were licensed required us to have that information available, in the unlikely event that it was needed. All I knew was that Sam and his clients wouldn't give that information after three requests by my staff, and the rules demanded that I file an S.A.R. (Suspicious Activity Report) and ask them to move their business elsewhere, which is what I had done.

Now the Feds wanted to ask me about my report as Chairman of Sterling Trust, against their targets, Sam Currin and his clients.

Glad to do my part. As a licensed financial officer, it was also part of my job to cooperate with the authorities. I hoped that it wasn't just some fishing expedition by the U.S. to create a crime. I had heard of these things happening.

As I sat waiting for the electronic gate to open at the farm so I could be on my way, I began thinking about the FBI. Years ago, I had wanted nothing more, for a while, anyway, than to number amongst their ranks. While most of the boys I knew were thinking Army or fireman, I was thinking pure "feebie".

You see, my great-uncle, Greer Woltz, had been an FBI agent. In fact, he was there even before young J. Edgar Hoover had become its director, and was one of the few "Dickies", as they were called, that J. Edgar retained after he took over the helm.

They were called "Dickies" because of some ridiculous, fake turtleneck *thing* that they all wore under their jackets. It was probably a throwback to the Frenchie, Director Bonaparte, a direct descendant of old Napoleon himself, whom President Teddy Roosevelt had appointed as the original director of his federal bureau of investigation back in 1908.

Now, they're just called "Dicks", but for non-apparel related reasons. But I digress.

So Uncle Greer, the "Dickie", became a "Dick" when J. Edgar took over "the Bureau" (as he always referred to it, in quite reverential tones). Greer traded in his turtleneck for the thin black ties, white shirts, and non-descript dark-grey suits he would wear until he became a dead "Dick" in the 1970's. J. Edgar, or "the Director", as Uncle Greer always called him, did significantly improve the image of the outfit, which was best known for sneaking through Congressmen's mail (Senator Tillman being the first victim for opposing them back in 1908). He also made sure that they were all professionals; every agent had to either have a degree in accounting or law. They also had to be good at going through Congressmen's mail, as well as that of other citizens, but they had to look good doing it.

By Uncle Greer's day, Congress had lightened up on the Bureau, considerably. They'd given old Teddy quite a battle over it back in 1907 when he first brought up the idea because a national police force is patently unconstitutional. It was then, and it still is 100 years later, but Congress doesn't get upset about little things like constitutionality anymore.

Senator Tillman and other constitutional scholars in Congress pointed out to old Teddy, that such was not an allowed duty of the federal government under Section Eight of Article One of the United States Constitution. Further, it is forbidden by the Tenth Amendment, which clearly states that any duties not specifically granted to the federal government in the Constitution are reserved for the states or local people. James Madison was pretty clear on the subject.

But old Teddy "Bull Moose" Roosevelt didn't sweat the small stuff like the United States Constitution, and created "the Bureau" anyway in 1908 using something called an "Executive Order". I say that in quotation marks as my hero (and author of the U.S. Constitution), Mr. Madison, wouldn't have recognized that term either.

You won't find "Executive Order" anywhere in the Constitution, especially in Article Two where the powers of the Executive Branch are granted government by the People. That's actually legislating from the Executive Branch, which is *verboten*, but like I say, they don't sweat the "small stuff" like legality anymore.

We're up to about 13,000 of these illegal "Executive Orders" last I heard, but you won't hear a peep out of Congress about it, because roughly 99.9% of their own legislation is outside the boundaries of federal government's clearly stated purview as well.

You ought to read Section Eight of Article One sometime just for grins. The whole kit and caboodle only has seventeen granted powers at the federal level. Eighteen duties and powers are actually listed, like producing *Letters of Marquis*, and making Treaties with Indians; you know, Major stuff. Number eighteen "duty" just says that they can make laws to carry out the other seventeen.

I mean this is still the ultimate law of the land, but none of these people who swore to uphold the U.S. Constitution seem to have ever even read it. But I digress.

I had grown up hearing Uncle Greer's tales, of chasing old Ma Barker and her boys across the Midwest every Sunday for a few years during church. He and I would sit way in the back of the Fellowship Hall at what was called 'Central Methodist Church in Mt. Airy---because it used to be downtown---and during the arpeggio scores of the undulating sermon when the preacher was on a wind-up, he could whisper to me without hardly anyone knowing that we weren't paying attention. We just had to put things on hold during the quiet moments after the reverend's baritone surf had crashed upon our spiritual shores bringing the seraphim flotsam of the message to the parched sands of our souls. Anyone who has ever heard southern preaching knows exactly what I'm talking about.

But the quiet "valleys" didn't usually last too long and we'd be right back in the chase or behind the woodpile in the shootout while still earning our perfect attendance pins and credit for being in the House of the Lord at the appointed hour---or almost.

The real sanctuary was still under construction back then, and its completion pretty much ended the stories and my interest in becoming the second FBI agent Woltz....another "Dick".

The new sanctuary was huge, but acoustically designed so you could hear a mouse sneeze and all the seats in the long and narrow nave of the church left no back-bench space where we could hide and chat undetected. The ushers were no fools. They'd captured them before we ever got a chance.

So my childhood interest in the unconstitutional "Bureau" had long since faded, but my anticipation of meeting Agent Doug Curran and seeing the changes in "G-Men" from Uncle Greer's day to present was still there.

It wouldn't be long. I was on my way.

As the electronic gate swung open, I expertly nursed the car through the gap with a good inch to spare on either side. The fog was so thick that I couldn't see more than a hundred feet down the road.

Maybe it wasn't a bad morning to waste with these people and do my civic duty after all. My son John and his little Scottish buddy, Stewart Graham, who'd come up from Nassau with us for "Spring Break" wouldn't want to fish in this fog bank anyway.

And I'd be back in no time anyway. It would burn off by noon and we'd be slapping at the pond with our lures by one o'clock. No problem.

CHAPTER 2

THE FBI RUINS MY DAY

But the *feebies* and the U.S. Attorney's Office in the Western District of North Carolina had a slightly different plan for me on that foggy spring morning. It did not include fishing with young John and Stewart.

As I eased past the foxhound kennels, it looked like there was a white SUV parked behind it in the fog and two people - a man and a woman - were sitting inside.

Odd, kind of early for the fox-hunting "Tally-Ho" crowd to whom we'd leased the farm to be stirring about. From what I'd seen, they took their drinking much more seriously than their riding or hunting, which didn't make early mornings their best time of day. In fact, that spring morning, even their foxhounds looked a bit hung-over.

Odder, the SUV pulled in behind me in the fog. Maybe it was a young early "bird" trying to find a worm. If it was young lovers, I'd ruined the moment because the SUV slowly pulled out of the fog behind me.

Nothing like unexpected company to spook a worm!

Oddest, however, was when I topped the hill where our private farm road comes to the state road. It looked like a convention of poorly dressed, scruffy-looking kids and a couple of deputy sheriffs.

It looked like a 'rave' gone bad or something. Good to see the deputies in our neighborhood. It was a rare occurrence.

But as I got closer, I couldn't help but notice that the scruffy-looking kids were all in a fraternity or something. They had bright yellow letters on their parkas.

Whoops. The letters weren't Greek: *FBI*. Nope, don't remember a fraternity at good ole UVA with an 'F' or an 'I' in it.

Definitely was not a 'rave' and for darn sure they were not fraternity brothers. They all had Glock pistols and flack jackets, along with a twitchy sort of "make my day" look about them.

But why would they be here? I was on my way to a meeting with the FBI that had been set up since early March, in Charlotte.

I rolled down my window and was eyeball to eyeball with none other than Agent D. Curran according to his nametag, the same man I was to meet in Charlotte, North Carolina at ten o'clock.

"I'm on my way to meet you, Mr. Curran" I said, "Does this mean there has been a change of plans?"

"We decided to do it a little differently", said young Agent Curran, "Would you step out of the vehicle with your hands up." It was phrased like a question, but certainly didn't sound like one.

With at least seven Glocks, plus whatever the Davie County deputies had in their holsters, all within a few feet of my brain, it seemed like a fine idea to me, question or not.

The next few minutes were pretty much like what you see on TV, so I won't drag it out except to point out how reality is different.

For one, *Miranda rights*, as in <u>Miranda vs. Arizona</u>, "You have the right to remain silent. Anything you say, can and will be (twisted) and used against you in a court of law", and all that. Well, they don't really do that stuff anymore if they ever did. I mean there were nine of them and just one of me. All they had to do is say that they said it and no judge would believe the defendant.

Plus, the judges are all former prosecutors these days anyway, so they gave up on 'truth and justice' a long time ago when they first took that job.

I've yet to meet a single federal defendant who was ever read his rights.

Second, they take this little metal prod and stick it in a small hole in the handcuffs to "set" them at their usually snug position, which I've never seen on TV for some reason.

10

With the brief amenities and chit-chat out of the way, the next step is to stick you in the back seat of a car head-first with your hands cuffed behind you, which is kind of fun if you're into being off-balance and looking less than graceful.

That was after they stripped me of my jacket, wallet, $700 in cash, Swiss Army knife, Blackberry phone, and belt. If you're wondering about the belt, I learned that it was taken from me so I wouldn't hang myself there in the backseat....with my hands cuffed....from a sky-hook....with a beefy, young feebie sitting beside me.

Wish they worried as much about *truth* and *justice*, you know....the little stuff, as they do about keeping you alive so they can torment you.

And then we sat....as all the neighbors drove by gawking at this scene from a B-grade cop show, slowly, rubber-necking to see me in the backseat of the FBI car.

And Uncle Greer would have been truly upset by these young people. Their manners were pretty much like all kids these days, not very good. But old Greer would have had a conniption over the way they were dressed. They looked like anything from college kids in a bar--- a cheap one--- on down to hoboes. No natty, dark suits and ties. That went out the door with Miranda rights and constitutional amendments Four, Five, Six, Eight and Ten, I guess.

When I asked a couple of them whether they were lawyers or accountants, I just got a blank stare. Agent Curran, to his credit, knew what I was talking about and explained that agents were once pre-qualified for the job by having to be one or the other.

The big, goofy-looking one said with a guffaw, "Glad we don't have to do that no more". I wonder if they're required to speak English properly. Guess not.

Agent Curran seemed to be doing it all. He even had to play both "good cop" and "bad cop" while the rest of the kids drank coffee and let their adrenalin dissipate after the dangerous and exciting "capture" of the man who was already en-route to their office anyway.

I'll admit that I was a little bit numb. It was confusing, at best.

I'd volunteered to come and assist them as an officer of a foreign financial firm and from my sense of civic duty, yet here I was sitting in the back of an FBI sedan in handcuffs.

"Good cop", Curran, stuck his head in the cruiser disturbing my reflections to offer, quite kindly, to return my car to the house so it wouldn't be left in the roadway.

How nice. Maybe I had this young man pegged wrong.

"What's the keypad code to the electronic gate?" he queried.

Hmmm. Bells went off. "You can just leave it at the gate," I said.

"Don't you want your wife to know it's there and tell her what has happened so she won't worry?" he said with a very good impression of a sincere person on his face.

Agent Curran handed me my Blackberry, or should I say, put it to my ear, after he dialed my home number.

Ring, ring, my wife's sleepy, "Hello".

"The FBI was waiting at the end of the road for me. They're bringing the car down now," I said.

"Why? What for?" she shrieked.

"I don't have a clue. Just meet them at the gate and get the keys, OK? And let's try to find Doug Hanna and tell him what has happened when you get back to the house."

Doug Hanna was the lawyer from Womble, Carlyle, Sandridge & Rice who was en-route to Charlotte from Raleigh, North Carolina, for the scheduled 'meeting'. We'd uncovered a securities fraud and reported it twice to the Securities and Exchange Commission, who had never responded, so I had called Mr. David Levinson, former lead attorney for the SEC in D.C. to ask what to do.

David said that he had heard that there was an investigation into that same group's activities out of Charlotte, North Carolina being headed up by a young Asst. U.S. Attorney by the name of Matt Martens.

Martens showed no interest either, and wouldn't take my calls, so I had Doug Hanna, who had been retained by our trust firm to sue these people for fraud, to call Martens and offer assistance.

Hanna had reached the boy and set up an appointment for April 11th, then rescheduled for the 18th, as Martens was "so busy".

Screwing the American public is a full-time job.

Agent Curran, who was still playing good cop, said "I'd be happy to take the car down to the house so that she doesn't have to walk up to the gate to get the keys, if you'll just give me the code."

What a nice guy.

But sitting there with my wrists aching behind my back as the steel from the handcuffs cut into them, after being hoodwinked by these guys, I wasn't sure that I wanted this gang of poorly clad goons to all show up on our porch with their semi-automatic Glocks and flack jackets, traumatizing my family.

Plus, the farmhouse didn't have guest parking to accommodate this fleet of government vehicles that had been allocated for the capture of the dangerous outlaw trust officer and economist, Howell Woltz.

"I don't think so, Mr. Curran. After getting a taste of how you folks handle things, I'd rather have you just meet her at the gate."

And meet her he did.

A few minutes later, the storm troopers returned with another captive. Out of the back seat of yet another government sedan emerged my wife, jet-black hair askew, glasses on--- no time to even put in her contacts--- with a jean skirt wrapped around the long T-shirt she had slept in. We were on vacation for crying out loud.

"Good cop", my ass. Bad cop, bad man, doing evil things.

Now my wife can be absolute Hell to live with, I'll be the first to admit it, but nobody can rightly accuse the girl of criminal activity. That's a joke to anyone who has ever known her. Yet there she was in handcuffs too.

She had been "prefect" every year throughout her entire schooling in Trinidad. A prefect is the head student. Best grades, best at everything academic. You know, the one all the rest of us used to love to hate.

And fiercely proud, my girl is…fiercely proud. Even with my bad eyes, I could see the fire raging inside her from her posture and stance.

What were these people doing? Why were they doing it?

When they'd finished debauching her person, and had done the headlong "shove" thing to launch her into the back seat, Agent Curran came back to the car where I was seething on a slow, hot, burn. He had what we in the South call a "shit-eating grin" on his face.

I can't tell you why we call it that. I even doubt that anyone with a mouth full of it would be grinning at all. But if you're from below the Mason-Dixon Line, you know exactly what I'm talking about.

Anyway, what I'm trying to say is that the boy was pleased with himself. He'd almost single-handedly, with the help of just short of a battalion....or a small 'rave'....captured the wild and woolly Woltzes.

"Howell the Horrible" and "Vicious Vernice" were no longer a threat to polite society. They were safely in custody. The world could breathe a little bit easier.

For what, we hadn't a clue (and still don't), but abducted and cuffed, we were.

They hate it when I use words like 'abducted'. Even my own sycophantic "plea merchant" attorneys wig out when I do so and try to correct me.

"No, Howell. Don't say 'abducted', or 'kidnapped'. You'll upset them", as if I could give a hoot at this point. "Say you were 'arrested'." Look up the word, Jack. 'Abducted' has a meaning, for goodness sake. Just because it was your prosecutor buddies that did it doesn't change the meaning of the word. 'Arrested' indicates a process ....due process, in fact. Lying to a grand jury about fabricated charges, and setting up a kidnapping to hold two people as potential witnesses, because you can't do so any other way is *abduction*, plain and simple.

I mentioned to our efficient young 'abductor', Agent Curran, they had just left two unattended little boys asleep in the house who would have no idea what the government (or any other terrorists) might have done with Mommy and Daddy when they woke up.

"That's not my problem", was the reply, which sounded eerily like "I was just following orders", but I didn't point that out just then. He added, "My orders are to get you to arraignment, and that's what I'm concerned with".

I was blown away with that. "You mean leaving two little boys, ages eleven and twelve, alone in a house way out here, after you've taken both their parents without their knowing it is not your responsibility".

No answer. Fish-eyed stare. But slowly, there appeared a tiny spark of humanity that service to the Dark Lord had not quite been able to extinguish.

Kind of like Darth Vader, you know, when he said, "Luke, I am your father". Down under there, way deep, long before he had left the human race to become the prosecutor's "boy". It was there. I could sense it.

"Do you have kids, Mr. Curran?" I asked as calmly as possible.

I can't remember what he answered, but I think it was "Yes". More importantly, however, that tiny little spark flared for a millisecond and he began morphing back into a human being.

I needed to "close" the deal before the brief window of opportunity shut, and asked, "Would you let me call someone to check on them?"

"Who", he blurted out brusquely.

"Our local chief of police, a man named Robert Cook", I replied.

He dialed Robert's home phone number on my Blackberry, and held it to my ear.

"Robert, this is Howell. The FBI has taken me into custody. Vernice also, it appears. I don't know for what or why, but the boys are asleep in the house and won't know what happened to us. I need you to come get them."

"Be right there. Cheri and I are leaving now." No questions. That's the kind of friend he's always been.

With that, the whole fleet of U.S. government cars and two deputy vehicles left the scene of "the takedown", but not before everyone I'd ever known in the region had had at least one chance to drive by and see the circus.

They only thought they knew us all those years. Hah!

And incredibly enough, the tactical team had accomplished this dangerous feat without sustaining a single casualty, and only one 'off-schedule' occurrence.

The 'chick' feebie had to stop and winky-tink at the Seven-Eleven. When a girl's gotta go, a girl's gotta go, you know.

And off to Charlotte, North Carolina to another federal jurisdiction (in violation of the Sixth Amendment) we went, lickety-split.

Wouldn't want to keep the judge waiting, now, would we?

CHAPTER 3

THE ARRAIGNMENT

Other than the unscheduled stop for the female FBI agent to "powder her nose", the trip to Charlotte, North Carolina was without event.

The familiar scenery scrolled by but had a surrealistic look to it that morning. My mind was buzzing with questions.

Why had the U.S. Attorney's office changed the appointment from April 11th to today? What was he "so busy" doing? Convening a grand jury and making up a reason to hold us? Agent Curran had used the term 'arraignment'.

I was familiar enough with the process, having grown up in a law family and having an ex-wife that was a lawyer (now judge), to know something of how it works.

But I also knew that the grand jury was no longer an honest institution as it was at one time in America, whereby citizen-jurors were presented with facts by a neutral party seeking justice.

As incredible as this may sound--- and I swear I'm not making it up--- a potential defendant or target of the federal boys is not even allowed to have an attorney present at a grand jury hearing in America's federal courts today.

The "prosecutor" (U.S. Attorney), which, as an office, was unknown to our forbearers, can and does frequently lie, fabricate evidence, and present staged "witnesses" reciting rehearsed, false testimony, and they do so with impunity. The proceedings are held in secret, unlike the honest and open grand jury of yesteryear, and the transcripts of these kangaroo courts are "sealed" and cannot be seen by the victims of these outrageous and unjust affairs, so there is no one to catch them at their mischief.

It's probably not too hard to pick up what I think of this situation, and apparently, amongst anyone but the prosecutors themselves, I am not alone in my disgust.

A first-year law book I recently read stated that the all-powerful prosecutors had so befouled the beloved institution of the grand jury in America that they could "indict a ham sandwich", as the deck is so stacked in their favor against the citizenry.

Makes you proud to be an American, eh?

The more I cogitated on the situation en-route to Charlotte, it was obvious that this young Asst. U.S. Attorney had indicted two ham sandwiches and we were on our way down there to be his lunch.

We were easy targets. Just how easy and how misguided this blaming or targeting could be is something we had recently learned firsthand from a commodities scam in North Carolina wherein a crooked trading firm by the name of Tech Traders, headed by a guy named Coyt Murray, was over-stating earnings significantly. In fact, there had actually been losses and some of our trust company clients had been the victims. This somehow had resulted in our being targeted by a misguided government agency. A nasty little lawyer woman with the CFTC (Commodity Futures Trading Commission), Elizabeth Streit, whose job was to guard the victims' interests had instead attacked our firm and wasted one year trying to fabricate a case against us rather than going after the criminal trader and accountant that had scammed our clients and other investors.

Turns out we had the money, and that's what sweet 'Libby' Streit was after, as her salary and the CFTC's income are largely derived from fines. As disgusting as that sounds that is how our government now works.

The CFTC describes itself as a "quasi-federal agency", which must be re-authorized by Congress every five or so years. I suppose that's because they aren't listed as a legal duty of the federal government in the Constitution. I checked. They aren't in there.

The CFTC, SEC, even OSHA, are all given "seed" budgets to cover some expenses, but are then fully expected to bring home the bacon. They are now cash cows for the government. The SEC, as example, was given a seed budget in 2003 of a few hundred million, and brought in over a billion in cash. Their budget was almost doubled in 2004, as were their revenue expectations. These are moneymakers.

It is basically just a new form of tax, and these guys make the Sheriff of Nottingham in the tale of Robin Hood look like a light weight, as they scrounge the financial shires, threatening "investigations" unless firms pay fines to them. It's a shakedown, plain and simple.

Anyway, our financial firm and many other investors were snookered, because Tech Trader's financial statements were being independently audited by an outside CPA firm managed by a former state legislator named J. Vernon Abernethy. What we and everyone else did not know was that Coyt Murray was paying J. Vernon bribes, and making him large "loans" to purchase real estate (with our money), in exchange for verifying Tech Traders bogus statements.

As an institution, we relied heavily on this beady-eyed little skunk, just like the other investors, to independently verify the numbers.

But Coyt Murray had lost his shorts in bad trades, and the shifty little accountant, Abernethy, had lost his in a divorce, and so they were both broke. Libby Streit knew that there were no fines to be had from the real bad guys, so she decided to try to make some.

Our firm, thanks to fraud by both of these crooks, was unknow-ingly the largest victim with double-digit millions in the trading portfolio, which turned out to be nothing more than a Ponzi scheme.

If you don't know what a Ponzi scheme is, it's something like Social Security.

But Libby needed bucks, so she targeted the victims, and actually made the statement to a federal magistrate judge (according to our attorney), in defense of her unwarranted attack, "Well, these people are operating offshore, your Honor. They've got to be up to something."

Marty Russo, our attorney from New York, pointed out how ridiculous such a comment was. I mean, ninety-four percent of the planet's commerce is "offshore", but the court did nothing to rein in the banshee and make her do her duty. They just promised us that she would and denied our intervention. Perhaps they agreed with her condemnation based on geography, who knows.

They really ought to get out more. It's a big world out there and America is the only place where "Enrons", "Worldcoms", and "Tech Traders" seem to occur much less a Bernie Madoff. That's only in America.

It dawned on me that sweet Libby Streit may have slimed her way down from the Windy City and pressed these boys in the U.S. Attorney's office to assist her in her assault. But I couldn't make myself believe that, as we had no part in any crime. Heck, we were the "scammed".

But she had been pretty darn angry when our firm had filed to intervene in the case and told the presiding judge up in Camden, New Jersey that Ms. Streit was not protecting our interests. She had even gone so far as to seize an account worth over one million dollars at GNI, Inc. in Chicago, which was in the name of our trust company, a licensed financial institution, and we weren't even defendants in the case!

Welcome to Nottingham.

The financial officer at GNI, Inc., Tom Duffy, had told me (as a former CFTC officer himself), "She can't do that! It's illegal!"

But do it she did, just out of meanness (and to boost the pot), I suppose. That's just the way government here works now, unfortunately. No regard for the laws they themselves are charged with enforcing. I've seen it now at all levels.

So the wheels were spinning in my head, even with the shock of being in the back of an FBI car, handcuffed, tooling down Interstate 77 South on the way to a federal arraignment on God knows what charges.

Constitutional scholar that I am, however, I knew that there would have to be a bond hearing at which time I would post or personally guarantee an amount, not to be "excessive", and would then be released as the Eighth Amendment required.

I'd then be free to prove whatever they'd concocted was false and prepare for a Public and Speedy Trial as guaranteed by the Sixth Amendment. These were my inviolable rights as an American. Piece of cake, I'm thinking. No doubt about it. We'd be out of there fast, quick and in a hurry. Doug Hanna, the lawyer who should be sitting with the U.S. Attorney at the moment and who had organized the meeting would surely have it all worked out long before we arrived.

God bless James Madison and the U.S. Constitution. I began to relax a bit.

When our entourage reached Charlotte, the turn of events was far less encouraging. In fact, it was pretty darn bleak, to tell it like it was.

Not only was I denied my right to counsel, who was there in the building, I was finger-printed, photographed, checked for scars and tattoos, and then put in a booth and interrogated by some woman from "probation" who said that she was just there to collect information for the court and to "help me".

A little pointer here folks, no one from the federal government is ever there to "help" you, from my own experience, and this large gal was no exception to that hard and fast rule.

She was there to ask questions, get answers, and then apply those answers to questions she'd never asked to make me look like a liar.

Agent Curran had assisted in the set-up as well, by leaving me only one thing in my possession, my Bahamian driver's license, as my only ID.

"But I'm a resident of North Carolina, not The Bahamas" I'd said. "I want my North Carolina driver's license".

"This one is better", is all Agent Curran had to say, and the Lord only knows what happened to my domestic ID.

Curran had apparently been ordered to make me look as "foreign" as possible for some reason, and the marshals who booked me and this plus-sized babe from Probation were to add the trimmings.

"Why?" I wondered. No answer was forthcoming.

After all of that fun, and just when I thought it couldn't get any worse, it did. The next step was to throw me into one of the standing-room only "holding cells" with the prisoners awaiting court.

Fortunately, that group was entranced by a fiery, young man nattily dressed in a dress shirt and black trousers who happened to be representing himself in court. All the others were dressed in these horrible bright orange jumpsuits with MECK CO JAIL in huge letters on the backs of the shirts and down one pant leg.

No doubt those guys were guilty. You could tell by the clothes.

The nattily dressed, young Mr. Howard, his mother, and his brother, had been charged with operating an illegal call-girl service where the debutantes in their employ were slightly under what the government considered to be the age of consent.

He was a pimp. And he was engaged in a boisterous debate with one of the young ladies, who were a couple of cells down the line, presumably where they had put my wife.

I was actually quite grateful to the young man, as he allowed me, the only white guy in the place besides the marshals, to ease over to a section of the "bull-pen", near the open toilet, without getting too much unwanted attention.

It was quite a show, and I learned some words as well as urban terms of endearment, previously unknown to me in the fifty-two years of my sheltered existence.

Ken Howard was certainly exercising his Sixth Amendment right to confront the witnesses against him. He told all of us, his "captive" audience, that he would consider anything under a sentence of sixteen years to be a "victory".

Wow! Murderers don't get sixteen years. What did this guy do?

The entertainment was therapeutic, and kept my mind---and thankfully, everyone else's---off of me.

I heard my wife's voice down the corridor over the din of the prisoners' banter, giving the U.S. Marshall pure Hell as they "processed" her, and could only wonder what these people were doing to us and why. Hoping to awake from the nightmare at some moment and find that it had all been nothing more than a bad dream, I passed the waiting in a state of near shock.

Everything seemed to be in slow motion. The surreal patina still shaded the scene.

After what seemed like hours, our names were called. We were shackled and led away in chains, criminals that we were, and then unshackled, about fifty feet away, in the presence of U.S. Magistrate Judge David W. Keesler, where we could be made to look as guilty as possible for dramatic effect.

My wife was still in her sleeping T-shirt, bra-less and humiliated beyond words. We simply looked at one another, not knowing what to say.

I guess I was just numb. My heart broke to see her like this. But it put a fire in my soul that has yet to be extinguished. How these animals could do this to innocent, or even guilty but un-convicted people, was unfathomable, but they do it every day, at the incredible rate of two hundred and ten, every twenty four hours, Monday through Friday.

The experience in the courtroom was nothing short of outrageous. The attorney that was scheduled to meet me at the U.S. Attorney's office, Doug Hanna, was at the defendant's table. He looked as distraught as I must have by that point. I could only imagine what was going through his mind.

They read off the charges against me and my wife. They were unrecognizable activities; "obstruction of justice", "perjury", "conspiracy to defraud the United States government"!

When in the hell had we done all of that? We'd never been witnesses in a case. Vernice was from Trinidad, for crying out loud, and our business was in The Bahamas. When were we supposed to have done all of this.

But as we would soon learn, little things like guilt and innocence, or even true charges have nothing to do with a federal indictment any longer. The trick for these young AUSAs (Assistant U.S. Attorneys) is to stack up enough charges of any kind so that they can convince the judge to deny bail. It works now in 77.1%[1] of all federal cases. Though you may have thought the Eighth Amendment guaranteed you the right to a reasonable bail (as did James Madison, who wrote the Bill of Rights), you would be wrong in the magical new world of the "Incarceration Nation".

The Feds decided after the little two hundred year experiment of doing it the constitutional way that James Madison really didn't mean that you were actually supposed to be out where you could prepare a case, he meant for you to be in jail where you were helpless.

That certainly works for the Feds. The simply hold you in jail, until you wear out and will plead guilty to anything, just to get some clarity, and get out of the nasty county jails they like to hold un-convicted citizens in now during this excruciating process. 68.5%[1] are never allowed out a day to prepare and are sent straight to prison.

My mind was trying to take it all in that day in the federal court room, and understand the un-understandable. The drifting of thought stopped, when I heard the lawyer, Doug Hanna, all but disavowing us to the court and judge. Looking around wide-eyed, stepping closer and closer to the U.S. Attorney's table, and away from us, the body language was unmistakable.

---

[1] Sourcebook of Criminal Justice Statistics 2004

"Them?"...."I'm not with them". "Well, I sort of represent their trust company on something, but I know nothing of their criminal activities!" He really helped us out. Lawyers, Humph!

Poor lawyer Doug continued babbling at the judge trying to distance himself from us, but finally, seeming satisfied with the light-years he'd put between him and us sat down and shut up.

Judge Keesler read off the charges very sternly and the unbelievably high number of years that would be required to be served under what he referred to as the "sentencing guidelines". According to his little chart, I was facing forty-five years in prison!

My wife's little chart had her at thirty-five years of prison time----all for fabricated charges. We touched each other's fingers under the table and held on for dear life. It is impossible to describe the feeling of facing something such as that when you know in your heart and mind that you have broken no laws and committed none of the "crimes" for which you are charged.

I do remember taking a long look at the two young attorneys the government had fielded against us, however. The one closest to me appeared to be a young kid in his twenties. He had bright orange hair and an expression of pure, unadulterated joy on his face at our misery, I must assume. Another bonus on the way he must be thinking. The other, somewhat older persecutor to his right was a small, thirty-something fellow with a look of smug self-satisfaction on his visage, clearly pleased with how his day was going as well.

I remember looking at them and wondering how anyone could derive such apparent pleasure from destroying people's lives like these two kids were doing to ours. That question has yet to be answered.

They had to know that the charges against us were false and contrived. Hell, they must have been part of their fabrication. How people could do such terrible things and be so gay about it was beyond my comprehension and still is, though I understand their motivation for such evil deeds much better now than I did then. That's how they get ahead in the corrupt organization they serve. I remember thinking that there wasn't any "Department of Justice" in the U.S. Constitution either. These boys were as unconstitutional as the FBI.

"Do you understand the charges against you, Mr. Woltz?" Judge Keesler said, bringing me out of my meditations.

"No sir. I don't understand any of this at all", I said, much to the chagrin of the scared little bunny rabbit with a law degree sitting beside me.

He jumped to explain that this was all just a normal procedure and I should just say, "Yes sir".

But there was nothing "normal" in my mind about being falsely accused of unrecognizable and made-up "crimes", which put me and my wife in prison for the remainder of our natural and productive lives; nothing "normal" about that at all.

I finally yielded, and played the game, as did my wife, and it was over. We had been "arraigned" by the government of the United States of America, the country I had loved.

Looking at the Bill of Indictment was truly distressing, if not frightening.

The United States vs. Howell Woltz

The only way I can describe the Indictment was bizarre. I was being accused of "conspiring" to defraud the United States government, with the Honorable Samuel T. Currin, whom I had reported for possible improper activity, and forced to take his business elsewhere. It seems like they should be giving me a medal rather than indicting me, if Sam had really done wrong.

They also named an attorney from Wilmington, North Carolina, Rick Graves, as a "co-conspirator" in this unrecognizable crime of thought. I'd only met Rick on a couple of occasions and he had referred us a couple of clients over the years. No crime there and we'd turned down the last ones.

I couldn't even imagine how these government boys could have massaged anything I had ever known or done into one of their Kafkaesque "conspiracies" to do anything, much less defraud them. It looked like I was the one suffering the fraud, sitting in a federal courtroom being arraigned on unrecognizable and uncommitted "crimes".

My "overt acts" in the indictment were "taking U.S. Air to Nassau, Bahamas" and attending required trust conferences for my continuing professional education hours (CPE) to maintain my license as a TEP (Trust and Estate Practitioner).

How was I supposed to get to work, swim? My office is on an island in the middle of the ocean for crying out loud. When did going to the office become a criminal act? No "crime" was ever described in those "overt acts" because none had ever occurred and the pettifoggers knew it.

But they hadn't stopped there. They'd added several equally unrecognizable charges, as bargaining chips, I would later learn, having no basis in reality. While the indictment was mostly about Sam Currin, I was also charged with "Obstruction of Justice" for not accepting a deposition subpoena for someone else, which would have voided it under Rule 45 and is not anything even approaching a crime, but doing so may have been. They also had a charge for "perjury" though I'd never testified in a court, and every word I'd said in a civil deposition was absolutely true (until a corrupt CFTC agent, Elizabeth Streit, had redacted the transcript to give it the appearance of untruth, for which she has probably gotten a raise rather than going to jail as she should).

When they had nothing more to redact or falsify, they just plain made them up. There was a charge of "Obstructing Due Administration of Law", but they never said how, and the thing ended with another "Conspiracy to Obstruct", that was redundant and blank. I was later told it was just an "error".

Error! No kidding! The whole damn thing was an ERROR!

Clearly not much thought had gone into it and they had certainly not wasted any fact or truth in it. It was a completely fabricated sham, but I was going to be sitting in jail because of it, that part seemed certain.

What country was this? Had I been gone that long, like old Rip Van Winkle? Did we lose the Cold War to the Communists after all? Hell, the Soviets couldn't have gotten away with nonsense like this.

But there it was, The United States of America v. Howell Woltz, just as bold as brass.

What that Bill of Indictment was saying was that the entire nation was against me. I was to be tried and ruined for uncommitted crimes by my own people if the little boys in suits at the next table had their way.

The process had started. An unstoppable avalanche had begun, which would obliterate our former lives---the lives we were living just hours before that very day---and would never be able to return to again.

CHAPTER 4

THE FIRST NIGHT

My honeymoon with the Feds was something else. It included all the usual elements...trepidation, anticipation, surprise, anxiety, and a good screwing.

Fortunately, the last was figurative and metaphoric in nature, though younger, more timid men are often not so lucky in that regard.

After the arraignment, I was unable to focus enough to even read the thick Bill of Indictment, and just enjoyed the gregarious company in the holding cell while more "justice" was being dispensed by the court on a one by one basis.

Nobody came back happy, and no one got bail. Not a very good sign. I made a mental note to re-read my Constitution and see if perhaps I'd misunderstood the Eighth Amendment.

At long last, the court ran out of "justice" to dispense and called it quits for the day. My new friends and I were chained, handcuffed, and shackled once again for the short ride to the Mecklenburg County Jail in downtown Charlotte, North Carolina.

My earlier confidence in our highly-paid attorney, to have us home in time for dinner was a bit shaken. It was looking more and more like a night or two in the sheriff's custody, as a bond hearing was scheduled for two days hence on April 20th, before the same judge, the Honorable David W. Keesler.

Oh well. That would give us something to talk about at Christmas! My ancestors had arrived in Virginia in 1615, well ahead of the Mayflower, and not a one of them had ever darkened the door of a jail. I was breaking new ground after nearly four hundred years, but they had probably skedaddled across the pond for reasons of injustice or to avoid imprisonment over in Jolly Olde England, any dam way. They'd probably understand wrongful incarceration better than anyone.

Once our felonious company was well-chained, trussed, cuffed, and secured by armed guards, we shuffled our way into elevators and down steps in biting leg cuffs to be piled and packed into a small van. It had been parked out in the hot sun in the middle of the loading dock area of the federal courthouse and must have been one hundred and thirty degrees inside. The officer held me until last, which I greatly appreciated, and silently thanked him for the small kindness.

But as I would soon learn, when you're singled out by a Fed, it's not to receive a "kindness". They've been told to give you special treatment, yes, but not in the "good" direction.

They rolled our last companion out in a wheelchair. He was a young, black man with shoulder-length "dreadlocks" as they call the twisted locks of Rastafarian origin that are so popular on "the street" and in prison today.

Due to a bullet in his spine, put there by his own brother, his bowels were uncontrollable, and the poor fellow had soiled himself. The guards had saved me to put in last beside him, evacuated bowels and all.

They shoved me in and set the young fellow "on" as much as "beside" me, barely on the seat, without control of his legs (in addition to his bowels and bladder) and slammed the van door shut. As best we could, shackled and trussed as we were, we scotched him in place so that he wouldn't fall to the floor. One of the black fellows placed his shoulder to hold him from behind, and I held on to his sleeve from his left, which was all I could grab as my handcuffs were attached to a waist chain.

The chubby officer laughed, pointed at us, and yelled, "Is it warm in there?" He then went to the inside of the glassed-in front and made a show of fanning himself and enjoying the cold stream of air conditioning in his separated section of the vehicle.

The smell was overwhelming and combined with the heat it was all I could do to not retch. But not one of these tough, street-wise guys said a word.

The young man's obvious humiliation at soiling himself, in addition to the intentional effort by the federal officer to degrade and demean us all, left the group silent, yet quietly forged into brothers.

It was clearly "us"....the white guy included....against these cruel and indecent federal officers, and we would quietly suffer the stench and the guards' senseless derision rather than give them the satisfaction of any response or acknowledgment of their inhumane behavior.

My attention was diverted from my own discomfort as I saw them lead my wife in a slow and painful shuffle-step from that place of injustice to a waiting sedan. That was a defining moment for me, watching the mother of my children and partner of eighteen years plod slowly along in leg chains, waist chains and handcuffs in the hot sun, still in the clothes in which she had slept the night before.

The cruel buffoons charged with our safety and care were bragging to my wife's guardians about putting the young crippled man (sitting in his own feces) in our transport in the heat and leaving off the air-conditioning. What a joker. He'd be a real "hit" at the Feds' watering hole tonight telling that one over his Pabst Blue Ribbon.

A welling-up of something close to pure, unadulterated hatred for these people began to form at that moment. The picture of my wife, painfully inching her way across the hot concrete in chains was indelibly imprinted on my brain.

Once mobile, the driver of our van, egged on by the chubby one, rocked us from side to side as he drove, while gunning the engine and riding the brake alternately, in an attempt to throw the young paraplegic into the floor.

They reminded me of the sick little boys one hears of that enjoy pulling the legs off insects and setting animals on fire.

Not a word was spoken by "us" on the way to the jail until arrival.

Checking in at "Mecklenburg Manor" was anything but a streamlined process. There is no express lane.

We were held in even smaller rooms than the courthouse featured, for hours. Benches lined the walls and there was the ubiquitous open toilet in the corner. Every time the jailhouse guard would come to take another one of us to be finger-printed (again), photographed (again), and questioned (again), I'd ask when I would be allowed to see my attorney, who was outside waiting on me. We'd arranged it as I left the court.

After getting no answer the first few tries, I said it more forcefully and stood up while doing so.

Big mistake!

"You'll see him when I'm damn well ready for you to see him. Are you threatening me?" asked the large black officer in question.

"No, I'm not. But he's been waiting for me since nine-thirty this morning and it's now seven P.M. He's just outside there, sir", I said in my most polite and non-smartass tone of voice.

No response, but about forty-five minutes later, he came back in to take me for the next round of torment and I asked...politely... if he had seen the lawyer or had any idea when I could see him.

"He say he have to go. Drivin' back to Raleigh or somewheres", was his response.

The "Raleigh" bit let me know that he had spoken to him, as we were in Charlotte, and Raleigh was hours away. The deputy wouldn't know that he was from there unless he had talked to him. That was good news.

The bad news was that I'd been denied access to counsel, unnecessarily, and had no idea what was going on. I felt better about Doug in a way. He had hung in there for seven or eight hours waiting to see me after the court proceedings, as he'd promised he would, but these people were apparently intent on preventing me from having the benefit of counsel.

Another few hours after being photographed, fingerprinted and so on for the second time of the day, we were put on an elevator, in small groups and taken up a few floors in the jail high-rise.

"Now we're getting somewhere", I said.

"Don't count on it, man. You jes'gettin' started", responded one of my companions. "The long wait is up here".

I assumed he was joking, as the "short" wait had already been five hours, after waiting all afternoon in the holding cells at the courthouse.

But he was not kidding. And it was worse. The size of the rooms got smaller yet again. We were now down to closet-size, with nothing but a toilet and a bench that would hold two---two if they were small--- but four of us were put in there, one big and three averages.

The three desk officers were supposed to be producing plastic ID bracelets, but they rarely moved other than to go to the bathroom or to get something else to eat. In fact, I never saw one of them do a thing.

The four of us took turns on the tiny bench. I got the first fifteen minutes, as I sat down immediately upon entering, and the large, black gentleman with the tattoos on his neck took the next four hours and forty-five minutes. It worked out fine. He was sleepy, and I had some heavy thinking to do. I think better on my feet. I really do.

And in only eight or nine hours, we were "processed", and ready to move on.

We were given our ID bracelets and taken ten at a time to trade our street clothes for those handsome, bright-orange, "I'M GUILTY" suits that I'd been admiring all day (which was "yesterday" by that time of the early morning), over at the courthouse.

We were forced to shower in the presence of a guard, where we were told to lift our scrotum for his inspection, bend over with spread buttocks cheeks and cough. Cavity and inguinal check complete, with a rinse-off, we donned our skimpy jailhouse attire, got a two-inch toothbrush, a tiny tube of toothpaste just a bit larger than a tube of Super-Glue (with about the same taste), and a bar of soap from The Republic of China.

No deodorant. This was a "budget" operation, at least when it came to the prisoners.

Then, off like a herd of turtles we went and were taken up into the higher floors of the massive jail facility to a housing "pod".

A "pod", by the way, for the uninitiated, is a double-decker, completely enclosed housing unit, with forty-eight to fifty-four cells, two TV's, a recreation area about the size of a living room----a small one----and stainless steel dining tables with fixed metal stools.

We were given a small sleeping "mat", two tiny pieces of fabric, which I was told were sheets, and another piece of fabric about the size of a face cloth that was to be my towel for the foreseeable future.

She....yes, the jail guard was a she... was a chunky, black woman with breasts that reminded me of the bumper guards on an old DeSoto automobile. Her hair was pulled back so tight that her eyes looked Oriental.

I asked where the pillows were, after she called out our cell numbers. She just stared at me. The other prisoners laughed, so I laughed too. I was a real hoot and didn't even know it.

One of them, who had figured out by now that I didn't have a clue, told me quietly, "Roll up your pants, and use that as a pillow." Good tip.

By then it was after one A.M., and I'd done enough thinking on my feet for one day.

Miss DeSoto(s) had assigned me to a cell on the upper deck and took great pleasure in slamming the large steel door shut behind me the second I cleared the threshold. It makes a chilling sound; I can tell you if you've never heard it yourself.

I felt a frisson go up my spine.

I'd never seen so many people in one day that took such great pleasure in their work.

My eyes were killing me, as I had "one week" disposable contact lenses in that were already three days old when I'd put them in the day before, and a cheap pair of "readers" I'd kept on so I didn't have them taken away. Without both of them, I couldn't see my hands in front of my face.

The contacts were +2.0, which were great for distance vision when I was driving, or to keep me from running into walls, and the readers were also +2.0. Together, I had +4.0, which was necessary for me to be able to see something up close. I'm blind as a bat.

I'd nabbed a small, plastic pill cup off the counter while the she-guard was feeling us up for contraband - which was ridiculous after a humiliating strip-search and cavity check - but she seemed to enjoy it, and that was to be my contact lens case.

No contact solution, but the previous guest in the miniscule 6' x 9' suite had been something of a pack-rat, and I found a tiny paper package of salt, along with a couple of packs of sugar, mustard, and black pepper in the steel frame when I was making up my....well, I guess it was a sleeping platform, as it certainly didn't qualify for a bed.

I'd just finished making a saline solution for my contacts with the salt packet, removed my "eyes", and put them in the little plastic cup when I heard the keys turn in the lock on the steel door. Turn-down service, perhaps?

Nope. Big Bertha was back.

"Shakedown", she said in a far less harsh tone than before, with an almost Ertha Kitt growl to it. "Put your hands up against the door, and spread your legs."

It hadn't been fifteen minutes since she'd done this to me before. She must really enjoy it, I thought to myself.

Her pat-down on 'round two' was more of a 'rub-down', and when she got to the groin area, she literally grabbed manhood, testicles and all, and whispered, "Looks like I got me a rich, white boy here in my hands".

I said, "Yes, it looks as though you do".

Pretty lame, I know, but it was my first experience at being sexually harassed and "felt-up" by a female prison guard. I had absolutely no idea what Emily Post or Amy Vanderbilt would have recommended as proper etiquette in such a situation. I mean, what do you say to a woman jailer on a power-trip with ready access to a 50,000 volts taser gun and your "manhood" in her hand?

And as the rest of my day had shown already, things could get worse.

She went in and tore up the tiny cot I'd just made up, looking for God knows what, and took the mustard, pepper, and my little lens cup. She threw the liquid into the toilet bowl, contacts and all, just as I was saying, "Don't", but it was too late.

"Those were my contact lenses".

"Oh. Too bad", she said, and put the empty pill cup back on the tiny steel shelf above the toilet. Without further pleasantries or even a good-night kiss after our intimate encounter, she again slammed the steel door with a resounding clang, and was gone.

Not being able to see is a terrible thing, and I think that was just about the last straw in a load of them. It had been a very, very, lousy day.

I sank to the floor by the toilet and put my head on my hand at its rim.

"Please, God. I'm sure all of this is for some purpose, but don't leave me where I can't see. Please."

Perhaps I've been at worse points in my life than sitting on the floor of a nasty jail cell with my head on a prison toilet, praying, but I can't pull it up out of memory right now if there was ever any to beat it. It was a pretty low moment.

As I was wheeling and dealing with the Lord over my eyes, the dead silence of the cell-block was broken by a scream followed by a wailing sound from below. Had Big Bertha squeezed too hard and held on?

"Let me out! I don't belong here! Please!" "Let me out", and so on continued for some time into the night until the wails turned to whimpers and then to silence.

I lay there against the toilet with my eyes closed, vacillating between self-pity over my situation on the one hand and appreciation that I hadn't broken down and been the first to "crack" like the guy downstairs, on the other. I hadn't broken or shed a tear and I promised to myself at that moment that these people would never elicit either response, nor would they break me.

When I opened my eyes some seconds later, I could see 'blurs', which were drops of the homemade saline solution on the toilet seat, including one large, perfectly round one, reflecting in the light. I put the reading glasses on and squinted.

Could it be? When I touched the 'big drop', it stuck to my finger. It was one of my contacts. I immediately put it in my eye and searched the floor, the toilet, and even in the bowl itself for the other one, but to no avail.

One would do. I'd begged the Big Guy to let me see, but I didn't say with how many eyes. Should've been more specific, I guess, but my prayer had been answered nonetheless.

And at that moment, a certain indescribable peace came over me. I knew that I would survive this, no matter what they threw at me. There was some reason that all of this was happening, and I needed to begin looking out for what that reason was rather than focusing on my own misery.

It was freezing in the tiny concrete and steel cell in the short sleeved top and pants jail outfit. I balled up on the mat atop the steel plate, covered myself body and head with the thin blanket, and fell into a deep, but peaceful slumber.

It was chilly without my pants, but they did make a pretty good pillow. The old boy knew what he was talking about.

CHAPTER 5

THE INFAMOUS MECKLENBURG COUNTY JAIL

My sleep was deep but short. Really more of a nap, as a strange sounding "pop, pop, pop" started at some distance but was coming closer and getting louder. When the Gatlin gun sound came closest, I also heard a hiss as the air-lock on the cell door popped and sprang open, automatically.

I had no idea where I was at first, or what that strange noise was, but upon opening my eyes, it was clear that the nightmare of the day before had continued into the new one.

Before I could come to terms with it, however, my new *amour* with the chest-mounted nosecones was screaming for everyone to get down there for "roll call". As hard as I tried to block out her abrasive voice, as she went from cell to cell screaming, in hopes of slipping back into the warm comfort of unreality, it was clear that Ms. Nosecones was having none of that.

My pillow quickly reverted to elastic-waist, orange prison pants once again and found their way onto my body.

"Salt", I told myself. "Salt to make contact lens solution, remember to find salt".

My brain was slowly beginning to function.

She made us all line up in alphabetical order and she started calling the roll as if we were in kindergarten. And then, she immediately called it again as she handed out heavy, molded-plastic trays with skimpy portions of grits, powdered eggs, and two slices of white bread.

"Should I tell her that I prefer whole wheat?" I thought to myself. Probably not!

I sat down at one of the nine steel hexagon tables and just looked at the tray.

An older sort of homeless-looking black man across the table was watching me stare at the unappetizing offering, and said, "Hey man, ain't you hongry?"

I just shook my head and slid the tray across the table to him.

In words that I would now find offensive, and with an attitude that would perturb the "new me", I said, "I'm not going to be in here long enough to get hungry for crap like this".

One of the men seated at the table said in a far kinder tone and gentler demeanor than I deserved, "Man, you best eat. You in Mecklenburg County now with a Fed bracelet on. You ain't goin' nowhere".

In my arrogance and self-assuredness, I decided to let this comment slide without response. This guy apparently knew nothing of the Eighth Amendment to the Constitution and its guarantee of a right to bail. Mr. James Madison, its author, never envisioned an American citizen not getting bail. The point of the Eighth Amendment was simply that it not be "excessive" in amount and must be affordable to the individual defendant and his unique circumstances. That's all.

I'd actually read quite a bit about this during my constitutional studies for something I'd written when I was a columnist years ago. I'd won more than one argument with my attorney buddies who generally thought that they knew everything. In the early years of our nation, there was no such thing as pre-trial detention, no matter how heinous the crime.

Mr. Madison and the other founding fathers (with the possible exception of Alexander Hamilton), would have considered such a thing anathema to a free people and reminiscent of old King George holding his victims and enemies in the Tower of London until they agreed to plead guilty to uncommitted crimes.

But there was little need to waste my constitutional knowledge on these people.

The one that could speak said to the others, "He don't know no better", apparently speaking of me, "He don't even know where the Hell he is yet".

A couple of the non-speakers chuckled at this and shook their heads in silent agreement.

He then said directly to me while looking into my eyes with a calm but piercing stare, "Man, I hate to be the one to have to break it down for you, but you ain't goin' nowhere 'cept prison from here. Feds don't do bond no mo'. You best get that through yo' head and get comf'able, cause dis is yo' new crib".

Though I knew that he was dead wrong, his tone was sincere. I was pretty darn sure that he was telling me without equivocation that bond would be denied me on the morrow and that this cell block was my "home" until I was sent to a prison.

Hmmm...

I remembered the precise wording of the Eighth Amendment. It was unambiguous. "Excessive bail shall not be required, nor cruel and unusual punishment imposed".

James Madison was not a lawyer, so his words were crystal clear and void of duplicity. In fact, in a book I wrote on the subject I said, "It takes a lawyer to misinterpret the U.S. Constitution, and nine of them in black robes to completely ignore it".

"Little Jemma", as George Washington called this tiny 5'4" intellectual giant, did not twist words or obscure meanings.

This brilliant man clearly never contemplated a defendant not being released on bail. He wrote the amendment to protect the People from the government setting an amount that was prohibitively expensive in the individual's particular financial situation.

For lawyers and others who have difficulty in understanding plain language without nuance it may be hard to decipher, but history backs up my take on it in spades.

How? There was not a single "jail" in any of the thirteen colonies back when "Little Jemma" wrote those protections against tyrannical government, so there simply was no place to hold what is now called a "pre-trial detainee". That's how.

Law school and history books on the justice system, such as Popular Justice by Samuel Walker, describe the founding and opening of America's first jail by a committee of Quakers (of which Benjamin Franklin was a member), in 1790, the year before old Ben died.

The Walnut Street Jail opened as an "experiment" in Philadelphia, Pennsylvania well after Mr. Madison had penned the Eighth Amendment, but never held a "pre-trial detainee". It only held convicted felons. Holding a defendant in jail prior to trial would deprive him of his right to prepare his defense. That would have been unconstitutional. It still is.

So I knew for sure that this poor fellow was wrong, but why was he so confident in his words? How come he spoke with such conviction?

By then "breakfast" was over and Miss Maidenform had ordered us back to our cells.

I'd forgotten the damn salt to make lens solution. Oh well.

It was only 4:45 A.M., so returning to my rudely interrupted slumber would be no problem, though the conversation over powdered eggs had been somewhat disconcerting.

But no sooner had I re-entered the comforts of the subconscious than I heard the Gatlin gun staccato sound commence once more and the raised voice of Miss Groin Groper yelling "Shift change! Shift change! Get down here now for shift change!"

As the men slowly began assembling, she assaulted them with continuous instructions, "Shirts tucked into your pants, and get yo' hands out of them. I don't want to see no asses hangin' out of them neither! Anybody that ain't down here in line in two minutes is locked down for the day!"

And so on.

The clock on the wall read 6:30 A.M.

"Didn't we just do this?" I thought to myself.

But I've always been pretty good at lining up alphabetically. In fact, I'm what many would consider a natural at it. Being a "W" helps, I can tell you. I just head to the end of the line and I'm generally in more or less the right place.

But the Crotch Queen wasn't up for taking any chances, so she went slowly down the line, mangling the names of most, and verbally abusing her captives to get even with all of those men who had mistreated her in the past. At long last, satisfied that she had settled a few scores with "man" kind, she retired from this laborious process to her "work station" to await the next shift.

Someone in line said, "Man down", which indicated that the replacement guard was at the "slider", and everyone got deathly quiet.

The heavy glass and steel doors of the "slider" opened and in walked a near carbon-copy of the night guard, with the exception of her hair style. This one had it piled up on top of her head in shiny waves of shellacked locks that wouldn't come loose in a cyclone.

She and the Shakedown Princess swapped a few words and twittered a bit. When they were done with the chit-chat, however, an austere, almost angry look took over the day guard's visage and she began doing the alphabetical "thing" all over again.

I guess that they were so proud of having learned it, that they were just anxious to show off their knowledge at every opportunity.

But this time we were instructed to file by her, show her our "armband" and take a seat at a table for her "Orientation".

Once we were all filed, inspected, seated, and in place, she began reading to us from her notebook in a monotone voice, mumbling and mispronouncing as many words as she got right. It was the longest twenty minutes of my life....to that point, at any rate.

Occasionally, some of the prisoners would begin whispering to one another, I guess to stay awake. She would either threaten to begin her "Orientation" all over again (a clear violation of the "cruel and unusual punishment" clause of the Eighth Amendment), if she couldn't tell who had done it, or she would send the perpetrators to their cells to "lock-down" if she could discern the source(s).

Once she finished, she asked if there were any questions about her "Orientation". No one was stupid enough to ask anything that morning, for which I was grateful.

And again, for the second time in less than three hours, we were locked down. I could return to my sleep, but not for long. The Charlotte-Mecklenburg County Jail, like many others in America today, strives to make and keep its "customers" as off-balance as is humanly possible. Therefore, they make it impossible to sleep for more than four continuous hours.

Sleep deprivation and disruption are powerful tools in any totalitarian or despot's kit. The CIA and other terrorist organizations have used them for years. Now, the County Mounties who hold the Fed's victims for them employ these methods in their subjugation and demeaning process too. That is the paramount goal of "modern" incarceration.

Now I know that sounds a little bitter OK....a "lot" bitter, but it is quite true. "Rehabilitation" and all those touchy-feely 1970's "things" to prepare a prisoner for his or her return to society went out in the 1980's and were officially abandoned by the penal system in the early 1990's. By 1994, it was just a memory.

It's now just human warehousing, which has pushed the numbers of mentally ill prisoners to extraordinary and frightening levels, and has ramped up the rate of recidivism to nearly seventy percent.

The Department of Justice itself has published the results of this bizarre turn away from sanity in public policy and has proven that a person who has spent as little as six months in a U.S. jail or prison is 300% more likely to commit a crime (whether they were guilty or not), than if they had never been in jail before.

They are nothing short of crime schools and social networking sites for future criminal activity.

And the prosecutors love it this way, as they are now compensated in most venues on the number of "convictions" on their scorecard at year-end (rather than "justice" being done), and how many years they cause their targets to be sent away (rather than fair and equitable sentencing to match the offense).

Even worse, perfectly sane individuals that enter this Byzantine and cruel system, which does not even attempt to rehabilitate or assist its victims in improving their chances at productive living, have become production lines themselves for mentally disturbed people and violent persons, who will almost all be returned to society one day.

The tremendous "savings" in education and rehabilitation expenses since 1994 have run up a bill in terms of human damage that may destroy the fabric of our society one day quite soon.

Mental hospitals are no longer where the largest populations of these poor souls can be found. In fact, number one in the entire world is now the Los Angeles County Jail, where roughly 3,300 seriously ill mental patients can be found on any given night scattered without care or caution amongst the other inmates. The taxpayers must love it. The jail spends over ten million dollars a year just in psychiatric medications! The number two and three mental "institutions" on the planet are also U.S. jails....Riker's Island in New York, and Cook County Jail in Chicago, respectively. That's pretty scary.

That bit came from an article by Thomas N. Faust in Corrections Today back in April 2003.

And this "up" and "down" business I was experiencing at the hands of these poorly trained, generally cruel and insensitive minimum-wage sort of folks, with serious mental issues of their own was about to make me crazy too.

And I'd only spent a night there!

By nine A.M., it was "up" again. The "lady" also announced that even though it was only sixty-four degrees Fahrenheit in the place, and we were just a thin piece of poplin away from being naked, we could not use our blankets until that night. I was freezing.

We played alphabetical line-up again at eleven A.M. to get our "lunch", which I gave away again, then locked down again for a few hours, "up" again at two P.M., alphabetical line-up at four P.M. for "dinner", "down" again after that, then "up" again for another alphabetical line-up for yet another shift change at seven P.M.

Wow. No wonder they go crazy. The repetition of useless and irritating rote actions would do it on its own. Glad I was getting out the next day on bond.

But as I spent my last evening in that horrible place, I had to confess to myself that this brief "glimpse" of what these men suffered, had been enlightening. The nonsense I'd seen wasn't "tough on crime", it was a carefully contrived and insensible regimen intended to break down the human spirit. It was sick. And these people hadn't even been convicted of anything, yet they were treated like criminals.

I couldn't wait to be out of there the following morning, back to my life, wife, and family.

Before going to sleep that night, I promised God that I would never forget what I had witnessed in there and would try to do something about it....if He would just let me go home.

But just in case....I'd remembered the salt at dinner. That little disposable contact just might have to last another day or even two – best to be on the safe side.

CHAPTER 6

THE BOND HEARING - PART 1

There are only two good things about a federal court appearance in Charlotte.

One- you don't have to worry about being late for court, because the "Feds" will have you in jail already.

And Two- You won't have to stand in alphabetical order and be treated like a child the first four or five times they do it each day, because you'll be in court, not in one of those horrible "pods" with those nasty guards.

You always have to look on the bright side, you know. Other than that, there's very little good to be said.

On the morning of the bond hearing, my cell door popped open in the early hours. It was April 20th. No Gatlin gun sound. No screaming from the guard. Just a voice over the little speaker in my tiny, concrete palace, "Woltz, you got court this mornin".

"Night court", I thought to myself, as I fumbled for my reading glasses. I needed them to find the little cup with my contact lens. It's Hell being blind, I tell you.

The homemade lens solution was a bit more saline than the store-bought version. "Ouch!" It burned my left eye. I was glad for a moment that I only had one contact left. Once it was in, and the tears from the burning had abated, the +2.0 lens allowed me to see what had been a "blur" before.

The clock down in what the guards called the "Day Room" showed the time as being 3:45 A.M.

"Hmm", I thought. "This judge gets started early".

"Woltz! Hurry it up. Don't want to keep the judge waitin", came over the speaker.

"Yes, dear", I said sarcastically, but quietly, I had thought.

"What was that, Woltz? I don't need no lip off you this mornin'. You got two minutes to get in that slider".

Disheveled and in need of a cup of hot, black coffee, I piled out of the cell in my bright-orange "I'M GUILTY" suit and Chinese thong flip-flops.

When I got downstairs to her work-station, I asked, "Where do I change into my clothes? Here or are they taken over to the courthouse with us?"

She looked at me as if I was from another planet, which is exactly how I felt at the moment, and said, "You in yo' court clothes far as I know".

"I can't go into court looking like this! I look like a.... criminal in this thing!"

"Well you ain't in here for yo' good looks, Woltz. Musta did somethin'. But that ain't my problem. Gettin' yo' butt in that slider over there is."

Conversation over, she pointed toward the "slider", which was an enclosure with one set of doors opening into the cell-block, and another which opened onto the hallway. Further discussion with this gal seemed fruitless.

She caused the inner doors of the "slider" to open, whereupon I entered and joined the other gentlemen ready to celebrate and enjoy their constitutional rights in the American justice system that morning.

After a fairly long wait in the "slider", a guard turned up at the outer door, and slid his ID card down the electronic key-gate. The outer door opened.

All he said was, "Follow me, single-file, right-hand side of the hallway", and off we went toward the elevator.

The same ID card was required there, as well as a key. Quite a bit of security! "I must be with some serious desperadoes" I thought to myself. "I wonder who they killed. How many did they kill?"

But then it occurred to me that I was with them, and other than my traffic ticket for speeding at the age of seventeen, I'd never knowingly broken a law. Heck, even the speeding ticket had been reduced to "improper equipment".

My companions all still looked asleep and not very worried at all. Perhaps these guys knew more about their constitutional rights than the man at breakfast had the day before. Like me, they knew that they were just a small bond deposit away from going home.

Their nonchalance was comforting. I began to relax. We had plenty of time to change into our dress clothes and groom ourselves for our appearances in court. It was quite thoughtful of these people to give us a time-cushion, so we weren't hurried.

It was only a few minutes after four A.M. when we got downstairs to the main floor. Plenty of time, indeed! I could visit with Doug Hanna, and be looking sharp.

I had not been able to call Doug Hanna to confirm anything or find out what was going on as I'd never been allowed to use the phone. The jail is required to give prisoners phone access so they can contact their attorney and family, but the number or"PIN" that I had been issued was invalid, so I'd been unable to reach anyone.

They also tape and eavesdrop on all calls between these un-convicted citizens and their attorneys, families (and anyone else they happen to call), but we'll get to that later.

All I can say is "Welcome to America".

But even without being allowed my phone rights either, I was sure that Doug Hanna must have recovered somewhat from our drubbing on Day One and would have everything smoothed out for my release and trip home today.

But when I got downstairs that morning, instead of a changing room and preparation area, we were packed into an already full holding cell known as the "bull-pen".

More men could have had a seat I suppose, but the benches were strewn with the stretched out, slumbering bodies of the early arrivals. They must have brought down the big ones first. There were some healthy young lads, each displaying considerable artwork on their exposed arms, necks, and even their legs in some cases. I was the only man in the room without a tattoo.

They all looked so peaceful, I decided against waking them to let them know that they were tying up needed seating space by lying down. Standing was good. As already mentioned, I think better on my feet anyway.

About an hour later, the door opened and even those that had appeared to be dead asleep shot up and moved towards it. Something was happening.

Fortunately, I was standing near the entrance and a guard shoved a paper sack into my hands and said, "Hold the bottom. It's wet".

The former sleeping beauties were grabbing bags, and then circling back for another. In jail, it appears, he who hesitates goes hungry. Those in the back of the line began shouting at the guard when he ran out.

He just held up his empty hands and said, "I had one for each of you. If you can't get it, that's your problem."

The sleepers had to sit up to eat, so I grabbed a corner on the benches, and opened up the bag. I was starving. Even powdered eggs would have looked good by Day Three of my adventure.

There were four slices of white bread, compacted to the width of one, and a slimy, plastic, baggie with two slices of mystery meat and two pre-packaged slices of partially-hydrogenated soybean oil squares with yellow dye, made to look like cheese.

The salvation of the meal, however, was the orange---small, but real. There was also a sugary juice drink, which was much to the other gentlemen's liking, and good trading stock. I traded the sandwiches and sugar drink for more oranges. A fruit breakfast; it could be worse.

When the door next opened and the guard came to pick up the trash from our hearty breakfast, I asked him, "When do we change for court? I have a bond hearing this morning and need to get dressed."

He just looked at me, shook his head, and said, "You pretty funny, man", and left.

There I was back to being a stand-up comedian again. If only I could 'get' my own jokes.

"You're in your court clothes", said the only other white guy in the holding cell. "It takes a court order to get these guys to let you wear your own, and that's not happening in Charlotte, North Carolina. These guys want you looking as guilty as possible every time you come into that courtroom."

"That can't be legal", I said, indignantly.

He just shook his head and said, "Man, this is Charlotte, the most corrupt federal jurisdiction in the United States. The 'Law' is the last thing these cats worry about".

I started to ask him if he was kidding, but about forty eyes were on us by then and it had gotten quiet. I would just accept that he was not kidding.

There was a window looking out on the hallway. I stared out it. The clock said it was almost eight A.M. We'd been waiting for almost four hours.

"Don't want to keep the judge waiting, do we?" The judge probably hadn't even gone to bed yet when they got us up.

And I was really upset over the clothes thing. It was just inconceivable to me that the courts and prosecutors were allowed to force un-convicted citizens to wear chains and prison uniforms into such proceedings.

It couldn't help but prejudice all that saw them, including the judge.

While I was still trying to absorb this horrendous fact, the U.S. Marshalls arrived with their leather tool bags full of chains and cuffs.

They brought my wife out of the women's holding cell. She looked as if she had cried all night.

I watched them put a long chain around her waist, leg chains and shackles on her bare ankles, and hook handcuffs through the stout waist-chain so she couldn't move.

The look of defiance mixed with sadness and humility on her face reinforced the anger in my heart at what these vicious and immoral people were doing to us.

I caught her eye, and we just stared at one another through the glass. There were no words....

Once all of us hardened, un-convicted, citizens were rendered unable to even scratch our noses, the orange and red clad chain-gang set out the door to board the transport to the federal courthouse.

Upon arrival, we were brought in through the rear of the building and put into the same holding cells as two days before. We were getting to be regulars.

I'd been unable to speak with my wife. They had told us to stay apart, and when I'd tried to get near her, the guards had intervened.

So, again, we waited and we waited.

The screaming between the cells and the rude, loud, boisterous jail house banter was at its usual fevered pitch that April morning. The juices were flowing.

A marshal came to the cell. "Woltz?"

I was on my feet in a second and at the door, thinking things had all been worked out. As sorry as I was for what all of these poor fellows were being forced to suffer, I was ready to part company with them and get back to my world.

But the euphoria was short-lived. I was only taken across the hallway to the same little room where I been interrogated by the large woman from the Probation Department two days prior.

A somewhat familiar face was on the other side of the heavy glass, but I couldn't tell exactly who he was.

He pointed to the phone. I picked it up.

"Howell? I'm David Freedman, an attorney with Fred Crumpler's office in Winston-Salem. Laurie called and asked me to be here today."

Laurie was my ex-wife (and a judge in Forsyth County, North Carolina). Fred Crumpler had been my fellow pilot friend and hunting buddy for twenty years.

Things just might be looking up.

"I thought you looked familiar. I've seen you at Fred's office when I've been by to visit him".

"Right, I thought you might recognize me. Well, we only have a minute, so I'll tell you about myself. I was recently named the best criminal attorney in North Carolina by the State Bar magazine. Laurie has suggested that your family retain me. Do you have any problem with that?"

"None whatsoever. I'm just glad to have somebody come to get me out of here", I said.

"Well, that's what this morning is all about. How do you plan to plead, guilty or not guilty?"

That threw me a bit. "Not guilty, of course! We didn't do anything! I don't even understand why we're in here!"

"Well they certainly seem to think you did something, but we'll deal with that later. Are you sure you want to plead Not Guilty?"

"Wow", I thought to myself, "How does this guy know what they thought?" I wondered.

Now I was getting concerned. This guy was no Fred Crumpler. He was dry as burnt toast, and a smile would break his face. He also didn't know me like Fred did. He would likely have been as incensed at these ridiculous charges as I was.

I was getting angry. "Damn right I'm pleading Not Guilty. I'm telling you that what they've charged us with is nonsense. I don't even know what they are talking about!"

He gave me one of those "Yeah, that's what they all say" sort of looks and our in-depth discussion of the case, and our preparation for the bond hearing were apparently over.

I could tell because he got up and signed off saying, "I'll see you out there in just a few minutes", and he was out the door.

I was so surprised that I just sat there holding the phone as he walked out. This was not looking good at all.

"Thank goodness 'bond' is an inalienable right", I thought to myself. "If I was counting on this guy to know anything about me or the case, I was up the proverbial "Creek" without a paddle.

Within minutes of being put back in holding, I was called out again, chained up to my teeth, and marched with my similarly clad and restrained wife, fifty feet to the Magistrate's Court.

The ladies' prison tailor had chosen a lovely, deep, blood-red for the female "I'M GUILTY" suits instead of our bright, glow-in-the-dark orange, but other than that, we were a matching pair. Same clothes, same "jewelry", heck, we had the same indictment!

As I entered the courtroom for the second time in my life and that week, I saw my dear mother, brothers, ex-wife the judge, our friend-Robert Cook (the Chief of Police) who had taken care of the little boys when the FBI had abducted us and left them unattended, and others.

This was quite a showing for no notice since I'd never been allowed a single phone call.

We were unchained in front of the judge for maximum effect. We already looked every bit the criminals in our respective bright orange and blood-red prison uniforms. The chains were just topping on the cake.

My poor mother was blinking back tears as she watched this carefully orchestrated spectacle. Our eyes locked, and she mouthed the words, "I love you", from the seats in the gallery, where she sat with my brothers, Jim and Thomas.

And then the "real" show started.

First up was the young prosecutor with orange hair that looked to be about twenty-five years of age. He introduced himself (Asst. US Attorney Kurt Myers) as representing the entire nation against my wife and me.

It was hard to believe that you were all so mad at us at once, and even more difficult to believe that if you were that angry, you'd hired this kid to do your dirty work.

But that was just the beginning of his harangue in <u>United States v. Howell & Vernice Woltz, et al.</u>

I was in shock at what I heard come out of his mouth. I still am.

He began by waving small sheaves of paper around in the air, claiming that they were our extensive criminal records.

"Whoa! We don't have any criminal record!" I blurted out as I came halfway out of my chair.

The "best criminal lawyer in North Carolina" was just going to let it pass. He pulled me back down in my chair and told me not to do that anymore.

"But he's lying!" I said.

But Judge Keesler had caught what I was saying, and seemed far more interested in the truth than my attorney, and certainly, more so than the young man representing the entire USA. He ordered the prosecutor to bring what turned out to be blank pages (except the top one) for him to read for himself

My wife had no record at all of any convictions, and the only one I had was a citation for speeding at the age of seventeen.

"Come on guys. Speeding reduced to improper equipment?" Judge Keesler asked of the government's young guns.

The young fire-engine red prosecutor had just been caught in a boldfaced lie to the court, but they're allowed to do that. He just rolled on as if nothing had happened, unabashed and unashamed of what would have been a crime if I had done so.

And that was just his warm-up.

He told the judge that we were "conspirators" of international note, but with no details. He said we owned financial firms in various countries (which was the only thing he said that was true), and made that sound like criminal activity. He claimed that we had accounts in Bermuda, Switzerland, and places like that....another lie, but it sounded good.

He said that I was buying a jet, which was news to me. Hell, the last time I'd flown a plane was when Freedman's boss, Fred Crumpler, and I were flying his plane back from bird hunting in Cawker City, Kansas. I hadn't been "current" or had a medical in fifteen years or so. But that didn't stop these boys.

Next, we were 'residents of The Bahamas', which was an absolute falsehood, but that's where the FBI agent leaving me with only my Bahamian drivers license came in. "Residency" is a legal status, like someone from Mexico having a "green card". It is also a status I've never enjoyed, and these people knew it, but were trying to paint us as a "flight risk".

To cap off this category of falsehoods, the young representative of the United States government boldly stated that there was no extradition treaty with The Bahamas, which took the cake.

Therefore, when I stole a plane (since I used to be a pilot long ago), and flew us to our place of 'residence' (where we couldn't stay because we weren't 'residents'), then we could not be extradited, because there was no extradition treaty.

The Bahamas' Extradition Treaty with the United States was one of the first acts of Parliament after the new nation became independent of Great Britain back in the 1970's.

Had any of what the young fireball AUSA Meyers said been true, he may have had a point. Had I really been current as a pilot, (and owned an airplane), and really lived in a nearby foreign nation as a legal resident, that really did not have any extradition treaty with the U.S., then I might have been a potential risk, if I had a criminal record or such tendencies in my past.

Having nothing of the kind, they decided to make it up. They lied so boldly and with such audacity that even the judge didn't buy it.

All I could think of at that point, however, was what these young professional prevaricators must have told the grand jury to snooker them into indicting us, if they were lying this openly in front of us! How far had they gone in their "secret" grand jury room? I could only imagine what 'whoppers' they'd told those poor suckers in the seclusion of the kangaroo court where they indict ham sandwiches on a daily basis.

As each of young Kurt Meyers' "windies" were being expostulated, I was punching this Freedman guy and telling him to object.

"That's a lie!" I'd tell him. "Say something!"

"Shh! Not now", was all he would say.

It was obvious he had a great memory, because he wasn't noting any of their statements that were false.

And then for his *coup de grace*, the young cullion prosecutor turned and fired his beady eye on us, pointed his freckled finger and said that my wife and I were a "threat to the community" and while shaking his head and jowls, "DAAANNNGGGEERROUS PEOPLE!!!"

My little West Indian wife looked at me and pointed at us both quizzically, as if to say, "Is he talking about us?"

We were the only people in the courtroom wearing "I'M GUILTY" suits and leg shackles, so all I could do was nod in the affirmative.

But even that wasn't enough for the young man. He ended by claiming that I, your humble reporter of these events, was "an economic threat to the United States of America!" I kid you not. The jerk actually said it!

The whole United States economy quivers at the mention of my name, according to this imaginative young knave.

He even said that I was so powerful, that I had an enormously wealthy "Watchdog" that would sweep out of the sky and whisk me away to a safe haven even if it took a million dollars.

Wow!!!

Throughout all of this the "best criminal attorney in North Carolina" had sat on his ass as if he were glued to the chair. He never raised a single objection, but one. That was in regard to one of their least important lies about our ownership in a bank in St. Lucia. I couldn't get the man out of his seat on the critical stuff.

I was incredulous at what I had just heard. It would be funny if our freedom was not hanging in the balance. All I could do was shake my head. It was bizarre.

But I noticed that Judge Keesler was also shaking his head and had a similar expression on his face. And by Jove, he told them exactly what I'd been thinking too.

He told them that their story was "bizarre", the same word I'd been thinking and ordered us released on an "unsecured" bond!

Victory! In spite of the worthless attorney and lying federal prosecutors, the judge had heard enough to know that their tale was nonsense, and was releasing us without our having to put up a penny.

See? I wasn't wrong about the Constitution!

But before I could finish hugging my wife in celebration, the spalpeen from the U.S. Attorney's office was shouting out to the judge, with a raised arm like a Nazi salute, that the government was appealing his decision to grant bond. He said that we must be held in jail until that time.

"What? How can they do that?" But do it, they did.

Before I could say "Bob's your uncle", marshals were all over us putting on chains once more. They'd never even removed the leg shackles, so it didn't take long.

My mother came up to the "bar" and said, "I still love you".

"You didn't believe any of that did you, Momma?", either came out of my mouth or went through my mind. I really don't know which. I was in shock. But I was glad there for a moment that she couldn't be on the jury!

My heart broke looking back over my shoulder as they dragged me away, seeing my own flesh and blood staring back at me with a collective look of shock, shame, sorrow, and resignation that I must be a crook.

"Yep, we only thought we knew old Howell for the last half-century. It must have been that speeding ticket back in 1971 that started him on his life of crime. He just bloomed late, but it finally manifested itself!"

My wife and I were so blown away by what had just been done to us that we couldn't even speak as we waddled back to the holding cells in chains. If this lawyer had been voted the "best", it was apparent that only prosecutors had been allowed to vote. He'd never get a client he'd treated that way to say he was anything but a shill for the prosecutors.

So much for my beloved Constitution! Our Eighth Amendment right to bail had been violated. The U.S. Attorney's young hit-team had told over seventy lies in less than an hour in an attempt to paint us as a 'danger' to the community and 'flight risk'.

Even with all of that, however, the judge had seen through their ruses and ordered us to be freed.

But these young jackals were relentless. There was something bigger afoot, and I just couldn't figure it out as yet. They had obviously appealed to give themselves time to go find a judge out there somewhere that would do their bidding.

And sure enough, "judge-shopping" was the next crime that young Meyers and Martens would commit.

It only took them a couple of days, and they found their boy.... two federal jurisdictions away.

CHAPTER 7

FIRST WEEKEND IN JAIL

One of the toughest things about the Fed's extra-constitutional way of treating folks these days, is not knowing what is going on, or when anything is going to happen, or what they're going to do to you next.

For those who have never experienced this and think that their lawyer is going to help them with any of this, well, think again.

Lawyers in federal criminal cases are about as useless as breasts on a bull.

You are on your own against the full force and power of the United States government. Your attorney is far more concerned about his relationship with the U.S. Attorney's office than with helping you. The lawyers that are exceptions to this rule could fit into a phone booth in most federal jurisdictions.

Of course, that is why the founding fathers made sure that defendants wouldn't be stuck in a jail where they couldn't prepare a defense; and similarly that's why the Feds have undercut the Constitution and keep you where you can't prepare one or fight them. It is simply impossible to do anything from the inside of a jail and they well know it.

So all you can do is sit and wait.

Back in the "pod", I was greeted by well-deserved and expected ribbing from the other inmates after my cocky attitude on Day One. At breakfast, the old, homeless guy was out of luck. No extra breakfast from me. Powdered eggs and grits were looking better and better with every meal on the county's starvation diet.

My tormentors were still playing games with me on phone access. The PIN access was a fake, and hardly accidental. According to my new friends and advisors in the "pod", that was standard operating procedure when you were a guest of the "Feds".

"They play dirty, man. Feds don't want you talkin' to nobody", I was told, and my experience bore out my new friend's words as being full of wisdom and truth.

It was the weekend, and the "pod" was void of reading material except for Seventh Day Adventist and Nation of Islam tracts, so I walked in circles in the tiny recreation room until the Chinese thong sandals had eaten into the skin on the dorsal side of my feet.

A nice, young, black gentleman by the name of Eugene slowly opened up a conversation during the second hour of my circular trudging around the tiny room.

Eugene was doing inverted push-ups, standing on his hands with combat boots up on the wall. He was doing lots of them, which was a marvel. Little did I expect to be living one of those foreshadowing moments we've all seen or read in books and movies. Eugene, it seems, led me gently – Alice in Wonderland style – into a conversation of brutal honesty and accuracy of predictions that as I look back seems to have been contrived. It was my first taste of reality and honesty since I left my farm some five days before.

"What are you doing in here", he asked. "You don't exactly look like you belong here."

He had nothing of the "street" lingo or dialect in his words and voice. He wore small-lens eye-glasses which gave him the look of a young professional or possibly a professor --- a strong one.

"I don't know", I answered as honestly as I could. "I really don't".

"If that's true, which I don't doubt, then they want something from you", he said casually, between rounds of being upside down. They must want you to testify against somebody else. They've got you in here to squeeze you so you'll do what they tell you to do".

Not really being ready to spill my guts to a stranger quite yet, I shifted the conversation, "How about you? How long have you been here?"

"Nine months".

"Nine months!" I shouted. You've been waiting in here for nine months?! They can't do that!"

Eugene laughed softly, and said, "Many others have been here much longer than I have. You'll realize pretty soon that they do anything that they want these days. These people don't follow any rules. You either do what they want you to do, or you sit in jail until you've had all you can stand."

"There's an old man from the Dominican Republic that they've had in here for several years," Eugene continued. "He won't say what they want him to say, yet they can't take him to trial because they don't have any evidence against him for what they accused him of in the first place."

In my naiveté, I asked, "Why don't they just let him loose and say that they made a mistake then?"

Eugene broke into a pleasant smile and said, "You really are new to all this, aren't you?"

"Yes", I answered, "I guess I am".

"If they let him go after all of this time, he could sue them for false imprisonment, so they've got to just wear him down now until he agrees to plead guilty to something, anything really, so they can justify holding him".

"That's so insidious", was all I could muster in response.

"I've been in here for nine months because I won't plead guilty to something I didn't do and won't lie on the stand for them about people I don't know and things I never saw or knew about. Just trying to wait them out now", he said.

"What could they possibly want from me?" I asked. "I work in the financial industry down in The Bahamas."

Eugene smiled again, "Well, you can bet that they want you to say something about somebody you know or you wouldn't be in here."

"They've got my wife in here too", I said, opening up to this stranger more than I had intended to do.

"Then they really want you to say something and figure they need some leverage on you", he said. "That's pretty common these days. They grab somebody you love and put the pressure on that way. Then they can make you say anything they want, true or not. It works."

"How do they get away with that?" I asked, sounding more like some Pollyanna every minute.

"People don't care what they do to people in here unless they've been in here and experienced it themselves," he said. "Let me ask you. Before a few days ago, did you give a darn whether they treated people in jail fairly or not, or care even a bit about what happened to folks accused of a crime?"

He answered his own question before I could, "Of course not. My guess is that you were a 'Get tough on crime', hard-core Republican until about three days ago", which stung, because it was so near the mark. "Whether the cops and prosecutors followed the law, or respected the rights of defendants, was the last thing on your mind, because you never thought you'd be one of us. Am I close?"

I was silent in acquiescence and thought. The young man before me had just read me like a book, cover to cover.

"But, my wife", I said.

"My guess is they want you to lie if they've got her in here. If all they wanted you to do was tell the truth, they wouldn't need her for leverage. Having you would be enough. They do that to make sure they get what they want. Who are your co-defendants?"

"Co-defendants" I asked. "You mean the other people listed on the indictment?"

"Yes. Those are your co-defendants. Is there anybody they might need you to help them convict?"

"Well, one is an attorney down in Wilmington that sent us a couple of clients, and the other is a former U.S. Attorney and judge from Raleigh", I answered.

Eugene chuckled. "You've got a U.S. Attorney, who was also a judge, and you're wondering what they want with you? Man, he's a trophy to these people. I hate to tell you this, but they'll do anything in the world to keep you on ice until they need you. It makes sense now."

I really didn't like hearing what he was saying, but it did make sense in a perverse sort of way. I said, "I'm beginning to think that too, after talking to you", I said. "We got bond---unsecured, in fact---from Judge Keesler yesterday, but the prosecutors appealed it. I didn't even know that they could do that", I said.

"Like I told you, they do anything they want these days. I'm surprised that Keesler gave you bond, as a matter of fact. Even the judges are scared of them anymore. If they appealed it, then you can bet they're out looking for the right judge now, so they can hold you", he said.

"They can't do that. That's judge-shopping. It's against the law", I said.

Eugene just gave me a look like he felt sorry for me for not having a "clue".

I didn't want to talk about it anymore. It was too depressing on a variety of levels. It was time to change the subject.

"How did you get the combat boots in here?" I asked.

"I clean the place. Medical gave me a shoe pass", he said.

"Can I help you today? I've got to have something to do or I'm going to go crazy in here", I said, wishing I'd left off the last part of the sentence.

We spent the next few hours scrubbing showers, sweeping, mopping, and cleaning the whole place. I enjoyed the work and talking to Eugene. He was a very bright young man, whose passion was art. He showed me some of his work after dinner, and a crowd gathered.

He was very talented.

One of the men was quite upset because it was his son's birthday, and he'd told him that he would get him a card made with his favorite character on it.

Eugene had agreed to make it for him, but the little boy had chosen a cartoon character by the name of Sponge Bob Square Pants. Neither the little boy's father nor Eugene had any idea who this character was or what he looked like.

The poor man was near tears, as he'd promised the boy the card, and he wanted it to be just as the child had requested it.

I sat a table away, observing, and was touched by the scene. Seven black men were huddled together trying to work out what to do about a little boy's birthday card.

He wasn't their child, or even related, but they could relate to the man's emotional turmoil and empathized with him.

Eugene drew a few other characters, but they weren't Sponge Bob Square Pants. None of the group had ever seen the cartoon except one, and he couldn't explain the figure's appearance adequately for Eugene to construct a representative drawing from his words.

The man was so distraught that I really thought that he would cry. The others were tough-looking, street-wise men from the 'hood', but their compassion for this father and their understanding of his dilemma was palpable and engaging.

While the father and his advisors lamented, Eugene was rapidly sketching on his pad. Just when it looked as though disappointment was inevitable, he slid the work over to the father, and tapped him on the shoulder, to draw his attention.

When the father saw the sketch, a broad grin came to his visage and replaced the sad look that had preceded it. "Pooh Bear!" he exclaimed, as everyone "Oohed" and "Aahed" over Eugene's work.

"Every kid likes Pooh Bear", one of the men said.

Eugene had captured the essence of the world's best loved bruin to the "T", walking along with a balloon tied to one hand and a honey-pot held close to his chest with the other.

"Pooh-Bear's always been his favorite. He'll like that just fine, Eugene", the father said, and everyone began to relax. The crisis was over for everyone but the artist....and me.

Eugene had to finish the card, and I had to absorb and integrate what I'd seen.

These tough, mostly young, street fellows walk, talk, and live in a manner intended to be threatening and even menacing. I had always assumed that they were that way because they were just naturally vicious or mean. I was unduly prejudiced, to be honest.

Seeing the episode that had just unfolded before my eyes, however, had given me a glimpse under that rough exterior, and was cause for momentary pause and reassessment.

It dawned on me that their actions and demeanor which were usually so extrovert and violent in appearance (or perception), may actually be necessary to their survival in the hostile environment of the "street", as they called it.

I'd just witnessed a tender moment where the real nature of these fellows had shone through. I would never see these men or any of the street-wise blacks in the same light again.

In their extremely violent world, survival may very well depend on how they're perceived. The menacing behavior they often displayed was actually defensive in nature. "Don't mess with me or you'll regret it", was the message.

The tougher they looked and acted, the less likely they were to be attacked themselves.

It was something of an epiphany for me.

After Eugene's advisors had departed so he could finish his work, I sat down to watch him.

"You've got talent, Eugene," I said to make conversation.

"I hope to get some formal training when I get out of here, and maybe go into commercial art," he said.

"When I get out, would you like for me to send you some art books?" I asked.

He looked up from his work. "'If' you get out. Sorry to be negative, but it sounds like we're in the same boat. If they have your wife as a hostage, you may be in worse shape than me. You might be in here too, and the sooner you start realizing that and getting your mind wrapped around that thought, the better off you'll be."

That was the first time that it had occurred to me that I may actually be denied my right to bail and be stuck in here for years. Not a very comforting thought.

What in the world would I do with myself?

Eugene had already told me the stories about men being lost indefinitely while the endless process of wearing them down dragged on interminably. Not very comforting either.

As if Eugene was reading my mind, he said, "You need to find something you can do to distract you or to keep your mind busy. What do you like to do?"

"Not much that I can do in this place," I responded.

"Start drawing", he said. "It'll keep your mind off of what's happening to you and your wife."

"That little boy would cry if he saw a Pooh Bear I'd drawn, Eugene," I said.

"Well you need to think of something, unless you want to waste your time in front of the TV like most of these guys do," he said.

Very slowly, the reality of my situation was coming clear to me, and it was not good. The cockiness was pretty much gone and was being replaced by a growing 'sick' feeling in my stomach. It was not exactly nausea, but rather a horrible sense of foreboding. Our lives were slipping away from us. Powerful and seemingly unstoppable forces were behind it.

I needed some spiritual solace. This was all getting bigger than I could handle, and my young friend was right. I needed to find something to hang on to. I needed something to focus on to keep my sanity in an insane situation.

Meditation had been a part of my daily routine for years since spending time amongst the Hindus in India back in the 1990's.

I knew that I needed to get focused on looking for the purpose in all of this. There had to be one. And I needed to figure out how to survive it, and not just physically. It was a tough environment, no doubt, and more than a bit disconcerting to be one of the only white guys, and most senior as well.

But I'd lived through nine coups and revolutions in Haiti, been through some things none of these young fellows would believe and lived to tell about it. Plus, I'd seen a different side of these men, and unless something stupid spun out of control, I'd be OK.

The real danger and challenge would be to muster the mental toughness to make it through, and even the toughest of these guys had to be dealing with those issues too.

But the scrubbing and mopping had served two purposes that day. The nasty condition of the facility had been greatly improved by our efforts, and I'd worn myself out physically, so I knew the mind would soon rest and I'd be able to sleep that night.

I washed out the dirty prison uniform in the shower, along with the boxer shorts I'd worn ever since they'd abducted me.

For the sake of my dear mother who will inevitably read these words, let me also state for the record that I washed them every day--my boxers that is. You know how moms are about clean underwear.

Those were the only clothes I had, so I put them back on, wet, to return to my cell.

It was freezing.

"The meditation will have to wait until morning", I said to myself.

I spread out the wet clothes as best I could in the tiny cell in hopes that they would dry by four A.M. I got under the thin blanket, naked and cold, hoping to get warm enough to sleep, and said a little prayer asking for guidance and direction.

CHAPTER 8

ROAD TRIP WITH THE U.S. MARSHALLS

Four a.m. rolled around once again, and the ridiculous ritual of "line up and scream" replayed itself for another day.

The usual powdered eggs and grits were replaced by oatmeal gruel and a single, tiny waffle square.

It was the Sunday special.

Other than minor changes in the starvation diet, one day was already becoming indiscernible from another.

My little routine was falling into place, but that was just in time to be disrupted. Morning meditation had been completed during the early morning lock-down after "breakfast". Next on the new schedule, replacing the hour formerly occupied by "self-pity" was walking briskly in a circle on the minute recreation yard.

I'd only walked long enough for the uniform to more or less dry out from being washed the night before in the shower, when the "CO" (the name the inmates had for the guards) started yelling for me.

"Woltz! Pack your shit and get your ass in the slider. You got five minutes. Marshall's are waitin' downstairs. Don't make 'em come up and get you".

Somebody always seemed to be "waiting" according to these people.

It didn't take long to pack. All I had was a thick indictment of unrecognizable crime, but I had to pack up the fine bedding they'd given me and place it in a plastic bin which had been issued to hold all of my worldly goods.

Everything fit with room to spare. Packed and ready to leave in two minutes. I had three to spare.

Once the guard or "CO" had me in the slider and out of her hair, the rush was apparently over. I stood there with my bin waiting for nearly a half an hour before someone finally came to escort me downstairs.

I had no idea where they were taking me or what they were planning to do with me.

That's the Fed way.

Once downstairs with linen and bin disposed of, I was put in the holding cell again, alone.

Shortly thereafter, I saw my wife pass by with a guard and caught her eye. She shrugged her shoulders as if to say, "I don't know what's happening either."

They put her in a holding cell nearby.

In a surprisingly short amount of time----in Fed time, that is----we were hustled out of the holding cells and told to get out of our "I'M GUILTY" suits and put on our street clothes.

They had been wadded up carefully and thrown into plastic sacks. We were given tiny booths in which to change, and exited in our wrinkled clothes, exchanging glances cautiously, still trying to figure out what they were doing to us now.

An older gentleman with grey hair had come. He was wearing a fishing vest over a knit shirt and khaki pants, and had a short, dark-haired young woman trailing behind him.

Everyone seemed to know the man and like him.

He was U.S. Marshall Jimmy Spivey, the only decent "Fed" I had----or ever was----to meet throughout this ordeal.

He was very polite to my wife----also a first and last----and even through cuffing, chaining, and trussing us up like animals, he did it in a way that treated us in as human a way as such an unnecessarily ruthless and demeaning thing can be done.

Marshall Spivey told us that we were not supposed to sit together or speak to one another, and he did put us in separate seats. B u t en-route, with his music playing in the front, I was able to put my head against the back of my wife's and speak to her from behind.

We asked each other the obvious but unanswerable questions about "Why" this was being done to us. I'd thought of a hundred things I wanted to say to her and ask her about over the past five days, but all I could do at that moment was nuzzle my head into the back of her neck and long, black hair that smelled so familiar, and enjoy the physical contact, head touching head.

We rode in silence up Interstate 85, back to our home jurisdiction, which was the Middle Federal District of North Carolina. I had more or less figured out that they must be going to Greensboro where the U.S. District Court was for our constitutional venue.

We'd never done business in the Western District or lived there, so I knew from my constitutional studies that they had violated the Sixth Amendment "venue" clause by charging us in Charlotte. I was quite sure by then that they were correcting their error by transporting us to the proper venue, which would be the Middle District, for the second hearing.

But we sailed right through Greensboro, after passing within just a few miles of our farm, and continued east toward the coast.

Three and a half hours after we'd left Charlotte, we were pulling into the underground garage of the Wake County Jail in downtown Raleigh--- two federal jurisdictions away. Well, it was the state capitol and certainly the jail conditions and people had to be an improvement over Charlotte/Mecklenburg County.

But it was getting clearer and clearer to us that our U.S. Attorney boys, Martens and Meyers, had gone to a lot of trouble to find a judge that would do whatever they asked.

We had sped right through the Middle District, past all of the Middle District judges, to go right into the very district and courthouse where Samuel T. Currin, my "co-defendant", himself had been the U.S. Attorney!

I tried as hard as I could to think of how this might be "good" for us, but couldn't come up with anything positive. Only negatives came to mind.

Sam had not been well liked in Raleigh. He'd had a lot of enemies. In fact, when he had attempted to get an appointment to the federal bench himself back during the Reagan-Bush days, he had failed, as much by resistance from his own political party, as the other. He'd been passed over.

The federal judges themselves had fought his nomination.

The thought of now going before one of those same judges for an appeal on bond as his "co-defendant", in the notoriously corrupt Eastern District of North Carolina was in itself chilling.

Knowing that my crooked young persecutors from Charlotte had picked a particular judge so far, far away in Sam Currin's old judicial stomping grounds was paralyzing.

If it was a Republican-appointed judge, then there was a very good chance that he was one of the men that had prevented Sam from getting appointed to the bench under the Reagan and Bush I administrations, for it was the judges of his own party that had blocked him. They disliked him intensely.

If it was a Democrat, then they would simply hate him— and us by association. Sam Currin had been Senator Jess Helms' fair-haired boy back in the 1970's and there is nothing an Eastern North Carolina Democrat hates worse than Jesse Helms unless it's a U.S. Attorney who used to work for him.

I had to admire the young prosecutors from Charlotte. What they had done was immoral, unethical, and probably illegal. But by the same token, it was ruthless and brilliant.

They'd put us in a no-win situation. We were far from home and jurisdiction, in a hostile environment for any case having to do with Sam Currin, going in front of a judge that either (a) had kept him off the federal bench because he disliked him, or (b) hated him because he had been Jesse Helms' protégé.

And we had been represented to the court as his close associates and co-defendants by the boys back in Charlotte.

We were so screwed.

Mr. Spivey and his young marshalette un-cuffed us, un-trussed us, and placed us in the custody and care of Wake County's finest.

As seemed to be the ritual in these jails, we were put into holding cells (his and hers, of course) for a long, long time, then stripped again of our street clothes and dignity.

I had to do the scrotum show, and spread my buttocks cheeks (and cough) for Officer Ramos, to make sure that I wasn't packing in some contraband from the Mecklenburg County Jail via means I'm sure you can only imagine.

The only thought more repulsive than the idea of transporting something in such a manner, is the idea of using anything that had been carried there.

I really couldn't believe that anyone would do such a thing, leaving the only other alternative that it was for the guard's pleasure, and to demean the prisoner.

Butt-check complete, I was issued the most god-awful "I'M GUILTY" suit imaginable. Wake County had gone out of its way to assist the corrupt prosecutors and judges down in "good ole boy", Eastern North Carolina to make their victims look as criminal as is humanly possible.

The V-neck tops and elastic-waist pants sported six inch alternating bright-orange and white horizontal stripes.

Put your choice of saint, prophet, or savior in one of these babies and just choose your crime. I swear he'd be found guilty and hung in a week in North Carolina.

I was beginning to see how these people down east had gotten their reputation for judicial chicanery. They didn't take chances. No siree.

Fairness and equity were just quaint, archaic terms that went out the door long ago with "innocent until proven guilty". Make 'em look guilty from the start and hang 'em high!

Can't take a chance on the prison farms running short of free labor, can we?

Another couple of hours after the butt-check and "I'M GUILTY" suits, we were taken to see the "nurse" so she could ask us lots of personal and invasive questions. There was no one else waiting that evening, which was unusual, so we had zipped through in half-time. She ascertained, verbally, that we were healthy enough to survive a couple of days in the High Sheriff's care.

In a record four or five hours, I was "processed" and taken upstairs--- re-chained, of course---just to ride the elevator five floors.

Word must have spread that young Assistant U. S. Attorney Meyers had called us "ddaannnggerroouuss people!" in court up in Charlotte. They certainly weren't taking any chances on the Wiley Woltzes that was for sure.

When the guard and I arrived on the fifth floor, he unchained me and ordered me to "grab a mat" out of a filthy room that was once used to fulfill the legal requirement that inmates be allowed to exercise five times each week. It was now a storage room for mats, "linen", and hygiene items that had been stuffed into little grocery store bags. A soap, toothbrush, toothpaste, towel, and sheets were in the bag. The "mats" were strewn all over the place on the dirty floor. I had my pick.

Sleeping mat and a baggie full of hygiene items in hand, I was ordered to enter what looked like an insane asylum from the outside.

Once inside, it looked, sounded, and smelled like one.

Two of the orange candy-striped inmates were screaming and cursing at each other, ready to fight over one of the two telephones. They ignored the guard's momentary presence, and he ignored the fact that they were ready to kill each other over who was in line to use the phone.

At least sixty men in bright orange and white prison uniforms were screaming, shouting, gambling, cursing, exercising, and sitting. There was not a place to kneel, much less to put down my little sleeping mat.

It was an absolute zoo. Never in my life had I witnessed such a scene.

I turned to ask the guard where I was to sleep, but he'd shot out the door like a rabbit. I was on my own standing there gawking while the mad house went on around me as if I were invisible.

The fifth floor had four "pods", blue, yellow, green, and red. I guess calling them by colors kept the highly qualified staff from needing numbering skills.

In the center of this floor of cuckoos' nests was a round "bubble" as they called it, which was a glassed-in observation center where the jailers slept, ate, and whatever else, behind darkened glass.

From there, they could watch the madness in complete safety.

Standing by the window and sliding door, I could see the similar scenes in the Green pod, which was straight across for the Blue one, and the Red pod, cater-cornered but partially visible around the "bubble".

Only the Yellow pod beside us was occluded from view. It was an unwordly sight like an M.C. Escher "off-kilter" drawing full of lunatic Waldos in stripes.

Turning my attention to the unit that was my temporary home, I was shocked by how small it was. It was a double-decker with one stairway to the upper deck, so crowded with men that it was impassable.

I was counting the number of cells when a young white man came over and said, "You look lost".

"I am", I responded "Where do all of these men sleep? There seem to be at least twice the bodies in here as places for them. I see only twenty-five rooms".

"Twenty-three", he said. "They're superstitious here. No room thirteen anywhere in the building. And there are far more than just twice as many men as rooms. There are about sixty in here so far tonight, and it's still early."

Sure enough, he was not kidding. The room numbers skipped from #12 to #14. At least sixty men were in view.

"I'm Michael Sprackland", he said as he put out his hand. "The only place left to sleep is the balcony upstairs. The floor down here is covered. Come on. I'll get somebody to slide their mats down a little so you can squeeze in".

I looked up around the balcony and sure enough, there were men littered all over the walkway, sitting on their mats, hanging through the guard rail. The scene was like some Hollywood exaggeration in a B-grade late movie where the story took place in a 1930's prison or insane asylum.

But this wasn't a movie. It was so real that it hurt my eyes and ears. It was the most shocking evidence of American government's complete disregard for the human beings it was feeding to the prison industry I'd yet witnessed.

Michael politely asked the men littering the stairway to make way, and I followed him up the metal staircase, trying my best not to bump anyone or hit them accidentally with the mat hanging over my shoulder and start a riot.

The "balcony" nearly encircled the pod, hanging off the wall on the three long sides and near the end, furthest from the stairs, there was a small gap which Michael encouraged the neighbors to widen enough to insert my mat.

When my mat was in place, the entire balcony was encircled with them, and every corner was full. Men were head to head or head to toe all the way around.

The lower floor was even worse, seeing it from above. There was nowhere to walk for the sleeping mats spread all over the floor, and even stuck between the metal tables, which were bolted to the concrete.

But for the brightly colored prison togs and the plastic mats instead of ones made of straw, the scene could have been from a medieval dungeon. I could not believe that what I was seeing and experiencing could possibly be in America.

But it was. I was an un-convicted citizen of the United States of America, detained unconstitutionally and being treated in a manner unworthy of a third-world despot.

It was as real as it got.

Another fight broke out over the phone.

No wonder. The facility had been built for a maximum of twenty-three men and if Michael's count was correct, we were two and a half times that number.

"When you get your mat put down, come on back downstairs if you like," Michael said, "and I'll tell you about this crazy place."

He had that right. It was definitely a crazy place.

"Thanks", I said. "I'll do that".

I picked my way through the bodies and found my way back down to a table where Michael was sitting with others.

A very nice-looking black gentleman asked one of the other men to give me a seat. He did so without question or comment.

"Welcome to the Nut House. I'm Edwin from Angier, North Carolina. Where are you from?"

"The Bahamas according to the Feds", I said, "but I'm originally from North Carolina.

"Bahamas! Damn, man. They're grabbing people from everywhere these days, aren't they?" said Edwin. Michael nodded in agreement.

Edwin was serving an exorbitant sentence, I learned, for a small quantity of crack cocaine, which had been "enhanced", as he called it, due to an old pistol being found by the police up under the clothes dryer in the laundry room, in an illegal search.

That had been several years ago. His wife was now estranged and living with another man. He had lost touch with his children and would be destitute and homeless when the Feds had finished with him.

He had been trying to earn a few dollars extra one Christmas so he could buy the children presents long ago, and the dealer that supplied him the drugs gave him up to get a time cut on his own sentence.

Michael Sprackland was from Fayetteville and had been charged with "conspiracy to launder money", which I couldn't quite understand that night, and still don't "get" as it is simply a bizarre Reagan-era law intended to circumvent due process.

Rather than charging citizens with the actual commission of a crime, (which requires some proof), the Feds now charge them with a "conspiracy" to commit some offense in over ninety percent of federal cases, and can put the person away for more years on this outrageous charge than if they had actually done something.

Michael had been a financial advisor by profession and the government had claimed that some of the funds his clients had him handle were proceeds of crime. By being the manager of those funds, he became a "conspirator" and was facing years and years in federal prison under what he called the "sentencing guidelines", which were unconstitutionally mandated ranges of years Congress ordered the judiciary to apply to certain crimes.

He was the first to explain to me how the system really worked.

"Everybody ends up taking a 'plea', he said, and Edwin nodded in agreement. "If you don't, then these guys will put you away for life. You can't fight them and win. They'll just keep on making up 'conspiracies' and keep making charges against you if you say you're going to trial. Nobody goes to trial any more, because you just can't win against them. I'm telling you the Feds win 95%[2] of the time, whether you're innocent or not doesn't matter. You have to take a plea."

Edwin continued to nod in agreement.

I countered, "But neither my wife nor I have ever knowingly broken a law. We don't even understand what they've made up in the indictment. I can't just say I did something that I didn't do and go to prison for it. That's wrong."

"You're right. It's wrong", Michael readily agreed. "It's not only wrong; it's against everything this country was supposed to be about. But that's the way it is. The sooner you understand that, the better off you'll be. When they come at you with a plea deal, which they will very soon, you'd better listen."

Edwin concurred. "I know it's crazy, but he's telling you the truth."

Michael added, "They'll come at you more than once; usually two or three times. You don't have to take the first deal, but for God's sake, don't just blow them off. Tell them you'll think about it."

"Third visit is about it, though. That's the best deal you're going to get. If you don't take that one, they'll destroy you, whether you did anything or not. These guys don't care about that. It's irrelevant to the Feds. They just want convictions, 'cause that's how they get raises. That's how they get paid," he said.

The conversation overwhelmed me. Pretty much everything I'd ever believed about my country was being challenged through personal experience.

I was locked in a filthy mad house, hearing that I was going to have to confess to uncommitted "crimes and conspiracies", and go to prison for several years....just to avoid the inevitable alternative of being crushed by them and spending the rest of my life there. Several years…or life.

---

[2] excluding dismissals, per the Department of Justice statistics for 2007 actual statistic was 96.3%.

Where is door number three when you need it? Numbers one and two were horrible. You have to lie about being a crook, or be sent away from your family for the rest of your days, just so some arrogant little assistant U.S. Attorney can get a raise?

It looked like old George Orwell had been dead on target with his book, <u>1984</u>. The only thing he got wrong was the year. He was off by about twenty or so. Big Brother had definitely taken over, if what these guys were saying was true, and I fully believed that it was, after my brief taste of what I'd seen from the Ministry of "Justice" so far.

Michael asked, "Who is your judge?"

I replied, "I don't know. We have property and are residents of the Middle District, but for some reason, they actually charged us in Charlotte over in the Western District."

Edwin said, "That's probably because your co-defendants are from there."

"No, that can't be it. One is from Wilmington and the other is from here in Raleigh. If that were the criterion, the case would have been here in the Eastern District", I surmised.

"That doesn't make any sense at all," said Michael. "Something is going on. I've never heard of that."

Not comforting.

I asked who their judges were. Both said, "W. Earl Britt".

Michael knew all about him. He said that Judge Britt was a big Democrat, appointed to the bench by President Jimmy Carter, back in 1980. "Judge Britt has been on the bench here for nearly thirty years", he said.

Thirty years on the bench in "good ole boy", Eastern North Carolina, may not be a good thing. It was also, not very comforting.

I'd been a commissioner under Gov. Jim Martin back in the 1980's and had gotten a good taste of North Carolina politics back then. It was a bare-knuckle, no-holds-barred, dirty, business. I had resigned in disgust before my term ended.

"It would really help if you were a Democrat. That matters down here," Michael said. "It matters to Judge Britt."

Ouch. That was downright discomforting. I'd been a founding member of Ronald Reagan's "Task Force", worked tirelessly in the Republican Revolution, and as recently as 2002, been on President Bush's Presidential Roundtable, and a member of the Senate Selection Committee with Sen. Bill Frist and former party chairman Haley Barbour.

It hadn't been too long since my wife and I were having lunch with Karl Rove at the Mayflower Hotel in Washington.

All I could think of to say was, "It might not be the best for us to have Judge Britt, then."

The young man's knowledge of his judge went way beyond anything that could have been gleaned from simply reading the Raleigh News and Observer or watching WRAL on the TV. Michael knew personal details and habits of the man, which amazed me.

"How did you learn so much about this guy, Michael? You sound like you know him, personally?"

"I ought to," he replied. "I've hung around over at his house all my life. I used to mow his lawn. He's been like a father in a lot of ways."

"How in the world did that happen?" I asked, shocked that a federal judge that familiar with the defendant had not recused himself from the case. That was pushing it, even for Eastern North Carolina.

Michael answered, "Oh, my mother has been his stenographer forever. I've known him all of my life," he said.

"He can't be your judge, Michael," I said. "He'd have to recuse himself for sure if your mother works for him!"

"Well I know that. He's supposed to, I guess, but you know how things work down here. Plus, I don't think he wanted to take a chance on my getting sentenced by one of the other judges. They can all be pretty nasty. He'll be fair with me. The others might not be. He didn't want that to happen."

Just when I thought that I'd heard it all, I learned that I hadn't.

We chatted awhile longer, but the day was catching up with me. The screaming from the crack heads, drunks, and crazies was more than I could yell over any longer.

I bid my two new friends "Good night", and thanked Michael for his kindness in helping me find my own twelve squares of tile on the floor earlier, so I could sleep.

Depression is a great sedative, and the conversation had definitely put me in such a state.

Even with the profanity being screamed back and forth, and the TV blaring at an eardrum-shattering decibel level, I found escape in sleep.

CHAPTER 9

BOND HEARING II

4:40 AM RALEIGH, NC- The Wake County Jail- Monday

"Woltz! W-O-L-T-Z. You've got court. Get moving. The judge is waiting", a guard yelled in the door of the "Blue Pod".

That "somebody is waiting" nonsense must be taught to all of these county jail people, I thought to myself.

It took a minute to realize where I was, geography-wise, at any rate. It was easy to tell that I'd slept on a hard floor. My left leg and arm were both asleep from the nerves and blood-circulation being cut-off from direct contact with the concrete floor all night.

The "zoo" had finally quieted down a few minutes before the guard had yelled to wake me up for the 'waiting' federal judge. The loud and obnoxious tales about "bitches", "'ho's" and violence from the still-high crack heads that had been added to our company during the night had provided constant entertainment until the drugs had begun to wear off and they'd drifted into a stupor, one by one. The last one had been talking to himself, and then quoting rap lyrics, which blessedly wound down to silence.

The Wake County Jail had none of the silly line-ups and "counts" like I'd had to put up with in Charlotte five times a day, but on the other hand, Raleigh was unwatched by guards, and therefore more violent. It was also a twenty four hour....well, twenty three hour party....complete with crack, cocaine, and marijuana. I saw all three being used that night in jail.

There was such unbelievable confusion and over-crowding that the guards didn't want to be in the pods any more than we did, I supposed and would rather allow it, than to come in and try to stop it.

I'd been able to avoid the toilet thus far, other than urinating, as the starvation diet in Charlotte---apparently a state-wide jail tradition---left nothing to eliminate.

Our 'shared' toilet was a hodge-podge of unpleasant sights and smells. There was alcohol-scented vomit, urine where they'd either missed or not even tried to hit the toilet, feces....don't even know 'how' it got where it was....and wads of used toilet paper scattered about all over the floor.

It was a visual, olfactory, and gustatory phenomenon that words cannot adequately describe.

I barely made it through urinating that morning without nausea overcoming me. There was nothing to throw up, I guess. I hadn't seen even a half-full plate of food in a week.

About half an hour later, a guard came back to get me for the 'waiting' judge. He'd assembled a small chain-gang of other un-convicted citizens and had them handcuffed together. I was added to the line-up, cuffed to another man, and we were all marched down to the elevator. We snaked out, as we had snaked in, and were marched down to and put in a holding cell together.

There we waited...and waited.

About seven A.M. or so, the guard brought in small brown bags as they had done in Charlotte. Knowing 'the drill' this time, I body-blocked and shoved my way to get a bag before the thugs got mine.

It was hardly worth the trouble, but every calorie was becoming precious.

Another hour and half, and the marshals showed up to transport the day's victims to the infamous District Courthouse of Eastern North Carolina.

My wife was on the same van, but we were unable to speak. We were placed in holding cells once inside the courthouse.

The crowded, loud, boisterous scene in the Eastern federal 'bull-pens' was a replay of the wild chaos I'd witnessed the week before in the Western court in Charlotte.

They removed the handcuffs but left the leg-irons, as no 'classification' is done anymore. Everyone, regardless of their supposed "crime", is thrown together. Everything from traffic violators on federal roadways, to murderers or terrorists (if there really was such a thing), can all be found ecumenically packed together, convicted and un-convicted, in the bullpens across America.

I guess that they think leaving the legs restrained might prevent a Bruce Lee-type from wreaking havoc. One fellow-prisoner opined that it was to make our "plea-merchants" (the jailhouse term for a defense lawyer), feel better about having sold us out to the prosecutors.

"Between these funky clothes and bein' in chains, we damn sure all look guilty! Makes 'em able to sleep at night after sellin' us down the river, you know," said the wise rural sage.

"That actually makes more sense than my Bruce Lee idea," I thought to myself, though the real answer would obviously be to follow the Constitution and not detain un-convicted citizens. End of problem.

But my wife and I were there for the second chance at our Eighth Amendment right to bail, and would know shortly if U.S. Attorneys Martens and Meyers' little tricks had been successful.

After hearing all that my new friend, Michael, had said the night before, all I was hoping was that the 'boys' had not had W. Earl Britt on their judge-shopping list. My "Mommy" had not been his stenographer, and I did not vote for Jimmy Carter, though in retrospect, with Reagan's "conspiracy laws", I wished that I had at that moment. I wouldn't be sitting there facing contrived and false charges.

'Anybody else but W. Earl', was my mantra that morning. But I had that sick feeling in my stomach, that deadly accurate physical manifestation and harbinger of impending doom, that no matter whom it was we were facing revocation of bond and a 'chosen' judge.

These boys would not have dragged us two federal jurisdictions away, unless they had cooked up a 'sure-thing' with this court, and that was for certain. They weren't taking any chances on our being free to defend ourselves or prove innocence.

By that April morning in Raleigh, it was clear that my "nation of laws" had been replaced by two prosecutors willing to violate any law or principle to keep the incarceration machine filled....and we were next in line.

The blatantly dishonest behavior of these young prosecutors was surprising, and the depths to which the legal profession itself had sunk, especially "criminal" defense lawyers, was also shocking.

I knew that morning that our number was up. The marshals called our names; shackled us at every joint a chain or cuff could be attached, and led us the fifty feet to the court in our orange-striped "I'M GUILTY" suits at a slow pace, as if we were on our way to execution. In a way, we were, as they had already destroyed our former lives just with the outrageous charges that they had filed, and the incarceration, not to mention the compromising of our assets, which left us penniless and dependant on others to hire and pay attorneys.

Upon entering the court, I saw my mother, brothers Jim and Thomas, our chief of police from home, and assorted other friends who had come to testify on our behalf, to insure that our bail was not revoked. Little did I know that not one of them would be allowed to speak.

Doug Hanna, the attorney that had arranged the meeting in Charlotte with the FBI and the U.S. Attorney's office, was there to counter the lie Assistant U.S. Attorney Meyers had told in Charlotte a few days before about no meeting having been scheduled.

They had been desperate to cover up the fact that I had willingly come to assist them in a case, and paint me as a desperado that they had captured. They had already proven that they would do anything, including lying in open court to a federal judge, and now judge-shopping two whole jurisdictions away, to get who they wanted.

But I also thought that maybe I had been too tough on this guy Freedman, as it looked like he had gotten Doug Hanna to come and prove that AUSA Meyers had lied and to show these young prosecutors for what they were. He couldn't be in their pocket, as I'd suspected the week before, if he were willing to do that.

Maybe we were going to be OK after all, I thought.

Another attorney came up and sat with us also. I recognized, but could not place him.

"Hi Howell," the man said as he put out his hand in greeting, "I'm Don Tisdale from Winston-Salem, and I'll be representing your wife."

I had no idea why anyone thought we needed another lawyer. Don had been District Attorney some years before when I'd lived in Winston-Salem and I'd seen him at various functions from time to time.

He had a drinker's face....beet-red at mid-morning, and swollen. Some of the best lawyers I've ever known were drunks, so that didn't bother me, but something about Don did, and I couldn't conjure up the memory of the bad association with that uncomfortable feeling.

Too late, there was nothing that could be done about it anyway. The 'show' was about to start.

Freedman came up and sat beside me at the last moment.

"David," I whispered. "When can we meet so we can plan what we're going to do?"

"Shh! We'll talk later," he said.

"Who's the judge?" I asked.

"Judge Britt," he said, as old W. Earl came out of chambers and climbed the stairs to his massive, elevated bench.

"All rise", cried the U.S. Marshall/bailiff, but my knees had become wobbly at Freedman's answer. Britt?

 "This is not good," I whispered to my wife, who had no idea what I was talking about. I sought out her hand and squeezed it.

 "Who would keep our children? How long would this horrible nightmare last? When would we be home with our kids," I wondered,

David Freedman tugged at the sleeve of my prison suit. Everyone else had already taken a seat while I was lost in deep reflection and worry.

And then it started.

W. Earl was wearing a spiffy little bow-tie, pretty much like the one in his oil portrait, which was hanging over his right shoulder on the massive wooden wall of the courtroom.

He had a high-pitched voice and appearance that reminded me of a character on one of those lawyer shows on TV. He sounded quite cantankerous as well.

Nothing was warm and fuzzy about W. Earl that morning.

He began by admonishing the young government pit bulls against reviewing or revisiting anything they had said in Judge Keesler's court the week before in the Western District where we had been granted bail.

"I've read it all and don't need to hear it again," he said, and then proceeded to allow the government boys to drone on for what seemed like an hour, reviewing and revisiting every single word and more.

They went through the same lies and added some. We were residents of The Bahamas, so we would flee. I was a pilot years ago, so I would just run out and steal a plane somewhere and fly away. There was a rich "Watchdog" with a million dollars to sweep in and protect me at a moment's notice....I really wish that there had been even a speck of truth to that one....and on and on, *ad nauseum*.

And just as before, I punched my plea merchant, David Freedman, the do-nothing lawyer—the "best criminal defense attorney in North Carolina"—and just as before, he refused to raise his gluteus maximus an inch off the chair or challenge a single untruth.

It's little wonder that one in every thirty-one American adults is in the corrections system if David Freedman is considered the "best". I'm still sure that only the prosecutors got to vote.

No anger here. Really! I'm completely over it.

And Judge Britt never interrupted the young government fireball's ranting a single time to remind him that he was doing precisely what he'd warned him not to do.

A horrible thought struck me. W. Earl didn't come off as the kind of guy who would allow some young turk to spout for the better part of an hour after he'd just told him not to. In fact, he wouldn't have tolerated even one minute of it unless the warning had only been for show and all of this was just for the record before he revoked Judge Keesler's order for us to be released.

My wife's new lawyer Tisdale, whom I still couldn't connect with the bad memory or event that his name had sparked was as worthless as Freedman. He didn't make a peep.

All we got to our whispers telling them that every word these guys were burying us with was a lie, was, "Shh, later" or "Not now!" For the record, I'm still waiting for 'now', cause it darn sure never came that day or later.

I could not believe that these two overpaid attorneys (Tisdale also got $35,000 I heard), were going to just sit there and let these young punks hang us like this.

For that kind of money, one would think they'd have spent the weekend with us, learning about the case, or preparing to counter what these professional prevaricators had said the last week.

It was clear that they had done no preparation at all. They couldn't have, because no records existed in the United States, and neither of these high-priced fellows had spent one second discussing our case, charges, business or even the weather with us. This was either a set-up, in which they were participating, or they didn't care or both.

Neither was a pleasant thought.

Doug Hanna's testimony would therefore be our only hope to counteract them. If I had to stand up myself and demand it, I was ready to do so.

I turned around to tell him what I wanted to do, but Doug's seat was empty. He had gone.

"David", I asked in desperation. "Where is Doug Hanna?"

"Your brother Jim had asked him to come, not me. I told him that we didn't need him, and he could go," he said.

"You did what!" I said, losing control. He could testify as to the meeting I voluntarily scheduled with the Feds!

Yep. We were sunk. This guy was worse than no lawyer at all.

The young, red-headed prosecutor finally wound down and ran out of nonsense to spout. W. Earl nodded gravely as if he had just heard Marcus Tullius Cicero give one of his famous orations like *In Toga Candida*, or *De Finibus*.

Now it was our turn. Attack!

But David Freedman did nothing, and said nothing.

The only help I had at either of these bond hearings had been from a pretty, young, Hispanic-looking public defender who apparently had not known that my family had wasted all that money to get the "best", and had actually brought law books with her and was trying to show David the legal argument that could prevent our illegal detention.

He ignored her, and when she wouldn't quit, he blew her off like a fly, and let them sink us without any fight at all.

My family had paid this dolt $35,000 to "go to trial", and David couldn't (or wouldn't) even stand up for me at the bond hearing.

It had gone from dismal to dark.

W. Earl Britt retired to chambers after refusing to hear any of our eight witnesses. When I complained about this, David explained that he wanted no redundancy from Judge Keesler's court.

"But David," I exclaimed, "He just let that lying government jerk go on for a bloody hour spouting the same crap! You're not going to say a word?"

"Shh! Not now."

But it was too late anyway. W. Earl's robe had already disappeared behind the big oak door of his chambers.

Minutes later, he emerged with his well-considered decision, from a balanced hearing of both sides and ordered us held till trial (or till Hell freezes over), whichever came first.

I can't say that I was shocked. The sick feeling in the gut is never wrong. What I couldn't believe, however, was how we'd been harmed as much or more by these ridiculous attorneys of our own sitting idly by, while the prosecutors waxed slanderously on with untruths, than by their words themselves! It was agreement by silence.

The rest of the day was pretty much a blur, with one exception. The "crowd" in the bull-pen had cleared out by the time W. Earl and his *'Hole in the Law'* gang had finished with us and I was put in a cell alone.

I could hear a man in the next cell talking. It was almost a replay of what I'd heard in Charlotte, where a guy named "Bailey" had been explaining the fine art of "snitching" to his "home-boy". Here in Raleigh, the same thing was happening again. This time, another man was explaining "snitching". It was almost verbatim. Apparently, that was how the Feds got all or most of their victims. They would simply get two people to say anything they told them to say, no matter how outrageous, against another person, for a "time-cut". It was horrible.

It was reminiscent of the Roman historian, Tacitus, who wrote in his *Annals* about the closing years of the reign of Tiberius Alexander, who ruled over Judea and Palestine during the time of Jesus' crucifixion:

"Among the calamities of that black period the most trying grievance was the degenerate spirit, with which the first men in the senate submitted to the drudgery of becoming common informers; some without a blush, in the face of day; and others by clandestine artifices. The contagion was epidemic. Near relations, aliens in blood, friends and strangers, known and unknown were, without distinction, all involved in one common danger. The fact recently committed, and the tale revived, were equally destructive. Words alone were sufficient…Informers struggled, as it were in a race, who should be the first to ruin his man; some to secure themselves; the greater part infected by the general corruption of the times."

Tacitus could have as easily been describing the corruption and ruinous atmosphere, not only encouraged, but demanded by the "justice" department and its prosecutors today. The courts hand out decades of "time" like candy. The only way to get these horrifying and unjust sentences for minor offenses reduced was to hand the corrupt prosecutors the scalps of others, their guilt, being of no concern at all. A conviction was a conviction, was a conviction to the U.S. Attorneys.

The target in my case was clearly Samuel T. Currin, former U.S. Attorney, which would make a trophy scalp for these young prosecutors. It was also rather obvious that I was expected to be one of their "snitches" to help them bury Sam.

The only problem was I didn't know what he and his client, Jeremy Jaynes, had done. But that wouldn't matter to these Fed guys in the least. I'd heard from my new friends that they coached their snitches and even wrote scripts of lies for them to read on the stand in court under oath, no less. The government extorted citizens into committing perjury 'to ruin his man', as Tacitus wrote, in exchange for immunity or a shorter sentence for themselves.

I'd just witnessed first-hand how unscrupulous they were and how little regard they had for the truth. They'd do anything to win.

Listening to the master snitch and his "Grasshopper" next door, a conversation came to mind from a few years before. I had been given a preview of how corrupt the U.S. Attorneys were by none other than the former U.S. Attorney, Sam Currin himself, back in 2004 over dinner one night at the Buena Vista Restaurant in the old part of Nassau near our offices in The Bahamas.

Sam is not much of a conversationalist, and the three of us—Sam, my wife, and I—were having a glass of wine before dinner.

My wife, who is a wonderful conversationalist, was trying to cover an awkward silence asked, "So, Sam, how did you like being U.S. Attorney?"

The innocent question provoked a dramatic and unexpected response.

Currin's face took on a pained expression and he actually looked for a moment as if he was going to cry.

"Vernice, before I die and go to meet my Maker, I'm going to have to visit every prison in the Southeastern United States, get down on my knees, and beg the forgiveness of the men that I put there."

Vernice and I stole a furtive glance at one another, "Whoops", I thought. Wrong question!

But I was so shocked by Sam's answer that I had to know more. "Sam, why would you say something like that?"

He responded, emotionally, and in real pain, "Howell, we made up charges, fabricated evidence, gave informants time-cuts to lie on the stand in court, falsified evidence....we did any and everything to win. And I put a lot of people in prison that have absolutely no business being there, I can tell you that now, and now, I am ashamed of it."

"Why would you do something like that, Sam?"

"That's just how it's structured now, Howell. Advancement is based on only two things---how many convictions you get each year and how many years they're sentenced. Nothing else matters and we did anything we had do to, breaking the law ourselves, in order to accomplish those two things."

"Come on, Sam," I said, "Don't tell me that. What if somebody was innocent? There has to be recognition of a prosecutor finding that out, doing the right thing, and letting that person go."

"That's the problem with our justice system," he said. "It just doesn't work that way anymore, and I regret what I did now. But I can tell you for certain that anyone trying to do 'the right thing' won't work for very long in any U.S. Attorney's Office these days. It's all about winning convictions and long sentences. Nothing else matters."

A silence fell on the table. Little did we know then that Sam's sins would soon come back around and smite everyone sitting there that night. The same horribly corrupt and unjust weapons that he had used against innocent victims for his own advancement and personal gain would soon be deployed against him.

We would also be destroyed just for being near him in his successors' zeal to make their own mark in the halls of injustice, just as Sam had done himself not many years before.

He'd gone from hunter to hunted, and he was soon to be a trophy on the wall of young AUSA Martens, the next generation of ruthless, unscrupulous, prosecutors that Sam himself had helped to spawn.

He would be eaten by his own. He would be mutilated by the same sword which he had so cruelly wielded against others.

I was brought out of my deep thoughts by Vernice's voice calling from a cell down the corridor.

"Howell? What does this all mean?" she said through her sobs of anguish. "Now that they've found the judge they want, are they going to keep us down here in Raleigh? What's going to become of us? When will I see my children again?" she cried mournfully, as the sobs became uncontrollable. "Why are they doing this to us, Howell?," and then nothing as the unanswerable questions gave way to the sounds of a young mother's heart breaking at the thought of being taken from her children by these vicious, heartless animals.

I had no answers to give. There were none, other than the one Sam Currin had supplied over dinner a few years before. We were there to add to the reputation and pay-grade of two ambitious little boys who wanted to be another Elliott Spitzer, or Alberto Gonzalez, and nothing, including the loss of their own souls, was going to stand in their way.

We were returned to the jail in chains, and after the usual endless hours waiting in the holding cells below, were returned to our respective cell-blocks to sleep on the floor of the Wake County Jail with that day's collection of drunks, drug-addicts, and violent arrestees from the streets.

Michael and Edwin were waiting when I came back in the Blue pod, but the report to my new friends would have to wait until morning. They could tell by the look on my face what had transpired.

I balled up on my thin mat, and covered my eyes with the little towel against the 24-hour lighting and found escape once again in sleep.

CHAPTER 10

OUT OF THE FRYING PAN AND INTO THE FIRE

A day or two after the "tag-team" of my own defense lawyer, the, prosecutors, and their chosen judge had conspired to deny our right to bail, we were on our way, back to Charlotte, in a U.S. Marshal's van, in chains.

The Wake County marshals delivered us to the Raleigh/Durham Airport, along with a van full of the Feds' most recent victims. The United States government has a 98.6% conviction rate, per AUSA Matt Martens, which is higher than any totalitarian, communist, or whatever our leaders are calling the current "evil" or "satanic" empire of the week, so these vans rarely have an empty seat.

We waited for hours, cramped and crammed together, sitting on the tarmac. "Con-Air", as it is affectionately known, was late bringing another load back from Oklahoma City, and picking up another crowd for the round-trip.

That probably needs some explanation for the uninitiated, who don't understand how the prison-industrial complex operates. Prisoners, which are the fodder that keeps the enterprises fed and growing, are shipped out to Oklahoma City, Oklahoma. They are kept there for a couple of months in a detention center, only to be brought all the way back to the East Coast---- probably to this same airport----and carted to some nearby prison.

If you're thinking that this makes no sense, then you understand it completely. And that is what I was thinking that day. It makes no sense at all----unless you look at who is "getting paid" by this craziness.

You see, the conviction/prison industry is now the nation's fastest growing. Really, it makes you proud to be an American, right?

We don't make anything anymore (except bombs and the means of dropping them on peaceful nations), but we whip everyone's butts when it comes to putting our own citizens in the "Pokey".

In fact, we're so far ahead in that regard, that no one could ever catch us, if they started rounding 'em up and throwing everyone in prison today.

Between the cops, guards, 18,000+ separate police organizations, and the whole prison/jail industrial-complex, our nation spends in excess of $300 billion on arresting, convicting, and incarcerating its own people, each and every year.

We didn't have $2 billion to fix New Orleans after Hurricane Katrina, but we have money to burn if you want us to put 'em all in prison...$300 billion, in fact.

When this book was started, the government admitted that one in every 138 Americans were in jail or prison, which was already a historical and world record. No madman or tyrant, since Adam & Eve, had ever thrown so many of his people, or such a large percentage of them, into prison.

It was said to be 2.2 million then, which was eight times the population of the entire 700 islands of The Bahamas, in jail or prison, here in the "Land of the ....uh....Free."

By the time this book had been completed, the government's prosecutors like Martens & Meyers, the "defense" prosecutors like Freedman & Tisdale, and the judges like Earl Britt, had crushed millions more lives and swelled the ranks to 3.3 million souls in jail, one in every 99.1 Americans...in less than two years according to government, but that was a lie. The truth is 7.3 million, or one in every 31 adults in the country is in the corrections system today.

Now folks that is not a "trend", or "getting tough on crime, it is psychopathic geno-carceration and yes, I did make up the word, as I can't find one that describes this unspeakable act.

Not meaning to sound shrill, but that _addition_ to our already record-shattering prison population, in just two short years, was greater than the entire number of prisoners in communist China.

And don't even try the argument, "Oh, they just kill them", because that is not true. There are only six nations left on earth that still murder their own people as punishment for crimes, and we are the fourth most prolific in that dark activity, even though we only have 300 million people. China is number one in that insidious club of six, but they also have 1.4 billion people, and are not that far ahead of us, statistically. Their prison population totals only one in every 1,272 Chinese. When compared to our one in thirty one adults, it really hits home just how "out of whack" we are compared to the rest of human kind.

An American adult is roughly thirty-five times more likely to be in prison here in the "Land of the....uh....Free", than a Chinese citizen is in his communist homeland...and only slightly less likely to be executed by his government!

Makes you proud to be an American, doesn't it? At least we're still the best at something.

But it does have an upside economically, which is all it takes to make it sacrosanct in our society here in America.

This $300 billion a year "industry" is making lots and lots of people filthy, stinking, rich, and as everyone knows, that makes it better protected than the Spotted Owl or clean water in America.

Just try to stop this log truck from running downhill and you'll get run over in a heartbeat.

The prison industry is passing out money to politicians like it was candy at Halloween, and the states are now spending more on packing their own people into little cells----by far----than they spend on educating them. It is bizarre and frightening, both at the state and the federal level.

Money is a powerful thing in America. Let's be honest, it's the most powerful thing, and whatever is in second place is so far behind that it doesn't even count.

And sitting there on the tarmac at Raleigh/Durham Airport in chains, I was trying to sort this entire mess out. Some of the people on the van had already been sent out to Oklahoma one time, and were on their way again. It made absolutely no sense.

But when one realizes that "Con-Air" is a private contractor for the government, and makes about one thousand dollars, a "pop" for carrying these American citizens back and forth across the country for no discernable reason, it all starts to come clear.

They ride their quarry around in ancient 737's, MD-80's or leased jets from Pan Am...yep, the one that went bankrupt back in the 1980's (and other assorted junk)....at prices that would make any airline company in America profitable. They've got one of the worst safety records on the planet in terms of "incidents" but they've never lost a "bird" yet.

"PATS" or Prisoner Air Transport Services is its real name, but everyone calls it "Con-Air". It's a license to print money, taxpayer money, as is the rest of the prison-industrial complex.

Each week when the plane comes through, U.S. Marshal vans, county sheriff "dog-box" trucks, and prison buses from all over the state converge on the private FBO (fixed base operation) at the RDU airport to exchange prisoners.

The marshals are the lead dogs, but the other badge & gun-toting "law" men and women also gather as if it were a convocation of Twainian dregs, in reference to Samuel Clemens line:

"If you ever want to see the real dregs of society, go to your local jail....and wait for the shift-change of the guards."

Can't argue with old Mark Twain on that one, and nothing has changed in that regard. The weekly meet for prisoner exchange by these prison guards is a circus. There's more testosterone amongst them, men and women, then one can imagine.

It's like "Show & Tell" for new gear, guns, and toys of human torture and degradation.

I kid you not one chick marshal even had designer pastel handcuffs she was showing off that day to the other little boy and girl cops. It was a hoot to watch.

Once Show & Tell was over and the plain-wrapper, white 737 had lumbered into the parking area and stopped, the prisoner exchange took place.

The poor, shackled, citizens who had been sent west weeks before were unloaded, and the ones that would make the round-trip back in a few weeks, were put on board.

My wife and I were traded to the Mecklenburg County U.S. Marshals who had brought a load of prisoners to ride to Oklahoma and re-shackled by them.

Hours later...and many hours since being allowed to use a restroom, we were returned to the Mecklenburg County Jail.

Now a normal person would expect that two high-profile felons like us, who had just left the "joint" a couple of days before, would simply be booked back in, and sent to their cells.

But that would be too easy, too soft on the (innocent, and as yet, un-convicted) citizen; and reduce employment beyond acceptable, "over-staffed" levels.

It actually took longer to get in and back upstairs the second time than it had the first. There seemed to be a plethora of new inductees in various states of chemo-kinesis that evening, and when no one does anything anyway, it can really stretch out "booking-in" an overload of new citizen-victims.

Though all was already on file, we were re-photographed, re-finger-printed, re-questioned, re-manhandled, and re-booked. They wouldn't let my wife and I sit together, but we could see each other across the large room, and just looked at one another, wondering when we would ever have that opportunity again.

No need to bore reader and prison voyeur with the details again, but this seemingly endless, mostly unnecessary, and decidedly unconstitutional process takes up to fifteen hours…every time.

But I felt warm inside, even as cold as they had the room, knowing that I was helping to provide "work"…or let's say a salary…for all of these well-fed officers sitting around who were unfit for other employment. It made me feel good about myself and the world in general.

After many, many, hours, I was back in another cell-block, with a whole new group of "detainees", and a different, hostile environment, where one wrong move or word can cause disaster.

That was the worst part of being shuffled around, and the Feds knew it, I'm sure. That's why they did it so often.

The insufferable routine of line-ups, and verbal abuse from the "Twainian dregs" became daily life again, for a few days, at any rate.

Every other person in the cell-block, or "pod", was taken from the place in small groups a few nights later…except me. The same affectionate "ball-grabber" was back on duty that night, and she had left the doors of the cells unlocked and told me to clean the cell-block.

Expecting another unwanted advance, or confrontation, I busied myself on the upper deck, sweeping and mopping. Before another incident could take place, however, a male guard came into the pod.

"Where the Hell is Woltz?" he yelled at the startled guard.

"I sent 'em all out of here," she said. "Guess that one wasn't listenin'," as she pointed upstairs in my direction.

"Woltz! Pack your shit and get your ass in the slider. I don't have all night," shouted the male guard who had come in search of me.

I guess it was my fault. At least no one was "waiting" this time.

Once "packed"…a short process…I was escorted to the second floor, alone, leaving Sweet Thing to her own devices upstairs, and put in a tiny pod designed for a handful of medical inmates. There were eight, double-bunk beds, and tables for just sixteen people.

But the place was wall to wall men, and the only available floor-space was beside the toilets, against the adjacent wall.

I reminded myself to send a thank-you note to the Feds for another set of lovely accommodations. My caretakers had removed me from a place with 54 empty beds, each having an accompanying toilet, to put me in an over-crowded medical pod on the floor beside two open "potties". Nice.

No one knew where to find me, and the fake PIN number for phone access was no closer to working than the one they had given me the first go-around. There was a 350 pound Sumo wrestling sized black man screaming karate noises every time he made a move in a chess game, and my new "neighbors", who had made room for me in the toilet corner, were an assortment of vagrants, homeless fellows, drunks, and panhandlers.

These were the same people that I had ignored on street corners and urban thoroughfares the world over. I was now sleeping with them, on the floor of one of the reputedly worst jails in the region.

The one to my left croaked, "Scooter's the name. Want something to read?"

"Thanks," I said, taking a well-worn Tannenbaum novel about the corrupt justice system.

"Scooter's" diction was good, and other than his burned-out voice, he could have passed for a regular guy in any setting.

We began to chat and I became fascinated by this little man. His real name was Henry Miller, "Like the author," he said, "He wrote the *Tropic of Cancer*, and *The Tropic of Capricorn*," which I'd never read, but heard of. He opened up and began to tell me his story, which was fascinating.

The child of two desperate alcoholics, Henry grew up fending for himself on the streets and reading. He was a prolific consumer of the written word, and there was little about which he did not know something, which he dropped out casually, with no intention to impress.

Occasionally, he would break out into a cacophonous laugh, which was infectious. I completely forgot my woes and worries talking to Henry.

He told openly of the various harsh liquids he had poured down his throat, some of the same which had partially robbed him of his ability to speak, as well as his elixirs of choice when funds were available.

Henry Miller "Scooter" was what he was and how he was by choice. He was an urban Henry David Thoreau, and downtown Charlotte was his Walden Pond.

He lived as he wished, where he wished, and followed no man's bidding. On occasion, when in need of extra sustenance, heat, or a break from the rigors of his "profession" as a sage of the streets, he would buy a tall can of cold beer with donated funds, and stand on a street corner sipping it openly until he taunted a police cruiser into stopping.

If they were hesitant to arrest him, he would threaten to throw up all over the back seat of their police car.

"Works every time!" Henry shouted, breaking into his high-pitched laugh.

Gradually, others joined our company on the floor. Garfield, a young gymnast/drug dealer, had grown up as an Air Force brat. He was the child of a pair of Uncle Sam's armed junkies. He'd lived all over the world and been dealing since his early teen-age years to support his deadbeat parents, who had long since left the armed forces.

David Wu, a gregarious Vietnamese businessman, whom the Feds had been holding for nine months because he wouldn't sign a plea of guilt for an uncommitted crime, also joined us. The Feds couldn't take him to trial, as they had no evidence, nor had they been able to line up other Vietnamese snitches (yet), to set him up for conviction, by lying. So there he sat.

The huge Sumo wrestler-sized black man came by to speak as well. His name was Terry Streit, and like a Sumo wrestler, he had a perfect knot on the back of his head about four inches wide and round. But rather than hair, Mr. Streit's knot was flesh.

His imposing figure belied an almost childish and quite polite voice. His sentences were punctuated by "Sir", and other terms uncommon to most of the men I'd met in both Charlotte and the Wake County Jail. He even came offering books and any sundries that may be needed.

Garfield, the gymnast, entertained us by doing hand stands between the chairs and tables, flips, and other amazing feats.

A friendly Hispanic fellow told me that I needed a haircut, which was true, and shortly, I'd been barbered, given books to read, food to eat, and had enjoyed a fascinating evening.

I was dying to brush my teeth and get the taste of the meager jail dinner and snack out of my mouth, but had not been given any hygiene items upon check-in. The jailer had said they were "out".

My new neighbor, Scooter, gave me an indigent pack, containing everything that I needed—a comb, toothpaste, toothbrush, soap, and a small deodorant.

It was quite touching, actually, and I felt a wave of self-revulsion and guilt wash over me. I'd stepped over and avoided the Henry Millers of my world for years and couldn't recall ever giving even one of them a dime or the time of day in all my life, yet here was one of them giving me easily half of his worldly possessions without a second thought or moment's reflection.

The kindness of these poor men was overwhelming. I felt humbled that night and began the long process of reassessing who I really was and how blind I had been to the needs and lives of others.

Comfortably successful in my world of finance and international business, I had separated from my fellow man in my own mind, and mistakenly viewed myself as above many of them. But at that moment, I survived and was maintained out of their largesse and kindness, which I had always denied them, and did not now deserve myself.

Henry and I read books until early morning, as Mr. Steit's snoring shook the small pod with its thunder, which made sleep unlikely. Occasionally, we talked about his life on the streets. I'd rarely met such interesting people as those friendly men in that tiny little room that night.

There would be thousands more to come, as the Feds moved me around the country on "diesel therapy", and most would not be that wonderful. My world, however…and my view of it…was about to change forever.

CHAPTER 11-

THE OTHER SHOE HITS THE FLOOR

The stay in the medical pod with the pleasant group of men was short-lived. We were watched constantly by the guards from a "bubble". The one in this (former) medical pod had one-way glass, behind which the guards were free to carry on however they wished, as we could not see them.

An openly gay guard, Mr. Federson, was on duty that weekend. He was a flamer. Big, bald, black, and he sashayed when he walked like a street hooker, but I'll never forget him for what he did for me.

Unable to reach anyone via phone, thanks to the fake "PIN" number that I had been issued, I sought his help and assistance. When I'd explained what they had done to my wife and me, and told him about the number, he pooched out his lips in disgust and said, "That's just not right! These people don't play very nice, do they? Let me call my friend in communications and see if we can't get this fixed somehow."

Sure enough, good to his word, Mr. Federson's *friend* showed up shortly, and the two of them went into the 'bubble' via a side door. About a half hour later or so, the two emerged laughing and having a good time. I had a working number.

I never found out which of the corrupt government people had added such an unnecessary torment to an already ruthless denial of rights and fairness, the FBI or U.S Attorneys or perhaps I'm just paranoid and both times were simply accidents. But I'll always remember Federson for getting it fixed for me. That first call was heart-rending. No one was at my home, of course. The Chief of Police in our community, Robert Cook, had come to get the little boys after the FBI had abandoned them when abducting us. Robert had kept them for us.

But I was unable to reach him at the time, as he had not set up his phone to accept collect calls from the outrageously expensive jailhouse phone system. It was $25.00+ just to call home, once we finally got it working and someone was there. This is just another absolute rip-off of the poorest and most vulnerable by our "justice" organizations.

And on top of the usurious rates, all calls—even those with prisoners' attorneys--- were monitored and recorded! No Sixth Amendment rights for these un-convicted citizens in Charlotte and Raleigh! No siree. Hold 'em in jail till they plead guilty and monitor every call they make, even Hell...*especially*, with their lawyers!

But I was finally able to reach my sister-in-law, Jenny Anthertz down in Florida. She signed up on the sickeningly expensive system and spent over $600 that first couple of weeks just fielding calls from myself and her broken-hearted sister, calling to find out about our children.

It is common knowledge that the jails and/or sheriff's departments get huge kick-backs from these despicable phone systems like Evercom and ITI, which parasitically bleed the victims of this perverse system.

It is truly unconscionable, but only one of the many affronts to the citizens unlucky enough to be caught in this wicked web of what presidential candidate, Ron Paul, so correctly dubbed the "New American Police State".

Jenny became our lifeline for those many months, and shortly after our abduction, took in our youngest son, Jonathan, who was only 12 years old. She cared for him while these evil people played their games that year.

Our older son was taken in by Chief of Police, Robert Cook, (his godfather and our dear friend) who had rescued John and his little Scottish buddy, Stewart Graham, when the FBI left them. These two people, Jenny in Florida, and Robert in Davie County, North Carolina, will always be remembered in my heart. They raised our children that horrible year as if they were their own. May God bless them forever for what they did, and may He do whatever He thinks appropriate to those that made it necessary!

Yep. Still just a touch upset. I'll admit it folks. But I'm trying hard to let it go. I swear I am.

But back to the story, the Feds had better things in store for 'Howell the Horrible' than laying up like a groundhog down in the friendly, little (former) medical pod. Once again, a less than kind voice was heard early Monday morning, "Woltz! Pack your shit now, and get your ass in the slider. Now, Woltz! Move it!"

I bid adieu to my new friends and joined the manner-less, overweight deputy in the enclosed glass slider. Off we went to pod 6800, which I'd already been warned was the "murderer's" cell-block. Great - this was going from very bad to very worst in a hurry.

When we entered the cell-block, there was no podium or visible guard. Like the small medical pod, but on a much larger scale, there was a spooky-looking, one-way mirrored 'bubble' where the officers could hide from view. There were 54 solitary confinement cells, on two tiers, and other than the many faces staring through the tiny windows in the cell doors, it appeared to be abandoned.

This place would be my home for the next nine months while they tried to break me, though I never would have believed it at that time.

The cell door to number 34 on the upper level popped open, and once inside, a voice came over the in-cell speaker telling me to close the door. The place was automated. A frisson shot up my back when the door's air-lock popped into place.

No books. No newspapers. No paper and pencils. No diversion. The tiny cell consisted of 312 cinder-blocks and a tiny metal cot, crammed beside a postage-stamp sized table with a swing-out chair underneath, and a sink/toilet 'combination' which I'll leave to the reader's imagination. All I could think of at that moment was my hope that the ruthless people that had gone so far outside of law and constitution to put me in that sordid cage would one day have the pleasure of spending time in one for their own crimes against the American people.

The ceiling was quite high, maybe twelve feet. I later learned that was because prisoners were required by law to have a certain number of cubic feet of living space. Rather than waste any precious footage that could actually be used by the poor, un-convicted citizen, they fulfilled the mandate by trapping unusable air-space.

Boredom and depression, a prisoner's constant companions, quickly set in. It is hard to describe what it feels like when you come to realize that everything you had ever believed in about your country was bogus....a sham. A little time sitting alone in a cell for an uncommitted crime can get you there in a hurry. Not only had they done this to me, they'd taken my wife as a hostage. My own government had done this, not some foreign terrorists but my own people using terrorist tactics.

A kangaroo court had indicted us on charges that the prosecutor knew to be false, not through any fault of the grand jury's, but because the perversions of the judicial process allowed prosecutors to lie and present false testimony with impunity, as there is no oversight or governing authority. We would not even be allowed a copy of the transcript in order to prove their misdeeds.

All of this kept spinning through my head. I'd already seen scores of men trapped in jail until they simply tired of the horrible environment and became part of the 98.6% conviction rate...highest in the world or history...by pleading guilty. The only country that was even close was Japan, who had copied our "government always wins" conviction machine.

America and its buddies in Tokyo had left every tyrant and despot in the dust on that score.

The pain was deep and desperate, and I wallowed in self-pity until I fell asleep.

CHAPTER 12-

DEALIN' WITH THE DEVIL- PART 1

Mornings started later in the murderer's pod. No need to rush things there, apparently. No one was going anywhere for a long, long, time...including me, unfortunately.

Everything was different. We were only allowed out of the solitary confinement cells at certain times and for meals, though that was also not consistent. Sometimes we were fed through a slot in the door, affectionately known as "the bean hole", for days at a time, especially during holidays.

But we were usually allowed out for a couple of hours prior to lunch and dinner in pod 6800, and in the evening about 8:30 P.M. for an hour or two. The rest of the time was spent in the solitude in our cells.

The inmates were far less friendly. Many, if not most of them were in there for murder or seriously violent crimes. Not a very "chatty" group on the whole. My being there could not be an accident.

The prosecutor's hand was definitely at play. And he wasn't long in showing that hand, either.

Before I'd even had a chance to settle in well, I was taken out of the cell-block early one morning for a "contact" visit. This was their term for a meeting in a room with people, without having a piece of bulletproof glass with imbedded wire between you and the visitor and a telephone to talk over.

My so-called attorney, David Freedman, had not come to see me or shown any interest in learning about my case since my arrest on April 18th. By then, it was April 27th.

I thought that perhaps he was my contact visit, now that it was too late to help me get bond. He'd let us get Shanghaied two federal jurisdictions away without a whimper or word, but maybe he was finally coming with a plan.

The guard took me by elevator down to the second floor to a locked metal door. The sergeant opened it with a large key, with a red dot of paint on the part held. I was thoroughly frisked and patted down. A guard then entered the small hallway with me, and the door was locked again. Only then was the other door opened. I must truly be a dangerous man, I thought, for all of this "security".

We then entered an area with four meeting rooms. I was told to stand by the door until "they" were ready for me. I had to wonder who "they" were.

Walking toward the room, I could see that it was full of men. The FBI agent Curran who had abducted us and the main prosecutor, Matt Martens were visible through the glass. Martens was talking excitedly about Sam Currin and Judge Britt. There were others in the room, but I couldn't see or didn't recognize them. I was put outside the door, out of their view, "to wait".

Martens' conversation was clearly audible and quickly got my attention, however. I was shocked at not only what I heard, but at my own attorney, David B. Freedman, being one of the quite interested listeners. Martens was bragging about getting Judge Britt to take our case, in concert with the Clerk of Court, Frank G. Johns, aka "Johnsy".

"He and Sam Currin are 30-year blood-feud enemies!" Martens exclaimed. "I can't believe we got him to take it," crowed the young servant of *justice* and *the people*.

He certainly wasn't talking about anyone else's case, if he was mentioning Sam Currin, so I waited for Freedman to say something, as this had to be illegal. If what I was hearing was true, then Matt Martens had just admitted to my own attorney that he had gone "judge shopping" for W. Earl Britt to hear the case, as he knew that he would be hostile to my "co-defendant", former U.S. Attorney, Samuel T. Currin.

And if Judge Britt was a "blood-feud enemy" of Sam Currin's, that certainly did not bode well for me and my wife either.

But Freedman said nothing, and once the laughter died down, I was ushered in by the deputy. Martens was all smiles, and friendly as could be. Everything was obviously going his way.

The only empty chair was beside David Freedman, whom I asked, "Aren't we going to have a chance to talk alone?" I was anxious to discuss what I'd just heard.

"Oh, I don't think that's necessary. Once you hear what we've come up with, I think you'll agree that that isn't needed," Freedman answered.

Martens then picked up the conversation. "Mr. Woltz, I know these last several days have been really rough for you. They must have been terribly difficult for you and your wife. But you're not really who we're interested in. We are sure that you can help us, but you're not our target."

He paused, smiled broadly and said slowly, "How would you like to get off of this merry-go-round? Just step off, and be done with it. Hmmm?"

A million thoughts were going through my head at that moment.

A half dozen government men whom I knew were not my friends, were all smiling at me as if they were, sitting around the table, waiting on my answer to a very loaded question. I could have kicked Freedman, if he'd been close enough, for throwing me to these wolves with no warning or chance to speak privately to him and find out what he was doing. They were giving me no time to make an informed decision, and apparently, my suspicions had been correct. Freedman was definitely working with them. What he was doing to me was unconscionable. This was our first meeting and he was holding it in front of the enemy.

"What do you think, Mr. Woltz?" Martens said. "You'd like that, wouldn't you?" Of course I'd like it, you idiot, I thought.

But why was Freedman, my own attorney, selling out to these guys? I'd written him a line-by-line rebuttal to the indictment, telling him how we could prove every charge and statement false. Being allowed no paper, I'd done it on the back of the indictment itself and told him we were going to trial. My wife and I were completely innocent.

But I also remembered what Michael Sprackland and Edwin had told me in Raleigh and thought I'd better see what Martens had to say.

"I suppose so," I said as non-committal as I could, even though I'd been committed already by David. "What are you proposing?"

Martens pointed back to his tag-team partner, my lawyer, who answered that question. "Howell, I've been doing this a long time, and I've got to tell you, what Matt is offering us is really unbelievable. It's without a doubt, the best 'deal' I've ever seen for someone facing the charges you're facing and the number of years in prison." What? Freedman hadn't even talked to me, or asked me a single question about guilt or innocence, and here he was telling me I'm going to prison, if I don't take his buddy's deal.

"But I didn't do anything!" I interjected. "I just came up here to help them and they grabbed me. I don't even understand why I'm here."

"OK. OK. Calm down. That really isn't important right now," he said, almost cooing as an adult would to quiet a child. Not important? How could false charges be "not important"?

"Let's put that aside for the moment", Freedman continued.

"But how can we put that aside"..., I tried to speak.

"Howell. Stop. Hear us out before you say any more," David said, interrupting me. "Suppose I told you we've come to an agreement whereby this all ends, or as Matt has said, you can get off the merry-go-round now. Now keep in mind that you've been indicted by a grand jury...."

"But..." I started, and David held up his hand.

"Let me finish," he said. "This is not going away. But we've come to an agreement, and as I said, it is an unbelievably good deal that you're being offered, where this can end soon and with as little pain as possible."

I wanted to run out of the room but knew I couldn't and had to hear what he was saying.

"Matt and I have agreed to this, we only need your approval. Now as you've probably already figured out, you're going to have to take a charge, and admit to having done something. Something small..."

"But I didn't do any of this!" I blurted out. "They've got to know that if they've done any investigating at all." It was like being in a bad late movie.

The FBI agent jumped in then and said, "Well a grand jury sure thinks you've done something!"

"Then somebody had to have lied," I shot back immediately.

Martens raised his hand to silence both of us like we were two sprats squabbling. "Go on Mr. Freedman," he said.

"OK. Howell, you're going to have to plead guilty to something...."

"Anything, really," Martens interjected.

What was this all about? It didn't even matter what I pled guilty to having done? This was getting worse.

Freedman jumped back in before I could speak, "But let's leave that for a moment. Let me tell you what we worked out. There are four items. First of all, your wife can go free immediately, if you agree to help the government. Second, there will be no forfeiture of any assets. That's got to please you." What...it's a great deal not to be robbed by Uncle Sam for something you never did? They were really nice guys after all. "Third, you'll serve little or no time. You help them and you're almost home now..."

"Wait. You said 'little' or 'no'," I interrupted. "Which is it? It's already too late for 'no' time. I'm in jail now."

"That's part of what we'll discuss, but let me finish. And the fourth part is there will be no new charges of any kind. This is the end of it, if you agree to help them against Currin."

"Let me make sure that I understand what you're saying, David. You want me to help with Currin. And in return for doing so, I'm guaranteed that:

1) my wife goes free now

2) there is no forfeiture of any kind

3) I serve little or 'no' time....I prefer 'no' to 'little'

4) no new charges of any kind will be added

Is that right?"

"That's pretty much it, but keep in mind that you will have to plead guilty to some small charge," Freedman said.

"Why?" I asked. "Why do I have to plead guilty to something I didn't do?"

Martens took the tag from his partner, Freedman, on this one, "First off we not only want your help with Currin, but also his client, Jeremy Jaynes. We'll expect you to testify against both of them, and it will add to your credibility with the jury if you've pled guilty to something and say you were working with them. It will make you much more believable."

"But I didn't know what they were doing, and you know that. I sent you the affidavits from our case in the Supreme Court of The Bahamas against the girl that Jeremy Jaynes was paying to do whatever was being done. She stated in her own affidavit that my wife and I knew nothing of what they were doing," I said. "You know that we didn't know anything from those documents."

Martens quickly said, "Oh but we can't use that. It's under seal with the Bahamian court."

"Under seal" I said. "It never even went to court. Her lawyer agreed to pay us to settle. The information is on the Web. Why do you say it's 'under seal'?"

"The cover sheet of the documents you sent us says it's under seal, so I can't even look at them," Martens said.

This was the same cat that had kidnapped us on fabricated charges, lied to a grand jury to get the indictment, told a federal judge seventy- six mistruths and outright lies to deny us our constitutional right to bail, and now all of a sudden, he was an ethicist, who could not look at information about me that was completely exculpatory. It was on the Web, for crying out loud!

"That case is not under seal!" I said sharply. "Why is it that you can accept Elizabeth Streit's nonsense, which is completely bogus, and charge us with it, but when there is something that proves we're innocent, you can't look at it? And it's on the Web?"

The meeting was coming off the rails in a hurry. Freedman jumped back in to save his tag-team partner, the prosecutor. "Now, Howell, this isn't going to get us anywhere. Calm down, and listen to me. If you go to trial, you're risking spending the rest of your life in prison. The government's conviction rate is 98.6%[3]. You need to listen to Matt. Let's leave the part about the charge for a moment, but let me assure you, that you need to hear this and give it serious consideration."

I wanted to ask how any honest government could possibly win 98.6% of the time, but the question was the answer. An honest government couldn't win that often. I was living the "how". Kidnapping, extortion, threats, and holding you in jail until you cry "Uncle". That's how they do it, but saying those words were not in my best interest at the moment. "How does my being guilty of something, or being a convicted 'felon', possibly make me more credible? That makes absolutely no sense. The opposite would be true. You think the jury is more likely to believe someone that says he's a crook? I don't get that at all."

Freedman and Martens exchanged glances and they faltered on that one. My radar was going wild, but I also didn't want to lose the conversation if they were agreeing to let Vernice go and not steal everything we had.

After a silence, David said, "I'll try and explain that to you later, Howell, but you're just going to have to trust me on that for right now. That's the deal, and I've got to tell you...it's the best you're ever going to get, and it's certainly the best I've ever heard of."

The boys in Raleigh, and all of the other horror stories of what these people had done to other innocents led me to believe that he was right on that, as wrong and odious as what they were doing might be.

"Can I see a copy of your agreement?" I asked David.

He and Martens exchanged glances again, as if waiting for the other to speak first.

"David?" I said warily.

"I don't have a copy with me," he answered.

---

[3] Confirmed by the Dept of Justice to be 90.7%, but when dismissals are included, that number is actually 99.6%

"But this agreement has been reduced to writing, right?" I pressed.

They looked at each other again.

"I mean you do have letters back and forth or e-mails or something memorializing this four-point deal, right?"

Freedman answered, "Yes. It has been memorialized."

"In my world, David, 'memorialized' means that something has been reduced to writing. Is that what you are saying? Are you, as my attorney, telling me that I am covered on this?" I asked.

"Yes. Yes, you're covered," he answered.

"So what do we do next?" I asked.

Martens took the tag again from his partner, "If we're in agreement Mr. Woltz, then we'd like to ask you a few questions now that we have that out of the way."

Freedman looked greatly relieved.

Rather than answering Martens, I said to David, "I'm counting on you. If you're telling me that you've got this deal in writing and I'm 'covered', then I don't have a problem with that, but what assurances do I have that what I say won't be used to make up more false charges against me?"

David reached in his briefcase and produced a document. "We have a 'non-affinity' agreement, which I've also got to tell you, Howell, is the best that I think I've ever seen. It says that nothing can be used against you, nothing. You're free to talk openly, once this is signed."

I took the agreement from him and scanned it quickly. "But the agreement items that you and Mr. Martens worked out. Can't I see them first before we do all of this?"

"You're just going to have to trust me on that, Howell. All of these people are here to talk to you now I'm not sure we can get a delay. This is your opportunity." With that, David looked at his watch, and said, "Look, Howell, I've got something really important to do this morning. I promise you all of this is set. But I've got to go, so let's get this signed so you can start helping these gentlemen, all right?

"Something really important", I thought to myself. The son of a bitch had been paid $35,000 to go to trial, I'd never once been able to talk to him alone, and now he was about to abandon me to half a dozen or so Feds, without the assistance or advice of counsel. I'd been put in an untenable position.

"David, I'm counting on your word that all of this is set and I'm protected," I said.

He stood up to leave, and said, "Howell, you need to focus on how you can help these men now. You just made a very good deal. Now it's time for you to do your part. You're covered. This is almost over. But I've really got to go now," and with that he was out the door.

It was incredible. My attorney had just sold me down the river after being paid to go to trial, and made a deal without ever talking to me once, or even knowing what the case was about. At least we'd get most of that huge retainer back, I thought. He certainly wouldn't try to keep that, after doing nothing for me.

And as soon as the door closed, the mood of the room changed quickly and palpably. They all exchanged glances. It was like being the only sheep in a room full of wolves. And then it began.

FBI agent, Curran had an associate with him, whom he did not introduce, but another man did speak up and say, "I'm Scott Schiller with the IRS. I was the agent on this case and the 'sting' operation in The Bahamas," he said.

I had learned at the bond revocation hearing that this man had sent two undercover con-men (illegally) to pose as potential clients. Though The Bahamas is not under their jurisdiction in any way, and neither are their outrageous "conspiracy" laws or tax regulations recognized there, they had circumvented the law and attempted to lure our firm into a "conspiracy" with their own agents to "defraud the U.S. government" though it was unclear how they may have imagined that to have occurred.

The con-men had proposed a transaction to sell gaming rights that had been granted by the sovereign government of Antigua, to a corporation in Georgia. The due diligence was to be the responsibility of the attorneys in the United States. We were simply to establish a corporation and trust in the region where the rights were owned through our trust company in the British territory of Anguilla, to accommodate the offshore transaction. Had the transaction ever occurred, it would have been completely legal in every way, under Bahamian, Anguillan, Antiguan, and even U.S. law.

But the proposed transaction had never been consummated and the con-men had been rejected as clients due to our staff being uncomfortable with their lack of honesty and openness.

Their funds had been returned, and the attorney that had referred them to our firm had been informed that they had been rejected. The attorney, a tax specialist in Wilmington, North Carolina by the name of Rick Graves, had agreed that they seemed to want to skirt the laws of the U.S. or step over into the "gray" areas that we chose to avoid, even though we were not under U.S. jurisdiction. In fact, we had quit taking U.S. clients just because of the crazy tax laws and even crazier so-called "enforcement" of them.

This was the same Rick Graves on my indictment, whom I'd met over lunch a few years before, who had a Masters in Tax, was a patriotic soldier (U.S. Special Forces) and had volunteered to go back and help out during Desert Storm (and did so).

What on earth were these government thugs thinking? Charging an American hero who knew far more about the tax code than they did could backfire on them.

But Graves had smelled a hint of dishonesty as had we, and the con-men of the U.S. Government were turned down as clients of our firm. We didn't deal with crooks and these guys fit the bill. A bit sleazy, slick-talking, with shifty eyes. . . .you know, government types, though we just thought they were common run of the mill crooks at the time, not knowing they worked for the most corrupt agency on the planet – the IRS.

Attorney Graves had dutifully notified the undercover agents by letter at our request, that their business was not welcome. We never heard from them again, so we considered the matter closed, never once suspecting that they were con-artists sent down to entrap us into an illegal act, which we refused to do.

Civilized nations do not have conspiracy laws, and no such law is recognized by our neighboring nations. Neither the Canadian government nor the Bahamian government will extradite people charged under such an outrageously unfair law back to the United States, as there simply is no defense against "conspiracy". It is an imaginary 'inchoate' crime of thought - thinking about a crime, not committing one.

But there I was, charged on the indictment anyway. Graves, the tax attorney who had referred them and I were charged with "conspiring" to violate the *reporting* laws of the U.S., which only apply to individual taxpayers not us, and we had refused to deal with them.

My attorney had sold me out and dashed out the door, having never investigated the case at all, or having ever asked me a single question about it. We'd yet to have our first meeting. I would later learn that he had never taken the time to read the indictment and did not know the 'crime' for which I had been charged and arrested.

The bizarre Kafkaesque world I had entered would only get darker that day.

CHAPTER 13

DEALIN' WITH THE DEVIL- PART 2

So my lawyer had taken a hike, and I was now facing the two young pit bulls, Martens and Meyers, who had so boldly lied to their "co-conspirator", the judge, to deny us our right to bond. I really did not want to deal with them for fear that my temper might flash, so I addressed Schiller, the IRS agent, on how he had contrived a charge against me.

"But Agent Schiller, you know that these are reporting requirements. I'm a trustee with a licensed, foreign trust company. These laws only apply to individual U.S. taxpayers. How can I possibly violate such a law?"

I continued, "It's actually against the law for me to report any client matters to anyone as a trustee. Each such disclosure can carry a fine of up to $500,000 and 10 years in prison."

Agent Schiller was on the spot. I'd figured out by then that all of their charges had been contrived just to hold me to use against their targets, Sam Currin and client, but I wanted someone to admit it.

"All right," Schiller said. "We know about the laws in The Bahamas on privacy. But our position is that had a transaction taken place, and had profits been realized, taxes *might* not have been paid on them."

"But Agent Schiller, you know very well that no transaction ever did take place. In fact, we refused to do business with the con-men and returned their deposit. You know that. And had....", but that's as far as I got. Agent Schiller interrupted me.

"Agents," he said. "They're agents, not con-men."

"Whatever you want to call them is fine, Mr. Schiller, but the fact is the transaction never did happen, and we never did business with them. And had all of this hypothetical activity taken place, it would have been legal, and I think you know that." He just looked at me and said nothing.

"Plus, the transaction proposed wasn't even under U.S. jurisdiction or taxable authority," I added.

Schiller looked left and right, conspiratorially, as if to confirm that my lawyer had really left me to them, and said, "OK. That's true. But here's our take on it. The structure was to have been a corporation owned by a trust, right?"

"Correct, but what does that have to do with anything?"

"The beneficiaries of that trust were to be Americans, so if there had been a distribution of those profits through the trust, at some point, they might not have reported them on their U.S. taxes."

I was incredulous. "What on earth does that have to do with us? What could that possibly have to do with me?"

"OK. I admit it's a bit of a stretch," he said smiling, "but it doesn't really matter now, does it? You've agreed to work with us."

But I wasn't ready to just let it go. "Just let me make sure I've got this right. You've just ruined our lives over a transaction that <u>never</u> happened, in a foreign jurisdiction where you have no authority; And you're saying that if one <u>had</u> taken place, which it didn't, and <u>had</u> it been profitable, which it wasn't because it never happened, that the trust <u>might</u> have declared a distribution of some of these non-existent profits, under its sole discretion. And had the beneficiaries, being U.S. citizens, decided not to report these monies, it's somehow my fault? It would be up to your con-men to pay their taxes! We've got nothing to do with that."

"Agents, they're agents," he said sternly. Any trace of humor left him, and he hissed, "But as I said, none of that matters anymore. You're working with us now."

Not a nice fellow. But then again, I've never known IRS agents to be described as "warm and fuzzy".

With the 'non-affinity' agreement signed and my lawyer gone, I felt like I'd sold out to the devil in a bad bargain. I wanted my soul back.

Like Dante's <u>Inferno,</u> I was sinking into the circles of Hell, expecting to see old Ugolino, the one who ate his own children and grandchildren down in the Ninth Circle, at any moment.

They'd had enough of my impertinence. They owned me. The questions started. The rest of the morning, they tried desperately to make a crime out of their charges. The CFTC biddie, Elizabeth Streit, had apparently worn out the phone and carpet of Agent Doug Curran's office at the FBI, pushing vindictive charges against me and my wife.

Agent Curran had quite apparently done no investigation of her charges of "perjury" and "obstruction of justice", and battered me to admit to things that had never occurred, or to agree with their perverse take on what had transpired. He was using the old standard TV-inspired bad-cop badgering techniques, in hopes that I'd break down and cry, "Yes. Yes, Agent Curran. I did it! I tore the tag off the sofa cushion that said, 'Do NOT remove under PENALTY OF LAW.' I did it! I'm so sorry!"

But I hadn't torn the stupid label off the sofa cushion, nor had I committed "perjury", nor had I "obstructed justice" in Elizabeth Streit's civil case where our firm had been the largest victim. And why did they need for me to "confess" to things I'd never done anyway, if we had a deal? None of it made any sense, and my sorry, worthless, lawyer was not there to ask any questions.

"Why would my wife and I want to 'obstruct' anything where the two crooks that cost our clients millions of dollars are concerned, Mr. Curran? That just doesn't make any sense. I hope Ms. Streit fries little Vernon Abernethy and Coyt Murray," I said, "but we didn't do anything and Agent Schiller just admitted it."

The young Assistant U.S. Attorney had watched this interchange quietly, but couldn't resist. "Oh you've done something, Mr. Woltz. We believe that all of you out there have done 'something', we just haven't gotten around to you yet," said Matt Martens, smiling.

All I could think was, "You sick bastard." And who was this "we" I'd like to know. Big Brother, Inc.?

"Mr. Martens, we tried to help the CFTC in their case. Before anyone else or any domestic victims had responded, we had already put together all correspondence with Tech Traders, Abernethy's bogus monthly return statements, and everything else we had. We delivered it to the Receiver, Stephen Bobo, the week after they'd shut them down, right to his hand, at Tech Traders' office, which he'd seized.

"But Ms. Streit isn't after the 'bad guys'", I continued. "She's after fine income and Murray and Abernethy didn't have any money, so she tried to make us out to be the 'bad guys' instead. I think you know that, Mr. Curran. She's also mad because we tried to intervene in the case when she refused to do her job and guard our interests, which was her <u>real</u> job. This is just payback. It's vindictive, plain and simple."

FBI Agent Curran wouldn't directly confirm that, of course, but he did smile and say, "She surely did push us to try and get you on something. I'm just glad to have her off my back."

"And on to mine, Dougie?" I wanted to say, but figured I'd better not push it.

But it was clear that Libby Streit had started this vindictive prosecution. Of that there was no doubt. Whether the 'sting' by IRS had been because of her referral, or just part of their campaign of terror against offshore financial firms, we may never know, but she was surely the reason that they had come down our chimney and tried to tie former U.S. Attorney and North Carolina Republican Party Chairman, Sam Currin and his young "spammer" client, Jeremy Jaynes, to us. In the deposition where she claimed perjury had been committed, she had desperately tried to make Jeremy and Sam a part of everything we did rather than just clients.

We discussed the perjury charge where Ms. Streit had asked me who the directors of Sterling Bank in St. Lucia were, which I had organized and helped to found. I had given her the names of those that had been approved by the Regulator, which is the only way anyone can get on a bank board, even though that information was completely immaterial to her civil suit against the crooked traders and accountant folks in the Tech Traders scam. Who the board members were of a non-defendant company was totally irrelevant to her U.S. case. The St. Lucia bank had a small investment with Tech Traders as well, but they were a victim.

"But you left out some names," Curran replied to my statement that I had given the list of board members correctly. There had been no 'perjury'.

So I shot back, "That's not true. Perhaps you should have read the transcripts rather than taking Ms. Streit's word for it, Mr. Curran. Did you contact the Regulator in St. Lucia to verify what she told you? I know the answer to that is 'No', because he would have told you the same thing that I told her."

I well remembered the deposition where she kept trying to badger the name of Jeremy Jaynes out of me as some sort of business partner. Jaynes was Sam Currin's only client, and had the infamous distinction of being the world's first person charged with spamming, by the Commonwealth of Virginia, or anywhere else for that matter.

Libby had been hot to tie us to any wrong-doing or wrongdoer she could. Not only had I given her the correct names, I had added, "And if you're wondering why I didn't mention the name Jeremy Jaynes, it's because directors and board members have to be approved by the Regulator. Jaynes removed his name, and was not approved." It was on the transcript, but she had withheld it to make up a charge of perjury with the FBI. It was a provably false prosecution had anyone ever taken the time to look. This had all transpired long before the bank license had been issued. It wasn't in business back then, but I'd added the information anyway so there would be no suspicion we were trying to hide anything.

But Libby had failed to show these young boys that part of the transcript apparently. I could tell it by the looks they were exchanging across the table.

So Curran went back on the offensive, "What about the obstruction of justice charge then?" he asked aggressively.

"What 'obstruction of justice'?", I asked. "Not taking someone else's subpoena? I took mine. No one had to chase me. Or was it telling a process-server that my wife was not at home, when she was not there?"

He knew that one was a dead-end as well. It wouldn't have even been legal service if I'd taken a subpoena for someone else. Libby Streit had just made up some charges as retribution, and abused her position and authority by filing them against the victims, while giving the real criminals a "pass" for helping her against us. They gave Vernon Abernethy, the CPA and confessed crook in the commodities scam that cost our clients millions of dollars, immunity from prosecution for changing his own testimony and lying to the grand jury. However, the grand jury was only allowed to hear Vernon's staged version, which contradicted his own testimony in the commodities trial where he was convicted. None of these pathetic people cared. It was obvious they were scalp-hunters and not truth-seekers.

It didn't take a genius to see the wormy little accountant's fingerprints on all of it. He had actually been Jeremy Jaynes' accountant. I was quite sure that he'd never told Libby Streit or the FBI about that. The only way I'd ever known was because he had called me a few months prior to the CFTC suit and thanked me for introducing him to Sam Currin again. He mentioned then that Jeremy had hired him.

In Vernon Abernethy's deposition in the CFTC case against Tech Traders, I'd read where Streit was trying to get the little miscreant to explain some point about what he'd done in fudging the numbers in the Tech Traders scam. She kept pressing him to say something specific, but he just wouldn't or couldn't understand the point, and even a corrupt government type like Streit knew that she could not just tell him what to say "on the record".

Finally, little Vernon had said something to the effect of "I don't know what you want me to say, Ms. Streit. Just tell me and I'll say it."

Yep. Vernon Abernethy was her boy, and for once, he had not been lying. "Tell me what you want and I'll say it." I could just see him reading her script at the grand jury hearing. Four of the five witnesses had one story - we were innocent - but the grand jury went with Vernon's version which countered his own previous testimony.

CFTC Attorney Libby Streit had cut a nefarious deal with this little beady-eyed bean counter to lie about us in exchange for not being prosecuted for a real crime of major proportions.

The CFTC's own web-site had called it 'one of the biggest commodities trading scams of the year', but I don't know of a single one of the defendants that ever went to jail over it.

The nasty little woman had decided to abuse her federal power and go after the victims instead; just because we had correctly pointed out that she was not doing her job.

But that's the way it works now in America, the feds have so much unconstitutionally allowed power, and no oversight.

Elizabeth Streit knew that and pursued us to get even, because no one was monitoring her. She could do so with impunity. She also knew then, what I was only learning, which was that truth made absolutely no difference in the U.S. Justice system any more. If she could just get the indictment, she'd ruined us, because the Feds *always* win. They have unchallengeable power and use it ruthlessly without discretion. Every case, they go for the jugular.

If they don't have anything at all, they fall back on "conspiracy", the blunt tool of tyrants throughout time. There is no defense against conspiracy, as it's not something that you do, it's supposed to be a crime of intent. It's something you supposedly <u>think</u>. Old George Orwell had once again called it right in his book, <u>1984</u>, written years ago, when he foresaw the "Thought Police". I was sitting with them in that little room.

The Feds now use that terrible tool of "conspiracy" in over 90% of all federal cases today. That why they always win…actually 99.6% of the time, is the exact statistic. You can't win when the government decides what you were "thinking". That's why civilized nations without dictators or emperors have always avoided such laws.

But my musings came to a close as the 'Thought Police' then attacked my wife, since they were having no luck getting me to admit to uncommitted crimes. FBI Agent Curran picked up the mantle again.

"I guess you're also going to tell me that your wife didn't take anything from Vernon Abernethy's house when you had a secret meeting. I have a witness that says your wife took records and a computer back-up tape from Abernethy's home." He looked triumphant. Aha! Gotcha!

"Then someone is lying," I said.

What secret meeting? If it was "secret", he wouldn't know about it, but Agent Curran had just confirmed my suspicions. Libby Streit had swapped Vernon Abernethy, the crooked accountant, a free pass for bilking people out of millions in exchange for telling self-exculpatory lies to a grand jury to help them indict us so we could be held as witnesses against Sam Currin and not return to The Bahamas.

Curran parried again. "I have it on good authority that your wife took something from that house that night."

"Good authority?" I asked. "The only people there were a convicted Ponzi scheme trader, a convicted accountant that falsified his returns, and our consultant who was there to verify that the other two were crooks. Who's the 'good authority', Mr. Curran? Walt Hannen was there to confirm whether or not the CFTC's claims that they were crooked were correct."

"And what did he determine?" asked Curran.

"That Abernethy and Murray were crooks! It took Walt and my wife about ten minutes looking at the original commodity account statements to see that Tech Traders had been falsifying returns, and that Abernethy had been rubber-stamping the fakes, never even looking at the originals, as his monthly certified statements had said.

"Why", I continued, "would we want to do anything to help either Coyt Murray or Vernon Abernethy when we'd just learned for certain that they were crooks? I wanted to hurt them, not help them, especially Vernon Abernethy. We had counted on his accounting firm for an independent review of the returns. Without such as that, our trust company could never have invested with a small firm like Tech Traders."

The only reason we had gone to Vernon's meeting that night was because he and Coyt Murray, the crooked trader, had come to our home at the farm begging us to give them another chance.

Coyt continued to swear his innocence and that all of the money was really there if we would just believe him. If that were true and our clients could be made "whole", then we had to give them a chance to prove it. Coyt lived in South Carolina so it was agreed that we would meet at Vernon's home in Gastonia, but it was agreed that they would bring the original statements from the commodities trading firms to be inspected by my wife, a CPA, and Walt Hannen, who we'd hired as a consultant to our bank in Saint Lucia (Sterling Bank Limited), trained by the FBI in forensic accounting, according to his resume.

My answer was still hanging in the air, and Agent Curran was waiting for me to blink. I didn't and he knew I was telling the truth. He blinked.

The room was quiet. "So you took nothing from his house that night," Curran said.

"Absolutely nothing. The only thing I wanted to 'take' that night was to 'take' a swing at somebody. Plus the original statements had been subpoenaed by the CFTC and were to be delivered the next day. That's why we had had to come to Abernethy's house that night to see them. It was the only chance we would ever have to see them ourselves and know for sure whether or not they were crooks. That night, we learned that they were. Murray had been running a Ponzi scheme, and Abernethy had been verifying the false returns."

"How about the computer back-up tape?" Curran pressed.

"Why on earth would we want to take a back-up of Abernethy's computer?" I asked. "Tech Traders was fudging the numbers. Abernethy wasn't doing anything but writing down whatever they made up."

The whole conversation was bizarre. I couldn't help but wonder what these people thought was on this silly tape, or why we would have any interest in it. They seemed mighty anxious to get their hands on it or know what it was. But they were asking the wrong guy.

The consultant that had come that night to go through the records, Walt Hannen, was probably the one they should be asking. We would later learn that Walt had been working for Sam Currin and Jeremy Jaynes and had actually been doing the laundering of their penny-stock funds through an account in his own name at Bank of America though he would never be charged for it. We on the other hand, had no part in it and we were in jail.

The back-up tape that they kept talking about had been Jaynes' accounting information, I later figured, because Hannen ended up with it at his home along with Vernon's accounting records that he had wanted to hide from his CFTC buddy, Ms. Streit, but blamed my wife.

Walt had actually told us about it himself. He said that Vernon had shown up at his Lake Norman home in the middle of the night back in April of 2004 with "a shaving kit and a box of financial records". Walt said that Vernon looked like a "scared little rabbit" and wanted to spend the night. He was afraid Ms. Streit was going to have him arrested.

Vernon had spent the night, departed the next morning after breakfast, according to Walt, but he had left the "records" with Walt, which I'd thought was odd at the time.

A few weeks later, Walt had asked if we would take an envelope to Nassau for him. He was the consultant for Sterling Bank, so this was not an odd request. We met Walt en-route to the airport, on our way down I-77 at his Lake Norman exit.

When we stopped, Walt said "hello", handed Vernice the sealed manila envelope through the car window, and off we went to catch our flight to Nassau. We never thought twice about it until some months later when our attorney in New York, who had handled the "intervention" attempt in Ms. Streit's CFTC case, called to ask about "a tape from Vernon Abernethy." We didn't know what he was talking about as all we had gotten from Vernon Abernethy was bogus return statements on Tech Traders' earnings! Walt had indicated that the envelope was for Sam Currin, not Vernon Abernethy. It was actually Jeremy Jaynes' accounting records by Abernethy, I now believe.

But our attorney called back a couple of weeks later and asked about the "tape" again. He said that sweet Libby Streit was harassing him, claiming that we were "hiding evidence" that was key to her "investigation". That was news to us. We'd given the nasty little woman and the Receiver everything we had.

To avoid a charge himself, I assumed that little Vernon must have decided to tell another fib and claim that he had given his tape to us, rather than telling Attorney Streit about his midnight visit to Walt Hannen's house with his shaving kit and file box. Dishonest but smart. "Put it on the Woltzes." I could just see his shifty little face in my mind.

But Walt may have told him to bring the items to be hidden from Streit. I couldn't be sure, but somewhere along the line, it came out that Walt had 'wiped' Vernon Abernethy's hard-drive clean of all data, using some sophisticated military program from IBM (or so Walt had told us). That really would be "obstruction of justice", I suppose, but Libby wasn't interested in the wrong-doers, just us. We had embarrassed her.

Walt's interest in helping little Vernon scrub his computer and hide files had been a mystery for a while, but eventually it was what cemented in my mind the idea that what he was really doing was covering for Jeremy Jaynes and Sam Currin, whom we later learned he was actually working for.

If the Feds had gotten hold of Vernon's records and found that he was Jaynes' accountant, and seen what Jaynes was doing, it could have been bad news from what we later learned. But I hadn't figured that all out by then. I was there sitting with the 'Thought Police' being grilled about taking this silly tape from Abernethy's house, based on someone's lie to cover their own misdeeds. How do you counteract a lie?

If I'd put the pieces together earlier, and figured out that Vernon Abernethy and Walt Hannen were in service to Jaynes and Sam Currin…and that what they were really doing was covering for *their* boss it all would have made more sense.

But all I could think of at the moment was to ask Agent Curran why we would want to help little Vernon do or cover up anything. We wanted him in jail where he belonged.

Agent Curran hadn't been able to answer that.

Martens, the prosecutor, had tried several times to steer the conversation back to getting information on his trophy, Sam Currin, and his spamming, penny-stock trading client, the infamous Jeremy Jaynes, to little avail. Until I got it clear who had done this to us, though, I wasn't switching gears.

But the morning had passed. The pudgy deputy came in and told them they would have to leave. It was "feeding" time. That was jailhouse vernacular for lunch.

Martens and crew promised to return that afternoon.

"Oh goodie," I thought. I get to spend more quality time with the dishonest U.S. prosecutors and corrupt agents without an attorney.

When I got back upstairs for "feeding", it was slices of white bread with an indescribable lunch meat and "partially hydrogenated soybean oil", cheese substitute squares.

Who could possibly ask for more?

CHAPTER 14

DEALIN' WITH THE DEVIL - Part 3

It didn't take long to enjoy my "mystery meat" sandwich back in the murderer's pod. A fellow can hardly complain about fine food like that. Only the best for Uncle Sam's "detainees"!

But I was dreading the afternoon session with the federal boys and getting angrier by the minute at David Freedman for abandoning me to them in the first place. What was he thinking? Or had he sold me out since before the bond hearing as it seemed?

The picture of what this was all about was coming clearer by the minute, however.

The charges were obviously contrived, even made up. They'd been cobbled together hastily once I'd offered to come up to North Carolina and assist them on the case. The grand jury had been held only days before the scheduled meeting so they would have an indictment to hold me, so I could not return to The Bahamas. They had made up charges against my wife as well...the same ones that Libby Streit had "shopped" in our home jurisdiction, (the "Middle District"), to no avail, so Vernice could be held as a hostage to force me to say whatever they asked of me.

They had been absolutely clear about *who* and *what* they were after. They wanted former U.S. Attorney Samuel T. Currin and his client, Jeremy Jaynes. As Sam had also been a judge and Chairman of the North Carolina Republican party before his star had fallen, he would be quite a trophy for young Asst. U.S. Attorney Matt Martens…a fine trophy indeed.

And Sam was vulnerable, as his star *had* fallen. He had little if any political clout left, and his practice was on the rocks. He would be an easy kill for Martens. His political protection was gone.

The best lawyers are recruited by the big firms right out of school. The next tier of students goes into smaller firms or private practice. Those that can't make it there try to become judges or go into politics. Sam, unfortunately fell into that last category.

Sam was a politico. But he'd had a good run, joining up with Senator Jesse Helms right out of law school, on Jesse's very first bid for office back in 1972. That's where I'd met Sam. I had been a campus coordinator at the N.C. State University.

Sam Currin had gone on to become Helm's chief of staff before becoming a U.S. Attorney, judge, and state chairman of the Republican Party. Then he ran out of gas.

By December of 2004, he was down to just one client, Jeremy Jaynes. He had confided to me that he was concerned and that both his partner, Thom Goolsby, and his wife, Margaret, were complaining. Jeremy Jaynes, spammer-extraordinaire and penny-stock trader, was his only bread and butter.

Sam had been targeted along with his sole remaining client, and was going to become a trophy on young Asst. U.S. Attorney Matt Martens' office wall, hide and all. That was the plan.

If Martens had been telling the truth that morning about Judge W. Earl Britt being Sam Currin's "blood-feud enemy", then the conspiracy extended two federal jurisdictions away, and as high as a federal district court judge. The fact that my own attorney, the FBI, and IRS agents all heard it and did nothing about it is itself illegal. Misprision of a felony is a crime (18 U.S.C. §4).

Back in 1980, Jesse Helms was very much opposed to the nomination of Judge W. Earl Britt, and had given Sam the task of seeing that the other 99 Senators didn't vote for his confirmation. Sam had taken on the task with vim and vigor; and spent the next couple of months vilifying him in every possible way to prevent his confirmation.

A quarter of a century later, it was pay-back time. Matt Martens had done his homework well. I had to give him that. He had also abandoned all ethics he may have ever had, and sought out the one judge in all of America who should never have been on this case....W. Earl Britt.

I'd already confirmed in Raleigh for myself that Judge Britt was culpable in matters of recusal, being trial judge for his own stenographer's son, so paying back Currin was little different. He'd taken young Martens' bait and signed on to the case down in far away Raleigh. Revenge is one hell of a thing. It's quite a motivator, I suppose. Judge Britt has proven himself to be as frail and human as any of us. He had accepted the case knowing it to be a violation of the Canons of Ethical Conduct.

But this was good old North Carolina, where politics and revenge are indiscernible. Politics is a contact sport in North Carolina. It's a good thing Lady Justice is blindfolded, because she surely wouldn't like what she saw if she'd gotten a glimpse of this set-up.

And we were caught smack dab in the middle of it between Scylla and Charybdis...betwixt a rock and a hard place. The deck was stacked against us before the game began.

With that undeniable conclusion in my mind, I was taken back down to the interrogation room on the second floor for more torment.

Martens wasted no time setting the stage for how the afternoon would go. I'd asked all the questions that I was going to get to ask. The afternoon belonged to him. I was to talk about Sam Currin and Jeremy Jaynes, the two scalps that would make him famous.

So I started way back at the beginning, in 2002 or so when Sam had brought Jeremy Jaynes down to Nassau to play golf and they had dropped by our office for a visit.

We had had a short meeting during which I explained how our trusts were formed and reviewed the legal aspects with Sam, as Jeremy's attorney. Jeremy was very quiet and showed little interest.

I thought no more about them after they had departed Nassau, but Sam called back within a couple of weeks and said that his client had been very impressed and wanted to come back down with his attorney from Colorado.

The next visit was short but active, as Jaynes' attorney, T.J. Agresti, was extremely aggressive in issues of U.S. law, far more so than our trust company cared to be, but I did have time to visit with Sam. In our private talks, he claimed that Jaynes had been voted young businessman of the year in the Raleigh, North Carolina area and had amassed a fortune of $20+ million, mainly in Internet advertising.

When I said the number "$20+ million", every agent in the room grabbed his pen and started writing. I immediately regretted having said it as we certainly never saw that kind of wealth from Jaynes ourselves, and that may have been "puffery" on Sam's part.

I continued, however, telling them that Sam had described Jaynes' advertising activities as "travel and leisure", "natural pharma", and so on, where his company actually made the sales and collected their fee, with the residual going to the customer.

Sam assured me that it was not pornography or anything that would embarrass us or our Regulators in Anguilla or The Bahamas.

Jeremy joined us at some point, and I remember his pointing toward the harbor and saying, "You see the harbor over there full of cruise ships? Our advertising filled over half of those berths. We use fax, printed mailers, and internet advertising all together. It's very effective."

On the "natural pharma", Jaynes explained that included natural 'Viagra-like' products, vitamins and supplements, which he said was a booming sector of internet growth.

So far, so good!

He then explained how his company managed the payments, which were almost exclusively credit card charges. Then we started getting to the real meat of what he wanted. The banks were a major problem for his company, as they not only took high transaction fees, but also withheld a large percentage of the payment against potential charge-backs, on which they earned interest, but paid nothing to him or his clients. It was very restrictive for growth as well, having so much money tied up in the charge-back withholding. He wanted to make a major change.

Sam picked it up from there, and broached the subject of his real interest, which was getting a banking license, so the company could process its own charges through a related institution, reduce the unnecessary withholding levels, and earn the fees instead of the large banks.

It was an interesting plan, and one that intrigued me, as I'd been on the committee that had written the E-Commerce plan for the government of The Bahamas a few years prior, and knew a bit about the need for banks that were savvy in the ways and nuances of E-Commerce, of which there were very few offshore at that time.

Sam knew that I'd started a bank in the Far East a few years before, and he had recommended to Jeremy that they get me to assist in establishing theirs, and participate as a partner. It was only then that I learned that their first trip had actually been about trying to reactivate a license that one of Sam's other clients had once owned in The Bahamas, but they had been unsuccessful. The Central Bank of The Bahamas was not licensing new banks at that time.

Many people come to the island nations with big ideas and plans. Most fizzle or stop when it comes time to put up capital. I told them plainly that getting a bank license was a difficult and time-consuming process. I'd done it. And I would not consider even researching the matter, much less, beginning the process unless the required bank capital and all anticipated start-up funds were in place prior to doing so.

Sam assured me that the capital was available, and he, as Jaynes' attorney, would guarantee that it would be in escrow and ready as needed, upon call.

I arranged meetings with KPMG, the largest accounting firm in Nassau, and also with the Deputy Director of the Central Bank of The Bahamas, Mr. Kevin Higgins. KPMG wanted huge fees just to "research" the issue, but Mr. Higgins was quite honest and advised us that The Bahamas was simply not issuing bank licenses to anyone unless they were first licensed in another country. Our money would be wasted.

Once he understood what the goal of the bank would be, which was to basically be a clearing house for Internet charges, Mr. Higgins suggested that we arrange to meet with Visa-Latin America in Miami, Florida, and ask them what jurisdiction would be not only best for licensing, but a jurisdiction that they would approve.

I knew from our research on the E-Commerce committee that Visa was roughly 73% of all credit card business worldwide, so this made great sense.

A meeting was arranged in Miami, and Sam and I met with the Visa-Latin America executives, as suggested. Meanwhile, through Sam, Jaynes had us set up companies for his internet advertising business, for each region of the world, to segregate it by market. We also established a trust structure for him, which would own the various entities.

The meeting with Visa went quite well. They were keen on the idea, and our credentials impressed them. Their suggestion was to look toward the relatively new banking jurisdiction of St. Lucia in the eastern Caribbean, as an excellent place to license a bank.

We were further assured that if we did so, Visa would work with us and approve the bank for credit card processing. The only caveat was that we would also have to issue cards, which was not our interest, but those were the rules.

One of my partners in our trust company in Anguilla, Mr. Joseph Brice, was a prominent St. Lucian, and had excellent credentials and contacts in his home nation and joined in my efforts to establish a bank there.

Joe is a huge black man, with a deep, gentle voice. Joe had been educated in the United Kingdom at the University of Edinburgh, and then on to law school. Afterwards, he had been recruited by the United Nations and had worked on projects in Chile and Trinidad, before being hired away by the British Virgin Islands to establish that territory as a corporate center.

Under Joseph Brice's management as Registrar General, the British Virgin Islands went from zero international companies, to 150,000.

He was hired by another British territory, Anguilla, to duplicate this miracle, which he did, making tiny Anguilla the first "on-line" corporate registry in the world. That is where I had met him when my business attorney, Hiram Martin, and I had traveled to Anguilla to meet with the regulators to research the island territory as a potential site for a trust company.

Hiram and I had been as impressed with Joe Brice as we were with lovely Anguilla and the quality of its Regulators, so the decision had been quite easy to establish our trust company there.

Sterling Trust was born after the required regulatory review and application process, and Joe Brice had become the local managing director and a partner in the business.

The idea of starting a bank back home in St. Lucia had appealed to Joe, and shortly thereafter, a trip was arranged to meet with the regulators there and explore the possibilities.

On that trip, Jeremy Jaynes, Sam Currin, and Sam's law partner, Thom Goolsby, joined Joe and I. We met with the regulators, accountants, local notables, and even the Prime Minister, Dr. Kenny Anthony, who was a close friend of Joe Brice's.

Once established as a plan, I took over and began the drudgery of the lengthy application process, which consumed a great deal of the next two and a half years.

Jeremy Jaynes put up the initial exploratory capital, as agreed, for the set-up cost, and I did the work.

Other than a brief meeting in North Carolina, where I was introduced to Jaynes' Canadian partner, Bryan Kos, I didn't hear from Jaynes for the following year or so, more than once or twice. All communication came through Sam Currin, or my secretary, Fertina Turnquest, who seemed to be dealing more and more with Jaynes and Kos on their advertising business.

But no revenues seemed to be forthcoming. Every time she was needed, it seemed that she was "doing something" for Jeremy Jaynes or Bryan Kos.

I mentioned this to Sam Currin once or twice, as my staff seemed increasingly occupied with Jaynes' advertising business, but the huge cash-flows promised (on which we were paid), had never materialized.

Their business was actually costing us money. Sam continually promised that the situation would soon change, and I was so busy working on setting up Sterling Bank and managing our other clients, that I really had little time to deal with it. Having known Sam for 30+ years, I trusted him, which was a terrible mistake that would cost me dearly.

And then all hell broke loose. In the early summer months of 2004, we began receiving lawsuits from a network of lawyers all over the United States, via fax, mail, and threatening "shake down" calls from the business equivalent of the ambulance-chasing variety of lawyer, hungry for a quick buck.

The lawsuits were claiming that our corporate management firm, Sterling ACS, Ltd., was a "fax-blaster" and sending unsolicited advertisements, which was in violation of some U.S. law. It was also very untrue.

We had absolutely no idea what these shysters were talking about until one of them called from Ft. Lauderdale, Florida. I overheard my assistant, Fertina, talking to him, and told her that I wanted to speak to him to find out what this was all about.

He began his little tirade of huff, puff, and bluster, but I quickly cut him off at the knees by reminding him that he had no jurisdiction in The Bahamas but demanded to know what kind of scam he and his "network" of blood-suckers was running, as we didn't have a clue what he was talking about. Plus, I told him, "fax-blasting" from The Bahamas, at the outrageous phone rates Batelco charged, would be a silly proposition to begin with.

"You really don't know what this is about, do you?" the attorney asked.

"No I really don't," I said. "Please edify me."

"Are you near a computer?" he asked.

"Yes," I said, and with that he led me to a website called 'Tucows.com', which was a website registration company. Someone had registered a website, in *my* name, called *winningstockpicks.net* or something similar to that with our company address in The Bahamas.

I was livid.

The lawyer then explained that a rich guy out in California, by the name of Steve Kirsch, had created the network of lawyers, who sued "fax-blasters" when Kirsch advised them to do so. They would file or threaten the suit, then agree to drop then for a couple of thousand dollars. It was a cheap way to generate some money when business was slow.

"But what does this guy Kirsch get out of it?" I asked the lawyer. "Do you pay him a percentage, or what?"

"No. We don't pay him anything," the lawyer said. "None of us can figure out what his angle is."

Interesting, I thought. We parted ways with the agreement that he would drop his lawsuit, though we both knew that he and the others had no jurisdiction. It was just a "shake-down", plain and simple. But what was this Kirsch guy up to? That didn't make any sense.

I immediately called the number on Tucows.com's website and got some zoned-out Internet type on the line and laid him low, demanding to know how my name got on his website and how fast he could get it removed.

He said that he could not do so unless his "re-seller" that had registered it approved.

"And where in the hell is this re-seller?" I demanded.

"Raleigh, North Carolina," he replied, and gave me a number in area code 919. Raleigh, North Carolina...internet...fax-blasting...it all came clear.

We only had one contact in Raleigh, North Carolina and that was Sam Currin's client, Jeremy Jaynes. I yelled for Fertina, who very sheepishly came into my office. Only a plate-glass window separated us, and she had seen...and heard...my anger.

"Get Jeremy Jaynes on the line now!" I said.

"He's not available. I've already tried," she said, which I found odd. Why had she been trying to reach Jeremy Jaynes? "Then get Sam Currin on the line," I barked.

"Don't you think you should wait and talk to Jeremy first?" she asked. She seemed to be protecting him. That was even odder. I picked up the phone and called Sam myself.

Sam sounded as mystified as I was by all of this, but promised to find out what was going on.

I then called this "re-seller" in Raleigh and unloaded on him. I told him that he had one day to straighten out his mess and get my name off that website, or he and everyone involved would be getting sued, but even with that, it seemed as though he had been forewarned...expecting my call. He had refused to give me his name, even before he knew why I was calling....

The only person that knew what was happening was...Fertina, my assistant.

By the time I hung up and went looking for her, she had gone. The receptionist said that she had "left early for the rest of the day." No answer on her cell-phone either. I tried 20 times.

I was furious, but nothing like what was coming.

CHAPTER 15

THE OTHER SHOE HITS THE FLOOR

What happened next would change my life.

At that point in 2004, I'd built the basis for a small financial empire. We had our trust company in Anguilla, corporate management firm in Nassau, the beginnings of a bank in Saint Lucia, and had also gotten into the insurance business in Anguilla, having recently been licensed as Sterling Casualty & Insurance, Ltd.

We had also been approved as the recognized dealer for Latin America and the Caribbean by the government-owned Perth Mint of Australia, and had established Sterling Precious Metals Ltd. to handle sales of gold, silver, and platinum in our region, which was the southern half of the Western Hemisphere.

Our trust company had purchased a portion of Batterson Venture Capital in Chicago as well, and the "Sterling Group of Companies" offered more or less every service a serious international investor could want. We had been approached with buyout offers by John Deuss, the seventh richest man on earth, as well as UBS Bank's Private Banking Division out of Geneva, Switzerland. Both had been turned down and come back. We were talking a deal.

But everything I had built would soon be toppled through no wrong-doing on our part.

The first leg was kicked out from under us within a couple of days after the fake website registration of Jaynes' stock site had come to light, and because of it, as well.

Another website, called "*junkfax.org*", which was run by the scam lawsuit promoter, Steve Kirsch, published what he called "research" on "The Anatomy of a Stock Fraud". It was the most scandalous trash I'd ever read, with hardly a word of truth in it. It was pure slander.

And I was right on there as a key player in a "penny-stock fraud", according to the libelous Mr. Kirsch, including my picture.

He'd found a snapshot on the Web where I'd been the keynote speaker at an S.T.E.P. luncheon in the Eastern Caribbean (Society of Trust and Estate Practitioners out of London), and put that over his article of untruths.

I was livid. Within five minutes of seeing Kirsch's trash, I had forwarded a copy to our regulators in both Anguilla and The Bahamas, and notified Sam Currin that he and his penny-stock promoting clients had better appear in Nassau within 24 hours to explain themselves.

And they did. Jaynes, Kos, and Currin arrived the following day, and I invited the Deputy Director of the Central Bank, Mr. Higgins, to come to the meeting and hear their explanations first-hand, so he could determine what should be done.

No one had ever mentioned "stock promotion" as an activity of Jaynes and Kos's "advertising" operations. This completely blindsided everyone except my assistant, Fertina Turnquest, whom we would later discover had been doing their secret bidding since February of 2004, where she and her husband, Mark, were being paid as much as $38,000 per month to set up trading accounts, coordinate transfers with U.S. law firms who were involved in Jaynes' operation, and most importantly...she was to keep it all hidden from us.

But in the meeting that day, as the story unfolded, Jeremy and Sam had been very convincing about the company's activity.

"We promote stocks. That's true," Jaynes admitted. "And sometimes, we're compensated with shares for doing so. But these aren't our companies. We just provide the service of 'investor awareness' for them."

He took us on his website and showed us what he was doing. Sure enough, venerable companies, such as General Electric and its stock were being promoted, along with other large-caps, mid-caps, and a couple of penny-stocks.

"But, what about this Kirsch guy?" I asked.

Jaynes and Kos both burst out, "Steve Kirsch is nothing but a short-seller! He 'short-sells' shares of companies whose stock he doesn't even own against 'margin' and then publishes his lies and distortions to drive the price down. The price plummets as everyone dumps shares when they read his stories and then Kirsch jumps in and buys them back for next to nothing to 'cover'. He's the biggest crook in the business and makes millions doing it."

"Why doesn't the S.E.C. (Securities and Exchange Commission) go after him?" I asked.

"They never seem to go after the short-sellers," Jaynes said. "They make themselves look like 'investigators' and 'whistle-blowers' like they're guarding the public's interest. The S.E.C. actually follows their lead. Meanwhile, they're destroying companies and shareholder value, all just to make millions for themselves. It's a rich man's game, and the S.E.C. is too stupid to see what's really going on."

Sure enough, we went on Kirsch's junk site, "*junkfax.org*" and you'd have thought the guy was the Lone Ranger. Jaynes also took us to an "I Love Me" site, as he called it, where Kirsch had pages of praise for himself. He even bragged that he had given Al Gore over a million dollars, the day of and the day after the election of 2000, to make sure that the vote count "went the right way".

"The son of a bitch tried to buy the election," one of the boys said.

"But what about the stock stuff," I asked. "Is any of it true about what you're doing?"

"How much of what he said about you is true, Howell?" Bryan Kos asked me.

"I counted 22 falsehoods or outright lies in the one page he did on us," I answered. "He claims his 'research' shows that companies are 'here and there' in places that we've never even started a company. It's all trash except for the address of our farm in North Carolina. He got that right, but all anyone would have to do is call directory assistance to get that."

"Well, he's just as accurate on Jeremy and Bryan, Howell," Sam interjected. "This guy Kirsch is nothing but a short-seller. He's no good."

That was pretty strong stuff coming from a former U.S. Attorney, judge, and lawyer.

"We're thinking about going to the S.E.C. ourselves," Sam added.

"I think that's the thing to do," I said.

Mr. Higgins, who had been quiet up until that point, said, "That's the last thing you need to do. And Howell, you need to stay completely out of it. You're not a policeman; you're a financial services provider and a trustee. I agree with Judge Currin. These gentlemen have done nothing wrong. Unless they've been indicted for a crime, your job is to provide them a registered office and trustee service, nothing more."

My thunder had been stolen. I'd been put in my place by the Regulator.

"But what about our reputation?" I asked. "This guy, Steve Kirsch, has put absolute lies out about us for the entire world to read."

"So sue him," Mr. Higgins said. "Isn't that what you Americans like to do?" With that he chuckled and added, "This has nothing to do with us. These people have broken none of our laws, Howell. Just do your job."

It was quite a put-down, but I had to listen to my Regulator. What about Anguilla? Would the regulator there, Mr. John Lawrence, see things the same way as Mr. Higgins?

I could not afford to take the chance. I organized another meeting in Anguilla, and required Jaynes, Kos, and Currin to meet with the Regulators there as well.

The meeting was depressingly similar. John D.K. Lawrence and his assistant, Carlyle Rogers, relied on Judge Currin's credentials and assurances that all was legal and above board.

Mr. Lawrence and Mr. Rogers certainly knew that what this Kirsch character was saying was untrue, as all of the companies he mentioned had been incorporated right there in their own Registry, while the 'investigator' Kirsch was claiming that his 'research' showed Trinidad or The Bahamas, and so on, as the home jurisdictions of the companies. He had clearly done no 'research' other than looking at the Edgar database on the S.E.C. registration on his targets and making up the rest.

Mr. Lawrence ended the meeting with just two comments:

First, he was relying on Sam Currin's credentials and expertise. If anything untoward happened or if the activities of his clients ever edged into areas which may be of questionable legality, he was to notify Mr. Lawrence directly and immediately.

Second, like Mr. Higgins in The Bahamas, Mr. Lawrence warned me that until that happened, I was to quit trying to play policeman and satisfy myself with being a trustee.

Put in my place a second time, by a second regulator, I had to just lick my wounds and comply.

But I wasn't done with Mr. Steve Kirsch yet, and I was still extremely angry that Jaynes, Kos, or one of their people had used *my* name and *our* company address for their investor awareness site that had brought so much unwanted attention.

Because of that, this Kirsch guy had splattered my picture and these very damaging lies all over the world. There was no way to estimate how much business this little man would cost us or how many potential problems he would bring our way, just so he could buy the shares he claimed to be seeking (at a bargain) to make more money.

But I had to agree with Jeremy and Bryan on what this guy Kirsch was, because he had himself admitted to looking for shares on his own junk site. He claimed to have spent hours calling brokers and dealers everywhere looking for shares of one of the same companies that he had spent weeks trashing on his web-site which was designed solely to drive down the prices of the target stocks it seemed. Every claim he made about our company had been untrue.

Why would a man that claimed the company and everyone that had ever had any involvement with it were crooked...be calling everywhere looking for shares?

Bingo! The only possible explanation was that he needed to find shares to buy in order to 'cover' his short-selling. I could think of no other reason. Kirsch had to be a crook. It was clear that he was an imaginative liar, who could take a small core and weave a very damaging tale around it, but his own words gave away the real truth. Nothing else made sense.

I copied Kirsch's admission from his junk site in case he ever realized that he had basically admitted to being a stock fraudster, and later tried to remove it.

It was then that I began the long and arduous process of suing Steve Kirsch from The Bahamas for his slander and defamation of my character.

I soon learned that was something that had hardly ever been done in The Bahamas, but that is where the damage had occurred to my name and that of our business.

The ramifications from Jaynes and Kos's misuse of my name were almost immediate. I received a subpoena from the CFTC lawyer, Elizabeth Streit for a deposition in her civil suit; a subpoena from the S.E.C. in Miami for a deposition regarding Kirsch's diatribe on the Web; a grand jury subpoena from North Carolina for the following year; and a phone call from the trash-man himself claiming to be an agent of the S.E.C. Steve Kirsch told both myself and our attorney, Marty Russo that he was calling under the auspices of the U.S. Government. The boy had no scruples at all.

Jeremy Jaynes was indicted by the Commonwealth of Virginia for 'spamming' under their new law, which AOL had garnered from the state legislature (with massive donations to politicians) and the world that we had so carefully built began to crumble all around us.

Regulators and attorneys warned me against any disclosures of client information, the mere mention of which could cost me years in prison and fines of several hundred thousand dollars.

The S.E.C. deposition had come first. Marty Russo came down from New York to attend it with me. We met at their headquarters on Brickell Avenue, and I spent the entire day being interrogated on nothing but Steve Kirsch's propaganda.

The head of litigation, Mr. Chih Pin Lu, and his assistant, Julie Russo, questioned me, not on any investigation that had been done or real information; but on Steve Kirsch's trash from what Sam Currin called his "short-selling site". I could not believe what I was seeing. Every question came from his wild allegations, about people I'd never known. They weren't even coy or secretive about using web-slander. They were reading directly from a copy of his crude and libelous ranting about companies with which I'd never dealt, whose stocks were allegedly being promoted by Currin's clients.

I began to think that Steve Kirsch may work for the S.E.C after all, since he was able to get away with his highly questionable stock activities, claim he was a government agent, and not be indicted himself. Either that or he had something on someone that kept him protected…political donations, perhaps?

When he had called me on my cell phone, I had actually been with Marty Russo. After Kirsch claimed to me and to Marty that he worked for the S.E.C, we contacted Mary Romano (of the California S.E.C. office), who assured us that Kirsch had no affiliation with any S.E.C. office, nor had he ever had any.

Steve Kirsch was running around gathering trash for his "short-selling site", posing as a federal agent…and the S.E.C. was doing nothing about it. It sounded very fishy to me.

But sitting there with the S.E.C in Miami was quite worrisome, as I'd been warned, in writing, by our Bahamian counsel, about the very strict rules on client confidentiality, and had a very difficult task ahead of me. There was a thin line between the privacy laws in the nations where I worked and held financial licenses (The Bahamas and Anguilla), versus possible contempt or perjury charges in the United States.

I had been advised by counsel that Jaynes and Kos were *not* even clients of our firm, technically, and that was the line I must follow. They were beneficiaries of foreign grantor trusts, not *clients* or *owners of anything*.

But I actually learned more from them than they learned from me, as they had the data from S.E.C. registrations and showed me documents I would never have otherwise seen. It was clear that my assistant, Fertina Turnquest, was neck-deep in Jeremy Jaynes' business, working from inside our offices for him, while being paid to work for our firm. She was a dangerous turncoat.

I learned that she had put my own in-laws from Trinidad as directors of companies involved in Jaynes' "advertising" business, which is how Kirsch had gotten his so-called 'research' so wrong. He was using the directors' addresses, and wildly assuming that the corporations must be domiciled there also. He had done no 'research'. He'd made a guess and run with it. It didn't matter. All he wanted was to make the stock price go down. The truth was irrelevant.

Jeremy and Sam had apparently been correct about Steve Kirsch and what he was.

The next deposition I was subjected to was with the lovely Elizabeth Streit, the morally withered lawyer from the CFTC who had been re-invigorated in her witch-hunt by Kirsch's postings on his "short-selling site". None of that had anything to do with her case, but her hope was that she could make us into bad guys by showing that we knew some, I suppose.

Nothing that day had anything to do with the commodities fraud of Vernon Abernethy and Coyt Murray, or Tech Traders. This was a lynching party, plain and simple; a federal fishing expedition to try and entrap some victims.

Marty Russo had joined me for Libby's party as well, and we had caught her lying before the proceeding had ever begun.

Libby had a speaker on the conference table of the deposition room. Marty asked her why it was there.

"Who's going to be on the speaker, Beth?" Marty asked (Beth was what she preferred to be called. We just referred to her as "Libby" out of spite, I suppose).

"Oh, nobody but Joy McCormack up in our Chicago office. She couldn't make the trip," she'd replied.

"Is she alone? Will she be the only person listening?" Marty asked, "Or is there going to be anyone else?"

"She's alone", replied Streit. "It will only be her".

"You are alone, Ms. McCormack?" Marty had asked.

"Yes. Yes. I'm alone", she'd responded over the speaker.

"And you'll notify us immediately if that changes?" Marty asked her.

"Yes. I will", she answered.

Not thirty seconds more had passed before we clearly heard a male voice in the background over the speaker.

"Who was that, Beth?" Marty asked. "You promised that no one else would be listening. I clearly heard a male voice just now. Who is it?" he asked Streit, then turned to the speaker and said, "Who's there?"

Streit just blushed and stammered. She'd been caught lying and we hadn't even started yet.

She had Joy McCormack tell us that she was alone...which we later figured may have been true...because the male voice was from the FBI agents listening over the speaker in the next room!

They were definitely in the law offices Streit claimed had been "loaned" to her by old friends for the deposition, as FBI agent Doug Curran was standing in the hallway that night as we left.

Libby spent the entire day asking questions, not one of which had anything to do with her case or the criminals that had robbed our clients of millions. It was clearly an abuse of federal...or in her case...."quasi-federal" power. She was misusing a deposition of a victim in a civil case as a fishing expedition for another agency. It was an attempt to entrap.

She asked all manner of immaterial and inane questions about who was on our boards, about credit cards, and so on. I answered every question honestly.

Where she was shopping for the name Jeremy Jaynes and it didn't fit, I gave it to her anyway. I was going to be sure, I'd decided, that she couldn't claim that even one word had been untrue or incomplete. I was not worried about Jaynes. We'd come to the conclusion that we did not want his business, and I had planned to notify Currin the following week that they would have to find new trustees due to Sam's refusal to give us source of funds information.

But these were the Feds. The truth didn't matter. Libby Streit would claim perjury anyway. And the FBI agents in the next room would follow her lead without checking even one of her bold lies. Feds don't investigate any more. They either expect you to plead guilty, which is the case in 93.6% of all federal adjudications[4]; or they nail you at trial with "compensated witnesses", (a.k.a. "snitches"), who are saying whatever they tell them to say for a "time-cut" in their own sentence.

Vernon Abernethy, the crooked accountant who had cost our clients millions, had avoided prosecution altogether by agreeing to lie about us at a grand jury hearing. That's just the way it works in America today. His testimony directly refuted that he had given at his own trial (as well as four other witnesses), but the Feds went with it anyway.

---

[4] 2008 U.S. Sentencing Commission Final Quarterly Data Report

And what a day it was. Long after dark, and long after the legal limit for a deposition had been exceeded, Libby was halted. Her last weak attempt had been too much. She'd held up a piece of paper, making yet another false claim of some sorts, saying that my signature was on it. I think she'd been watching too much TV. I guess she'd seen a scene like that where a savvy cop drew "the truth" out of a "bad guy" with a trick like that. But this wasn't Hollywood, and she was no savvy cop. I snapped.

"That's a damn lie!" I'd shouted. "Let's see it!"

Marty had called a halt because she couldn't produce any such document. She'd gone too far. Libby slipped the blank piece of paper back into her file. We were done.

But she wasn't. On the way out of the room, FBI agent Doug Curran was standing in the hallway with a grand jury subpoena.

"That's dirty", is all Marty said to him, and we kept on walking.

It wasn't hard to piece things together from there. It was Friday night, just before Christmas, in the locked office of a private law firm, way after hours, and Agent Curran had been waiting in the empty hallway with a grand jury subpoena.

It didn't take much to figure from there who the voice on the speaker had been when Streit had lied about Joy McCormack being the only listener.

Feds. You just can't trust them to ever tell the truth. I've learned that the hard way.

But I never got to the grand jury. Marty had called Agent Curran at the FBI before it was held and asked him if I was a witness or a target of the grand jury. According to Marty, Agent Curran had gotten a bit huffy, and refused to answer.

"Well if you don't know what you want with my client", Marty had said, "then I must advise Mr. Woltz to take the Fifth Amendment and say nothing, as it sounds like another one of your fishing expeditions."

Curran had exploded at that, "Well if he's just going to take the Fifth, then he doesn't need to come at all!"

"Good. I'll tell him that," with which Marty hung up and very wisely memorialized the conversation in a letter to Curran so he couldn't later lie about it and claim that I had just failed to appear.

But after this spate of federal interest and being trashed by scummy short-sellers, we'd had our fill of Jeremy Jaynes and Sam Currin. A whirlwind of trouble seemed to surround them.

The bank we used for our trust clients, First Curacao International, had advised us of the same decision. They no longer wanted any business related to Jeremy Jaynes after his spamming conviction either. He was toxic.

December 17th of 2004, I drove to Raleigh, North Carolina, and advised my longtime friend, Samuel T. Currin, that regardless of what our regulators said, we were not going to continue doing business with him or his clients, even indirectly as trust beneficiaries. Sam, as the "Protector" of the various trusts and related entities, was given six months to find new trustees for transfer of any remaining assets, or we would forward them to the court of Anguilla for disposition.

Sam was furious. He told me that I could not do that, and actually filed the first and only complaint we ever had with our Regulator in Anguilla, Mr. John Lawrence, over our demand that they move their business. But rather than tell it like it was, Sam claimed that we were stealing Jeremy's money, and demanded an audit, which was a clever move, as it would delay any disposition of the assets in the interim.

Sam had been a U.S. Attorney and Fed. He had learned from the best how to deal dishonestly.

The audit showed only one error...we had undercharged our trustee fees under our agreement, and were due considerably more money from the trusts before moving the assets. Every penny and property was in its proper place and accounted for.

But the day I was firing myself at Sam's office had been a busy one for my wife, Vernice, as well. Things were hopping down in Nassau. Perhaps sensing our investigation of her since the S.E.C. deposition had taken place, my assistant, Fertina Turnquest, had stolen $40,000 in cash, from our vault. She had also taken many private files relating to Jeremy Jaynes, and fled the office, according to the staff, after receiving a call from Sam Currin's office.

Vernice had ordered that she was not to be readmitted, if she returned. She did return, desperate to retrieve something from her desk, but she was not allowed to enter. The locks were changed that day, along with the combination to the vault.

The "motherlode" was found, hidden behind the file drawer in her desk. It was all of her direct orders from Jeremy Jaynes and his attorneys in the U.S., dealing with his activities and trading accounts that had been kept from us, the trustees.

Fertina had been no dummy. She had made Jaynes fax her signed instructions to do each and every crooked act, and his attorney, who according to the documents was a Mr. Jere Ross, of Bush Ross Gardiner, up in Tampa, Florida, had done the same. He'd been Jaynes' middle-man between the trading accounts they had opened and our accounts at First Curacao for trusts and companies.

All we saw were small transfers from a law firm, having no way of knowing what was going on behind the shield.

We had our smoking gun.

One of our other corporate officers, Dematee Mohan, called CIS, the criminal investigation service of the Royal Bahamian Police, and reported the theft of the cash and files by Fertina and her husband, Mark Turnquest.

Our attorneys at Davis & Co. were instructed to file an action against them in the Supreme Court of The Bahamas, forthwith, and put a seizure on the funds her own files showed had been diverted from our company accounts.

Over $200,000 still remained at First Caribbean International Bank, and was attached by court order. Supreme Court case, Sterling ACS, Ltd. v. Fertina & Mark Turnquest, became case 001 of 2005.

Fertina had diverted $1,016,000 of funds to her personal accounts. Not bad for a girl from Cat Island, who'd never even finished high school.

She and Jeremy Jaynes were a matched pair.

Vernice and I spent our Christmas that year sorting through her files, learning of what had been going on behind our backs for the better part of a year, and meeting with CIS investigator, Sergeant Miller.

Fertina and Mark Turnquest were ordered by the Royal Bahamian Police, not to leave the island, but they knew the jig was up. They decided to try anyway, and were arrested on-board the U.S. Airways flight to North Carolina, just before takeoff, attempting to flee the nation and to get to their benefactor, Jeremy Jaynes. They were put under house arrest by the Bahamian police.

But Fertina did us a favor in the Supreme Court case against her and her husband, which may ultimately give me justice in my own case if an honest Fed ever investigates the corrupt prosecutor and judge that put me where I am today. In her own sworn affidavits, as well as exhibits from the complicit attorney in Tampa at Bush, Ross, & Gardiner, she cleared us of any involvement and clearly stated that only she knew of Jeremy's activities, which she ran through her and her husband's company, 1st Consultants.

And Matt Martens, our prosecutor, who was sitting across the table from me as I recounted this tale, had already been sent a copy of all of this exculpatory information before the grand jury hearing, but had failed to produce it, which was a violation of the federal law, itself.

We would later learn that the reason Martens didn't dare produce this information was he had used Fertina Turnquest, whom we had tried for theft and multiple other felonies, sued in the Supreme Court, and ultimately forced to return the cash and gotten back $200,000 from her accounts at First Caribbean...as the star witness against us!

The truth that she had sworn to in the Supreme Court case affidavits in The Bahamas, would have proven that what Martens told her to say about my wife and I to the grand jury in North Carolina so he could falsely charge us, were lies, so he had to sequester the exculpatory evidence, even though it was available. This is a crime... but no one cares. The Feds do it every day and get away with it, because there is no oversight, and the grand jury of today is little more than a kangaroo court.

He would also hit me with a superseding Bill of Information and charge me with "conspiracy" (which just that morning he and my lawyer, David Freedman had assured was contractually forbidden in writing), by claiming that I knew about these activities when he knew that I did not.

And I would sign that false statement in exchange for my wife's freedom a few months later, when she was near death, so she could be freed to receive proper care and be reunited with our children. The prosecutor, Matt Martens, and myself, would sign that lie, knowing it to be one.

In the federal system, the truth will never set you free. Only a lie about yourself or someone else will do that. Like it or not, that's the way the federal system works today in the Land of the Once Free. That's why our system is now the least just in terms of fairness and equity of any on the planet, statistically.

I had spent the entire day being interrogated by these agents, and we hadn't even gotten to the part of my tale that had brought me to Charlotte to assist them at our prescheduled meeting in the first place.

Having admitted that we had committed no crime, they were desperate to have me 'confess' to something...anything. FBI Agent Curran said, "Surely you have done *something* wrong. Tell us about that."

The only thing that I could think of that I had ever done in my professional career which caused me discomfort was stating to the S.E.C. that Jeremy Jaynes was not a "client". This was technically and legally a true statement, given on the advice of both U.S. and Bahamian counsel, but I had felt that it was less than candid.

They all excitedly made notes and though I was promised that anything I said could not be used against me based on the non-affinity agreement I would soon see a grossly distorted version of my words in a document stating that I had "confessed" to perjury.

But the boys finally had a "crime", though it was not one that could stand the least scrutiny or any adversarial testing, as my statement had been the truth under law and stated on the advice of counsel. "Discomfort" does not perjury make. Lying under oath does.

But the day was gone. The sight of the overweight deputy coming to run them out of the interrogation room was a welcome sight.

It was once again "feeding time" in the Mecklenburg County Jail, and not even these FBI, IRS, and DOJ thugs had the juice to override that.

Deputy Dawg and I rode back upstairs in the elevator in silence. Even on starvation rations in that nasty jail, I could not muster an appetite that night.

I felt dirty having been around those evil people all day and showered instead of eating. The hard, metal bunk may as well have been a feather bed that night I was so tired. Once again, I escaped my misery in a deep sleep, wishing it could all be a bad dream.

CHAPTER 16

LIFE IN LIMBO

Life in federal custody has been described as hour upon hour of sheer boredom, punctuated by moments of stark terror. That's about right.

But living amongst a bunch of known killers can spice things up even more, I can tell you. You just never know who is going to flip out, or over what.

Several of us....the Fed's guests that is...were in the 'murderer's pod' for another and very specific reason. We were supposed to become so scared and miserable that we would sign anything just to get out of there. It actually works quite well. It's immoral, unethical and unconstitutional, but they don't worry about things like that anymore.

But the "bad guys" weren't all bad. The first one that I met in Pod 6800 was a man accused of more murders than Jack the Ripper. He's now on death row, but he used to loan me books and be my spades partner. His name is Mike Sherrill.

But several of the men in there did not belong. The stories came at me like bad dreams. A white man with glasses is presumed to know something of the law. Why, I'm not sure, but that's the way it is. After several young, black men had come to me with legal questions, I simply asked one of them, "Why me?"

Without hesitation, he replied, "Because you're a white man with glasses." And so it went. But because of that, I was forced to see that my case was anything but unique. In fact the sordid tale of our unjust detention and being falsely charged was something that many of these men had lived with all of their lives.

Even those that had done "something" were subjected to illegal searches, illegal seizures, warrantless arrests, and bizarre and unconstitutional treatment.

In the case of my then neighbor in Pod 6800, Antonio Delrae Smith, who had been caught with a small amount of crack cocaine in his pocket, and a weapon, he had broken a law. But how had his arrest come about?

As with every case I ever read, "snitches" had given the police his name, in exchange for a time-cut, or the dropping of one of their own charges.

The police had used this information to get a search warrant for Smith's home. He was not there when they came to his house, but was later seen at a convenience store miles away from his home by an officer. She called in "back-up", and with no probable cause of any kind, the small army of officers drew their weapons and threw Smith to the ground.

They found a small piece of crack cocaine in his shirt pocket and a gun that he had in the car for protection, as is allowed under the Second Amendment, and was his right.

Smith was promised to only be prosecuted on a minor offense and returned home if he would cooperate. His court-appointed counsel (Trobich) encouraged him to do so, claiming the deal was secure.

But after nearly two years, when I met Antonio Delrae Smith, he had yet to ever be sentenced. When they finally took him before the judge for his "no-time" deal, which had escalated to a "5 year" plea agreement for the tiny rock, he was sentenced to 16 years and 8 months in prison.

I've never yet, out of the hundreds of cases I've reviewed, ever heard of a prosecutor or agent telling any of these men the truth. They seem incapable of being honest with the citizenry they are employed to serve.

More out of complete disgust at the injustice rather than choice, I began learning what I could of the law. My sister-in-law became my angel and supplied me with copies of law books and the tools I needed to learn something of the way the system was supposed to work, as it was clearly broken and not functioning as a free nation (or our constitution) required.

And she didn't just send them one time. They were frequently stolen by the guards in targeted "shakedowns" or each time the prosecutor, Matt Martens, had me taken on another joy ride, or "diesel therapy" as it is called.

My first success was intoxicating. J.R. (Fitzgerald) Stephenson had been held on an impossible charge for 21 months when I met him in Pod 6800. I say "impossible" because J.R. is a 6 foot 6 inch black giant, weighing 275 pounds without an ounce of fat on his body. Further, J.R. Stephenson had a deformity from a terrible car wreck, where his neck had not been set properly after being broken. It was 36 inches in circumference. It was larger than my waist, after a couple of months on the 'Mecklenburg' diet.

When I read the police report, however, the suspect was described as a small, 5 foot 10 inch, clean-shaven man weighing approximately 165 pounds. The victims further described the man as having no distinguishing marks or features.

When people saw my boy, J.R., their jaws dropped. He was that big. And the neck was so obvious, that the fellows sometimes called him "turkey-neck" behind his back. Way behind his back, that is.

We wrote to a minister who had once been in jail whom we heard had also done some investigating for prisoners who couldn't afford to hire such. He wrote back and agreed to help us.

Meanwhile, in my law books, I'd read of an old act passed back in 1871, and signed by Pres. Ulysses S. Grant, which was called the "Ku Klux Klan Act". 42 U.S.C.§1983 had been designed to allow blacks in the post-Civil War south who could not get justice from the local courts after the Fourteenth Amendment had guaranteed equal protection to them, to apply directly to federal courts where cases of injustice could be adjudicated.

But was it still active law?

I wrote the local U.S. District Clerk of Court to ask, and received a curt reply in the affirmative. It was still active law. So far - so good. But I hadn't a clue what to do about it, so I wrote back asking if there was a form for such.

After a few tries, I finally got the entire packet to file a federal suit for J.R. which could have been sent in response to the first letter, but these people make everything that helps government's victims like pulling teeth.

The preacher/investigator found that the "confidential informant" was Adam 1 telling Adam 2 as they drove down the street, "Let's get that big guy." There had been no informant. The two arresting police officers had lied.

And the witnesses, three of them, had never been shown a "line-up", as is required by law, they'd been faxed "head-shots" from chin to hair, quite intentionally excluding the neck. And only one of the three had given my boy, J.R. the nod, and then only "maybe". The other two had picked someone else, and were sure about it.

But little things like that don't get in the way of "American Justice" these days. They had their man, and the prosecutor was the last person on earth to make them do the right thing. They'd decided to just let J.R. sit in jail until he too agreed that he had done it. That's just the way it now works, as it did in my own case.

When these two officers got their subpoenas delivered by U.S. Marshals and the chief of police got his for the constitutional violations of Mr. J.R. (Fitzgerald) Stephenson's rights, it changed things considerably. After we'd mailed it out, my own prosecutor had taken me on another senseless round of diesel therapy, and when I got back, J.R. was gone. They actually put me in his old cell, #52, when I was returned.

We had sued them for $950,000. All charges had been dropped and J.R. had been set free. The last I heard from him, he was planning to open "J.R.'s Kountry Kitchen" with the money, he said, in his thank you note for my assistance, though I never heard whether he got paid or how much.

That was my first win and it felt good.

But there were some real killers in there too. Not everyone was innocent, though the percentage of wrongfully incarcerated would shock even the ACLU or anyone else if they'd lived with these men.

For example, there was Serrano, the Salvadorian assassin who had been trained by our government, but had decided to become a "private contractor." He'd been charged for 8 murders, or "bodies" as the boys called them, but was quite pleased with the deal his former masters had given him, as there had been more. Many more, he said.

And at my "feeding" table in the pod was Bayliss Shamun, the Syrian-born killer who'd been caught on video executing a Seven-Eleven clerk over $50 that he wouldn't hand over.

He'd gotten away with it until his own mother had seen the footage on TV and recognized him. She called the police herself and turned him in. He was on thorazine so heavily that I'm not sure whether he knew where he was or not much of the time, but when they forgot his medication, or had sold it to someone else (as happens), he could be seen on the tiny recreation yard in his own little violent world, pretending to blow adversaries away with a pump shotgun, or at the opposite emotional extreme, praying and crying.

Then there was Mills, who was my neighbor after I moved into J.R.'s cell. He was shacking up with a little Rastafarian midget a few nights a week, while they waited to go to prison.

I could hear them singing love songs to each other between rounds of homosexual sex through the speaker box in the wall that separated us.

They called it the "down-low" instead of homosexuality, and it was rampant. One young punk named Gartland was in a different cell every night it seemed. He'd done a drive-by shooting into a car full of people as a gang initiation into the Hidden Valley Kings, and killed one of them.

Gartland would end up going home, as he'd turned snitch on the gang, including his own cousin. Mills would get twelve years even though this was his *third* murder. I got seven years and four months, and they still can't tell me what I did wrong.

And there was Derek Harris, the leader of our pod's Christian group that would meet on the little "rec yard" twice a day. Derek or "The Bishop" as we called him had already served 3 1/2 years for raping and then murdering a woman. Arrested on another crime, his picture popped up one day in the Charlotte Observer announcing that two more young women had been exhumed, with his DNA on (and in) them. Two more rape/murders for "The Bishop".

But Mr. Harris never missed a single prayer meeting, and continued to tell his flock that he was going home any day. He also encouraged them to follow his example and stay close to the church when they got out.

Derek Harris had certainly done that himself. The two girls had been found in shallow graves near his church. He'd stayed close all right.

And so it went. Double murder got eight years. A triple got twelve, and singles went from six months for manslaughter up to about six years for a good, cold-blooded killer. The national average as of 2000 for murder, rape, robbery, and aggravated assault is only forty-nine months. Seeing this minimal sentencing for the maximum crime, I began to wonder what I was doing there, when they couldn't even tell me how I'd violated a law of any kind.

Real killers get less time, by far, than marijuana smokers in my experience of reviewing many cases. And the accused killers aren't always killers either. A good example (among many) was another man at my table, Mr. Jimmy Myers, from Statesville, North Carolina. He was in jail awaiting trial for the attempted murder of his wife with an assault rifle. She didn't know it. He didn't know it. But a nosy neighbor heard the gun go off behind his house (shooting a tire) and called the police saying he must be trying to kill his wife . . . attempted murder. Neither Jimmy or his wife had any idea what the police were talking about when they came to arrest him (without any investigation), but he would sit in the Mecklenburg County Jail's "murderer's pod" until they made him plead guilty to "something" or he died there waiting (which he almost did).

And in 2006 the sentences for "real crime" became even shorter as the prisons were being emptied of "real criminals", to make room for people like me, who had been sentenced under Congress's outrageously unconstitutional "Sentencing Guidelines" for ridiculous conspiracies and couldn't be released, by law, until their sentences had been completed in full, while murderers could be released early.

That's "justice" in America today. And it was an eye-opener. The more I learned, the more I was shocked at just how out of control the entire system actually was, and how the corruption of law enforcement, prosecutor and judge was not an isolated event, but rampant and the rule instead. And the cases just kept coming.

Another §1983 suit I prepared was for a young Mexican man, Noe Moreno, whose brother had been driving their car with his best friend in the back seat. After a head-on collision had left their friend dead, and themselves broken up and unconscious, the top of the car had been peeled off like a sardine can to extract their bodies.

The attendant police, EMS medics, doctors, and every person in the chain had correctly identified Noe's brother as the driver, and he had also said so when he regained consciousness at the hospital. The fact that his body had been removed from the driver's seat was also a pretty major clue, since he was unconscious.

But the following day, as the detective related in his own (amended) report, "after a call from my sergeant", the driver was changed to Noe, because he had a DWI on his record and would be a far easier conviction for the prosecutor because of it. The fact that he was the wrong man, or innocent, made absolutely no difference to the prosecutor and police, as "drunken Mexicans" had become a political issue, and the conviction would look good in the news.

His court appointed lawyer would not address the issue, or question the prosecutor and police on any of these glaring discrepancies, as is common for both public defenders and private counsel as well. I'd gotten the same treatment from David Freedman and his successors.

The last I heard, Noe took the charge and agreed to a sentence by plea agreement to protect his brother. He was on his way to prison for seven years for a crime he'd never committed, for the prosecutor's public profile enhancement. It is questionable whether a "crime" had been committed in the first place, but that has no bearing in the prosecutor-run courts of today.

The horrible stories I witnessed and worked to correct would fill another book. This few months of studying cases and seeing the injustices first-hand from the case records and victims' own mouths was a life-changing experience. I would never be the same. And I began to realize why I was there. It was not an accident.

CHAPTER 17

SOLITUDE

Concurrent with the education in law and injustice was a primer in the purpose of my life. The few hours each day when we were allowed out of our solitary confinement, were sandwiched between long hours of solitude.

I read voraciously for the first few weeks, anything and everything that I could get my hands on to distract my mind from where I was and what was being done to my wife and me. I was avoiding the present with everything I had. Closing my eyes to the "now" that I was living.

And that initial period was characterized by anger, self-pity and the general question one may expect, "Why is this happening to me?"

But that can be a dangerous question to ask if one believes as I do that we always get that which we seek. I got my answer.

Having been a student of meditation since days spend in India in the 1990's, many of those hours were consumed sitting cross-legged on the concrete floor of the cell trying to empty my mind of the harsh feelings and fears that had filled my consciousness in those early days of captivity and find the purpose in this experience.

I then tried to see my new life as a monastic one of reading, learning, meditating, and searching for meaning in what was transpiring. The violent atmosphere and hostile guards made my efforts difficult, but with time, I found that I could be content much of each day. The goal then became to increase that period of contentment each day, and meditate more and longer.

The search for meaning, purpose, and answers was intermixed with long hours of reading law, other detainees' cases, and legal history; delving more and more into the sources of injustice, and writing down my thoughts about how we came to this point as a nation, and what we might do to correct it.

There was no moment of epiphany that I now recall, but at some point, it became clear that what I was doing and learning may in fact, be preparing me for what I was to do with the rest of my life. It was the answer clothed in action as to why this had happened to me.

My dream fishing boat, the offer to buy my business, my dreams of a leisurely life of ocean fishing, writing, and travel were not to be. Those dreams were my life before I voluntarily came to meet with the Feds.

I had been plunged into another world by my own government...a world as alien to me as if I'd been dropped on another planet. It was a hostile world inhabited by corrupt prosecutors, agents, and judges on the one hand, and violent criminals and the wrongly accused on the other.

Taking inventory of me and my life at that point was painful. I'd spent my entire existence chasing business dreams and dollars. I liked to think of myself as a good person who'd always tried to help others and had been honest, just as most of us choose to do, but in reality, I would leave the world more or less as I had found it. I'd done little harm, but I'd also done little good, at least of any lasting quality or meaning.

My life to that point had actually been a complete waste. Building my little financial empire had done absolutely nothing positive for the world or mankind. No one's life had really improved because of my efforts and the disappearance of my business from it had left hardly a ripple.

It had been an enterprise of complete egoistic pleasure. My febrile attempts to build a financial fortress had sputtered and failed, and neither its success nor failure would ever leave as much as a slug track in the annals of human history. I had helped no one other than materially, and had not improved life on Mother Earth for my fellow souls as should have been my task. I had merely been a hoarder of its largesse for others and a consumer of its resources myself.

The only good thing I could say about my life was that perhaps I had done no harm by living it. But is that what life is about? Simply doing no harm?

I had worked hard on spiritual enlightenment, as a future based endeavor. I had studied all of the world's sixteen major religions, but I had done it for me, as an intellectual enterprise, not as a part of the connectedness of all life and living things.

Sitting in a jail cell on the hard concrete floor searching for my life's meaning and purpose led me to the inescapable conclusion that this experience was not accidental.

It was time for an honest inventory of my skills as well as deficiencies at that point.

The deficiencies were manifold. I'd been far too self-centered in how I lived my life, with the comforts of myself and my own family being of paramount concern...maybe even my exclusive concern.

I'd spent more on fine wines each year than it would cost to feed a village in other parts of the world (and probably drank way too much of it).

Though regular in donations of money to worthy causes, I could think of few occasions in recent years when I had gotten my hands dirty directly helping others.

And though at that point, sitting in the Mecklenburg County Jail, I was living amongst what society considers it's meanest, worst, and lowest, it came clear that my personal spiritual goal had to become a feeling of connectedness to them. Rather than thinking of myself as separate and apart, possibly even superior in some ways because of education or (former) wealth, I knew that at this point, having been body-slammed to the floor-mat of life, I could certainly claim superiority to no living soul on earth.

At that point, it became clear that I must learn to love and feel a connection with every living thing, including these rough and troubled young men with whom I shared my days and this space.

As I learned more of these individuals' lives through the review of their cases and the injustices they also suffered, a connection could not be avoided.

A certain joy began to creep into my daily existence and I was only disconnected from it when I was required to interface with the government rogues or my own lawyers.

This process of several months has been reduced to mere sentences in this narrative, which could be misleading. It was fitful, with many emotional vicissitudes and was characterized by stops and starts, but the goal had been established, and my 'purpose' had been glimpsed.

My life would become a striving for connectedness to all of life. That was the goal. I realized also that there was no way to plot and plan for this goal as I had in business and other areas of my life. The past was just that. The government's cruel and untrue press releases, along with Steve Kirsch's distortions and prevarications on the Web had ruined that life. It was gone forever. I could not go back.

I had no future that was discernable either. With fortune and reputation filched from me, planning a future was a fool's errand.

The only moment I had then...or had ever had, I began to see, was the present one. Only by living each moment of my life in this awareness and connectedness could I ever achieve anything.

And with that realization came joy; even the questionable, meager fare to eat including the viscid morning porridge was consumed with pleasure from then on.

The purpose of this new life? Well, I was unlikely to ever invent new sources of power or a means of feeding the world from its dwindling resources. My life of self-centered business activity and the relentless pursuit of a dollar had left me bereft of the skills that mankind urgently needed.

But I could cobble words together. I could write. And I was living the results of terrible government, which had been run for 100 years by people just like me; greedy, selfish, with an "all for us and none for them" attitude. I was living the nightmare that "we" had constructed for "them", and I was now one of "them" too.

So that became the purpose that drives me yet...to explore the sources of our distorted, greed-based American system and its resulting injustices, and work to right the wrongs that I had indirectly helped to create, with all that was left me. . .a golf pencil and eyes from which the blinders had been removed.

CHAPTER 18

CHALLENGING DAYS

The greatest challenge to this spiritual awakening turned out not to be jail or the people therein, but my own case and legal counsel. The murderers were fine, but just the thought of the terrible people with whom I had made my bargain and my own lawyer, who had led me into this devil's deal, made me physically ill when I thought of them.

After the initial meeting where I'd been abandoned by David Freedman, and left to the wolves, my brother, Jim, had called and directed him to do his job and to come see me in the jail, and explain what he had done.

He did, but hardly so one could notice. This very brief encounter came a couple of days after that first meeting, when Freedman came to Charlotte, North Carolina, to have lunch with the attorney who had represented Coyt Murray, the commodities trader in the CFTC case.

That's about all I got out of it. He couldn't have stayed in the tiny booth more than four or five minutes. By the time the explanation was finished, that neither his visit to Charlotte or his luncheon had anything to do with me or my case, he said that it was time to go or he'd be late.

He left his side of the enclosure with me hanging on the phone through which we communicated, still trying to get him to tell me when I was going to *see* a copy of the agreement he'd made with the prosecutor, Martens, on my behalf.

Rather than a direct answer, all I got was, "Don't worry, It's all taken care of."

The man literally walked out and left me with the phone in my hand, and what had to have been a terribly disgusted look on my face. I'd never been treated by anyone like that in my life.

But Freedman had done what he came for. He'd shared not one iota of useful information with me, his client, but he had a "visit" recorded on the jailhouse log, and could tell my brother, Jim, that he had come to see me.

What no one realizes until they have been put in this terrible situation themselves is that the whole deck becomes instantly stacked against the citizen-victim when the court allows the prosecutor to railroad it into denying a defendant his right to bail.

I now understand that that is the reason the prosecutors do it. The defendant will eventually have no option but to take a plea deal, as he will know that he cannot win from jail with a "Freedman".

A defendant cannot prepare for trial from a county jail. There is no way. He is completely dependent upon people like David Freedman, and sadly, most federal attorneys have slipped into the gutter with him. They're awful, and they don't give a tinker's damn about their clients.

And they, like my lawyer, are better off letting the Feds put the client in jail and keep them there, because then, they don't have to be worried about being bothered by them. Eventually, the poor client will figure out that he hasn't a chance in Hell, and will decide to take a 'plea' just to end the uncertainty of it all. It is cruel, unusual and very effective. It is also illegal.

I cannot adequately express the mental anguish and visceral level of anger this cruel treatment, which is now standard federal policy, causes a person. It is this exact situation that James Madison, the primary author of the U.S. Constitution, was determined to outlaw for all time in America by the incorporation of the Eighth Amendment into the Bill of Rights.

But every federal defendant (that is not one of the government's snitches), is claimed to the magistrate judge to be either a "flight risk", or a "danger to the community", by the U.S. Attorneys for the government. In our case, with no criminal history or background of violence of any kind, the two young government badgers had claimed to the court that we were "both"!

They even went so far as to claim that I was "an economic threat to the United States of America"! It's in the transcript. That's also about the time that Judge Keesler had called their story "bizarre" and ordered us released, unsecured, but as the reader knows, that didn't stop Assistant U.S. Attorneys Matt Martens and Kurt Meyers.

These two young prosecutors had a plan. They would convict their mothers to get a special scalp like Sam Currin's, and no canon of ethics, constitutional amendment, or law would stand in their way. In fact, I'm here to tell you that it didn't. They violated all three, to the great pleasure I'm sure, of their supervisor, the infamous Gretchen C. F. Shappert, former U.S. Attorney of the lawless Western District of North Carolina.

These boys were after the Golden Fleece...a U.S. Attorney's hide and head, and nothing was going to stop them. The sick feeling that these brief, meaningless, and unexpected sessions with my attorney, Freedman, brought on were painful, both mentally and physically. The dull ache in the stomach and sense of incredible hopelessness this illegal denial of my rights brought about made for miserable days and nights afterwards.

He would come frequently enough for the record to show visits, but he was always there for another meeting with someone else, or en-route to an "important meeting". It became clear that these drive-bys were just to make the jailhouse visitation record look as if I'd been represented.

And he never made it to a single session with the Feds for our little "chats" until the very last one. He simply left me to their vices, unprotected.

I was told at each of these brief encounters that the "agreement" had already been mailed, or he'd forgotten to bring it. He lied. It never appeared, and had been forgotten (that was true). He and Martens had "forgotten" to do it. There wasn't one.

The first hint of Freedman's duplicity and infidelity came in May when he told me that they wanted to meet with me again, and "might want to add a small 'money laundering' charge, in order to 'make me more credible with the jury'."

I blew up.

"No," I said, "absolutely not". We never, ever 'laundered' money, David. Plus, you and Martens clearly stated as one of the four items in our deal, no *new* charges'. That was the deal, and that's it."

"Martens feels really strongly about this," David said. "Just think about it."

"I feel strongly about it too, and the answer is 'No'. We made a deal, and I agreed to it. I've done my part already, now he needs to do his."

"Just think about it," David said soothingly, as he was yet again slithering backwards out the door to go do something 'important'.

"I've *thought* about it! No! No!", but it was futile. He was gone again. The frustration is beyond description. I see why the rate of mental illness stands at 45% in America's jails and prisons. A perfectly sane person could enter such a system, which is bereft of any semblance of 'justice', 'fairness', or any of the buzzwords taught in public schools, and simply through the futility of dealing with it, lose their grip.

But Freedman had told one truth. The Feds did want to talk to me again. They showed up. He did not. He never darkened the door, the bum.

And it was a much smaller group, with only 3 "suits", as my new neighbors in pod 6800 called them.

The young Asst. U.S. Attorney, Matt Martens opened the round with the words that would become his standard beginning, "Your attorney, Mr. Freedman, told us it would be OK to meet with you without him. He's got something important going on, and since we've got an agreement, he saw no problem with it."

"Oh, you have a copy of the agreement for me?" I said, and held out my hand. "I've been waiting for a copy since we last met."

Martens gave me a surprised look worthy of Peter Lorre; and said, "I thought Mr. Freedman had already given you a copy, so I didn't bring one."

If any reader is ever in a similar situation, which is very likely at the rate the government is arresting its people; this is the time to run. Just get up and run, screaming for the guard to let you out.

Feds, especially U.S. Attorney type Feds, are congenital liars. They're born with it, and then the government trains them until they are refined in the art. I've never yet had one of them tell me the truth about anything. They just can't do it.

But I didn't know then what I know now, so I gingerly said, "I'd really like to get a copy of your and Mr. Freedman's agreement before we go any further. And why is it that he can't be here? I'd rather have an attorney present."

Now at that point, by law and the Code of Professional Conduct, the meeting had to end, but Martens knew I did not know he was breaking the law and that my attorney was in league with him, so he coolly answered, "I think he had to deal with a client up in Greensboro," he said. "But don't worry about the agreement. Everything is set. We may just need to tweak it a little bit and add a money-laundering charge in there, but your 'time' will remain the same."

"I've already told Mr. Freedman that I won't do that. We never *laundered* any money in my life, and I'm not going to say that I did."

"I'm not saying that you did, Mr. Woltz. And let's not get side-tracked on that today," he artfully dodged. "I think Mr. Curran has some questions for you."

And with that, Doug Curran, who had led the abduction team, spoke.

"First of all, Mr. Woltz, since our last meeting, I've been checking out everything you told us. I've got to tell you, you're the most honest and forthright witness that I've dealt with in my career."

Martens visibly winced. This was apparently not something that he wanted Curran to say. I picked up a small current of discord between them.

"The only thing I'm having trouble with," Curran continued, "is that night at Vernon Abernethy's house when you and your wife were there reviewing the trading records. Are you sure that neither you nor your wife took anything from his house at all?"

"Absolutely positive," I answered. "The last thing we wanted to do was help the little crook, Mr. Curran. He'd helped Coyt Murray fleece our clients out of millions. I'd like to know when you guys are going to get around to doing something about *real* crooks like them. Can you tell me that?"

Martens grimaced again and turned slightly red on that one.

Curran ignored my question and said, "Well I've got someone that says you did take something."

"Then that person is lying," I retorted calmly. "All you need to do is think about it, Mr. Curran. What could Vernon Abernethy have that we would want? His records were falsified returns of fictitious earnings. Why would we want them? It was our clients who had been scammed by them. We wanted them to go to jail, not to help them."

"How about records from Sterling Casualty your insurance company? Wasn't Abernethy supposed to be helping you set up the accounting for that?" he asked.

"What records could there be, Mr. Curran? The company never got off the ground, nor did it do any business, because Vernon Abernethy stole the capital and put it into Tech Traders. There was nothing to 'account'." Curran knew that I was telling the truth. Little Vernon had lied about it to cover why he had not produced Jeremy Jaynes' financial records or whatever he had hidden at Walt Hannen's house to keep from "the CFTC witch" as he called Elizabeth Streit.

And then came the real reason for the meeting. "We really could use a little help, Mr. Woltz," Curran said sincerely. "If we could just get a couple of files from your office down in Nassau, we could tie this thing up with Sam Currin and Jeremy Jaynes."

"No problem, Mr. Curran. Get me out of this jail and we'll go down there together and get them," I said. "I've already done the 'little or no' time you promised me already." They all laughed.

"I wasn't kidding," I said. "How else are you going to get them?"

"Well, we thought maybe you'd let *us* go down and get them," he said.

It was my turn to laugh then. "No way! Not without me or my wife there." The conversation was not making any progress.

They also wanted the files on Gatelinx, they said, which was the stock trading scam that also included former U.S. Attorney Sam Currin, Jeremy Jaynes, and others, on which we had filed a Suspicious Activities Report as well. That was the case that I had come to meet with AUSA Martens and FBI agent Curran about when they abducted me.

But in the Gatelinx scam, rather than just putting my name on a website, as Jaynes had done on his penny-stock trading promotion, he and his scoundrels had falsified S.E.C. filings for the initial public offering (IPO) of Gatelinx Corporation, and used our trust company name as the owner of the shares of the shell company they had bought, which was several years old, to cover the true ownership. They had backdated and created original shares. The only problem, aside from fraud, was that the dates on those bogus shares were years before I had ever started Sterling Trust or licensed it. Sterling Trust hadn't even existed.

Our firm learned of what they had done from discovery documents in a lawsuit we had begun against Gatelinx for stock fraud, when we included their stock transfer agent, Holladay, in Arizona as a defendant in the case. They offered our attorney full cooperation against Gatelinx, their client, if we would drop them from the suit. We agreed, and received a huge pack of documents, in which the original S.E.C. filings proved the fraud.

We forwarded copies of the documents to the S.E.C. on two occasions, with a report of suspicious activity, and to AUSA Martens' office as well. They'd done nothing. The stock had been trading for almost a year by that point.

"Why don't you go after the real crooks, like these guys at Gatelinx?" I asked the assembled crew of prosecutor, FBI agent, and IRS agent. "You seem to have plenty of time for Ms. Streit's nonsense against people like us, but no time for the bad guys like Vernon Abernethy and Coyt Murray, or these Gatelinx fellows. When are you going after them? Abernethy and Murray cost people millions. These guys Brecher and Hagen at Gatelinx could run this fraudulent IP0 as high as $170 million. We reported that to your people in Miami last September, and nothing's been done yet."

Martens replied, testily, "We're looking into Gatelinx. In fact, $5 million traded through just one firm up in Vancouver in just one day. We're watching it."

"You know that, yet you let it continue?" I could not believe what I was hearing.

These were the same people who had admitted at our last meeting that we had "broken no law", but just wanted us "out of business". Here we were discussing what the CFTC had described as "one of the largest commodities frauds of the year", where Vernon Abernethy and Coyt Murray had cost trusting investors millions, and Gatelinx, which was trading $5 mil of fraudulent stock through one firm in one day but they were doing nothing about any of it. And we were in jail.

And I was working with these bums thanks to an inept, never-present, sorry excuse for an attorney, David B. Freedman, who at our last meeting had reminded me he would be going on an "extended vacation to Israel" after doing nothing for months.

The bastard hadn't had time to defend me but had time for "extended vacations" on my money. Now, he didn't even have time to protect me from these federal wolves. He'd taken our money and abandoned us to whatever fate may befall us.

I was fuming by that point, and I'm quite sure that it showed. The injustice of what was being done to us galled me, and the cavalier attitude of all the participants, both government and private attorneys, proved that they were so jaded and hardened to it, that it didn't even bother them to destroy people, or to let it happen. And they were being paid to prevent such injustices not create them. It was a sick system; immoral, depraved people advancing and profiting on injustice and other human beings' misery, while the lawyers got rich pretending to defend them.

The meeting was called to a close. We were getting nowhere and things were deteriorating quickly.

FBI agent Curran made one final pitch for the files on Currin, Jaynes, and Gatelinx, to little avail, and I rebuffed it unless it was under the supervision of my wife and/or me.

I could just see these federal cowboys rooting through my client files looking for more people to ruin without cause, or to "shake-down" for money.

Martens and the IRS agent, Schiller, began leaving the little interrogation room, but FBI agent Curran stayed behind.

He reached out his hand to shake mine, and said, "Mr. Woltz, I just want to apologize for what we have done to you and your family."

I was stunned. In my mind I was formulating a response like, "Then why don't you tell the truth about what's been done to us and set us free?", but Martens, the leader, was waiting at the door listening to this exchange.

"Come on Curran. We have to go," he barked, clearly angered by the FBI agent's confession, as it reflected on what he, Martens, had done to us.

But FBI agent Curran paid him no attention other than to nod his head in Martens' direction and say, "I hope you can understand that is all I can say right now." With that, he turned and followed the young prosecutor, Martens, out of the interrogation room leaving me to my own thoughts until the guard came to get me. That was the last of our meetings that FBI agent Doug Curran ever attended.

The IRS agent, Schiller, had admitted that we "broke no law", and that he knew it. Now, the FBI agent in charge of the case, had apologized for "what we've done to you." What kind of man was this Martens fellow? To continue this immoral and knowingly false prosecution was beyond criminal. Would he one day regret his sins against his fellow man as Sam Currin had come to do, I wondered? I thought back to the night in Nassau when Sam had nearly cried, and told us that he feared meeting his Maker without first making apologies, on his knees, to his victims. Had he been like the young Martens back then?

These meetings with the terrible government operatives, (and my own attorneys), always left me disrupted spiritually and devastated emotionally. The physical manifestation was a sick, hollow feeling in the pit of my empty stomach followed by lethargy.

I was quickly reaching the point that all federal victims eventually come to, where they'd rather do "time" for something they didn't do, rather than have further dealings with the corrupt agents, prosecutors, and attorneys that have hijacked our once respected system of justice in America.

That point was rapidly approaching. Getting away from the evil was becoming more appealing and important than fighting the injustice. I'd rather be in prison for something I didn't do and be away from these horrible people with government, and the lawyers that served them at our expense, than continue to have to deal with them. Every time I was around them, I took three steps backwards, spiritually. Something had to give.

CHAPTER 19

ANOTHER DECEPTION

It was beginning to be obvious that I'd been swindled by my attorney, David Freedman and his co-conspirator, the Asst. U.S. Attorney, Matt Martens. I grew up in a small town in the foothills of the Blue Ridge Mountains where people generally were honest and truthful. In a small place like Mt. Airy, North Carolina, a liar or a cheat couldn't make it very long before everyone knew he was a crook and had to either give it up or move on.

Mt. Airy was the little town that one of its more famous residents, Andy Griffith, made famous as "Mayberry", and it was a bit like that. It certainly had not prepared me well for the Feds.

I'd attended the University of Virginia, where the honor code is revered. My father, John Woltz, had been student body president when he attended UVA, as well as head of the student-run Honor Committee, and I'd been reared with its tenets as a child. I'd never dealt with men like Martens and Freedman.

My business career had been peopled with honorable attorneys such as Calder Womble[5] of Womble, Carlyle, Sandridge, and Rice; Fred Crumpler, who was my bird-hunting buddy as well as lawyer; Georges Talleyrand in Haiti; Frank Lightmas of Lightmas & Delk in Atlanta; and Marty Russo of Nixon-Peabody in New York; all honorable and decent men. They'd all been friends as well as counselors, which had ill prepared me for dealing with corrupt men in the criminal end of that profession.

---

[5] Years later, while I was in prison, Calder died, and my letter (and story about him) to his family was read by the minister as part of his eulogy.

I had learned to trust attorneys, as strange as that may sound today, but that's the way it was. I'd never had one of these fine men mislead or mistreat me. I'd never had a billing dispute, and I'd never felt that I'd been overcharged or underserved by any of them.

The corrupt, young US Attorney, Matt Martens, was a shock.

To learn, as I would, that David Freedman, my own attorney, was in a league with him, was heart-breaking.

But that is exactly what happened.

The weeks passed slowly while I waited on resolution. I begged and pleaded for a phone number to reach Freedman, but he refused to set up any line on the jail system where I could call him. He told me at one of his drive-by meetings when I became adamant about it, "I've got enough people bothering me without getting calls from jail."

I could see that he wanted to catch those honest words that had slipped out as soon as they left his lips, but it was too late. That was how he really felt.

But that was unacceptable. He kept claiming that his staff couldn't figure out how to set up the phone, while my eighty-one year old mother had no problem with it. He just would not do it.

My brother, Jim, became so frustrated with him (and my complaining about him, I'm sure) that he bought a cell-phone, set it up on the jail phone system, pre-paid $500 on it, and mailed the darn thing to Freedman.

He answered it one time, told me he was "busy" and never answered it again.

So, as previously noted, I began to write him, begging for a copy of the agreement that he and Martens promised me they had "memorialized".

I simply could not bring myself to believe that two officers of the court, under the professional code of conduct, would so boldly lie. But I was wrong. They would and they did, as I would soon learn after they used the "carrot" of the agreement that did not exist, to get the last thing they needed from me.... .....access to our office in Nassau.

I was still limited to my one disposable contact lens from the day I'd been abducted by the FBI, and unless reading, kept it in a small medical capsule cup, soaking in home-made saline solution in my cell, made from packets of salt from the meager meals we were served.

The latest "arrangement" that they had cooked up with our complicit attorneys was where both my wife and I would be taken out of the jail to the FBI's Charlotte office, where we would "monitor" the FBI's visit via phone hook-up with our office in Nassau.

Our Bahamian attorney, Michael Foulkes, would be in our Nassau office and open the vault as we gave him the combination. He would retrieve the three files that had been requested, and that would be it.

Then, the government promised, they would *really, really* keep their word this time and release my wife immediately thereafter.

But the selected day in early June came and went, and the guard kept me locked in solitary confinement all day. I'd waited anxiously from the early morning "feeding" time through the entire morning. Then "lunch" of a carrot and fake cheese sandwich came and went, but still no Feds. No lawyer.

I finally gave up by mid-afternoon as visiting hours were sacrosanct at the jail and took out my precious contact lens, and put it away.

About 4:15 PM, the guard "popped" the air-lock on my cell and ordered me into the "slider".

"Contact visit, Woltz", she said. "Get into the slider now."

Odd. It was only fifteen minutes until closing time.

A guard was waiting to take me down to the second floor interrogation rooms.

We entered the secured area quickly, with none of the usual rigmarole, and the prosecutor was there with a young FBI agent (not Curran) and my _wife's_ attorney, the infamous Donald Tisdale.

Just hostile government agents, and a hostile Tisdale, whom my wife's letters had informed me was encouraging her to lie about me to help these animals convict me of something!

And they were in a hurry.

I'd seen my wife in the hallway and figured they'd snookered me again. She'd been taken over there (to the FBI office), I guessed, alone, and they'd gotten the files. They'd lied again! We were both required to approve the release, and they had apparently pressured her into doing it without me.

All that I'd had time to ask her was, "How did it go?"

"Fine," is the only answer she could give before being hustled off.

With only minutes remaining and the guard waiting to close the interrogation area for the day, I was shunted into the little room with prosecutor Martens, the young FBI agent, and my wife Vernice's attorney, Don Tisdale. No David Freedman, as usual.

Freedman was consistent. He'd never been at one of these interrogations yet.

These guys were all smiles. Things must have gone well.

"So, Vernice said that everything went well down in Nassau. You got what you wanted?" I asked. "I thought that I was supposed to be present too."

No one corrected my obvious misunderstanding that the visit to our office had occurred that day as planned, when it really had not.

Martens, the prosecutor, just said, "We've only got a minute here, Mr. Woltz, and we need your signature here before we can use the files."

He slid a piece of paper across the table with a small, square box of 'jumble' printed on it. I put on my reading glasses, but without the contact lens on as well, I couldn't read it.

The "readers" just got me up to +2.0 diopters. It took +4.0 for me to be able to see anything up close. "I can't read it," I said.

"You've got your glasses on," Martens said.

"They're just 'readers' I had in my pocket when I was brought here. I need a contact lens with it to read. I had given up on your coming today; it's so late, so I took it out."

"That's true, Mr. Woltz," Martens said. "That's why we need to get this done now. They've already told us we have to leave."

"What is it?" I asked.

"It's just a consent form so that we can use the files," he said.

"So you did get them?" I asked.

He did not answer directly, so I can't say that he lied on this occasion. Martens cleverly replied, "We can't use them without your permission. This is just a consent form so that we can do that."

"Has David Freedman seen this?" I asked.

Martens hesitated. With a room full of people, that was too big a lie for even a U.S. Attorney to tell.

So the infamous former prosecutor, Don Tisdale, leaped into the breach for his comrade, the US Attorney, and blurted out, "Sure he's seen it. He's the one that wrote it. David just left here a few minutes ago. He had to be somewhere. He told me to have you sign it."

As a sidebar, you may recall, Don Tisdale is the worthless scum lawyer that wrongfully put away an innocent, young, black man by the name of Darryl Hunt in Winston—Salem, North Carolina for 20+ years for a murder that Tisdale knew and admitted that Hunt had not committed. There is a book about it, The Darryl Hunt Story, as well as a PBS special dealing with it.

But I didn't know this or make the connection at the time, I just knew that I had a visceral dislike of him, but still believed that lawyers were honest people for the most part.

"So David wrote this and left it for me to sign?" I asked the gang. "Is that what you are telling me?"

"Absolutely," said Tisdale.

"And if I sign this, Mr. Martens, we're really done this time? I assume that you have the agreement with you?"

He smiled broadly and pulled it half-way out of a folder. "Sure do," he said. "Just sign the consent form and that's it. We're done. You're almost home."

"What about Vernice?" I asked. "You promised that she would go free 'immediately' back in April when we first met and made this agreement. Are you going to keep your promise this time?"

The guard knocked at the door and pointed to his wristwatch. They wanted us to leave.

Martens leaned forward and said, "You sign that piece of paper and she can go home as early as tomorrow."

"Tomorrow," I reiterated. "Is that right, Don?" I said looking him in the eye. "You're her lawyer. Are they going to stick by this promise? They also promised us there'd be no forfeiture or new charges. Is that what it says? I'm counting on you to tell me the truth."

"That's what it says. You sign that consent form, and this is all over. She can leave tomorrow," Tisdale said, with a sincere look on his face. "They have to do it."

"And the agreement was that I would do 'little or no time', so I'm going to be right behind her, right?"

"That's correct. That's what it says," Tisdale assured me. "I'd really like to read that first and make sure that it says those things," I said. "Has David reviewed the final draft?" Martens and Tisdale both said "Yes", quickly, which was also a lie, I would quickly learn, as he hadn't a clue what it said.

The guard was back and pressing them to leave.

"You can review it with David over the next few days, and he and I can fine-tune it if anything needs to be changed," Martens said, "But we really don't have time for you to read it right now as you can see."

"Why did you wait until so late in the day?" I asked. "And why wasn't I included like you promised?"

I was getting cold feet and becoming reluctant to sign; whether, David Freedman had written it or not. And why had they made me wait almost two months to see it if it was "memorialized" back in April?

They could tell that they were losing me. Tisdale put his best arrogant, bully voice on and said, "Look here. Your lawyer has advised you to sign this thing. He prepared it. It will set your wife free. Isn't that what you wanted? Don't you want to get her out of this place?" and with that he slapped his chubby hand on it, slid it towards me and handed me the pen.

That worked, as he knew it would. "Show me where the line is," I said. "It's all just a blur to me."

Don pointed out the signature line. I signed it, and to this day, neither I nor David Freedman, whom I was told had written it, has ever seen what I authorized.

I certainly had no idea what this dandy bunch of cutthroats had done to me, and would later learn from a copy of the jailhouse log that David Freedman had never been there that day at all. They'd made it up. And Asst. U.S. Attorney Martens had met with me again alone, in violation of the law and the Professional Code of Conduct. Both David Freedman, as my attorney, and Matthew Martens, as a government lawyer, knew that it was a violation on both their parts for a person to be questioned without an attorney after indictment[6]. But these two crooks had allowed that to go on for months.

The pen had hardly left the paper before Martens grabbed it and stuffed it into his brief. They shot up and out of their chairs like burnt rabbits and headed for the door, leaving me alone.

"Whoa! Whoa!" I shouted after them. "What about the agreement?"

Martens was already to the exit door and half-way out of it before he handed back a copy of the thick agreement. There were far more than four little items in it that was for sure.

I held it as far away as my arms would allow, but could only read the large, bold headings. As I randomly thumbed through a page or two, however, I made out a heading that said "Forfeiture" in bold print.

"Wait! Mr. Martens!" I yelled through the closing door. "This isn't the right agreement. It says 'Forfeiture' in a heading. Ours doesn't have any forfeiture. This isn't our agreement!"

"Talk to Mr. Freedman about it," he shouted back, as I was being led away. "This is just a boilerplate version. He and I can work out any details." And he quickly escaped behind the solid door, which the deputy locked.

---

[6]Edwards v Arizona, 451 U.S.477, 68Led 2d 378, 101 S. CT 1880 (1981) "Counsel must be present at custodial hearings."

I couldn't wait to get back upstairs to get my "eye" in and see what these people had done to me. The feeling I had at that moment was near hopeless panic. I had signed, God knows what, on that piece of paper, and had gotten a document that had a big, bold heading, "Forfeiture" on it where none was supposed to be in the agreement at all.

When I got back in my little cell upstairs, my hands trembled as I tried to put the salty contact into my left eye.

It immediately brought stinging tears and I tried to let the anger go as they washed the lens to a bearable salinity level, so I could begin to see to read the document.

By the time I finished reading it, I was in shock.

My wife was not going free immediately according to anything in this document. She was their hostage until they _chose_ to release her and only then would she be set free.

The 'little or no' time for me had ballooned to over seven years in federal prison.

The "no forfeiture of corporate or personal assets" had become a complete forfeiture of everything we had ever owned or ever would, and a $1.2 million 'fine' on top of that, after they'd stolen everything else.

These animals even wanted to steal anything our children might ever have or inherit. It actually said so in the agreement.

And the "no new charges" commitment that I had been promised was 'memorialized', had become a charge of "conspiracy to commit money laundering" to try and tie me in to Currin and Jaynes' activities here in America, of which I'd never had any part or even known about.

The feeling of despair and anger against these corrupt government cullions and our own despicable attorneys was overwhelming. Any spiritual "progress" made since my last meeting with them was out the window. I was beyond consolation.

The only person that I could turn to once again was my dear brother, Jim. When he learned of the government's perfidy and Freedman's complicity with it, he was livid too.

"But they promised *no forfeiture of assets* he said. How did Freedman allow them to change it if it was in writing back in April?"

"The son-of-a-bitch wasn't even there, Jim! And how about the 'little or no time'? This thing says 87 months. That's 7 years and 3 months in prison for something that never happened!"

The cell block guard warned me to calm down, or threatened to lock me in my cell for the rest of the night. I tried to calm down and speak more quietly.

"Jim, they had me sign some piece of paper. They said it was a 'consent' to use the files they got in The Bahamas today, but I couldn't read it. I didn't have my contact lens in. I don't even know what it said. Don Tisdale and the prosecutor Martens said that David Freedman wrote it."

"Howell, they weren't in your office today. That's been put off until next week.

I was stunned.

"But they..." and I stopped, because it dawned on me 'they' had never actually told me that the visit had taken place. I'd just assumed it since that was the planned day, and no one had ever told me any differently. They had just let me think that it was over without correcting the misconception.

"Look, Howell. I'm going to get off the phone and track down this Freedman character. If I have to call him tonight at midnight at his house, I'll find him and make sure that he is there to see you tomorrow, one way or the other, OK?"

"OK, Jim," I told him. "I don't know what I'd do without you, brother."

"You'd do it for me," is all he said.

"That's true, but I hope we never have to find out. I wouldn't wish these people on my worst enemy. These people are pure evil," I said.

We ended the conversation and I went upstairs and locked my own cell door. I'd save the guard the trouble.

I begged my Maker for sleep to come take me away from this horrible situation. I'd always heard that God never gives us more misery than we can handle, but I was beginning to wonder about that.

At some point, sleep did overtake me, and I escaped again to the other world where I found relief.

CHAPTER 20

A VISIT FROM MY BARRISTER IN JAIL

True to his word, my brother Jim tracked down the elusive Mr. Freedman roosting in his lair the night of the meeting with AUSA Martens in the jail and excoriated him.

He naturally responded to my brother that I was suffering from jailhouse paranoia and had not clearly understood what was written in AUSA Martens' document. In other words, "Your brother's not only too stupid to understand, he's a little crazy right now."

Freedman may have been right about the paranoia, but that was because I was living with a bunch of violent men (thanks to him), many of whom were there because they had actually murdered someone, unlike me, and the incidence of truculent behavior was the norm rather than the exception. I was also lawyer-less for all intents and purposes, with a nasty, wicked little prosecutor from New York, who couldn't tell the truth if his mouth were stuffed with it, trying to destroy me.

As for the 'stupid' part, brother Jim must have unloaded on him about that because I'd actually read the forfeiture section to him over the telephone, and either we were both stupid or the government was stealing everything we had, which meant that David Freedman and the prosecutor had lied to me (and my brother) about their agreement.

It isn't "paranoia" when someone is truly out to do you harm, and my brother didn't buy into Freedman's evasive maneuver to make me wrong instead of him and his government buddies.

In fact, Jim must have romped on David Freedman, Esquire, pretty hard, because the poor excuse for a lawyer was at the jailhouse door well before lawyer-thirty the next morning.

We met in a small booth where lawyer and client were separated by a thick, plate-glass, reinforced with wire, and communication was via a phone handset.

This was probably not a bad idea that morning as I was ready to kill him. The violent atmosphere that he and his prosecutor buddy had me living in must have been rubbing off.

He began by telling me how I had not understood the plea agreement or the wording of it. I knew right then that the jerk couldn't have even read the thing.

"Stop! Stop right there, David," I yelled. "Don't waste my time trying to tell me that I can't read an agreement. I write fifty page trust documents for a living. This either says what it says or it doesn't. You apparently haven't read it yourself."

And with that, I slammed the page with "Forfeiture" heading a section up against the plate-glass with such a thud that the guard outside came to look in the window.

"Read it, damn it!"

He slowly read it through the glass and chicken-wire separator and began shaking his head. He turned a bright red.

"This...this...something isn't right here. Are you sure you have the right agreement?" he stammered.

"Am I sure? That's your job, David, and 'Hell no', this isn't the *right* agreement. You and that damn monkey from the prosecutor's office promised me four things. *FOUR THINGS*, David. And not a one of them is in here!"

I had turned down the corners of the relevant pages, and held them up to the glass, one by one.

"No forfeiture?" I asked. "Your buddies want to steal everything I've got and leave me with a $1.2 million fine, David. They even want to steal anything that my children might ever have."

"That's just positioning. We can negotiate..." he started but I cut him off.

186

"Negotiate! What in the Hell are you talking about, David?" I
shouted. "You promised me this was 'negotiated' before I ever
sat down with the bastards! The two of you lied to me. You're
working for them, not me!"

The guard knocked on the door and motioned for me to calm down
and quit yelling.

"Little or no time, David?" I said as I slammed the next page up
to the plate-glass. "Do you and this Martens jerk call seven
years and three months of my life 'little or no time'? Why don't
you do it, David?"

"I....I....I'm sure we can negotiate that too. We can get a 5k1.1[7]
and...."

I cut him off again. "You're not listening to me, David. You and
Martens lured me into your deal by promising me that this was
all done already written, 'memorialized' is the word you used. But
you and your buddy lied to me, didn't you?"

"Now wait a minute, Howell. You make it sound like I'm working
with them. I'm on your side."

"My side? How in the Hell would I know that, David? You
abandoned me to these wolves on *Day One*, apparently with a lie
about an agreement that hadn't really been written up, and you've
never once been at any of these interrogation sessions, including
yesterday. How can you do something like that, if you're on my
side?"

"Now calm down. I can negotiate with Martens. I'm sure he's an
honest...."

---

[7] 5k1.1 is known as a "downward departure", but
the government is not bound by their agreement to
keep their promise of one, and in my experience,
does not except in the cases of their informants.

"Honest?" I cut in. "He's a damn liar just like you are! What do you have to '*negotiate*', David? You need to trot yourself over to your 'partner' in crime's office and get that damn 'memorialized' agreement *memorialized* is what you need to do.

"Let me remind you what it said," I continued. "Four things were in it:

1)   *My wife goes free <u>immediately</u>. It's June, David. June. And the poor girl is still in this damn jail as a hostage.*

2)   *No forfeiture of assets. Remember, David? Not <u>some</u> or even 'a little'. No forfeiture, period. That was the deal.*

3)   *"Little or no time", David. Seven years and three months is not 'little' and it damn sure isn't 'no'. I should have been out of here already.*

4)   *No new charges. The two of you can take this new 'conspiracy' charge and stick it. We never laundered any money ever, and I'm not going to say that we did."*

There was silence for a moment. My chest was heaving. I was so angry I wanted to smash the glass.

"That's the one point that Martens seems to feel strongly about," David began to say. "We may need to give a little on that point."

"No!" I said. "He needs to stick with the deal he made and you need to make him do it. I still can't believe the two of you lied to me. I've done everything I was asked to do and more. I've fulfilled my side of the bargain completely. Now I find that you and your little partner snookered me. What kind of people are you?"

"Now don't lump me in with them," David protested. "I'm not on their side."

"Then show me a copy of your 'memorialized' agreement, David, or get over there now and get this ridiculous thing fixed so it reflects what you and Martens promised me. If you can't or won't do that, then you are on their side. That's the only 'conspiracy' I see, David. You and these government boys!"

He seemed to have gone from red to pale.

"And if you can't get this thing fixed by next week, I expect you to do the things I've written and instructed you to do. I want to go to trial or file to get this nonsense dismissed."

"What 'things' are you talking about," he asked.

"Don't you read my letters, David? If you won't take my phone calls so I can talk to you and you don't read my letters, how in the Hell am I supposed to communicate with you?"

"What 'things' are you suggesting?" he asked, again.

"I wasn't 'suggesting', David. I was *instructing* you as my attorney to challenge the grand jury. It's clear someone lied for these ridiculous charges to have ever been made in the first place. Elizabeth Streit at the CFTC concocted them out of revenge. Get me the grand jury minutes and I'll prove it to you.

"And I told you to challenge this venue. We have no business being in the Western District. It's only because this Streit woman couldn't get the U.S. Attorney in the Middle District to even look at her bullshit charges that they came to Charlotte. My attorney in New York told me that. They'll take anything here and hold you in jail until you plead guilty to it, but that's not right. It's not constitutional. This is the wrong venue and I told you to challenge it.

"I also told you to challenge W. Earl Britt as the judge. I heard Martens admit to judge-shopping with my own ears that first day. He said Currin and Britt had been *'blood-feud enemies* 30 years,' and was bragging about getting him to be the judge in Currin's case. You were in there with them!"

David jumped in on that one. "I must have missed that."

To admit that he heard Martens say that and hadn't reported it would be a problem for him as an officer of the court. It is a crime![8]

"I'll bet you did miss that," I said with a facetious laugh. "You seem to have missed a lot, David. I also told you in my letter that if you couldn't get me that agreement right away, I ordered you to file for a dismissal. That date is June 29th; it's in my letter of May 7th."

"They'll never agree to that," he said.

"Do it anyway. I'm beginning to see that the only fair treatment I or anyone else might get in this messed-up system is on appeal. The Sixth Amendment to the U.S. Constitution still says that I have the right to a public and speedy trial. If they deny me all of these rights, it will help me on appeal, because it doesn't sound like anybody gets 'justice' *here* anymore."

"Let me get this agreement sorted out," David said anxiously. "You don't want to go to trial, trust me on that."

"Why not, David? We never broke a single law. Even Agent Schiller admitted that in one of the interrogation sessions. Schiller said that they just wanted us 'out of business'. It would have been really nice to have you there to hear him say that, David. But then you'd probably have 'missed' that like you 'missed' Martens' judge-shopping admission, wouldn't you?"

"You've got to quit making it sound like I'm working with them, Howell."

"Then do something to show me that you're not, David."

"I'll get this agreement straightened out," he said.

---

[8] Failure to report a felony such as 'judge shopping' is known as 'Misprision'. It is a crime in itself under 18 USC §4, and should have put Freedman and the other agents of the government present that day in prison for up to two years.

"If you don't, then you need to read my letters and start the motions rolling, David, cause we're going to trial. I haven't even seen any evidence yet, but I'll need that soon" I said.

"You remember that I'm leaving for vacation this week and will be in Israel this month don't you?" he asked.

Though I did remember his mentioning that at the bond revocation "show" down in Raleigh, I could not believe that so many weeks had already passed. I never expected to still be in jail in June.

"You mean you're leaving this week?" I asked.

He nodded. "I'll be back before the end of the month."

"That's just great, David. So I sit in jail for another month while you're on vacation. You've done nothing I've asked you to do and you're leaving with a completely fucked-up agreement on the table after promising me something totally different to get me to help them. That's great, David. I hope you have a nice vacation.

"But either get this agreement fixed, or be ready to go to trial when you get back," I said.

"I'm going over there right now to talk to Martens about it," he said. "There are obviously a few errors here."

"A few errors, David?" I asked incredulously. "It's the wrong agreement! It has nothing to do with what the two of you promised me. Get it right, or get ready to go to trial. That's it. And file those motions, David. I need to start building a record for appeal."

"There will be no need for that," Freedman said, "I'm sure Martens is a reasonable guy. We'll get this worked out," he added as he rose from his chair to leave.

"I'm not kidding, David. Get it like it's supposed to be or we are going to trial."

With that he took his leave.

I could not decide whether Freedman was completely incompetent or whether he just didn't give a damn. Probably both.

But it was clear that I'd been put in a dangerous and precarious position by this man and he was unlikely to improve.

On the way back to the cell, I decided it was time to start looking for a real attorney, though I had no idea how we would pay one. I had to have someone that would work for me instead of the prosecutor.

I still could not believe that what Freedman and Martens had done to me was ethical or legal. Though I would have to find it on my own, and it would be too late by time I found it, I would learn that what they had done was neither, but that would not be allowed until I was already in prison.

Not only was it against the Professional Code's Disciplinary Rules for a prosecutor to meet with a represented person after indictment, it was also a violation for the person's attorney to allow it. They could both be disbarred but in Charlotte, North Carolina, no one seemed to worry about little things like that and as already mentioned before, the North Carolina State bar would prove to be useless.

And I would also learn that what they had done to me was a constitutional violation of the law and cases like mine had been overturned because of it. But again, none of this was about 'justice', the 'law', or what was 'right' or 'wrong' any longer.

The federal system of 'justice' was miasmic. Its poisonous atmosphere had destroyed the moral foundation of both its practice and its practitioners. I would have been far, far better off without any attorney at all. Had Freeman not lied to me about a 'memorialized' agreement, I would never have considered dealing with the Devil. What I didn't know yet at that point was that his replacements would be just as dishonest and worthless as he had been. The plot was just beginning to thicken.

CHAPTER 21

THE SEARCH FOR AN HONEST MAN

The Greek Cynic philosopher, Diogenes, used to walk the streets, barefoot, carrying a lamp in broad daylight seeking a "human being".

I can't remember if he ever found one, but the story has morphed into saying that he was searching for an "honest man". That's not the way it was. He was looking for a "human being", but the other way does sound better.

But like old Diogenes, I was looking for a "human being" also and my task was much more difficult than his. He could leave the tub he used to live under and wander all of Asia Minor in his search.

I, on the other hand, was stuck in the murderer's pod in Charlotte, North Carolina, and could go nowhere. To make it worse (if not impossible), the "human being" I was searching for also had to have a law degree and be licensed to practice in the State of North Carolina.

A human being _and_ a lawyer in the same body and person, no less; a nearly impossible task most would say, and from my experience, they would be right. I wasn't even allowed a phone book in the Mecklenburg County Jail to try to find one.

But I had no choice but to find another lawyer...or so I thought. I focused on the need to put the old "law of attraction" to work. "Ask and it shall be given," "Seek and ye shall find."

I had to seek, as it was apparent by that time that having David Freedman as an attorney was worse than no lawyer at all. My brother, Jim, was also frustrated with him, having fronted the money for us, and unable to get results or even the courtesy of a returned phone call from him.

But Jim lived in Roanoke, Virginia, and the best that he could do was scan the firms looking for one that claimed to specialize in, or knew something about, criminal law, which was random at best.

My 'search group' was cell-block 6800, the murderer's pod. Not exactly a treasure-trove of white-collar criminals. Most had 'public defenders' for attorneys, in fact, and even the ones with paid lawyers never saw them.

Once you're in jail, you're a captive client, if the reader will forgive the pun, and like Freedman, they know they can treat you like dirt because you can't do anything about it. It is very close to impossible to find another lawyer, by design.

Other than answering one brief call (on the cell phone that my brother had sent to him), where he said he was too "busy" to talk, I'd never been able to even speak to David Freedman on the phone, nor would I ever.

But I soon found that the criminal portion of the profession as a whole had descended into the quagmire as well. It wasn't just Freedman. They were all worthless according to their clients. The system was to take a poor guy's money--all they could possibly get out of him---then tell him they were going to trial, while knowing full well that they never would, and then push the poor fellow into a guilty plea through threats of life in prison for minor or uncommitted crimes, if he didn't. It was a dirty game.

"Better take a plea for 15 years. Otherwise, the prosecutor will make sure that you get life!" I was actually told that by the young attorney who replaced Freedman, so that is no joke. To this day, no one has ever been able to assign any criminal activity to me, nor had I committed any, yet I am still in Federal Prison. We went out of our way to follow not only the laws of the nations where we were licensed trustees, but all others as well, including the United States.

194

Finding an attorney that would do things differently, especially from jail, was tantamount to an impossible mission. My group in 6800 offered slim pickings for finding a 'human being' lawyer referral. Those who didn't have government 'public defenders' had plea-merchants as well. Some of the murderers hated their attorneys so badly that I suspected their next homicide may be their own counsel. From what I witnessed, they'd get less time in prison for that than if they'd been caught with a tiny rock of crack cocaine or an unused gun, or....god forbid....failed to pay a couple of dollars of tax to Uncle Sam's collector-boys at the IRS. According to the U.S. Department of Justice statistics, 'real' crime (murder, rape, robbery and aggravated assault) carry an average of just 49 months in prison,[9] as previously stated.

Having Freedman as a lawyer, I was beginning to see their point of view. He and his co-conspirator at the U.S. Attorney's office were trying to give me 87 months and knew that I had not broken any law! I'd get less time for murder!

But one day I heard my friend, Antonio Delrae Smith, saying something positive about his appellate attorney. That was news. In fact, I had never heard anyone in any of the 'pods' say a kind word about their own, or anyone else's lawyer yet.

Antonio Smith is the one, if you recall, whose lawyer (Trobich) had sold him down the river like my boy Freedman had done me.

But Antonio Smith had since found a young, aggressive, black, former-prosecutor by the name of Tolly A. Kennon III, who had seen the light and converted from the 'dark side' to fight judicial corruption instead of being part of it.

Bets among the fellows at the table were that he (Tolly) wouldn't last two years in Charlotte.

---

[9] Perpetual Prison Machine: How America Profits From Crime, by Joel Dyer. (2000) Westview Press, Boulder Co. and Oxford, England

"Gretchen Shappert (the U.S. Attorney in Charlotte, North Carolina) will run his ass out of town in no time flat!", said 'Big Easy', a prisoner from New York. "Gretchen ain't puttin' up with no honest lawyers that will fight 'em."

Big Easy's words would be prophetic.

I got Smith to call Mr. Kennon and ask if he would visit me at the jail. He told Smith that I would have to write him and tell him if I was represented or not first, and who was handling my case.

An ethical lawyer...now that was different.

So I wrote Mr. Kennon a note saying that I had been represented but if I could ever get the attorney to take a call or come see me, and that he was going to be terminated for refusing to follow (any) client instructions, or even investigate my case.

I told him I'd been lied to and wanted to fight. My attorney wouldn't do it, so I was looking for one that would, but wanted to interview his replacement _before_ hiring him.

I couldn't take another Freedman.

He agreed to the interview but said that he could not do any work for me or have any involvement in my case unless I was unrepresented, or he spoke to my lawyer first.

That worked for me, an ethical guy. And no worry about his ever talking to Freedman before I fired him, because he never returned phone calls anyway. Not even my brother, Jim, who had paid him all that money, could get him to return a phone call.

Smith had let me read a brief that Mr. Kennon had written to the court in his case. It was fiery and feisty-sounding. Kennon sounded like a real advocate for the client, but I feared that the boys were right. The U.S. Attorney's office was going to eat this fellow for lunch, so I'd better get him before they took him down.

And it wouldn't be the first time that Gretchen Shappert's wrecking crew had gone after the good ones. We'd been following the case of the FBI's local director of ethics, a man named Erik Blower. He had challenged some of her corrupt methods and suffered her retaliation for it. She'd proved him right. She responded by filing corruption charges against him, preemptively. She and her crew of gremlins chewed through his financial records and used every means at their disposal to destroy him, and did.

Using some credit card receipts from Vegas, where Blower had gone on vacation, she took him down like a wrestler on TV.

He was on the mat, drummed out of the FBI, and barely avoided jail before her vindictive prosecution was finished. She was evil on the hoof, according to all reports.

But Tolly A. Kennon III didn't seem scared. He was a big man and he was on a mission to clean up the corruption. He was well-spoken, friendly, and I liked him right off.

He said that he didn't want my case unless I was serious about fighting it. He had come back to North Carolina from a prosecutor's position in Florida because he saw that he was on the wrong side. The prosecutors no longer stood for law and order; they were only interested in convictions at any cost.

In his calls with legal professionals around the country, there seemed to be consensus that North Carolina was the place to come if you wanted to fight corruption in the federal judiciary. There was all of it you could stand in Charlotte.

While my home jurisdiction, the Middle District, was considered professionally run and fairly decent, the Western District, where I had been improperly charged; and the Eastern District, where AUSA Marten's had gone judge-shopping were, according to Kennon's sources, "the most corrupt jurisdictions on the planet."

Even with no previous experience in corruption or government gone crazy, I could believe that. I'd seen nothing but corruption and dishonesty at every level since my nightmare had begun there.

He agreed to take the case, but not until I had terminated my other attorney. He never even brought up money.

Yep, I liked Mr. Kennon. I liked him just fine. He was the 'human being' lawyer I'd been seeking. My spirits began to rise. So that's how we left it. My only problem then was finding this sorry fellow, Freedman, to fire him. He wouldn't take my phone calls, nor had he ever answered (or followed) written instructions. As I've already mentioned, I'd even gone to the lengths of sending correspondence to him through my brother Jim's secretary, Kelly Kiser, up in Roanoke, Virginia, as it became unbelievable that anyone could simply ignore a pre-paid client who had years of his life at stake for false charges.

I had begun to fear that Jim might begin believing Freedman's self-serving questioning of my sanity and version of events. But the ever-efficient Kelly diligently kept a record of the massive (one-way) correspondence and showed it to my brother.

The last time I had seen Freedman was in June on a 'drive-by' meeting after his vacation to Israel. Jim had wisely advised that I hold off on firing him until I had seen what agreement he got his pal Martens to come up with and if it was in line with their promises.

That made sense, as neither Jim nor I had found a replacement at that time, back in June 2006. On one occasion, Freedman and Tisdale (my wife's infamous lawyer), had actually been there the same day and I had spent a few minutes with both of them.

I started out by expressing my deep dissatisfaction with the fact that both my wife and I had been in jail for months and the promised 'agreement' had seemingly been a hoax.

"Why has there been no 'adversarial process'?", I asked. The answer to my question was because they were all working on the same team, but I knew they'd never admit that.

Tisdale was already red-faced, blotchy and puffy-eyed even though it was early afternoon. He looked as if his lunch had been in 'liquid' form, and my little speech about an 'adversarial process' set him off on a tirade.

He kicked the chair his feet were propped on, and stormed out of the little room saying, "I don't have to listen to this shit!" in a slurred voice, and never returned.

Freedman tried to cover for his 'out of sorts' comrade by calmly apologizing for his behavior and claiming not to feel that way himself.

But before I could get any answers out of him, he once again said that he had to leave and promised to come back soon.

"Have you filed any of my motions yet?" I was asking as he started out the door. He looked at me like he didn't have a clue what I was talking about.

"David, I've written you a number of times and I told you before you took off on your trip that if you couldn't produce the agreement you and Martens promised me, that I wanted to go to trial. Please don't tell me that you've done nothing yet!"

He gave me a sort of dumb, 'deer in the headlights' look and said nothing.

The thin veneer of civilization was about to be peeled away from me. I wanted to smash him and his little red-faced buddy. They were beyond pity.

We'd paid these fools $70,000. They owed us some level of professionalism or they should return our money and let us find some real lawyers. That was my naive take on it, at any rate. They would never give back a cent unless the State Bar forced them to, which was about as likely as the sun rising in the west.

But he was still standing there.

"David?" I asked. "Have you filed any of my motions? I've been writing you since April. Have you done _anything_? Please answer me."

"I've really got to go. Let me look through my file and get back to you," he said.

"How? When? I can't call you. You won't respond to my letters. How will you 'get back to me', David? When will you get back to me?" I asked.

"I'll get word to you through your brother," he said. "But I really have to go now," and he slipped out again, not to be seen for a month.

Though I should have been used to it by then, I was incredulous. In my entire career, I'd never dealt with people like this. I must have still been standing there with my mouth wide open when the guard came in to get me.

"Didn't go too good, Woltz?" he asked.

"No," I answered. "Not well at all. But I know why they call the sons-of-bitches *criminal* lawyers, and it's not because of the type of law they practice." The guard chuckled but I wasn't joking.

I went straight upstairs and wrote a letter to the clerk of court to request a status of docket sheet to see what, if anything, my worthless attorney had filed in my case.

It was time to begin learning how to do things myself, as it was obvious that this man either had not done anything, or had done so little as to not recall it. He had drawn such a blank when I asked, that I feared he had done absolutely nothing. I would soon learn that was precisely what he had done. Not a motion had been filed, and there had been nothing done to defend me. He would admit quite soon in a heated moment, that he had never taken the time to even read my indictment.

CHAPTER 22

MY EDUCATION BEGINS

After the letter requesting a docket status report from the clerk of court was finished, I began asking around to see if any of my fellow prisoners knew anything about how to actually file motions and "do" law work.

A very quiet fellow by the name of Ricky Graham was everyone's answer. All the others had just been abused by the law and its practitioners, but Ricky had decided to try and study it, in hopes of using it positively, though it had failed Ricky.

He spent his days and nights designing beautiful communities and buildings that would never be built, as the following year... after ten years already behind bars...the prosecutor would belatedly add a murder charge out of spite, and take the rest of his life from him the month he was to have been released.

But we didn't know that then, and the courteous Mr. Graham could not have been more helpful. He had me re-write the request for the docket status report, and gave me the address for the clerk of court. Even more helpful, he gave me some books to order and read on the law.

I called my brother's wife, Jill, and as Ricky had suggested, asked her to order the Georgetown Law Journal and any other law books that she could find that may help me learn how to protect and defend myself, if nothing else, from a crooked prosecutor and my own lawyer's incompetence.

I absorbed the books and began to ask questions. Much, if not most, of what had been done to us was illegal or unconstitutional I would learn, but through various political shenanigans and redistributions of power, the federal government had ballooned into the monster it is today and seized un-granted authorities from the States and the People.

I also studied books on constitutional issues, the history of the judicial system, Latin and research texts that went back to the founding of our nation.

I re-read the <u>Federalist Papers,</u> which were written mainly by Alexander Hamilton (with a few more sensible articles by James Madison and John Jay thrown in) and the obscure but far more informative <u>Anti-Federalist</u> responses, which had warned that federal power would collect in a ruthless central government if the federalists won the argument for the nation's soul.

We are living proof that the anti-federalists were correct.

I no longer read *for* escape. I began to read so that I could learn <u>*how*</u> to escape the injustice that had trapped me and so many others in the perverse web of the prison-industrial complex.

The prison rolls had risen by 60% under the Clintons, and had only continued their incredible ascent after the year 2000 under the prison owning junta of Bush, Cheney and crew.

The more I learned, the angrier I became at the injustice being perpetrated against the American people.

While 'real crime', as I call it--murder, rape, robbery, and aggravated assault--had been dropping for nearly 30 years, the politicians had been escalating their "get tough on crime" rhetoric.

Days came and went and I wouldn't even know where the hours had gone, as I soaked up cases, books on the system, and stories of the injustices caused by it. I'm sure that my fellow prisoners thought me mad, staying in my cell absorbed in studies and rarely showing my face for days at a time. I was a man possessed.

One night my Vietnamese neighbor, John Nguyen came into my cell and asked, "Mr. Woltz. You ever kill somebody?"

"Kill somebody, John? Not that I can think of. Why would you ask something like that?"

"Well, I think maybe you, me, Smith, and Mexicans only ones not kill somebody," he said in his Viet-English patois.

I had been so oblivious to my surroundings and the world that I had hardly noticed that fact until John brought it to my attention.

"Why do you think they have _us_ in here?" he asked.

I thought about it for a moment, but couldn't really think of any rational reason. "I don't know, John. Why do you think they're keeping us in here with the killers? It makes no sense, does it? What do they want from you?" I asked.

"They want my money. They say I am drug-dealer, but I run a tea shop for Vietnamese and a nail salon at the mall," he said.

"What money do they want, John?"

"My money and my mom's. Vietnamese not trust banks. Keep cash. They say cash come from drugs, but it come from fingernail business and tea. The policeman holds .45 automatic to my daughter's head and say I must do what he says. Police here bad people. What they do is not right. They steal our money and say it drug money. If I don't sign paper saying so, they put my wife in jail too. Is not right."

That hit home. "My wife is in here now," I said.

"Your wife, in this jail?" he asked.

"Yes, John," I answered. "She's two floors down and she's never broken a law. They told me for months now that she would go free, but they won't show me a copy of the agreement we made, or let me sign it. I'm beginning to think they've tricked me. Have you signed anything yet?"

"No. Same thing. You think they put us in here with bad people to scare us so we sign anything they want?"

I thought, "Wow. That's incredible." My Vietnamese friend had seen right through them while I had been completely clueless, not even realizing the underhandedness of their ploy, but that was part of my education as well - understanding their crookery so I could expose it.

"From what I've seen, John, that's a very logical conclusion. I hadn't even thought of that, but I'll bet you're right."

And we would both prove that to be correct, as months later, once our 'plea agreements' were signed, we were immediately moved to lower security pods with far less violent neighbors.

Bit by bit, I was peeling the federal onion, and it was getting uglier and more rotten with each layer.

During those days, I also read the U.S. Constitution over and over again, at least 200 times, and committed the Bill of Rights to memory. The problem was clear. We no longer followed our game plan. The Constitution only listed eighteen powers of federal government that were ever granted by "We the People" to them. Other than counterfeiting and piracy on the High Seas, Congress had no authority to pass criminal statutes. That was the exclusive purview of the States.

The Tenth Amendment to the Constitution had made that clear. "The powers not delegated to the United States by the Constitution, nor prohibited by it to the States, are reserved to the States respectively, or to the people."

The whole purpose of the various nation-states joining together had been for mutual protection and defense, a common currency, and free trade without tariffs, not to create a dictatorial regime at the national level.

The idea had not been to see how many citizens the United States government could imprison using laws that it had not been granted the power to impose either.

The whole picture of what had happened to our nation became clear to me over those months of intense study and constant research.

I realized that America is now at a crossroads for its soul like the blues player who traded his eternal life for worldly success, and the Devil is back to collect his due.

My mission became clear. My destiny was to write about the injustice I saw and expose it in hopes of our people awakening to what was going on before it was too late, if that time hasn't passed already.

In my own case, I decided to fight. The government had
plainly lied and my own attorney was in their service.
Prosecutor, judge, and counsel, were all in an unconstitutional
conspiracy...a real one...to circumvent due process and violate
our rights. They had succumbed to the age old pitfall of men
with too much power and no oversight. They believed that getting
anything they wanted, including revenge and fame, at any cost, was
their right and privilege.

But they were wrong. They may get away with it, but I would see
to it that the world would one day know what they had done,
and how they had gone about it.

CHAPTER 23

THE SHOWDOWN

I was pulled out of my studies and reverie one day in late July when the guard popped the air-lock on my cell.

"Get in the slider, Woltz," he said over the speaker in my cell.

It had been a month since Freedman had promised to return, and no responses had ever been received to my instructions to file the several motions.

The docket status report had come in, however, and I had learned that David B. Freedman had never filed a single thing in all of the intervening months in the case of <u>United States v. Howell Woltz</u>. He had not followed a single one of my written instructions, including my order to file for dismissal when our speedy trial rights were violated as of June 29, 2006. Had he followed just that one order, I would not be in federal prison today.

In the intervening weeks, I'd also decided, as mentioned, that I was going to fight these people, with this sorry lawyer or without him. The visitor downstairs had to either be the skunk himself or my persecutors, I thought to myself on the way down to the second floor. Probably the prosecutor again, I guessed, as Freedman had disappeared off the planet. He'd also always come to the little rooms on the sixth floor where we were separated by bullet-proof glass on his earlier 'drive-by' stops (which was probably not a bad idea given my feelings toward him), rather than using the "contact" visit rooms on the second floor where I could get my hands around his throat.

Hanging around with murderers was broadening my horizons. The study done by the Department of Justice that a person who spends just six months in a U.S. jail, whether guilty of a crime or not, is 300% <u>more likely</u> to commit a crime when he is released, than if he'd never been in jail at all, was true and I was becoming living proof.

Jails, like prisons, are just crime schools today since "rehabilitation" was thrown out back in 1994. Maybe homicidal tendencies were rubbing off on me.

So with these thoughts in mind, I was shocked to see none other than the sorry barrister himself when I was taken into the interrogation room by the deputy. Not only was Freeman there, but he had his co-conspirator, prosecutor Martens, as well as the young FBI agent that had taken Doug Curran's place after he had apologized to me.

Martens was all smiles. The weasel wanted something; that was for sure.

Freedman hardly spoke and avoided eye contact.

"How are you doing, Mr. Woltz?" Martens opened, dripping with feigned concern.

"Fine," I replied. "How do you think I'm doing you son-of-a-bitch?" is what I wanted to say, but held back.

"You're probably a little concerned about things, I suppose, as it's been awhile since our last meeting, so we wanted to get back together and assure you that everything is fine." He said with another big, fake grin.

"It's not fine with me, Matt," I said. "You and my lawyer over there lied to me. My wife's still in jail. I'm still in jail, and last time you came, you gave me some nonsensical agreement, which was anything but what you two promised me in order to get my cooperation that first day. How can you think that everything is fine?"

The grin lessened, but was still there.

"I think we've figured out a way to get everything resolved," he began. "You might be able to help us on something."

"It's already resolved on my end, Matt," I said. "I've done everything that you asked me to do. You tricked me the last time we met, and rather than getting the three files we had agreed to, your people stole eight to ten legal boxes full, and copied our hard drive down in Nassau as well, I understand. So I've already helped you and more. It's your turn now to keep your word."

Martens' fake smile was waning fast. He ignored my comments and said, "It looks like Rick Graves is going to trial."

Rick Graves was the attorney, you may recall, who referred the undercover IRS agents our way in the "sting operation", inadvertently, and was my "co-defendant", which is the stupid term the Feds use for someone they are railroading in the same car they've put you in.

"Good for him," I said. "He should. He didn't do anything wrong, just like us," I said.

There was no smile left at all after my answer.

Martens used his clever little line he had back in April, "We say all of you out there have done 'something', Mr. Woltz. We just haven't gotten around to everybody yet. Rick Graves, however, has been indicted by a grand jury. We just need you to corroborate a couple of things for us. We'll take care of the rest."

"What a despicable little rodent," I thought to myself. All of you out there have done 'something'?

"In other words, you're saying that you want me to testify against him in court," I said.

"That's right. We just wanted to make sure that you're clear on the... 'facts'," he said carefully, "before you get on the stand."

"In other words, you don't have any evidence against him," I thought to myself, "and you need me to lie to cover your butt for indicting him." Like us, they'd arrested Graves with no evidence against him, figuring that they could just make up something or get him to plead guilty like 95% of their victims do. But Graves wasn't in jail like me. He could fight them. And he was an attorney.

Judges rarely ever deny attorneys their constitutional right to bail, so Rick Graves was out where he could mount a defense. They also couldn't get away with taking his wife as a hostage as they had mine, so they didn't have any leverage on him.

208

Martens needed someone to lie, or he was going to lose this one, and that could hurt his goal of getting Sam Currin's conviction to build his 'rep'. Without me, Graves was going to be one of that tiny percentage that wins. No lie, no conviction.

"What could I possibly say about Rick Graves that would help you?" I asked. "I hardly know the man, and he never broke any law to my knowledge, just like we never did, and I think you know that. You claim to have tapes of all our conversations. Use them."

"Oh there's plenty on the tapes against you and Graves," he said. "I've listened to them. They're very damaging."

"Then you don't need me," I said.

"We may need you to corroborate a few other things," he said.

I remembered the meeting with the con-men from the IRS quite well, and knew that we had never suggested, or allowed anyone to suggest, illegal activity in our offices, or they would have been asked to leave. We'd made comments about U.S. taxes being outrageous, and the Government being completely out of control (as was evidenced by my present situation), but nothing was said that could be construed as remotely illegal....and we'd refused to deal with them and sent their money back anyway!

"Nothing was said or done outside of the law," I said. "Of that I am sure."

"We think you gave the undercover agents control over the trusts. That would make them a sham," he said.

"That's not true and you know it. They had no control at all over any trust, nor have we ever allowed any client to have control over a trust. I know you know that, because you have a copy of the trust deed. It is clear. Only the trustee has control and it is irrevocable." I said.

"At one point on the tapes, you even said that someone was more likely to get hit by lightning than for you to refuse to follow their instructions, Mr. Woltz," he snarled. "I heard it. Those were your exact words."

"You're a damn liar. That was <u>never</u> said," I shot back. I'd had enough of this guy's foolishness.

"Now Howell," chimed in my sycophantic lawyer, "Don't say things like that. We have something here that can help you. Just listen for a minute. Listen to Mr. Martens."

Martens went straight to it. His ploy hadn't worked. There was nothing on those tapes either Rick Graves or I had to fear and Martens knew it as well as I did. The IRS agent, Schiller, had even admitted it. We'd never broken any law.

"Here's what you're going to do," he said roughly, with no more phony Mr. Nice Guy facade or fake grin. "You're going to 'REMEMBER' a conversation with Rick Graves, either on the phone or in person, where the two of you agreed to give the undercover agents control over the trust."

"That never happened, and you know it," I said.

These guys were too smart to tell you to lie, instead they said, "You must <u>remember</u>."

"You're not hearing me, Mr. Woltz," he said sternly. "You need to listen very closely to what I'm telling you right now if you want your wife to ever leave this jail. Do you hear me?"

I heard him. I had to 'remember' something that never happened. He let that sink in for a moment, and then continued. "Now, you're going to 'REMEMBER' a conversation with Graves when just the two of you were on the phone or together, where you agreed to let the undercover agent have 'control' over the trust, and you're going to testify to that at his trial. Do you understand now?"

"No such thing ever happened," I said.

The nasty little rodent was threatening to keep my wife in jail if I didn't get on the stand in federal court, under oath, and tell a lie so he could convict an innocent man and get another notch in his belt. He sickened me, but he was clever. Rather than say 'lie', he said 'remember'.

But on the other hand, I knew I had to be careful, as my wife's letters were becoming more and more morose, bordering on desperation. I couldn't just blast him and say what was on my mind. I decided to act like I just didn't 'get' what he was telling me to do.

He came at me a third and last time. "I'm just going to say this one more time, Mr. Woltz, so you need to listen very carefully. You're going to 'REMEMBER' a conversation with Attorney Rick Graves where the two of you agreed to give the undercover agent control over the trust.

"Do you understand me this time?"

"No. I really don't understand what is going on. I don't," I said as meekly as the blistering fire inside me would allow.

Martens visibly reddened, and turned to his partner in crime, and said, "Mr. Freedman, you need to talk to your client and explain to him what's going on here. If you don't make him understand what he has to do, then all of our deals are off, not just this one."

All of our deals? Had I been traded off? "You can have Woltz, but look after my other client?" Was that what had gone on? I remembered Martens knowing about Freedman's 'other client' up in Greensboro at our last meeting when I'd asked why my lawyer couldn't be present. How had Martens known about him?

David's tongue came untied quickly after Martens threatened him with that.

"Howell, you really need to listen to Matt and...remember...the conversation," he said softly.

"Why?" I asked. "You two have misled me. You've lied to me. Why should I help you? Why should I do this?"

Martens handed Freedman some papers, with a case highlighted and Freedman then handed it to me, even though Martens was between us.

He looked at it for a moment, and then said, "See this case, Howell?" Freedman cooed. "Whitfield v. United States?"

"Yes," I said. "I see it. What does it have to do with me?"

"Just read it," he said.

I read the highlighted part. "No overt act in furtherance of conspiracy to launder money is required in order to be found guilty under 28 U.S.C. §1956(h)."

"What conspiracy?", I asked.

"He has evidence that could tie you into a conspiracy with Sam Currin and his client, to launder money," Freedman said, pointing toward Martens.

"That's a damn lie!" I said.

"Mr. Woltz," Martens began, "I have a copy of a signature card which was used to open a bank account at a Bank of America branch in Lincoln County, North Carolina. Your signature is on it. That's all I need under §1956(h) to convict you of being a part of the conspiracy, if you choose not to be cooperative on Mr. Graves."

His smile came back, and this time it was a real one. He was genuinely enjoying this.

"I'm not on their account at the Bank of America! I'm not on any of their accounts! I don't even know where Lincoln County is!" I shouted.

Martens giggled. "And I know you're telling the truth. I've even got e-mail between Sam Currin and Walt Hannen saying not to let you know about the account, so I know that you didn't know about it, Mr. Woltz. But that really doesn't matter. That one piece of paper is all I need to get a jury to convict you of being in the conspiracy and put you away in prison for twenty years."

From my experience thus far, he'd probably have sent me anyway after I did his dirt, were I the kind to do something like that. But I had no intention at the moment of letting him know that I would never consider such a thing.

His very presence was repulsive, and joining him in his crime against mankind would make me like him. There could be no more deviant behavior than knowingly putting innocent people in prison just to advance one's career. And doing so under color of government authority made this little man worse than any other sort of criminal.

Freedman broke the silence with his soft, almost feminine voice, "Howell, he's really got some very damaging evidence. You need to work with him on this."

"Let's see it then. Where is it? You must have a copy. And how can I be on an account under the KYC (Know Your Customer) rules, if I've never even been to the bank?" I asked.

"I'll send you a copy", Martens said, bordering on anger himself. "That little card is all I need to convict you, Mr. Woltz. You need to really think about this."

"David!" I nearly yelled. "You just heard him say that he knows I wasn't part of it, and you're helping him do this?"

Freedman said nothing. He just looked at the prosecutor, like a dog watching his master, waiting for his orders or to be told his next trick to perform.

Martens broke the silence. "You'd better get your client straightened out, David, or that's it, and you better have him in line soon or lots of things will change."

"I'm sure I can get him to understand what you want," Freedman nearly whispered, like I wasn't even part of the conversation.

I stood up on that. "I'm done here." I knew damn well what they were up to. I motioned to the guard and left the room with the conspirators still in it. But instead of feeling dirty and miserable like I usually did after being around them, I felt stronger and whole.

Not only would I refuse to be a part of their conspiracy, I would expose it regardless of the cost to myself, and I felt good about that decision. I actually smiled at the thought of it.

I couldn't have looked in a mirror had I been part of their immoral scheme. Whether I was in jail or at home, I'd still have to live with myself. Where I did that was just geography. If it was jail, so be it.

My soul was not for sale.

CHAPTER 24

THE CONSPIRACY IS EXPOSED

I had not yet confirmed Judge Britt's involvement in the overall scheme, and still labored under the belief that he might do the right thing if he was made aware of the prosecutor's illegal acts. In retrospect, I was quite naive.

He hadn't recused himself from the case of an old enemy, as the Canons of Ethics required, to avoid "even the appearance of impropriety." Had he and his old nemesis, U.S. Attorney Sam Currin, been friends instead of enemies after all those years of being in the Eastern District's judicial traces together, it was still inappropriate for him to have accepted the case. And accepted, he had. He wasn't chosen randomly or assigned it. The prosecutor, AUSA Martens, had admitted that he sought him out. An honest judge would have refused on that ground alone. Britt did not.

Furthermore, his reflexive revocation of our bond at Martens' request, without hearing a single witness or utterance, and after knowing that a capable judge in the Western District had readily and easily determined that it was appropriate to grant it, should certainly have been a clue to anyone of his impenetrable bias and determination to exact his revenge from Currin & Company. Unfortunately, in his eyes, I was "Company", and he would never be told that it was I who had originally written the S.A.R. (Suspicious Activity Report) about them.

And I, like most Americans, had bought the mythology of public school indoctrination about a "fair and impartial judiciary". If there ever was such a thing in America, it has long gone from our present federal system, I can tell you from personal experience.

And I was the key to Judge Britt's revenge, and could be valuable in that effort. I was simply collateral damage and an 'acceptable loss'. Sometimes these things happen. What are the lives of a few citizens, when compared with the needs and desires of a king? And make no mistake about it. These 'appointed-for-life' federal judges are just that---kings, or think they are. They answer to no one.

'Sed quis custodiet ipsos custodes'?

But in my Pollyannaish blindness to reality, and in defiance of the ready evidence at hand that the guard-dog at the chicken house door was actually a fox in league with their destroyers, I wrote the man himself, Judge W. Earl Britt, to disclose the crime I had witnessed first-hand.

I truly believed that Judge Britt, even if he had erred by agreeing to take a case where an enemy was the target, would be compelled to investigate the clear crime alleged against his co-conspirator, the ambitious, young 'procurer', Matthew Martens.

My letter to Judge Britt had carefully described the false lure by which my cooperation had been garnered by the prosecutor, his resultant frequent meetings with me (without counsel being present), and his ultimate demand that I lie against an innocent man before he would consider honoring his contract with me, which had been fulfilled in whole for my own part of it.

I'm embarrassed to admit that I actually anticipated investigators coming any day to interview me and look into the allegations. It's almost humorous to now look back upon the undulating desert I've crossed where justice is rarer than water, and think that I truly believed that, in retrospect, but I did, and I did so fervently.

So after days had passed and a visitor was announced on the Second Floor, I knew that my faith in the system had been justified....until I got down there and saw David Freedman alone, in the little room.

He had been sent as an emissary from none other than Judge Britt himself, who was apparently willing to do anything necessary to prevent his chance for retaliation against Sam Currin from slipping through his fingers after waiting a quarter of a century for this opportunity. If my allegations against the prosecutor were entertained at all, much less, seriously, he would have to order the young bulldog off the case.

The case, once tainted, and with no "offshore banker" or "tax attorney" to squeeze into corroborative or false testimony, re-indictment against Currin was unlikely to occur. And it seemed certain that Judge Britt was not going to let that come to pass.

Freedman was to the point. "Judge Britt has received your letter. He's asked me to come and ask you to withdraw it," he said, as he tapped his folder.

"Before we discuss that, David, I hope you have the plea agreement you've been promising with you, because I'm not interested in talking about anything else until I see it this time and make sure that it's what you and your buddy, Martens, promised me."

Freedman feigned a search of his brief and folders and said, "My secretary must have forgotten it. I know I told her to put it in here." This, by the way was in August 2006 and we had been playing this 'my secretary forgot' game since April.

And right then something clicked in my brain. I knew his secretary, Kathy Smith, and she was not only pretty and friendly but deadly efficient. Kathy never 'forgot' anything. She had been my dear friend, Fred Crumpler's secretary there at the same firm for many years. Fred was one of my best friends, and bird-hunting partners. Word was David was trying to take his firm over as he neared retirement.

That also explained why he made sure that I could never call the firm. He knew that I would complain to Fred, who was still the most powerful partner, even in semi-retirement, that Freedman was not only failing me, but aiding the prosecutor.

"If you don't have that agreement, David, then we have nothing to talk about, as I assume you've done nothing I've asked you to do in my letters."

"To be honest, Howell, I've not really read them," he answered. I was surprised by his forthrightness until I realized that he was just trying to shift my attention from the nonexistent plea agreement.

"Are you saying you haven't 'really' read them, or haven't read them at all?" I asked.

"Not really at all because none of that matters if we're going to make a deal. That will just upset Martens," he said.

"How many months have I got to tell you that there is no deal if you don't have an agreement? It's August and you still can't produce what you promised me was done in April. I've been asking you to go to trial since June, in writing. You and Martens have been lying all along. You're still lying. You didn't 'forget' the agreement, David you don't have it, do you?"

He dodged answering, "What matters right now is that you authorize me to tell Judge Britt that your letter to him is withdrawn. That's the only 'letter' that is important. And then you need to agree to do what Matt Martens wants you to do with regards to Attorney Rick Graves. You do that and they have told me to promise you that everything can go back like it *was* and there will be no retribution."

"Like it <u>was</u>?' David when you say 'They', I assume you mean Britt and Martens? Where were we? Let's see....no agreement, false charges, threats of more false charges and lies? Why on earth would I want it back like it <u>was</u>?"

"If you don't, they will see that you spend many years in jail," he said.

"Are you communicating a threat for your partners, David? Lie for the judge and prosecutor or go to prison for refusing? How deep into this thing are you with them, David? You're one of them, aren't you?"

"You've got to quit saying that. I'm just looking out for your best interest, Howell. I'm really on your side," he said softly.

"I don't believe that," I said and started to say what was on my mind about him, his judge, and his prosecutor, but I noticed two huge documents on the floor. My curiosity got the better of me and prevented the tirade.

He saw my eyes fix on the documents. "What are those?" I asked.

"They're not important unless you agree to help," he said very matter-of-factly, but he did bring them up from the floor and set them on the table to bait my interest. I'd been begging to see any 'evidence' as to why I was in jail for months, and in all that time, I'd never been allowed to *see* a shred of it. My mouth was almost watering to get to finally see something. Anything was better than nothing.

"If I were to take the letter back and agree to testify at Graves' trial, what would the deal be?" I asked, not out of any intention to do either one, but to play along until I could get my hands on those documents. I was pretty sure that they were transcripts from the IRS con-men's visits to Nassau, when they'd come wearing 'wires', trying to entrap us. I wanted them badly if nothing else but to prove that Martens had lied about what was in them.

"I think I can get us pretty close back to the original arrangement, but you'll have to agree to the money laundering conspiracy charge. Martens is going to insist on that. He needs that in his case against Currin," he said.

"How does my pleading guilty to something Currin did that I never knew about help Martens?" I asked. But I knew the answer already from having heard so many plea deals and immoral swaps of lies for time cuts. The Feds' trick is to get one person cornered into "confessing" to a conspiracy of some sorts, whether they were ever part of one or not, and then using that (and the threat of that person's false testimony), to extort others into taking a plea deal, and saying that they were guilty of it as well. It's a cruel, dishonest, illegal, and highly effective strategy. They use it in almost every case, and it is the single reason that so many innocent people are in federal prison. "Conspiracy" is not something you do, it's something you <u>think</u>. There is no defense if the government and two liars say you thought something. You're done. That's why civilized governments do not have conspiracy laws, and why our boys here use the charge in over 90% of all federal cases. No proof required. An indictment is for all intents and purposes, a conviction, as stated before, but worth repeating.

But David had taken my bait and did his little text-book prosecutor spiel about it making me a "better witness". I nodded as if taking in every word.

"What are those?" I asked as casually as I could.

"They're the transcripts from the undercover agents' visits to your office in Nassau."

"Bingo", I thought.

"And if you're on board with everything, Martens wanted you to review them so you'd know where the gaps are that need filling at trial. You know what he's looking for. He's out to prove that the trust was a sham, and that Rick Graves knew it," he said.

"Whether it's true or not", almost slipped out, but I caught myself. I had to get my hands on those transcripts.

"Yes," I said. "I know exactly what he needs. If I say they had 'control', and that Rick Graves knew it, the trusts become illegal. Such trusts are only legal if the beneficiaries have no control or ability to order distributions," I said.

"Well, you seem to have a good handle on that so review these," he said, as he slid the huge transcripts to me, "and see where any gaps are that need filling so Martens has what he needs at Graves' trial."

I took them, trying to appear nonchalant, and tucked them on the floor, on the side of the chair away from Freedman. He'd never touch them again.

"So when are you going to bring me the corrected agreement?" I asked.

"Oh, I'll get that in the mail to you right away," he said, as he was putting his things away to leave.

"When? Tomorrow? The next day?" I was convinced then that he had no agreement. Kathy Smith didn't 'forget' anything. He and Martens were consummate liars and he would do anything to keep in the prosecutor's good graces. He made a damn good living taking huge retainers and serving up his clients to be slaughtered. It was far easier his way than going to court or having to find out what actually went on in a case. He got paid whether it was a win, loss, or a draw.

I guess Freedman had given up. Why do the work if the government is going to win anyway?

But I'd paid him to go to trial and told him since June to do it, when it became clear that I'd been hoodwinked.

He answered, "I'll get it right in the mail to you. And we're clear on the letter, right? It never happened?"

"Let's discuss that when I get the agreement," I said. "If you're in a rush, perhaps you should bring it back down to me rather than mailing it." I even smiled for good measure, and stood up, with the transcripts locked under my arm.

He stopped his preparations to leave and said, "I'd really like to be able to tell Judge Britt that the letter has been withdrawn right away, and give Martens our assurance today that you're on board," Freedman said. I was sure that was true.

The allegations in the letter were as damning of Freedman as they were of Martens.

"And I'd really like to see how I'm being treated this time before I do anything more, so you need to hurry back down with the agreement, don't you?" I said, just a little too tartly. I never was a good actor. I'd put him back on the alert. The charades were at an end. I could tell by his reaction.

"Maybe I should hold onto those then until you decide," he said, putting out his hand for the transcripts.

"If you think I'm giving these back after begging you for five months to show me why I'm in jail, you've lost your damn mind, David. I'll read them and be better informed to make a decision when you come back with my plea agreement. If these are accurate representations of our conversation, then they're exculpatory and will help me at trial."

Freedman blanched a bit at that, "But what do I tell Martens and Judge Britt?"

"Whatever you please. Tell them what I said. That would be fine. I need to see an agreement this time, because not one of you, including Judge Britt, can be trusted," and with that, I turned and went to the door with the transcripts in a death grip.

Freedman was flummoxed.

The guard was standing outside and took me back upstairs.

Everyone was out of their cells when I returned, as it was near "feeding", as they called it, so I sought out Ricky Graham to ask him how I could make sure that the letter to Judge Britt ended up in the public case record in case he threw it away. "Did you keep a copy?" he asked.

"Of course," I answered.

"Are you sure you want to do this? I advise you not to because it is going to mortally piss off this judge and prosecutor. They always get even," he said.

"I've got to, Ricky. If this judge is part of this thing, which he must be since he's refusing to investigate it, then my only hope is on appeal. I want someone, someday, to be able to read what I reported and see that Judge Britt did nothing about illegal activity and prosecutorial misconduct."

"I'll advise you one more time not to do it, Howell. These people are dirty. Let God deal with them," he said.

"I'm sure you're right, Ricky, but God needs a 'little helper' on this one. Tell me what to do."

Ricky paused a moment, stared at me, and then relented.

"Send a copy to the clerk of court with your case number on it. The clerk is supposed to file everything, if it has the case on it," he said.

"How will I know if the clerk files it?" I asked.

"Oh I promise you that you'll know that quickly enough," he said with a smile. "The clerk will copy everyone in the case including your lawyer and everybody else's. You'll hear 'em yelp, I suspect!"

So that's what I did. I sent a copy to the Clerk of District Court in Charlotte, and the yelping began. I also sent a letter to David Freedman firing him for lying and copied the clerk on that as well.

CHAPTER 25

THE BARRISTER IS FIRED AND THE BRIDGES BURNED

My friend, Mr. Graham, was right. The letter to Judge Britt set the bells a ringin', but I felt better. There was no going back now. The bridge to temptation had been burned, and the court was on notice that Freedman was being terminated.

I then tackled the massive transcripts and read them completely through twice.

Two things were clear and one was suspected. Martens had lied. No surprise there. There was no such line as the one he'd quoted about lightning striking in either of the texts, which I knew already, but the confirmation was satisfying.

It was also interesting that other statements appeared, and some had disappeared from them as well. Tampering with evidence? You bet.

For example, the transcripts had me discussing a baseball game with the IRS con-men that had been on television. Having never watched a baseball game on TV in my life, and finding the idea of sitting in front of the TV doing so my best idea of boring, I was more than certain that was not likely to have happened. Other lines were equally suspicious, and I made a mental note to demand that the tapes be reviewed and matched to these false transcripts to prove the tampering that was evident[10].

And the suspected alterations included omissions of the many periods where both Attorney Graves and I had warned the con-men of what could and could not be done, legally, and the rules we would require them to abide by as trustees to insure that the trust was legally managed, within our laws in the nation of licensing, as well as the U.S., as it would not be a sham trust.

---

[10] I later had the tapes reviewed and tampering was confirmed. The transcripts did not match the recordings.

Each time these clear passages that I knew were said and should be on the page were reached, the section was omitted as "inaudible". They'd played with the tapes and falsified the transcripts. Crooked Feds! They couldn't play fair.

If this was their 'evidence', then I was looking forward to going to court and exposing their chicanery.

And now that I'd officially shed myself of David Freeman, I contacted Tolly Kennon - by phone, no less! He came to see me a couple of days later. At last a real lawyer who gave a damn. I was starting to feel pretty good for a man falsely accused and in jail for something he didn't even know about.

It was like a new day had dawned. Tolly Kennon was not at all shocked by what these people had done, as he saw it every day, dealing with crooks (government ones, that is, who were far worse than his clients on the whole). And he had that sense of outrage that had been so missing in the plea-merchants, who just suck money from government's unsuspecting victims, knowing that they will never defend them. He pledged to help us in our fight, all the way, and I believed him.

There was just one problem...he was so busy going to trial, unlike the plea-merchants, that he couldn't focus on the case and begin filing motions until October, as he had back-to-back cases in the month of September.

It was well into August by then. The nightmare had been going on for over four months which was well over the statutory maximum time for the Feds to have taken me to trial. The Speedy Trial Act of 1974 specified "speedy" as within 70 days. The part that I would later learn is that within that legislative act, 18 U.S.C. §3161, there is a codicil which says that if the defendant has not requested dismissal on the grounds that his Sixth Amendment right to a speedy trial had been violated, then he waives that right! How Congress could legislate that you have to ask for your constitutional rights before they must be recognized is beyond me, but that is the type of law that has placed us squarely in the jaws of tyranny. We haven't been swallowed whole yet, but one can certainly feel the saliva and smell the breath of the beast, and it stinks.

And of course, my sycophantic attorney, Mr. Freedman, had refused my direct orders to file for a dismissal, which under our lawyer-serving system, meant that I had waived my rights to Sixth Amendment protection, simply because he, an attorney whose interest was in currying favor with the prosecutor rather than defending his client, had refused to follow concise instructions. As unbelievable as that may sound, folks, that's the way your country is now run...and the lawyers love it.

To add insult to this injury, while the court and my own counsel were violating my right to a speedy trial, the Supreme Court was deciding that enough was enough and demanding that the illegal detention which myself and my wife were suffering, would no longer be allowed.

Keeping my wife and me in jail for more than 90 days had been a direct violation of federal law as well, I would later learn once I got to prison. §3164 (b & c) of the Speedy Trial Act require even "high risk" detainees to be released if they haven't been tried within that time period. Judge Britt broke the law . . . . again. No "excludable delays" had been cited, ever. He was holding us until his partners in the conspiracy could squeeze confessions to uncommitted crimes out of us. By federal law, we had to have been released by July 19, 2006.

Judges simply do not follow the law anymore in the United States, and Congress has shown no courage in removing them as the Constitution requires them to do for such "high Crimes and Misdemeanors". Illegally holding a citizen in a dangerous jail is about as High a Crime as I can think of and relieving the corrupt curmudgeons of their black robes would be a small penalty to pay for such horrendous and immoral conduct. They should be put in prison themselves.

But, almost every federal prisoner I've ever met was similarly violated by government and court in complete disregard of law and constitution, while Congress and the "Justice" department are asleep at the wheel.

On June 5th, 2006, the Supreme Court handed down its decision in Zedner v. United States, 126 S.Ct.1996,164 L.Ed.2d 749 (2006), wherein it stated, "that where a defendant has entered a plea of not guilty, the trial must begin within 70 days of his arraignment on his information or indictment." We were way beyond that. And Zedner went on to say, "The Court further held that where no such trial has commenced within the 70 day time period allotted by the statute, the indictment must be dismissed."

So even the Supreme Court agreed with what I was begging these attorneys to do, in writing, no less. And had they done so, the court would have been required to drop all of the charges.

The indictment must be dismissed, not "might be", or should be considered. Must be dismissed!

So why were we still in jail months later, even though the statute law, U.S. Constitution, and recent Supreme Court's Zedner decision demanded our release? Because, 18 U.S.C. §3162 (Sanctions) states, "Failure of the defendant to move for dismissal prior to trial or entry of a plea of guilty or nolo contendere shall constitute a waiver of the right to dismissal under this section."

Now without getting too deep into this and side-tracking our story, I ask the reader, what kind of damn fool would waive this right, and stay in jail, knowing that the government chews up 99.6% of its victims and spits them into federal prison for years and years on minor offenses, when they could just have it dismissed and go home?

The answer is, only a fool that doesn't know that his attorney is waiving this right by not filing for dismissal. To look back and realize that I had given five different attorneys instructions to file for dismissal and none had followed my orders, after Zedner had been decided in June of that year, has caused more than one sleepless night.

But I didn't know about Zedner then, and the plea-merchants have no need of keeping up with the law, because they have no occasion to ever *use* it. They're not going to go to trial, and they're certainly not going to do anything to upset their symbiotic partners in crime, the prosecutors, which filing for a legal dismissal would certainly do.

There is no doubt that Tolly Kennon would have done so, but fate and government corruption kept that from happening, so not one attorney ever filed my motion to dismiss under the Speedy Trial Act as they had been ordered to do. By the time I had learned about the Zedner case, I was on my way to prison. The first time I would ever be allowed in a law library to look up these laws, I was already there, though the law required them to grant me access to one at every stop. But as the guard in Charlotte admitted, they were told to never let me see the inside of one until it was too late. And they didn't.

So while Tolly Kennon was fighting his other cases in court during the month of September, back in 2006, I was biting my nails waiting to get started on a real adversarial contest with a corrupt prosecutor, and a compromised judge.

My brother, Jim, had continued his search, and was particularly concerned that I was again poorly represented, because each time he asked if I had spoken to Tolly Kennon, I would say "No". Though he had told me that he would be unreachable while at trial(s) in the month of September, as he was a sole practitioner, Jim was so worried that we had another "Freedman" that he was intent on finding a larger firm where communications would not be problematic.

He found a Charlotte firm by the name of Helms, Mulliss and Wicker, who claimed to have 'an experienced defense litigation team'. While I continued to assure Jim that I had what I needed in Tolly Kennon, and was not so keen on any other attorneys, he was emphatic that we have a big firm on board as well so I finally got what I needed to go to court and win my freedom. There has never been a more wonderful brother, or one that would do what this man has done for me, but that turned out to be a terrible mistake, though neither of us knew it at the time.

And though Freedman had been dismissed via letter and it has been copied to the court, it was still incumbent upon him to produce the plea agreement, because he had lied to us all about its existence.

My wife, however, was being told by her attorney, Tisdale, that I had it, but refused to sign it, even though doing so would set her free immediately. He was also encouraging her to agree to work with the government against me, and testify as to whatever they told her to say, to free herself. Don was still a corrupt prosecutor at heart. Putting Darryl Hunt away for all that time hadn't satisfied his blood-lust. He wanted me too, I guess.

She sent me a copy of one of his letters to her, which said that I was "taking her off the cliff with me", pressing her to join him and the other prosecutors against me.

Her mournful letters continued to ask why I would not sign the document so that she could go home and be with our children. When I called her sisters to ask about our children, they would also gingerly ask the same. Though far too polite to question my word when I told them that I had never received it, I could tell that they had difficulty accepting that Attorney Tisdale would tell such bold-faced lies. Perhaps they can ask Darryl Hunt about that one day. He spent twenty years in prison due to Don Tisdale's dishonesty. But it was straining already difficult and painful relations with my wife, so I finally asked her sister, Jenny, to call Attorney Freedman and harass him until he took her call, so she could ask him for herself and confirm that Tisdale was just baiting my wife in service of the prosecutor.

She did so and finally got the worm on the hook by threatening (politely) to not stop until he gave her an answer. Finally he took the call in late August of 2006 and admitted that I had never seen the agreement which confirmed that Tisdale had been lying to them all.

That volley prompted AUSA Martens to set a deadline for my signing the yet to be seen document, while he still had his accomplice, Freedman, in the picture. That date was to be the Friday before Labor Day September 2006.

I waited the whole morning for Freedman to show up that day. No one came. Mid-day "feeding" came and went. No Freedman.

As had happened before, I took out my precious contact (though by that time I did have a spare), as I'd given up on him once more.

"Woltz! Get your ass in the slider, pronto!" was heard over my little speaker in the cell. We only had an hour before closing time. Typical! That immediately alerted me to something being wrong. They were going to try to sneak something in on me claiming it was "now or never". But I was beyond that. The guard took me downstairs to the second floor.

I entered the room. Freedman was alone.

He handed me the plea agreement. I said, "You're so late, I'd taken out my contact. I'm not signing it without reading it."

"You're just going to have to trust me and sign it anyway," Freedman said. "Today is the deadline."

I laughed right out loud at that. "Trust you! Have you read your mail, David?"

"No, why?" he answered.

I'd written him over a week before and fired him, in case he hadn't gotten the hint from the letter to the judge (or didn't read that either). But at least he was running 100% as that meant he'd never read anything I had ever sent him since he had taken the big retainer, way back in April.

"Maybe you should read the one I sent you last week, David. It could save you some time," I said. "But since you're here, why don't you tell me what the agreement says?" knowing full well that he'd never read that either.

He looked dumbfounded, but began fumbling with the inter-office Department of Justice packet. He'd obviously come straight from his "partner in crime's" office with the thing and never even opened it. I've still got the inter-office envelope it came in -- Department of Justice, Matt Martens.

Freedman mumbled, "I...well....I think it's pretty much what we expected, so you really should sign it. If I don't have it back over there by 5 p.m., all offers are off," he said gravely.

"Then it's off, I guess, because I'm not taking your word for anything anymore," I said. "You don't have a clue what it says either, do you, David? And while we're on the subject, why did you leave that consent form for me to sign back in June, knowing that they were planning to trick me and ransack our office down in Nassau?"

Freedman looked at me like he honestly didn't have any idea what I was talking about, and said so.

"Tisdale and Martens told me that you wrote it," I said, "and that you had left it for me to sign. They told me you had just walked out before I came in. That was the day my brother, Jim called you at home raising Hell about the 'pro forma' agreement Martens gave me."

"Howell, I honestly don't know anything about any consent form, nor have I ever seen it. I really don't know what you're talking about."

I described it, and reviewed what had happened that day. He turned reddish, out of embarrassment or anger, I'm not sure which.

"Martens never told me about it," he said. "But that's not important right now, this is," as he put the agreement before me. "What are you going to do?"

"Read it when I get back upstairs, I suppose. I'll think about it over the weekend, and go with it if it's what we agreed on. If it's not, which I'm quite sure it isn't, I'm going to trial. I'm tired of you crooks and your games," I said.

"You've got to quit lumping me in like I was working with them, Howell. I'm on your side," he said as if reading from a script.

"The Hell you are, David. You're trying to get me to sign an agreement for Martens that you haven't even read yourself as my overpaid attorney. It hasn't even been out of the damn envelope since you left his office a few minutes ago I'll bet. And you wait until the end of the day, thinking that the two of you can trick me into signing it under pressure. It could be sending me away for twenty years, like he said he might do, and you don't care enough to have even read it, just like the last one. If I'm wrong, David, tell me what it says. You can't do it, can you?"

"I....well, I....it's pretty much what..."

"You don't have a damn clue, do you? You can't any more tell me what's in here than you could about any of the letters I've written to you. You've just sold me down the river and left me to hang ever since you took our money, haven't you?" I said, calmly. "Do you even know what I'm charged with, David? Did you ever read the bloody indictment?"

"Well, I know he wanted to add a conspi--"

"That's not what I asked you, damn it!" I shouted, not so calmly. The man was suggesting that I sign away my life on an agreement that he'd never even looked at, with no qualms or concerns about me. He just wanted it done; he wanted to keep the huge retainer for doing absolutely nothing for me, and leave me to my fate at his partner, the prosecutor's, hand.

"I...well, I...I can't really remember...."

"Did you read the indictment? Answer me, damn it!" I shouted and slammed my hand on the table. I noticed him glance at the door. There was no guard out there.

"Answer me you son-of-a-bitch. Did you ever even read my indictment!?"

He flushed red, and finally said, "No!"

He hesitated a minute, and then said, "It didn't matter what it said because you were going to plead guilty in the end like everyone else does! It didn't really matter what it said. It only matters what the prosecutor says and that's all."

He was flustered enough to tell the truth for once.

"You never read my indictment. You don't even know what I was charged with. You've never looked at a piece of evidence, read my letters of instructions, or discussed the case with me ever, and here you are at the last minute telling me to sign this agreement that could send me to prison for 20 years and you didn't even look at it first?" I just looked at him. My anger had almost turned to pity. A pitiful, greedy, poster-boy for all that was wrong with the legal profession in America sat before me. He was beneath contempt.

"You might want to read my last letter to you, David," I said as I got up to leave.

"Why is that?" he asked.

"It could save you another trip." With that I rang the buzzer for the guard.

Once back upstairs, I put in my *"eye"* and read the agreement thoroughly. It was as I expected, and nothing like what they had promised me.

"Little or no time", had become 7+ years in federal prison, with several years of supervised release. I'd be in jail or under their thumb for the rest of my life if I'd signed it.

"No forfeiture of assets, personal or corporate", had become a total forfeiture of everything we owned except our farm cabin, plus a $1.2 million fine, and any inheritance that we, or our children may ever receive. They wanted it all.

"No new charges" had morphed into an indefensible conspiracy to launder Currin and Jaynes' cash in places we'd never heard of.

"Wife released immediately" just wasn't even in there. The closest they came was mentioning that she was in the case also and would be released when they got good and ready, and not until.

That piece of human trash downstairs had tried to mislead me into signing the agreement without ever taking one look at it himself he cared so little. David Freedman was as despicable to me as the little rat he had partnered with over at the U.S. Attorney's office.

How such people live with themselves still mystifies me today, and I truly have pity for them, as they represent the least desirable traits of mankind.

The worst task was writing my wife and telling her what the agreement said, and that I could not sign it. It accomplished nothing, including her release. It had all been a lie.

The next and equally difficult task was calling her sister, Jenny, who was anxiously awaiting my call, thinking Vernice could walk out the jailhouse door that day, which is what the infamous Mr. Tisdale had led her to believe.

"They never intended to keep their promise, Jenny", I told her, and read the part about releasing Vernice....or more accurately, not releasing her. "They're crooked people, Jenny, and not to be trusted for a moment, including our own lawyers, unfortunately. David Freedman had never even read the agreement."

"But her lawyer, Mr. Tisdale, said they would release her as soon as you sign it," she said, almost in tears.

"Don Tisdale is a black-hearted liar," I said, and told her what I'd learned about the 'consent form' that Tisdale had represented as being Freedman's work, in order to trick me into signing it for his fellow prosecutor back in early June.

I could tell that she wanted to not believe what I was saying and that her sister would somehow magically walk out of the door if I would but sign the document. That's what Tisdale had told her, so she would pressure me to do so, but he had lied.

It was a troubled night, but I knew that I had done the right thing. Had I signed the agreement, we would not only be penniless, but in deep and eternal debt, and both of us would still be in jail.

The prospect of prison, however, became very real that night, and it weighed heavily on my heart.

CHAPTER 26

THE CONSPIRACY TAKES FORM

For months, I'd been desperate to get my attorney, David Freedman to respond or visit. Once I'd fired him, however, I couldn't keep him away.

His "last chance ever" deal on the Friday before Labor Day, had become "one more chance", then yet another, and so on, as Freedman ran back and forth to the Charlotte jail dangling revised bait and threats, in an effort to save his "other deals" which Martens had not so obliquely referred to in our final meeting.

I simply refused to go in the room the last time he came and told the guard that he was no longer my attorney, and asked that he tell him to stop bothering me. He quit coming after that.

September of 2006 was a difficult month, however, waiting on Tolly Kennon to be available once his trials were over, and worrying about my wife. Her letters were not accusatory, but I could tell that Tisdale must still be fueling the fire telling her that the plea agreement I'd refused, said something that it did not. He was encouraging her to help the prosecutors against me, the man who paid them. What a guy.

A leopard just can't change his spots no matter how hard he tries, and Tisdale had never tried at all. He remained a prosecutor. I would learn how true the "leopard" theory was once the other prosecutor, Matt Hoefling, came on board as my attorney.

The government must give them a lobotomy or put something in the water coolers. Maybe they brainwash them, I don't know, but once these prosecutors are breast-fed from the government teat, they are hard to ever wean. But bad lawyers and prosecutors weren't my only problem.

The joie du vivre that came with firing Freedman would be short-lived.

My home was still the murderer's pod (6800) and it continued to have change-over, which always meant a spike in violence. A new group of particularly thuggish, young offenders from the street had set about trying to control the phones and had established a theft network to steal other inmates commissary and belongings, meager as they might be, culminating in a free-for-all one morning during "feeding", complete with home-made knives or "shivs" to stab each other, and various other jailhouse weapons of choice.

Nine of them were hauled or carried out that day in handcuffs at one time, which would be a record in my experience until a similar gang-related incident came about in the overcrowded Wake County Jail the following month.

One of the new arrivals to replace the departing gangsters was a businessman from Tampa, Florida, who had escaped Colombia during the Medellin drug wars when the CIA was changing suppliers for its American market. His name was Walter Perez by that time.

He had changed it from Carlos H. Escobar, to escape the stigma of the name made famous by his cousin Pablo Escobar, of the drug cartel in his home town of Medellin.

Before leaving Colombia, he and his family had been attacked and Walter/Carlos had been shot by competing drug-lords or paramilitary, he wasn't ever sure which. While the name Escobar had been well-respected and even famous as the family name of a prime minister, the infamous Pablo had tainted it beyond safe use.

Governments assumed that those with that name must be involved in the cocaine trade and harassed them. Competing drug lords targeted and tried to kill them for the same reason, incorrectly making the same assumption.

Walter had survived the attack and fled to Tampa where he had become a major developer of real estate until the Feds showed up one day and accused him of a credit card scheme. They put him in jail while they tried to fabricate a case, as is customary in post-Constitution America.

234

There was no evidence, as he'd never known about it. The only thing that tied him to it was a tryst with a young Hispanic woman who had a fake credit card, but the G-men 'smelled' money, so they ignored the facts (or created their own), and made him a part of a "conspiracy" anyway. That's what they do these days, unfortunately.

Walter was educated, smart, and angry about the gross injustice done him. We hit it off right away.

A natural leader, he quickly set about organizing the Mexicans, Hondurans, Nicaraguans, and Salvadorians, who traditionally didn't get along (though Americans tend to lump them all together as some homogenous group), and formed a cohesive coalition to forward and make public the particular injustices they suffered as an ethnic group.

Sheriff Jim Pendergraph had perfected the art of sweeping up brown people with an accent back in 2006, and hundreds of these poor men were in jail, not understanding why. I never interviewed even one of them who had been arrested legally. Their doors had been kicked in without a knock. The Supreme Court had all but gutted the Fourth Amendment with its July decision of that year allowing evidence to be used in spite of illegal entry or home invasion by the police (Hudson).

The court said it didn't want to "tie the constable's hands". No worry about 'tying' them in Charlotte. The constable had a battering ram in his.

The rest had been profiled in illegal traffic stops, "license checks" and a myriad of other constitutionally odious methods, but the mission was being accomplished, as tawdry a mission as it was, and the local Charlotte Observer continued to pile accolades on the narrow shoulders of its local hero, who at the same time, was averaging the death of one of his captives a month, due to negligence, abuse, or just not giving a damn, at his local jail where he warehoused them.

The sheriff was even quoted as saying so in that same newspaper in an article about the 700 or so of us un-convicted citizens sleeping on the floor of his jail each night. "It's not about them" (the prisoners), he said, he was just worried about his guards being attacked! There was no problem in his book treating un-convicted citizens like animals. He didn't need to worry about them voting, as 99.6% of the Feds' victims would be convicted, guilty or not, so they couldn't hurt him at election time.

Yes, the inanition of the Western District of North Carolina had filtered all the way down from federal, through state, to the local constable. There was a complete absence of social or moral vitality and vigor. There in the shadow of the Bank of America headquarters, and sitting in the high-rise jail, hundreds of homeless were being turned away from food and shelter each week, yet the sheriff was looking for $130 million to build a third large-scale prison in his town, to lock up more immigrants and citizens simply going about their daily lives... and he'd get it, eventually. There's always money for more prisons in North Carolina, even when people are starving.

Against that backdrop, our campaign began to bring forth these issues but the letters I translated and sent to the Charlotte Observer for them were never printed.

We soon found out why. Walter got the telephone number for Franco Ordonez, a reporter at the newspaper, assuming that a Spanish surname would imply sympathy. It did to a certain extent, in that he took the call, but his hands were tied (unlike the constable's) and they were bound by the ownership of the newspaper for which he worked.

Walter handed me the phone to speak with him in "American" English. I asked why these properly worded, polite letters were not being published. His chilling admission was that the newspaper was reviewed by either FBI, Homeland Security, or both, he wasn't sure, but said that any articles or editorials that they found offensive, were not printed.

The ultimate owners of the company that owned the newspaper, quite removed from the local scene, were apparently more worried about getting their next big merger approved by the Feds than preventing the abridgement of free speech and press. They were voluntarily subjecting themselves to government censorship. However, it seemed to us, which was as frightening as any aspect of the rapid decline of freedom in America that we had witnessed first-hand, to be another constitutional erosion.

The canary in the coal mine was dying, or may be stone dead already. Old John Peter Zenger must be rolling over in his grave.

When it became clear that the regular press was compromised and wouldn't publish uncomfortable truths, we turned to the Hispanic press and had a similar but equally heart-breaking discovery. La Noticia, the local Hispanic newspaper, also failed us. Rather than government censorship however, they 'self-censored'. A spouse of management was an officer on the sheriff's own staff. No articles reflecting poorly on the cowboy sheriff would ever find its way into the publication's pages for fear of retribution, which was probably a justifiable and very real concern.

With no viable press available to us, we set about organizing our own publication, Despierta America! (Wake Up, America!), which was really a tribute to Walter's resourcefulness. How he organized the publishing of this beautiful newspaper is a story unto itself. He also began a Hispanic hunger strike. I was the sole "gringo" participant, and did get quoted in the paper, stating that we must guard each others' liberties, or watch our own soon perish.

I became the editor of Despierta, but the real effort was outside the prison walls, in Walter's family and business network, which spanned several states from New York to Florida.

But our operation was soon disrupted, as the 'snitches' in the jail let management know who the mystery publishers were, and Walter was jerked out of the cell-block at lunch one day, escorted by the Captain himself and two deputies.

He was moved to the North jail to separate us, but we continued our efforts by mail, and through phone, via his brother's fiancée, Nayibe.

The publication actually grew in spite of these set-backs. By our final month, we were distributing over 30,000 copies of <u>Despierta America</u> to prisons and jails across the Southeast, which was an incredible undertaking accomplished under the most oppressive circumstances imaginable. I take little credit for it, but am proud to have been a part of the effort, though it would cost me greatly in terms of personal comfort and health quite soon.

My own challenges were snapped back to the forefront, however, one Sunday, when without any warning, (as is the Feds' way), I was ordered into the slider. At first, I thought perhaps it was related to our publication, as they told me to pack my belongings, which had grown considerably and included quite a library.

But when I saw the U.S. Marshals, I knew it was case related. It was October 1st, 2006. We'd been in jail for one half of a year while the Feds tried to wear us down to say we had done something that we had not.

I was again subjected to humiliating 'processing', which entails being stripped of everything, and put back in the same, dirty street-clothes in which I had been abducted.

My wife *was* brought down there as well. We gave each other the usual questioning look, but neither of us knew what this was about. She looked gaunt, and I could tell by her appearance that the experience was slowly killing her.

I refused to leave without my legal papers. After an extended argument, they had allowed me to carry them, as they must by law, but as is always the case, they first try to intimidate the prisoner into giving them up, to keep him at a constant disadvantage.

My wife, as bony and thin as she was, rose to the occasion and also fought to keep her papers and files.

We were put into the Marshal's van, bound in chains by our hands, feet, and waist.

Once en-route, with tears in her eyes, she whispered, "How could you do this to me?"

I had no idea what she was talking about.

"Do what?" I asked.

"Mr. Tisdale said that you were going to tell lies about me for AUSA Martens to get yourself free. They've been trying to get me to do that to you for months, but I've refused. I could never do that to you, Howell. How could you...?" she said, but trailed off into sobs.

"I could never do anything like that Vernice. You know that. Tisdale is a lying son-of-a-bitch! How could you believe such a person? He and Freedman, both, are working for them, not us!"

"So you've never talked to them about doing that?" she said, tears giving way to joy.

"On all that is sacred to me, on our two sons, I swear it," I said. "You know me better than that, Vernice. The last time I saw that bastard, Martens, was in July when he tried to force me to testify falsely against Rick Graves. If he couldn't get me to do that, how do you think he could talk me into telling lies about my own wife? Don't you see what they are doing? They have no case against us, so they're trying to turn us against each other! Our own lawyers are helping them. I've read the transcripts. Unless one of us lies about the other, they can't convict us. We never committed a crime. The IRS guy admitted it."

She broke into fresh tears, but from happiness, rather than grief, and we gently put our heads together, just enjoying the moment of togetherness even bound in chains.

I told her all that had happened with David Freedman and about their "doctoring" the tapes and transcripts. We had a wonderful reunion and pledged to not let the evil-doers, especially those in our own employ, succeed in driving the divisive wedge further between us.

Vernice had evidence of her attorney Tisdale's attempts to divide us for the prosecutor in her files. We decided to "swap" them when we arrived in Raleigh, so she could read my notes and papers and I could read hers. We decided that we would claim each others, when the U.S. Marshalls dropped us at the jail.

Neither of us had any idea why we were being dragged down to Raleigh, but Vernice had made the decision to change attorneys and get away from this wicked Tisdale character, and advise the court of that, assuming that is where we were headed. My lawyer was just uncaring and incompetent. Don Tisdale had an indecent mean-streak and seemed to thrive on hurting people.

We would rid ourselves of them both and fight, we decided that day.

After the usual several hours of waiting in the grungy holding cells, and "processing", we were stripped for the second time that day, including the "butt-check", and put into the now-familiar, orange and white striped "I'm Guilty" suits, so we could never be confused in court with the un-convicted citizens that we were. We had to be made to look guilty.

I was put in the Yellow Pod on the fifth floor this time, and wondered if my friend Michael Sprackland, the son of Judge Britt's stenographer, was still in the Blue Pod beside it. Maybe old W. Earl had worked his magic and set the boy free. I hoped so.

Nothing could have prepared me for the scene that met me upon entering, however. There were scuffles and shouting matches going over the phones, to which the guard paid no attention. One group of young, black men with black nylon skull caps was hanging off the bars on one side of the second floor, taunting and threatening a rival group of blacks on the other side.

A young, long-haired teenage boy had been brought in with me, who walked up the stairs, around the rail, past the loud and obnoxious gang members, and prepared to jump. He was out of his mind on some drug, and thought that he could fly. In his mind, he had wings.

The police cameras picked that up, I suppose, because they ran in to stop him and took him out to the unused recreation area.

That gave the gang war some comic relief, which allowed me to find a space on the balcony....the only one left....between the warring gangs. The entire floor of the small "pod" was covered with the mats of men trying to sleep or come down off drugs. It was a zoo. I tried to count the men, but due to movement, fights, and general chaos, lost count each time as I passed 62 or 63.

The place was designed and built for 23 men. We were very close to triple that, with far more on the floor than in beds. The count was almost two to one, in fact.

It was all I could do to keep from vomiting the bologna sandwich we'd been given for dinner when I went into the shared toilet. It was worse than the last time.

The spot I'd been allotted by lack of other choice was just outside this odoriferous little room, and each time the door was opened, it slammed into my mat on the floor, making sleep nearly impossible. The room beside the toilet was filled with yet another gang that had been busted that night, all with long "dregs", into which they had woven packets of crack and powder cocaine. They traded it throughout the night to other prisoners for their commissary or food trays the following days. It was an unbelievable night. High on crack and cocaine, the place was like a Hieronymus Bosch scene on a psychedelic canvas. Surreal was the scene, but yet very much tangible, touchable, and deadly. The dangers were not imaginary.

The drugs began wearing off about 4:00 a.m., the next morning, and the party wound down to just rap lyrics and snoring. Just as I was getting to sleep, the guard did a replay of my last visit, and came in to get me up with the "Judge is waiting" line. In no hurry, I brushed my teeth, and did my best to make my legal papers and belongings look as uninteresting as possible, as I had to leave everything there.

My wife and I waited downstairs for hours, as usual just to be transported to the holding cells at the courthouse in chains, where we would wait the rest of the morning as well. When at long last we were chained up again for the fifty foot walk, so we could be presented to the court in our funny suits and chains, I was surprised to see Tolly A. Kennon, seated at the defense table. The red-faced Mr. Tisdale was with him. Apparently, everyone knew about the party but us, its victims.

At the prosecutors' table sat the Assistant U.S. Attorney Matt Martens, and his young 'associopath', Kurt Meyers.

Judge Britt began the session by saying that he was unclear who represented me, and that he had been <u>asked</u>, (was the implication), to convene the hearing to determine who my counsel really was.

Now that was clearly nonsense, as I had written Judge Britt and said that I was representing myself, <u>pro se</u>, as was my legal right, until further notice. I'd further asked to be a part of any <u>ex parte</u> conversations. His little chats with the prosecutor were killing me.

Also, Tolly Kennon had notified the court in September that he was coming on as counsel, so something crooked and decidedly detrimental to our interests was afoot. I couldn't figure out what, but the sick feeling was there, and it's never wrong.

Britt went through the charade, however, expressing concern that I was properly represented while he and Martens were hanging me. Tolly addressed his concerns and reiterated that he had notified the court of our association, but Britt kept looking to the back, and asked again if I was sure I had the representation I needed. It was so obvious that I turned around myself and looked back to see if F. Lee Bailey or Johnny Cochrane was standing back there. They weren't.

Instead, a young boy, tall and skinny, stood up and asked to approach. In a high, squeaky voice, which sounded as if it hadn't quite successfully navigated the rigors of puberty, Matthew J. Hoefling announced to the court that he had also been retained by my family, unbeknownst to me, and would be "on board". On which side of the board he would be was debatable, but on board, he was. And how had the judge known he was there?

Britt's relief at the sight of the young fellow was palpable, which put me on alert even more. Something was "up". No sooner had the little boy taken his seat than Judge Britt was ready to close up shop and run, but my wife nervously rose to her feet and with the wicked Don Tisdale at her side, she courageously told the judge that she must have new counsel, as she was not satisfied with Mr. Tisdale and was letting him go. Britt jumped at the poor girl and told her that if a lawyer wasn't in the room <u>at that moment</u>, and willing to stand up and agree to represent her, no changes would be allowed for the duration of the case for either of us, NONE.

She had been looking for a new attorney for months, but it is a nearly impossible task from jail, and these guys know that.

In fact, they capitalize on it. My brother Jim had been alerted to the proceeding, and had arranged for the lawyer he planned to hire for Vernice to be at the Raleigh hearing.

But the man had spent the morning with the old serpent, Tisdale, and he had apparently been successful in jading the guy. He refused to stand up and sign on, after driving three and a half hours to get there and do so.

Tisdale had effectively blocked counsel from coming to her rescue to protect his own disservice from being discovered, was our only possible conclusion.

The man confirmed our suspicions of subterfuge when he stood and refused to say that he was taking the case. Vernice was devastated.

In violation of law and the Sixth Amendment to the U.S. Constitution (and all morality) Judge Britt then did something which confirmed his complicity in the conspiracy in our view. He ordered from the bench, that we could not change lawyers from that moment forward, for the duration.

Once he and his co-conspirators had complicit counsel locked in for both of us, they weren't taking any chances on our disrupting their scheme by having a 'real' lawyer in the mix.

Tolly A. Kennon III had been an unwelcome surprise, but they knew how to take care of him fast, quick, and in a hurry. They'd ruined other good men besides Mr. Kennon, and had no reservations about doing it again. With the young former Assistant U.S. Attorney Matt Hoefling with the high pitched voice on the inside of my case as my lawyer, victory was secured. I would have no choice but to accept a plea as Hoefling was a pure prosecutor and I was his first defense case ever. He would refuse to look at the case, or help me, and would be talking "plea deals" before our very first meeting, though like Freedman, his firm had been paid and retained to go to trial. My brother, Jim, had even warned that there should be no plea discussions, but Hoefling had violated that order immediately.

The set-up was perfect. Illegal but perfect.

We were returned to the nasty Wake County high-rise style dungeon, confused and distraught. The full effect of what had been done to us by Britt, Tisdale, and Martens was far from clear, but we knew that the last thing on the court's mind that day had been protecting our interests. This had strictly been housekeeping to protect their own and assure our conviction.

At the end of the long day, after hours of waiting in the holding cells, we were taken back upstairs, where the writing was literally on the wall that explained the day's events. The writing wasn't exactly on <u>our</u> wall, but visible on the scrolling electronic marquee across from the jail on the front of the WRAL TV studios:

"FORMER U.S. ATTORNEY PLEADS GUILTY TO

TAX FRAUD"

Sam Currin had apparently taken a deal from Matt Martens. That deal would inevitably include his helping them fabricate a case against us. There was little question that he would do so, as he had admitted to Vernice and I over dinner in Nassau that when he was U.S. Attorney, he, like the young Martens, had done that for a living.

Perhaps when he made his tour of prisons of the Southeast, where he said he would get down on his knees and beg the forgiveness of those he had wrongly convicted, he would include a stop at whatever prison they put me in, and he'd apologize for what he had done to me as well.

Fat chance! A leopard doesn't change his spots.

I watched the newsreel scroll by for an hour on the front of the TV station across from the jail, and pondered how things could possibly get worse.

CHAPTER 27

THE BATTLE IN AND OUT OF COURT

My question on how things could get worse was quickly answered.

Upon arrival in Raleigh for the hearing to 'set us up', I'd been allowed to order commissary items. They were delivered to the zoo where I was being held, the day after the hearing.

My stash consisted of a few pre-stamped envelopes, a pencil, a Bic ink pen, and a pad of paper. Most of these were luxury items to me by then, as the military-style jail in Charlotte considered a ball-point pen or a full-sized pencil to be a weapon. The mere possession of one could result in a charge.

I hid these luxury items in the plastic grocery bag that served as my legal briefcase and chanced losing my meager breakfast by going into the horribly nasty toilet. I would wait until the need was unbearable, as nausea was an inescapable companion to relief, due to the sights and smells.

During the five minutes or so of absence, two events had taken place. One was good, and one was bad. Officer Saba, a decent sort of fellow in charge of the Yellow Pod that day, had yelled out my name, assigning me to cell #1. That was good. Most of the weekend crowd had gotten bail by then or been moved to the annex jail across the street, in anticipation of the next round-up of citizens.

But while I was getting relief in the toilet, I was also being relieved of my commissary purchases. That was bad. I only realized it had happened after moving my sleeping mat off the balcony, and into Cell #1, when I was preparing to write down the events of the week for my journal. No pen, no pencil, no envelopes. Only the pad of paper remained.

I'd had so many scrapes with thugs by this time that I'd lost the negotiating demeanor of my previous life, and immediately stormed out of my new quarters into the pod demanding to know who had robbed me.

The Hispanics had become my friends, and they were camped under the stairwell on the floor, just outside of cell #1.

One of them told me in Spanish which one of thugs had taken my things. He was a dusty-looking black guy, with a pock-marked face, and unkempt rat's nest for hair. Unknown to me, he was also a member of one of the gangs that had been rivaling each other on the evening of my arrival.

I marched up to him and demanded that he return my property, which shocked him more than scared him I'm sure, as he was significantly larger than I and a believer of the myth that middle-aged, white guys are scared of young black men.

He muttered and stammered denials, sprinkled with the usual connective invectives of "motherfucker", and threats that frequent the language of the street, but my Hispanic friends were aroused by then, and began a clamor behind me.

I'd put a copy of our jail publication, <u>Despierta, America!</u> in my legal papers, and had let them read it. When one of them noticed that I was the editor--a gringo--and spoke their language, I was quickly escalated to a compatriot; a very good position to be in at that moment.

But it was an awkward moment for all. The two (or three) black gangs had been warring each other and didn't have time to come together against a common threat; and my Hispanic brethren outnumbered any one of their individual gangs by several men.

A black man who would become my good friend at a later time, in another jail, Yari Leake, approached me and asked if he could broker a peace.

Being at the epicenter of an imminent battleground, with the guards ignoring the drumbeat of impending war; that sounded like an attractive offer.

A deal was struck, whereby the gang would keep one stamped envelope to retain face and maintain their "creds" as fearsome and lawless, but the rest would be returned to me.

Yari and I bumped fists, which is the universal jailhouse handshake, and peace reigned for the moment, though his dusty companion's glare indicated that it was far from over, if his leader ever departed.

The twenty-three of us who were fortunate enough to finally have rooms were locked in at nights and after each meal, which was a blessing under the circumstances. I could get some rest without having to fear an assault or worry about a sharpened toothbrush handle being stuck in a kidney in my sleep.

But even when the door was unlocked, my fierce friends from the South of the Border kept their sleeping mats in front of my door and assured me that no "mayate", as they called the gangsters, would ever cross my threshold.

But the following day, all Hell broke loose anyway. His gang fell on someone who refused to pay them tribute to use "their" phone and was beating him unmercifully, when the police finally put down their donuts and chicken biscuits and crossed the hallway to break it up.

My dusty adversary saw them coming first. He hit the poor fellow one last time in the back and came running to hide in my room, but I blocked him at the door and shouted, "Hell no, thief! You're not hiding in here!", and shoved him off.

All the rest of the gang, as well as the poor victim, were hauled out in handcuffs or wheelchairs by the boys in blue, except my adversary.

The dusty one was the gang's sole remaining member, and none to happy about it, I suspect.

Once the police left, he came out of hiding and must have headed straight for me. Our collision at the door had knocked my pad and pencil from hand and I was picking them up when he appeared at the door to finish what had started before.

Purely by accident of how the pencil had lain on the floor, and how it had been retrieved, I was holding it point forward in my fist, like a knife.

My would-be attacker jumped back and shouted, "Motherfucker tryin' to stab me!" Only then did I realize how it looked.

"Damn right I am if you try to come up in my room again," came out of my mouth without any forethought, and I moved toward him.

He retreated, which gave me great satisfaction to have appeared so truculent, until I turned back and saw the human wall behind me. Ten Mexicans and Hondurans were at my back, ready to rumble. I had my own 'gang' and never knew it.

"This ain't over," the "dusty" one shouted, over and over again, as he slunk up the stairs in defeat, a gangster without a gang. The brethren "de donde crecen la palma" shouted insults after him as he retreated, never to cause problems again.

The time came to leave my new friends. The pleasant U.S. Marshal, Mr. Jimmy Spivey, took my wife and me, along with a van full of prison-bound citizens out to RDU airport to meet CON-AIR once again. We were met by a female marshal, Colonel Barbara Troutman, and her male side-kick, for the return trip to Mecklenburg County Jail.

Mr. Spivey remains the only federal employee with whom I ever interfaced during the entire presentence period who treated my wife with the respect she deserved, and myself as a human being. Since being at the federal prison there have only been two others, the wonderful head of education in Beckley, West Virgina. Mrs. Barbara Fletcher, and my old boss at the welding shop, Tom Marabillas.

To the rest, an un-convicted American citizen or prisoner is to be treated like a dog, or worse. I suppose it comes from a system where all but 1 in 100 will be convicted anyway, guilty or not, through prosecutorial misconduct or the use of the outrageous and indefensible charge of "conspiracy". I don't know what it is, but they are generally an awful lot.

You're guilty until proven innocent in the federal system of today. Don't let any old high school civics textbook fool you. And as AUSA Matt Martens replied when I made the observation that the conspiracy laws allowed no defense, he crowed, "That's right! And we like it that way!" But we were on our way 'home' to the Mecklenburg County Jail, except for the stop at the airport to pick up more 'customers' for Sheriff Pendergraph.

Once the prisoner exchange was accomplished, and all of the marshals and Air Transport folks had finished chatting and comparing toys, Colonel Troutman and her assistant, who had long since packed us in the van, headed out on I-40 towards Charlotte.

I was able to sit directly behind my wife and we shared our thoughts about what had transpired in court, as well as what was to come. As bleak as it was, we had a great few hours together having learned from each others' files that our worst enemy to our relationship was not AUSA Matt Martens, but our own attorneys who were in his service.

We renewed our pledge to never again let them trick us into believing that the other would or could be turned to lie for them again. That vow held true to the end.

CHAPTER 28

BETWEEN SCYLLA AND CHARYBDIS

When I arrived back in the murderer's pod, I was greeted by great news. Room 52 was vacant. Other than meaning that I wouldn't have to sleep on the floor, that also signified that our 42 U.S.C. §1983 civil rights suit for my friend, J.R, must have worked.

Fitzgerald "J.R." Stevenson had been freed within a couple of days of the police officers and the department receiving their subpoenas for the violation of his civil rights.

One of the reasons that I had fought so hard to take my legal files with me when we were taken to Raleigh (to have our own rights violated by Judge Britt), was because I had the nearly completed suit documents for J.R.'s civil action in them, when the abrupt and unexpected call to "pack up", had come.

I completed the paperwork while living on the floor in the Yellow Pod, and mailed them to our preacher/investigator in Charlotte who had been helping us. He had filed them and J.R. had been escorted out of the jail, with the 21-month old false charges dropped like a hot rock according to the boys in 6800.

J.R. was a happy man. I was happy for him and me both, as I got his old room. It had no outside window, no warm water, and the lights were broken, but it beat sleeping on the floor, which is where I would have been otherwise.

A few days later, I received a beautiful thank you note from J.R. It was my first little victory against the evil that had stolen my country, and it felt darn good.

One down, 2.3 million Americans to go. (By 2009, they had admitted the real number of persons in the corrections system was actually 7.3 million).

The victory celebration lost its sweetness to my own bitter battle quite quickly, however, as the young boy, Matt Hoefling, who had left the prosecutor's employ to become my "trial" attorney, came to call on me at the jail the next Friday afternoon.

Page 250

He had an even younger, less experienced lad in tow, which I was told was "just in training". What they failed to tell me was that he was "just in training" on my nickel at $185 per hour, for every waking minute that he had my file in his bag. The inexperienced Hoefling's rate was even higher at $240 an hour. I guess their theory was that enough inexperienced boys at men's pay could equal one real lawyer with experience, but I can tell you that it doesn't work that way.

Out of compliance with the rules rather than any morals or courtesy, they had notified Tolly Kennon of their visit to do some gang-billing that Friday afternoon on the way home, so he was also in the contact visiting area when the deputy brought me down. This was my first meeting with the team Helms, Mulliss, Wicker had described to my brother, Jim, in its sales pitch as "experienced criminal defense litigators". They'd have looked more in keeping with their age (and experience) in baggy shorts with skateboards under their arms and Tony Hawk T-shirts, than briefcases and Brooks Brothers suits.

I'd done more "defense work" helping my big buddy, J.R., than either of these kids, it soon became obvious during our first meeting, but I couldn't bring myself to complain to my brother Jim. He had no way of knowing that he'd been snookered by these characters, and I was determined to give the young kids a chance, as long as Tolly was there too, so they couldn't do too much damage... or so I thought.

The young prosecutor took charge of the room and meeting, in his high, squeaky voice, as soon as I walked in, as if he'd been instructed to keep my real lawyer, Mr. Kennon, (who was actually lead attorney in the case), out of our conversation. Hoefling's voice proved that puberty had not come in the intervening week, but he had chutzpah, I'd have to give him that. He had violated all the Rules of Professional Conduct before our very first encounter.

Jim had been told to make sure that the words "plea bargain" didn't come out of my next lawyer's mouth. "We are going to trial," I told him.

I didn't even want them talking to Martens, the prosecutor, as that would weaken our position, and Jim gave them those orders in no uncertain terms – No plea – No deals.

Jim had assured me that the firm's business partner, Peter Covington, who had pawned these kids off on me, promised his man to be experienced and battle-ready.

After brief introductions, young Hoefling launched into his "defense" strategy, which can be summed up in one word, capitulate.

"Now Mr. Woltz," he started, "I know from what your brother told Mr. Covington that you don't want to even hear the word 'plea', and I can appreciate that. I also understand that you're not enthusiastic about our having discussions with Matt Martens at the U.S. Attorney's office either.

"But I felt it was my duty, as your attorney, to explore all avenues thoroughly, so I took the liberty of going to meet with Mr. Martens before coming over here and I've got to tell you, I think that with all the evidence against you, you should consider taking his plea offer."

I'm sure my mouth must have dropped to the floor. He hadn't "understood" too damn well, 'cause he'd violated everything we told him not to do before the first meeting. What was it with these guys? This one was as bad as David Freedman!

Tolly and I locked eyes and knew each others' thoughts in an instant.

The first thing that ran through my mind, once the initial flush of anger passed, was how in the Hell this boy could have possibly reviewed this "evidence" when it had been sequestered by the judge since day one, so we couldn't prepare a defense. I could tell Tolly was thinking the same thing I was. That troubling question had but one answer, as only the prosecutor had access to those files.

Brother Jim had told me that my "experienced criminal defense litigator" had once worked as an assistant U.S. Attorney, but how long ago, I wondered? I had assumed years ago, until I saw his little pink cheeks and heard the boy's voice. He must have just left there. How could he have had access to "evidence" in my case, unless he'd seen it there? The answer, again, was that he couldn't.

I thought then that this should be illegal, and would later learn that it was. I was completely blown away.

The best I could come back with in the blush of new acquaintance and trying to be polite, was, "You what?"

His rosy-red cheeks and bright blonde hair made him look like a poster-boy for the Hitler youth, and the red spots grew larger, as Tolly and I just shook our heads in disbelief at the arrogant young fool. At least he had sense enough to be embarrassed.

As there was no immediate response, I continued. "Your firm was instructed not to have any plea discussions, in fact, any discussions at all with prosecutor Martens, yet you did so before we even met? We're going to trial, Mr. Hoefling."

"Well, it's my duty as your attorney, Mr. Woltz, to explore every avenue...." I cut him off.

"I know, I know," I said. "I heard all that. That's why I had to get rid of the last attorney, and hired your firm, Mr. Hoefling. But is it not also your 'duty' to follow client instructions?"

"Well, in order to advise you properly, Mr. Woltz, we need to know all of the alternatives, and I really think that with all the evidence against you, that you should consider...

I cut him off again, "Whoa. That's another thing. How do you know about 'evidence' against me, when I haven't even been allowed to see it? My last attorney let Martens sequester it. How could you have seen anything to make such a determination?"

He glanced at Tolly, and the red spots on his cheeks grew and covered his face and neck. He turned beet-red. The little bastard must have worked on <u>my</u> case! He must have just walked out of the prosecutor's office in the last few months!

"Well, I, uh, I think Mr. Martens said something about there being quite a lot of evidence," he said unconvincingly.

"So we should just take the prosecutor's word for it and go ahead and sign a plea? Is that your recommendation, Mr. Hoefling?" I said sarcastically as Tolly and I exchanged glances. "What if I told you that I never committed any crime? Would that still be your recommendation?"

"Well Mr. Martens certainly thinks you did," he replied with a poorly placed chuckle. I didn't see any humor in my "new" attorney, who had been hired specifically to replace a plea-merchant, refusing to even consider either my innocence or the evidence.

Our first meeting would become the template for every such meeting thereafter, and I won't bore the reader with its repetitive content other than to pass on the "sticker shock" I experienced when the young prosecutor told me what his "great deal" was that I should take without fail, and with no review of "evidence", or consideration of actual innocence.

"And just out of casual interest," I said, still fully in a sarcastic 'I can't believe what I'm hearing' mode, "what great deal did you negotiate with the prosecutor, Mr. Hoefling?"

He's offered you a deal of fifteen years, and I think you really ought to ..."

Tolly and I burst out laughing.

"Fifteen years!" I shouted between paroxysms, "and you think that's a good deal? I turned down seven years last month as outrageous, and now you think I'll take fifteen for a crime I never committed?"

The beet-red face took over the rosy cheeks again, perhaps in anger, I don't know, but it was clear that his buddy, Martens, had not told him there was already a seven year deal on the table that was less than a month old, and I'd laughed in the last attorney's face when he told me it was "little or no time". I'd replied, "seven years is 'little or no time? Then you take it!" and told him to leave.

I had written Freedman a letter regarding the 'plea' which was also given to this next young boy by my brother, and would not resurface until late 2008, after they had all lied about its existence. (David Freedman is currently facing sanctions in Federal court and possible criminal perjury charges because of it). I wrote in August 2006:

"The plea is a lie. I am being pressured to sign a lie to get my hostage wife out of jail. That is the only reason there is even conversation going on about it. If I don't sign the plea, Martens said that he and the FBI would be on my doorstep for the rest of my life, indicting me until they made 'something stick'! That's a pretty big weapon to be threatened by when the bearer is the 'Justice' department of the most powerful government on earth."

These threats had been made in David Freedman's presence so he couldn't dispute what had been said (or written) as it was all true. Had it not been, he would have had to dispute it out of professional protection, but he couldn't so he lied about its existence instead.

What made this letter so important and made it necessary for these officers of the court to lie about it for 2-½ years was that a plea which was not true, or had been garnered by threats or false promises, is invalid under law. We were three for three on that score, so this letter could blow their whole deal with Martens to coerce me into this plea deal to get their money. That's right, they get paid by the U.S. Government for selling out their clients as a "part of the savings to the taxpayers for avoiding the expense of a trial," after the client paid them not to. It's hard to get more corrupt than that.

As for the young boy's 'plea' negotiations against our orders, I continued, "That's why you were instructed not to ever talk to him. You just cut any bargaining position we may have had right out from under us by going to him to discuss a 'plea' before you ever even met me. You were told not to do what you've already done for a reason."

"Well, he's awfully angry at you over that letter you wrote the judge," Hoefling retorted, in defense of his fellow prosecutor.

"That's why it's not the time to talk to him, Matt. That letter was reporting his misconduct as a prosecutor. Did you expect my reporting his illegal acts to make him happy?" I asked.

"'Alleged' misconduct," he said, flushing again. The little boy was like a blinking German light bulb---and jumping to his prosecutor buddy's defense, no less!

"Whose lawyer are you going to be, Matt, mine or his?"

And so it went, on and on. It was one of the most depressing, exasperating meetings I've ever experienced in my life.

It was Friday afternoon, and as badly as I wanted to talk to Tolly alone, it was not to be. The deputy came to run them all out at 4:30 p.m.

I was desperate to tell Tolly that I had no faith in this kid, as if he needed to be told that after watching him in action, but more importantly, I didn't want him to let them shove him aside as lead counsel, thinking that I wanted the "big firm" to take the lead. That was anything but the case. I wanted him, and him only, to represent me, especially after meeting the little boys that Peter Covington had sent to do a man's job.

I could tell from Tolly's uncharacteristic silence that he thought I wanted them in charge. These boys couldn't defend Mother Teresa. They'd have her pleading guilty to charity fraud and taking "15" years before she ever left the convent.

As soon as the guard deposited me back upstairs, I tried to call Tolly instead of getting in the "feeding" line, but there was no answer, so I got the much needed meal after all. It was force-feeding, though, as my body didn't want food at the moment, it desired justice, or even a vigorous defense. But I had to eat.

By that time, in October of 2006, I was a skeleton. My occasional visitors would chastise me for not eating enough, as if my captors gave me a choice. At each meeting, the visitation phone was monitored. Complaint would yield swift retribution, so I just nodded. The Mecklenburg County Jail's policy was to starve its victims until they were forced to buy the exorbitantly priced junk food on commissary, but I was too stubborn to do it for the first several months. At 5'11" and 155 pounds, I was a bone frame with skin over it and couldn't miss a calorie.

The weekend following the meeting was miserable. I couldn't reach Tolly to let him know that these guys were not my doing or my choice, and I simply could not call my dear brother who had worked so hard to find a firm to take my case, and had, no doubt, paid another 'king's ransom' to the blood-suckers to do so. They were a dreadful mistake, but I had to give it the best try before saying so to him.

The next week crawled by. It had taken a few days to get back into my meditation, study, and writing routine after being taken to the "zoo" in Raleigh, only now to be thrown into a another tailspin by the little boy plea-merchants who'd come "Trick-or-treating" for Halloween early, dressed up as lawyers.

When Friday afternoon rolled around again, the guard called my name, took me downstairs, and there was a not-so-instant replay of the week before. Almost the same words were said.

I'd been unable to reach Tolly all week, so the format was the same.

All the boy would talk about was his fifteen years "great deal" his cohort, Martens had offered. I couldn't get him off of it, even by rudeness. The Hitler youth thought was not far off the mark! He refused to consider my innocence, refused to actually request that the evidence be released (though he claimed to somehow know what was in it), refused to file for a dismissal, and so on. He wouldn't do a darn thing I told him to do.

It's hard to be "Zen" when you're watching the people in your own employ construct the gallows to be used to hang you.

His repeated references to various 'evidence' made it clear to both Tolly and I that he must have worked on my case before leaving the prosecutor's side. None of it had been released, other than the transcripts, which had only been given to me to help "fill in the gaps" back when Martens had tried to extort false testimony out of me against Rick Graves, the attorney who was charged as my "co-conspirator" in a conspiracy that a jury would rule had never been, six months later.

It also seemed clear from the boy's obstinacy that he was scared of trial, which led me to begin asking questions about his experience as a 'criminal defense litigator'.

He claimed vast experience in "cases", but got vague, avoided answering, or "had to go" rather than ever giving a straight response when I asked who he'd defended, and on what charges.

I was his first, by all appearances, and he wasn't going to "defend" me either. He was going to just feed me to his buddy, Martens. We later determined that he must have just come from the prosecutor's office before taking my case, and had left a wife, Jennifer, still working there as an Assistant U.S. Attorney alongside Matt Martens. I never confronted him about it, expecting him to disclose it at some point, but he never did.

Matt and Jennifer Hoefling became Assistant U.S. Attorneys under the infamous Gretchen Shappert, along with Matt Martens, my "other" prosecutor, in the same 'class' of 2004. It was 2006 when he had been put on my case. Not much time between those dates for any law experience of any kind, and zero time for "defense" of anyone or anything.

Attorney Bob Gleason had taken Karen Eady's place that year in the U.S. Attorney's office in Charlotte, North Carolina, and Matt Martens, Kimlani Murray, Ed Ryan, and Holly Pierson had been added as the freshman class, along with the Hoeflings...Matt and Jennifer, to the U.S. Attorney's staff.

The new class pitched in to do the grunt work on cases, like the young red-headed, Kurt Meyers had now become Matt Martens' "gopher", but they moved along as a class until being unleashed on the world, as Martens now had been on me.

It was quite possible we realized that as outrageously unethical as it might be, Jennifer Hoefling may very well still be working on my case as a prosecutor, at the same time as hubby Matt was playing at being my defender.

That should have set the North Carolina State Bar aflame, but didn't! Husband quits prosecuting a guy, and becomes his defense attorney to 'defend' against his own work, while leaving sweetie-pie behind, still working on the case!

No appearance of impropriety there; at least none to the lawyers' union known as the State Bar. I later tried and they found 'no fault'.

There was no doubt, however, that he was intimately familiar with my case which was impossible without some impropriety. He knew all about the genesis of it with the CFTC (Commodity Futures Trading Commission) and the little evil woman, Elizabeth Streit, who had pushed the charges out of spite. He knew about the "sting" operation by the IRS, and all about Sam Currin and Jeremy Jaynes, yet had never asked me a single question about anything. He didn't want to know anything about the case, unless it came from the prosecutor (or his experience there), it seemed, as he never asked me about any of it, and was uninterested in learning, no matter how many times I tried to tell him how he could easily prove our innocence.

Freedman, my previous attorney, had not even read the indictment, so he was an unlikely source of information and hadn't shown up at the hearing where Judge Britt had ordered the "evidence" sealed. He knew nothing to have told young Hoefling.

And each week it was the same except for a week in November 2006 when Hoefling (Matt), the "defender", and Hoefling (Jennifer), the prosecutor, took a vacation to South America. I felt like I was on vacation too. I finally reached Tolly by phone and asked him to come early so I could talk to him before the boy came one week. He did so, but he was a bit late and we were just getting into the matter when the Hitler youth look-alike, and his silent side-kick in training came in and interrupted us.

Tolly had only had time to tell me that my brother, Jim, had actually asked him to let the "big firm" take the lead, so he had done so. He was just following the instructions of the man who had paid him and had assumed that I wanted the same thing.

I didn't, and was in the process of letting him know that as they rolled in for their Friday afternoon drive-by, so they could bill me for their ride to the golf course, home, or bar, whichever may be their Friday evening destination.

The body language and silence were clear. They were young, but not stupid. For weeks and weeks we'd stirred the same old hash and I'd put up with it, out of not wanting to tell my brother that we had another Freedman, or maybe worse. We had a real prosecutor, who'd probably still be working the other side of my case if he hadn't been hired by Helms Mulliss Wicker (since absorbed by McGuire Woods, a large regional firm).

"Are we interrupting something?" young Hoefling asked, as he flushed a bit pink.

"Actually, Matt, I was telling Tolly here that I'm not satisfied at all with how this is going. You were hired to go to trial. You refuse to consider it, from everything I can see so far....", but he cut me off.

"Well I think the plea agreement is very reasonable and that you really ought to....", but I'd heard enough of his drivel.

"Then you take it, damn it! You do fifteen years!" He'd hit my button. I wasn't listening to that crap another time. "Let me tell you something, Matt. I didn't break any law. I didn't... ....", but he started again.

"Well Mr. Martens certainly thinks...."

"Stop right there! You want to talk about a plea or what your friend, Martens thinks, you do it on your own time. I don't want you wasting one more minute of my time, or my money bleating about a plea or Martens' opinions. You were told when you were hired not to do it, yet that's all you've done since the first day you came in that door.

"We're going to trial. If you can't do that, then I need someone who can and will. Do you understand me?"

"Well I think you should really consider...."

"Are you deaf, Matt? I've listened to your nonsense for weeks now. You're like a damn broken record. Maybe this 'defense' business isn't your thing. But if you're going to continue as my attorney, you're going to have to learn it," I said like the father I was old enough to be.

I turned to Tolly and said, "I can't take any more of this, Al"(his nickname). "If these boys can't or won't do the job, I want you to stay in the lead on this thing and start filing motions."

He nodded. (Little did we know that Tolly had already become AUSA Martens' new target for talking to me on the phone about filing charges of prosecutorial misconduct).

"And Matt," I said, turning back to him, "I'm going to have my brother send copies of the instructions that I sent to your predecessor, David Freedman. Those are now your instructions. I want to challenge the grand jury, challenge this crazy venue and Matt Martens' judge-shopping..."

"You shouldn't call it that!" Hoefling said in his pal's defense.

"I wouldn't if I hadn't heard him admit it himself!" I shouted back. "Whose side are you on, Matt? I'm having a very hard time telling."

He didn't respond, so I continued.

"I heard the man bragging to David Freedman that he couldn't believe that he'd been able to get Sam Currin's 'blood-feud enemy of 30 years', to agree to hear the case. It came out of his own mouth. That's judge-shopping and it's illegal. I intend to challenge it."

"All the judges in the Western District recused themselves because of Sam Currin," he began, as expected. "That's why they had to look elsewhere for a judge, because the ones here all had a conflict. They knew him when he was U.S. Attorney."

"And Judge Britt, from Sam's own home-court where he was the U.S. Attorney in the Eastern District didn't?" I asked, incredulous at the boy's stupidity, gullibility, or service to his master. "How big a fool are you Matt? You're saying that every judge in the entire <u>Western</u> District recused themselves because Sam Currin was an <u>Eastern</u> District U.S. Attorney? Even if that were <u>possibly</u> true, which it isn't, why didn't your buddy, Martens, try the <u>Middle</u> District judges then? I'll tell you why Matt, because the Middle District turned down this silly stuff to start with, and there isn't a judge that hates Sam Currin there, like Britt does. So what does your pal do? He goes all the way down East, to the same court where Currin used to actually be the U.S. Attorney, and picks Judge W. Earl Britt, the same man that he knew Currin tried to keep off the federal bench back in 1980, when Jimmy Carter nominated him! No conflict there, Matt? No appearance of impropriety? Or did Martens fail to fill you in on that little bit of history? Sam Currin was Senator Jesse Helms' top aide, Matt. It was his job to prevent W. Earl Britt's confirmation by the U.S. Senate. You don't think Britt remembers that? You don't think he will remember all the harsh statements by Currin against him and the political vendetta? This is pay-back time, son! The problem is, I'm just a piece of meat caught in the meat grinder, and I don't like it!"

I could tell by his reaction that he hadn't known any of this information. Martens hadn't told him what he'd done.

"Well, there isn't any way Mr. Martens could have chosen the judge, I can tell you that," he said, but he said it far less confidently.

"Let's find out," I said. "Let's challenge it. I'll guarantee you I'm right. I'll bet anything you want, that this was not a regular appointment. I heard the man say it himself!"

"I don't think you're right," he said, but I could tell for the first time that the boy was actually seeing the truth. His buddy was dirty.

"Then prove me wrong," I said. "I even wrote Freedman a letter about it when it happened. You have those letters, read them."

After hearing Martens bragging through the door of the interrogation room back on April 27, 2006, I'd written Freedman about the incident demanding that he challenge the judge as conflicted and go after AUSA Martens for prosecutorial misconduct. My brother, Jim, had forwarded all of these letters of instruction to young Hoefling, and I'd told him they were now his orders. Not one attorney except Tolly Kennon was ever willing to do so and he was destroyed by the government for even preparing to do so, I would later learn.

The letter was explicit. In August, just weeks before I'd written the attorney, after Martens had reneged on our deal, and ordered him to prepare for trial and go after Martens for 'judge shopping'. I wrote:

"I'd like to immediately file charges of judge shopping and use that as part of our motion for change of venue to the Middle District.

"All of you have said that Judge Britt and Currin are old political enemies from the days when Jimmy Carter appointed Britt and Currin was attacking him as head of the Republican Party."

"If all of you knew that, why on earth would all of you agree to drag a Western District Case, through the Middle District (where it should be), down to the Eastern District, to put us before a judge that really does have a conflict?"

Now knowing that I'm dealing with liars puts everything into question. We need to get this case out of here. They are crooked and Vernice and I have been railroaded for hidden agendas and the protection of the ones that did these things."

I reminded young Hoefling of what had happened on April 27, 2006 and that I had heard his pal, Martens brag of orchestrating Judge Britt's appointment with Clerk of Court, Frank Johns.

He was reluctantly coming around to the truth, though it pained him to do so.

"Our associate at the firm used to clerk for one of the judges and knows the clerk who assigns the cases. Maybe he can find out," he said, unenthusiastically.

"Then let's do it. Let's turn this thing around!" I said. "I didn't do anything. I didn't break any law, and the evidence will prove it, if you boys will ever get it released so I can look at it. I'm not going to prison for something I didn't do without a fight!"

After six or seven weeks, we had finally 'communicated' for a few sentences that day. I could not have made it clearer what was expected, and my brother did send Hoefling the instruction letters I'd sent to Freedman. I got confirmation from his ever-efficient assistant, Kelly Kiser. The boys had their marching orders.

No dimwit could have misunderstood what had been said by me or the written words of what was to be done. Or so I thought.

CHAPTER 29

WRONG AGAIN

But my euphoria lasted only one week. It was as if young Hoefling had never heard my words by the next Friday's drive-by, gang-billing op.

He went right back into his fevered pitch, sounding like Alfalfa of Little Rascals fame, telling me about the wonderful 15 year plea agreement that his partner, Martens, had warned him would soon be removed from the table.

My reply was, "Good. Tell him to do it soon, so I don't ever have to hear you bring it up again, Matt. I'm not sure you're ever going to successfully make this transition from prosecutor to defense. Did you not hear what I told you last week? And I know you got Freedman's letters of instruction. Jim's assistant sent them on Monday. That's all I'm paying you to talk about anymore. If you want to run on about Martens' 15 year plea, you turn off the time-clock, and we'll do it on your time."

He looked a bit stunned, but started to do it again. I tapped my wrist where my non-existent watch would have been and shook my head, "No. Don't do it."

The meeting was quite short as he'd done absolutely nothing he'd been told to do, and everything he'd been ordered not to do as we came up on the two-month mark. All he'd done was argue with me and attempt to pressure me into taking what at my age was statistically a life sentence for uncommitted crimes. My patience was at an end with this young boy and his silent partner (whom I later learned did not even have a bar card when Helms Mulliss Wicker had assigned him to my case as an "experienced criminal defense litigator", and former AUSA Matt Hoefling didn't even work for the firm!)

I called Brother Jim that evening and laid it all out for him. He was tired after a long week, but listened patiently.

"Why didn't you tell me this before?" he asked calmly.

I explained to him that I didn't want to seem like I couldn't get along with *any* lawyer. "I don't have any problem with Tolly Kennon," I told him. "If these young boys would listen to him, I'd be better off, Jim. He knows what he's doing. He's also a fighter, but these guys have pushed him aside. He said that you told him that you wanted them to take the lead."

Jim confirmed that, but said he was still convinced that we needed a big firm with resources and depth. "Plus," he reminded me, "Judge Britt ordered that you couldn't change lawyers, so we're stuck with these guys."

Not knowing at the time that Judge Britt's self-serving order was unconstitutional and completely against the law, we still assumed that we had to abide by it.

Jim also told me that he had received a communication from one of my clients in France who recommended a lawyer in Tampa, Florida, and had asked Jim to contact him to see if he would help me.

Jim said, "Britt didn't say that the family couldn't hire a consultant though, did he?"

"No he did not," I replied.

So Jim tracked down my client's recommendation and paid yet another large retainer for another attorney to come and make sure that the ones Britt stuck us with started doing their job.

Before we got off the phone, however, he hinted at the staggering bill he'd received from Helms Mulliss Wicker for the first month or so of "arguing".

That's also when I found out that the silent "trainee" was on my nickel, not theirs. He was assigned to my case before he even had a bar card, as mentioned before, at top billing price. The firm would prove to be completely dishonest in their dealing with us from beginning to end. I was disgusted by these people and their dishonesty.

I told Jim to call this Peter Covington character and tell him that the little boy, or rather little *boys*, he'd sent were not going to cut it. I needed a grown up with experience. One that would listen to me and do what I said - one, not two and not one to argue and one to watch. Though Jim was fronting the money, as the Feds had tied up all our assets, we were going to have to repay it some day.

These two little boys were wasting my money.

Though I, the client, would never be able to get a copy of these bills from this scandalous firm for almost two years, in spite of multiple requests, I would eventually learn that these two little boys had billed over $30,000 for their drive-by meetings those weeks leading up to our complaint in November of 2006, and had never yet carried out a single instruction from me, the client. They started sending me copies of the bills in 2007, and caused an orgy of complaints with each unearned hour. They would ramp up the bill to over $250,000 before they were done, and never carry out a single order.

But the cure for our complaint turned out to be worse than the disease itself. When the business partner, Peter Covington, was told of my deep dissatisfaction with the young prosecutor, but knowing we were illegally trapped by Judge Britt's order to keep them in our employ, he assigned yet another worthless bum to my case.

In the closing days of November, 2006, a pudgy, pimply sort of jolly-type fellow bounced into the Friday meeting to announce that he was the "cure"....but he was actually there at the jail to see another client....but I should not despair, as he was there. All would be well, as he actually had trial experience. A real lawyer he was, or claimed to be, and prepared to bounce out again.

"Whoa. Whoa," I said. "Not so fast. How much trial experience? Who were the clients? What sort of cases? How many of them did you win? We were told we were going to have an experienced criminal defense litigator. If you're finally it, I want to know something about you."

He babbled and burbled awhile longer, told me that he "knew of" my brother, Jim in Roanoke, through his wife's family, and so on, completely avoiding a straight answer.

I repeated my questions.

It turned out that my "experienced defense litigator" was one William C. Mayberry. Yep, Mayberry, like on the Andy Griffith Show. He could have been a character out of it, in fact, and he had as many trials under his belt as Barney Fife had bullets - one, to be exact.

There was almost no way to tie down this artful dodger on anything, a trait which only worsened during our short attorney/client relationship. I tried and tried to find out what his one trial had been about, to assess whether or not he had any experience at all relating to financial and tax matters, as had been alleged against me, but he would avoid answering.

The next Friday's drive-by billing-op included three of them; the "in-training" trainee with no experience, the prosecutor, who we thought had been pulled off the case after our complaint of his refusal to follow instructions and misleading representations as to his defense experience; and now a third wheel, Billy-Bob Mayberry. It was a disaster. The financial cost of this disaster was even more shocking, when I finally got to see it almost two years later. These monkeys were billing me $730 per hour for arguing with me and refusing to do what I asked during our meetings. This is criminal law today, and these are the real criminals.

To add usurious insult to that injury, they were averaging almost nine hours of chatting, meeting, reviewing, and contemplating their navels back at the ranch for every hour they spent in this group-abuse of me, the client, and they still wouldn't do a darn thing I asked them to do until Jim hired a consultant to force them to do it. Even then, they accomplished nothing for me or as I had asked.

I finally got it out of Billy-Bob Mayberry that his one criminal case had been a member of the "Outlaws", the nationwide motorcycle gang.

"How do you think that case prepared you for one dealing with financial matters, and alleged tax fraud conspiracies?" I asked him, a bit cynically.

"It was also a criminal case," Mayberry answered.

"I gathered that, Mr. Mayberry, but how did a motorcycle gang drug case prepare you for a financial trial?" I asked.

He mumbled and burbled some more, and ended up back on his Roanoke connections. He then threw out the name of the family there into which he had married rather than answering my question. I instantly recognized it.

My brother, his current paymaster, had also been married into that family. He and Mayberry were ex-brother-in-laws, but the marriage had ended in divorce, which is not generally considered the best recommendation for good relations and feelings. I was somewhat shocked, in fact, that Jim had hired this firm and man knowing of that background. Considering the other deceptions, it occurred to me that perhaps they had not been completely honest about that either.

"Does Jim know that he has hired his ex-brother-in-law, Mr. Mayberry?" I asked. "Did that not come up in your conflict check? I'm sure a firm of your size must do them."

He turned red, accentuating his skin problems, and said something to the effect that he didn't really see how it mattered.

It certainly mattered to me, and the gargantuan bills that he piled up were evidence of his complete disregard for fairness. Mayberry knew from inside knowledge that my brother was quite successful, and could afford the fees. But it wasn't my brother on trial, nor was he the ultimate paymaster. I was.

Each time they came, I warned him that only one of them was to be paid. No more gang-billings and I didn't want Hoefling, the prosecutor there at all. Yet each following visit, Mayberry claimed to have forgotten, and though he was told the bill would not be paid, he continued this unethical practice until his termination. I later learned that he had asked two of my brothers to sign guarantees of payment, and was milking the cow for all it was worth. Fortunately, after each bill-fest, I had written him of my continuing displeasure with his firm's refusal to do what I asked of them, and his gang-billings, which ultimately led to an investigation of his firm by the North Carolina State Bar but they again proved useless in protecting the public from their members. The Wicker of Helms Mulliss Wicker was apparently a past-president.

While my experiences with David Freedman had exposed me to the worst of unethical lawyers, Bill Mayberry and his billing crew showed me the worst of firm ethics. What they did to us over the ensuing months was nothing short of scandalous. Even after they'd been fired, for months and months afterward, bills totaling tens of thousand more dollars poured in. All I can gather in retrospect is that the buy-out talks with McGuire Woods were already under way, and the partners at Helms Mulliss Wicker had driven their minions to ramp up billings by any means to up the firm's price. Some days, more hours were billed than a work day has, and on top of the sky-high fees for these unrequested Friday drive-by gang-billings, they even charged a third of an hour for faxing over a form to the jail to reserve a room for these unwanted meetings.

All the while, not one of my instructions was ever acted upon until the consultant entered the picture, and attempted to force them to do their job, to no avail.

When I called Jim and told him that the new, so-called, trial attorney (with one "trial") was his ex-brother-in-law, he was livid. Mayberry had failed to report the conflict to the firm, and/or they had failed to report it to Jim, the man that had hired them. My client in France had recommended a large east coast firm based in Washington, D.C., by the name of Zuckerman & Spaeder, and a specific lawyer from their Tampa, Florida office, Jack Fernandez. Jack was hired as a consultant by my brother Jim after the first conversation - our sixth lawyer.

With his large east coast firm and offices in every major city, Jack came quickly to review this dyspeptic relationship, and organize a defense. We were still unaware that Judge Britt's order against changing counsel was unconstitutional, or these boys would have been sacked on the spot in October rather than our wasting the money trying to force them to do their job but we didn't know the order was illegal and none of the lawyers (including Jack), ever told us.

The first meeting was a free-for-all. I reiterated my client instructions, still completely ignored at that late date. I now had not only Beevus-Hoefling to argue with me, I had Butthead-Mayberry to mumble and burble inanities. The young third-wheel of the billing tricycle kept mum as always.

Jack sat expressionless through the entire show without saying a single word.

I ended the meeting, as I would every one of them, warning Mayberry, "Don't ever show up here with more than one of you again, and only come when I call you. I don't need three of you to come and do nothing I ask you to do, when just one of you can come for much less and ignore my instructions."

After Bill and his billing-crew had filed out, I turned to Jack, and asked, "What do you think? Is it as bad as I told Jim, or not?"

Jack had a somewhat shell-shocked look on his face by then, and just shook his head and said, "This is the most dysfunctional attorney-client relationship that I have ever seen."

We then met with Tolly Kennon, and Jack got to witness as functional a team of client and attorney as one could ask to see. He quickly realized that I only had trouble with those that I was paying to do something but refused to do it. Unfortunately, that included every criminal attorney I'd dealt with so far except Tolly "Al" Kennon. We got along like two peas in a pod and have never had a conflict to this day.

But Jack's instructions from Jim had been to "fix" the Helms Mulliss Wicker relationship, as we didn't know at that time there was a choice. He had us meet again, but this time, he interacted as well. He started by asking me to tell about the case and what had actually happened. Neither one of Freedman, Hoefling, Mayberry nor the silent trainee had ever taken a moment to ask me about anything.

Jack was a real lawyer.

He then asked me to run through my personal history. I did. Eagle Scout, God & Country Award, Boy's State, Commissioner under Governor James Martin's administration, President of the American-Caribbean Trade Association, Presidential Roundtable, Senate Selection Committee...and no criminal history of any kind. For the first time ever, Bill and his billing crew were quiet. They were watching a real lawyer do real lawyering as if it were the first time they'd seen it. He was getting to know his client and what had happened, rather than just trying to browbeat him into pleading guilty to something he didn't do so he could move on to the next victim and billing opportunity.

There was no screaming. There was no shouting. There was no cursing, just a couple of gentlemen trying to get to know about a situation so they could make an informed decision about how to handle it.

Jack instructed his new pupils to do what they had to do to get the evidence in the case before his next visit, and he left.

Throughout December, Jack nudged, cajoled, and embarrassed them into doing their job, reluctantly at first, but things started getting done at long last. He made them go through the evidence when it was received, by staying there with them at night until even Matt Hoefling had seen with his own eyes that Elizabeth Streit had manufactured false charges. I was not guilty and un-redacted copies of government's so-called 'evidence' proved it.

He admitted as much one day, though it almost killed him.

By that time, Jack had done what any good lawyer does. He had reviewed our case, after eight months of being held by the court for uncommitted crimes, which no other lawyer had done.

He saw so much wrong-doing by that time, that he then took a step for which my wife and I shall always be grateful.

Jack knew that Judge Britt's order was illegal, but he was not licensed to practice in North Carolina, so he called an old friend who was...J Kirk Osborn, one of the state's most famous. Things were about to change.

CHAPTER 30

A CHAMPION APPEARS ON THE HORIZON

It was a Saturday morning when Jack had called Kirk Osborn at home to tell him about our case and what the government had done to my wife and me. Kirk was so outraged by what he was told that he immediately got in his car and drove the 3-1/2 hours to Charlotte, to come see my wife at the jail.

This wonderful man did not know us and we did not know him. He came unbidden and un-retained, to do battle against injustice. Unlike the money-grubbers we'd dealt with in Freedman, Tisdale, and Hoefling-Mayberry billing crew, he never brought up money. As with Tolly Kennon and myself, my wife had to bring up the subject with Kirk Osborn.

A few days after this visit, I received the first hopeful letter from my wife that I'd seen since our abduction. She told me about their meeting and said that Kirk was coming to see me the following Saturday to discuss his strategy for us both.

For those readers who may not recognize the name, Kirk Osborn gained the national spotlight in the case of the Duke University lacrosse team members who were wrongly charged and publicly vilified by a nasty prosecutor in Durham, North Carolina, by the name of Mike Nifong.

Like many, if not most of them in today's perverted system of "justice", prosecutor Nifong had hidden exculpatory evidence, encouraged lying by witnesses, and set about destroying innocent people for fame and glory. Standard practice, as prosecutors can't be sued. They are above the law.

Mr. Nifong's misbehavior sounded dreadfully familiar to us. Kirk Osborn and two other attorneys had been relentless in their pursuit of this corrupt public prosecutor and eventually exposed his illicit activities, and had him stripped of his position in a very public and humiliating way. Nifong hired a prosecutor's best friend...Attorney David B. Freedman...my old lawyer, to fight to keep his license to practice law, but David did no better for the corrupt prosecutor than he did for me.

The miscreant lost his license and job as prosecutor, but could not be prosecuted for his own crime, which is a real crime.

While not nearly enough punishment to atone for such dark sins, it was a start.

Kirk Osborn planned and proposed to do precisely the same thing with the prosecutor in the case of United States v. Howell and Vernice Woltz, et al. After spending several hours with each of us separately, reviewing the record of the case, and learning all about it (something none of our attorneys ever took the time to do), Kirk opined, "This is the worst case of government misconduct I've seen in my career."

I asked him if that included his Duke lacrosse case and the corrupt Mike Nifong, he replied, "What these people have done to you and your wife is far worse." Coming from J. Kirk Osborn, that was strong medicine.

From the moment Kirk Osborn strode into the conference room, I knew that he was someone of substance who would have to be reckoned with by these wicked people. He was a silver-haired, handsome gentleman, somewhere between Gregory Peck and Sam Waterston in appearance, with even a more commanding presence. When he was in the room, the rest of its inhabitants became bit players and extras.

His only regret was that his long-time acquaintance, Judge W. Earl Britt, had participated in such a foul enterprise, but the ethics which Kirk held so dear, would be enforced, regardless of who the violator may be, and the chips must fall where they may.

I alerted my brother Jim that our savior had finally appeared. He immediately scheduled a meeting with Kirk and the consultant, Jack, who had advised this towering paragon of justice and virtue of our plight.

Out of courtesy, Jim copied the Mayberry-Hoefling billing crew on the notice of summit, as it was to be held in Charlotte, and allowed them to attend, but when Kirk Osborn strode into the U.S. Attorney's office to put the young prosecutor Martens on notice that there was a "new sheriff in town"...him...he told the "boys" to sit outside and wait. They weren't even allowed in the room.

What I would have given to see that!

Jim told me that it was one of the most impressive meetings he had ever attended, and Brother Jim is no slouch at such, himself. Kirk told the young prosecutor what he was going to do, and the timeline on which he was to do it. No "ifs", no "ands" and no "buts". And there was no time given for commentary or questions from the peanut gallery. When finished, he simply rose and strode out as he had entered.

And all of this was done within days, after months of incompetence and obfuscation. The only delay was my own sorry lawyers telling me that it couldn't be done. By that time, my wife's lawyer, Tisdale, wasn't even pretending to do his job, so Kirk laid out the plan for both of us to dovetail with his strategy.

Though Jack Fernandez had worked diligently to put together enough evidence using government's own records to free us and prove that the whole prosecution had been illegal by January 9th of 2007, the whole ballgame changed the following week. While we were strategizing "trial", my wife was dying.

We were stuck with the "boys" and having to shove them every inch of the way toward the courtroom door. Jack Fernandez was worried, as was I, that they would do us more harm than good, and may actually subvert our efforts (as Matt Hoefling had already done), in further service to the local prosecutor that kept them fat and happy, as long as they worked for him.

Jack was an outsider from another state, and saw AUSA Martens for what he was and didn't have to worry about next week's case.

On about the 15th of January, my world changed completely. Vernice had lost the will to fight which had been our decision coming back from Raleigh in October of 2006, and was losing the will to live. Coming from an honest nation (Trinidad) where one cannot simply be put in jail until they confess to things they never did, she didn't understand why we were still in jail.

She had been in the horrible Mecklenburg County Jail away from our children for eight long months. She'd been abandoned by her lawyer and Kirk Osborn had been honest with her about going to trial. "You'll win. But it will take us a year or more to do it."

The jailers had taken her to the Carolinas Medial Center "to die" once already, but she had survived. The thought of being in a small cage away from her children for another year took away her will to live.

The letter I received from her broke both my heart and will to fight them any longer. She told me that she knew me too well after all our years together to expect me to lie about someone else to save us, and she was not trying to change that. She accepted it. But she could not survive the time it would take to win. Her letter went on to give me her wishes for our children, as she would not be there when this ended.

I couldn't lie for Martens against Rick Graves, but I couldn't let the woman I loved die over my principles either. I had to make a deal. I got Jack to come right back from Tampa and we spent the weekend planning and he and Kirk worked out the strategy to get her free, by leaving me in jail. . . . for the time being.

They were to make sure that my plea contract clearly stated that agreement to it was predicated on my wife's immediate release at the time of signing. This was to show that she had been nothing but a hostage (so his later attack on the whole prosecution could be all the more virulent).

The three monkeys of the billing crew came to press me to allow removal of the wording from the contract, including the one who refused to see the evil (Hoefling), hear the evil (Mayberry), and the one who never spoke (the silent trainee).

"Matt Martens will never agree to that language," said the Mayberry Monkey. "He won't hear of it."

"I can't see the U.S. Attorney ever allowing it", said the Hoefling one.

And the third monkey said nothing.

I also forced them to insert language that the government knew that I had no knowledge of Currin and Jaynes' activities; I had them insert this into the new "charge" of a conspiracy to launder their money.

All I ever knew about was a transfer of all remaining assets after the S.E.C. inquiry years ago, of approximately $7 million in mostly non-cash assets, that our Regulator had ordered us to transfer to Currin's newly appointed trustee for Jeremy Jaynes, Mr. Walt Hannen.

The fact that I hadn't known of any criminal activity negated the charge of conspiracy to launder proceeds of crime. The fact that I reported it to the Regulators, and was told to move the assets anyway, as they'd never been charged with a crime, shows that I was never a part of any such thing. And lastly, but most importantly, the fact that neither Jaynes nor Currin were ever charged in this "conspiracy", left me, once again, as a "sole conspirator", which was a contradiction in terms. No honest judge or court would allow such a charge, or a plea of guilt to it.

But this was no honest court we were in, it was a (real) conspiracy to deny due process and get revenge, and our judge was a ringleader, so what the document said wouldn't matter. But it certainly would when Kirk got it to a real court.

See No Evil, Hear No Evil, and Speak Nothing At All were similarly vociferous in their opinion that this clause would also be rejected, but I wouldn't budge, and they knew better than to question Kirk Osborn.

"That would make the plea agreement illegal!" one squealed with new-found concerns for such things. "They'll never do it," Hoefling prognosticated, and so on.

"Everything about this prosecution has been illegal," I reminded them, "including choosing of a judge two jurisdictions away, and even before that. The charges themselves were illegitimate, even Matt here has seen that,"....but I caught a look between Mayberry and Hoefling that was like a caution flag. What had I said that had prompted such a warning between them, including the choosing of a judge?

The judge's appointment! Hoefling was supposed to check with his "associate" to disprove my contention that it had been contrived and judge-shopping.

"By the way, Matt, what did your 'associate' find out about the judge-shopping?" I asked. "I was right, wasn't I?"

One look at Mayberry's face showed that he was the 'associate'! These guys made it too easy.

"How about it, Bill, what did your friend say?" I asked.

He and Hoefling exchanged glances again, and finally he said, "OK, Johnsy (Frank G. Johns, Clerk of Court) said that it wasn't a 'normal' appointment. Are you happy?"

"Not normal means judge-shopping," I answered.

"He would only tell me that it was 'irregular'," Mayberry said.

"Judge-shopping, just like I said. Have you reported it yet?" I asked him, knowing the answer.

"I have no indication that it was illegal, just that it was irregular," he said.

Taking the minor win away from the field, I decided to let it go, and went back to the plea agreement conversation from which we had migrated. Kirk and I could deal with that later.

"So you think that a guy that would file false charges, lie to a federal judge to deny citizens their right to bail, and go judge-shopping is going to worry about a couple of words in an agreement?", I asked. "This bastard will do anything to get my signature on that paper, at this point, and if he wants it, he will have to put it in there. He'll do it. Just watch."

And sure enough, the young lion became a pussycat days later in the presence of the great Osborn, slayer of crooked prosecutors. He signed the agreements without a whimper when the time came.

And that day we executed the documents, January 26, 2007, was exceptionally cold. The IRS agent that had admitted I broke no law, Scott Schiller, was waiting downstairs at the jail with a female agent to supervise my wife when she went to the bathroom, I suppose, and a large young gun-toting goon was assigned to guard me. The only satisfaction I could muster, as they chained us up was that this would be one of the last times I would ever have to see my wife being treated in such an inhuman and unjustified manner. Having seen her ankles bleeding from overly tight chains, during long rides with such animals, I could only feel relief that what I was doing that morning would end such indignities for her.

The signing was held at the offices of Helms Mulliss Wicker on North Tryon Street, just up from the jail, but it was so cold that the agents bundled up in thick winter coats, and Schiller in his heavy Navy "Pea Coat" for the short ride to the my lawyer's illicit billing operation up the street.

We, even as un-convicted citizens, were in the skimpy, jail pajamas, and offered no coat or cover as these callous government minions chatted about whether the temperature would ever get above 20°F that day.

They were completely disorganized and couldn't find parking, so I was left in the sub freezing weather with the hulky young-gun, standing handcuffed in my bright orange prison pajamas on the corner of one of Charlotte's busiest intersections in early morning, rush-hour traffic, cars inching by two feet away, with the warm smoke from their engines steaming and billowing around us as it met the frigid air.

People would stare briefly from their cars just an arm's length from where I stood, as I would have done a year before, but they would avert their eyes quickly, when mine met theirs.

It was a strange experience, knowing in my heart that I'd committed no crime of any sort, yet standing there in public view, bent over from the cold and cramping handcuffs behind my back, and held firmly by a man with a gun, as a common criminal on display at this major intersection of America's banking capital as if in the "stocks" of days gone by.

The agents' planning skills were on par with their charity. The car pulled up about fifteen minutes later, which matched the temperature, and I was crammed back in amongst the heavy coats and blasting heater, unable to speak from being nearly bare for so long in the freezing cold.

Just a few feet down the street, we entered another parking garage, but thankfully, I was not deposited on yet another corner for more humiliation before the gawking public.

But once up on the open parking deck of the garage, there was further evidence of the dearth of planning skills, as none of the three agents had taken the time to figure out where we were going.

This time, they put me and my wife outside of the warm car while they conferred, until I demanded that they put her back in the automobile until they figured out where they were and where they were going.

Eventually, they did put her back in, but must have assumed that I enjoyed being nearly naked at 15°F, as I was left o utside for another lengthy period of time, while the three brilliant minds consulted within.

By the time we finally got in a building, I was near hypothermia. My dear brother Jim was there, as always, and had bought both of us suits of warm "normal" clothing to wear, so we could feel part of the human race while there that day.

But the IRS folks deemed this to somehow be a security risk through some unfathomable logic, and we settled for being allowed a sweater over our jail pajamas to thaw ourselves from the harsh treatment by the uncaring Feds, who were still complaining about the temperature outside as they undid their warm layers, not even thinking of what they were saying in front of us.

We met alone with my brother and Kirk to review the strategy. The "boys" weren't even allowed in their own conference room to hear it, as we considered them Martens' eyes and ears.

Once Vernice was free and safe, Kirk's efforts to shine "the disinfectant of sunlight", as it was once called by Justice Brandeis, on the whole illegitimate enterprise would begin in earnest.

The official signing of the documents before Judge Britt was already scheduled for the following week in Raleigh after which Jim and Kirk planned to get Vernice to a safe location. They would then give the "conspirators" a few weeks to think everything was OK, before Kirk hit them between the eyes with a 2" x 4".

The signing of the documents was uneventful, as mentioned, and we were returned to the jail to await transportation to Raleigh days later by the U.S. Marshals.

It was not until that night that I noted that Tolly Kennon had not been at the meeting. He was still lead attorney, and the only one of them I trusted besides Kirk, but he was technically my wife's lawyer for the moment. Had Tolly abandoned me, or had these nasty, little boys simply cut him out of the loop?

I couldn't blame him, after being attacked by the Feds just to neutralize our efforts to go after the crooked prosecutor, but thought it unlike him.

Later, I would learn that the big firm had not even let the man know that a plea agreement was in the offing, or copied him on documents of any kind. They had not advised him at all of our meetings, which I thought he had failed to attend, thinking I had chosen to sideline him, which was never the case.

A few days later, the U.S. Marshals showed up for our trip to Raleigh, and we were "packed out"; Vernice, thankfully, for the last time, while my meager books and belongings were put in storage until the Marshals brought me back to Mecklenburg County.

We'd been lied to and mistreated for nearly a year by then, and only Kirk Osborn's promise of making them live by their latest commitment gave us hope that Vernice would be free and able to begin picking up the pieces of her life and bringing our children, who were spread apart by this tragedy in three states, back together as a family.

The ride down was quiet for the most part. Vernice was tentatively hopeful of the end of her nightmare, and I was just enjoying our last time together for what might be years or forever.

I knew that I was entering the loneliest days of my entire life. The sense that while in jail together, (my wife was in the same building just two floors below) even as miserable as it was, it was a shared experience and kept my spirits focused.

We were together. I would touch the wall in my tiny cell, and know that through the blocks, steel, and concrete, her body was connected to me on the other end of those cold, inanimate elements.

I'm sure that sounds strange to someone never in such a situation, but months alone foster such thoughts as one seeks to find any way to remain connected with life and those you love.

But that connection was ending, and I was happy for her---and our children---that the bargain had been made. But what if something happened to our Champion? What if Kirk Osborn was hit by a train, or simply lost interest after freeing my wife?

I was signing a plea of guilt to uncommitted crimes for a sentence that could go as high as 87 months, or even higher if they'd lied again and ramped it up beyond the contract as they'd already done once before.

But the thoughts melted away as we came into Raleigh and were once more immersed in the tortuous gauntlet of "processing".

Many hours later, anal check complete, and dressed in the lovely Wake County bright-orange and white "I'M GUILTY" suits (3 sizes too big), we were separated and taken to our respective dungeons to sleep on the floor with addicts, drunks, pimps, and prostitutes, as well as a few assorted "real" criminals that really should have been there. There were always a few.

This trip, I was put in the "Green" pod on the Fifth Floor, which I would forever remember, as my days could have ended there.

The usual middle of the night call came, and I was rousted by the guard telling me that the judge was waiting. Chained and dragged through holding cells for hours and hours, as is always the way, we finally arrived at the "Judge Britt Show", where he was supposed to act like he was interested in whether our pleas had been voluntarily given as everyone in the room including him, knew was not the case.

Any fool, especially one that had been advised in writing of all the chicanery, threats, and misconduct of the prosecutor, like Judge Britt had and one that himself had conspired to bring this miscarriage of justice to this point, would know it was a coerced plea and illegal, but I guess 27 years of doing such wickedness makes one practiced at the "Show".

But the "Show" went pretty smoothly except for a couple of hitches in the script.

When I was asked by Britt if anyone had promised me anything I hesitated, and turned to Bill Mayberry and said, "I was promised that my wife would be freed."

Before Billy-Bob Mayberry could respond, however, Judge Britt realized his error and corrected himself, "or rather has anyone threatened you, Mr. Woltz, into taking this plea?"

I turned again to Mayberry, and said, "Of course they did. They threatened me with more charges against Vernice, if I didn't sign a plea." I well remembered when Martens had pointed to the FBI agent and said, "I'll have him on your porch every week with a new charge for your wife," on a few occasions.

"But not <u>you</u>," Mayberry said, with a sick smile. "He asked about <u>you</u>, not your wife."

They had not threatened me....lately....and I had to finish this thing for her. "No, your honor," I lied, and Judge Britt knew it was a lie, as I'd written him in a letter, which was on file saying so, but this was all for show and so that there was a record of my 'voluntary' plea to hide behind.

When I had hesitated, my wife squeezed my hand under the table so hard that it hurt. I had to choke back my anger and get it over with. I had to lie to set her free.

I had warned Mayberry before the "show" began that if they didn't release Vernice, <u>on the record,</u> before my plea colloquy was completed, I'd balk and refuse to finish it, as they had never told me the truth about anything yet, and I wasn't taking a chance on their doing what they promised this time on setting her free.

Mayberry had told Martens this at the prosecutor's table before we began. Martens had glared at me and turned slightly red, but knew his own record for dishonesty....100%....and that I was not bluffing. I would stop the proceedings.

The bailiff handed Judge Britt an *ex parte* note from Martens which I presumed was his "instruction" on this matter, and he followed the script---with a little prompting.

Judge Britt started with my plea, as planned, and switched to Vernice before it was over, as planned, but he did not set her free as planned. They were getting ready to do it again I realized, as we neared the end of the second phase of my plea colloquy. They had set us up, so I would plead guilty to fabricated crimes, and then renege on letting her go!

I punched Mayberry and warned him to do something, or this was ending quickly, up in smoke.

"Your Honor, may I be heard just briefly?", Billy-Bob jumped up and said, to save his thirty pieces of silver from the government he was going to be paid for delivering me up to them.

Judge Britt replied, "Certainly."

They were all on the same team.

Mayberry mumbled something about my sentence being at the bottom of some guidelines range, but then got to the meat of the interruption, "And Your Honor, at some point I would like to be heard or just join in with Mr. Osborn on the release of Mrs. Woltz. For now, just say that it's a <u>key element</u> of this plea agreement from Mr. Woltz's perspective."

That was an understatement, as my letter had said. It was the <u>only</u> reason a conversation was even going on about any of this, and Judge Britt got the message. I looked over at Martens and he was glaring again, but it was a clear signal that they had better let the hostage go, or I was going to blow.

And they did.

Judge Britt refused to allow me a transcript of the plea colloquy, but our investigator was able to get a copy directly from his stenographer. It had been altered, and entire passages left out or doctored, like when Judge Britt asked Martens about stopping my plea and switching to let my wife go. He said, "So you mean I have to stop Mr. Woltz's plea colloquy, go to Mrs. Woltz and let her go, and then go back to Mr. Woltz? Can we do that?"

Seven witnesses confirmed that this was said, as well as AUSA Martens' tentative response, knowing that the whole scam was illegal, "We think so, Your Honor?", but it was doctored in the transcripts, to sound like switching between them was Judge Britt's idea, not my demand, to protect the guilty.

When the investigator asked for a copy of the tape of the proceedings to compare to what the witnesses had told him, the stenographer, Sharon, told him that she had been told not to record it. There was no tape, though the rules require an electronic copy to be made to avoid such illegal activity, and only one person could have told her not to follow the rules – Judge W. Earl Britt.

But it all ended. Having no choice if they wanted me on record as saying I did something I didn't do, the corrupt little cabal of judge, prosecutor, and complicit "defense" attorneys, under the hawk-like scrutiny of J. Kirk Osborn, let my wife go.

Brother Jim, our constant guardian through our perils, was at the ready. He and Kirk whisked her out the door to get her to safety as soon as she could be checked out of the custody of the horrible Wake County Jail by the U.S. Marshals.

I saw her from my little holding cell downstairs, as she was preparing to leave, dressed in new clothes which Jim and his wife, Jill, had bought for her to drape her thin, bony body in after nine long months of inhumane treatment and starvation at the hands of the most corrupt group of people I've ever known----our own federal government.

Jim took no chances and personally flew her out of there on his private airplane to safety, away from the evil-doers.

I had high hopes that Kirk's plan would work, and I would soon be free as well, but something told me that my own torment may be far from over.

But she was safe, which was all that mattered to me at that moment.

CHAPTER 31

MY LIFE GOES ON TRIAL IN A HIGHER COURT

After her last wave that night, as I watched her leave the jail, I sat back down in the holding cell. I could no longer stand up. I thought perhaps I was just weak from the months of starvation, or depressed from having to sign a lie, but I was so weak that my legs would no longer hold me.

The freezing temperatures and exposure at the hands of the careless IRS agents had taken their toll, and a severe cold had resulted from it, but by the time I was finally taken back upstairs, I knew it was something far worse. My forehead was burning yet I could not stay warm. Even before going into the cell-block, I told them to get me an emergency medical form, as something was seriously wrong with me.

They did, and I filled it out on the spot, and gave it back, asking the guard to please get me to a doctor that night.

Outside, the temperature was plummeting and the jail was filling up quickly with the homeless and helpless who were intentionally getting themselves arrested as my little buddy "Scooter" had said he would do, just to get indoors for the night. Though Raleigh was the State's capital, and awash in money for wasteful spending and showy projects, none could ever be found for the poor. They had nowhere else to go but jail to keep from dying of exposure, just like in the "banking" capital of Charlotte.

Even with the overcrowded floor space rapidly filling up, room #8 was empty, as one of my Hispanic friends from an earlier visit to Wake County Jail informed me. He helped me in there, warning that it was very cold in there on nights like this, as it was on the building's corner and the block wall had no insulation. No one wanted it; that's why it was empty.

All I wanted was a place to be left alone and sleep. My own thermostat was so out of whack by then that I couldn't tell cold from hot.

My friend from last visit was Oscar Medellius, the former minister of finance of the nation of Peru under President Fujimora. Oscar came to check on me and brought me an extra blanket when he saw my condition.

I barely had strength to stand, but had promised to call my wife's sister, Jenny, and let her know that Vernice was free from these evil people at last. I don't really remember anything for some days after that other than bits and pieces, once I had made the call to Jenny. I was so deathly ill that even the gangsters let me skip the line and use the phone, so I could go back to bed.

Oscar and others came to check on me from time to time. The cup of water they had brought me had a thin crust of ice on top the next morning, indicating that the temperature behind my locked door had been below freezing. They later told me that it had been 8℉ outside according to the weather report, that first night while I was delirious.

My only real memory of those days and nights was a series of dreams where my life's continuance was on trial. There were arguments, carried out in a court-like atmosphere, but not of this world, which were very lucid and are still clearly embedded in my memory.

The "pro" side to continued living was that I could eventually be reunited with my wife, family, and remaining friends. Another well articulated and compelling reason for choosing "life" was made over and over again of the dire need for the corruption of these people and this system to be exposed, and the sorry state of the legal profession itself to be brought to light. The faceless, bodiless advocate said that this was now the purpose of this life, and the reason I'd had to experience the suffering myself. Were I to let life slide away, it would have all been wasted, as that was what all of this was about. I was to work to end similar suffering of others, by writing about it, by writing about the corruption and wrong-doing by government itself, by working for change.

And that was a "choice" I was now facing. That was clear. It was as if parts of my soul were presenting arguments to me, as to whether I should continue living this particular incarnation, or die and move on toward the next one.

And the arguments for the other side were darkly tempting and quite alluring. By choosing not to live any more of this life, I could quietly and ignominiously slip away in my fevered stupor, and move toward the next incarnation. The siren's song was sweet and fetching.

The unearned shame that had become my mantle would be left along with the shell of my body. I would rob the prosecutor of his scalp and trophy and my suffering, as I would never go to prison, if I simply let my grip on the thread of life go at that moment.

Like the "conspiracy" statutes, no overt act was required. I didn't have to do anything. By simply letting go of the thin thread that was holding me to this world, I would be free to sail out of my misery and pain, out of the squalor and filth of this dangerous and detestable jail, flying freely through time and space until called to experience human existence once more in a new form, for new lessons.

It was a debate that continued for the better part of three days and nights, before coming to a final verdict. The scale could easily have tipped either way that week, but the argument for "life" won out. I had a purpose to fulfill, and came out of the deep transformational experience committed to my new life, and determined to never mourn the old one.

I had died in a way, and my ephemeral visit to the ethereal world left a changed man with a purpose to drive his existence for years to come.

A reformer was born from the banker's ashes.

The eighth day of my sickness, after all danger had passed, a guard came to my door and asked if I was still interested in getting "emergency" medical attention.

My response is not fit for print, but it cemented my purpose. By all means possible, I pledged to work tirelessly to bring an end to the cruel, ineffective, and destructive machine that destroyed lives, families and spirits. That had become my life's purpose. To keep as many people as possible from having to go through what I had experienced.

The judicial system was corrupt; the laws themselves outside of constitution and conscience. The means of holding even those that had done something from which society needed protection, had become nothing but training grounds to teach them to do worse.

Senseless, needless laws were the root of the problem, and every branch and twig that grew from it produced a sour and bitter fruit.

Our nation had become everything we once hated. We had become like those we once fought. Our own government had become the enemy of its own people. I saw this clearly for the first time.

CHAPTER 32

RUNNING THE GUANTLET

Upon finally being returned to Charlotte and the Mecklenburg County Jail, I fell to writing more articles for *Despierta, America!* I was picking up the pieces of the little existence I'd carved out for myself.

Most of my books had been "lost", as they did not put me back in 6800, the "murderer's pod". There was no longer any need to try and scare me into signing a plea. I'd done it already, though they didn't know it was just a temporary step toward another plan of the maestro, Kirk Osborn.

Instead, they put me in pod 4200, which seemed to be some sort of federal holding and immigration set-up.

It was far less violent and I immediately made friends with a diverse threesome. One was Randy Martin, a gemologist from the mountains of North Carolina; a long-haired, former drug user with the most outrageous tales I'd ever heard, but I never doubted a word of them. Randy had lived them, no question.

Another was Ricky Seeley, also from western North Carolina, who had served thirteen years for minor possession of marijuana. He had joined the Native American circle at the prison in Butner, North Carolina, and was their medicine man before leaving there. We called him "Chief". His Indian title was actually "Hollow Bone", the medicine man's usual identifier, but we thought the promotion was in order, as we had no other Indians, or followers of the Native American religion, except me.

The fourth wheel of our crew was Michael Forchemer, an actor and gambler, originally from California, who the U.S. government had rounded up illegally in Costa Rica under laws which the WTO (World Trade Organization) Court had ruled invalid. The U.S. Government had appealed the ruling of this court (which it had forced on other nations), and lost again. The Court said the U.S. had no authority to regulate or outlaw on-line gambling in other nations, just to protect its own participants, which was the real purpose.

But they arrested Michael anyway, for answering the phone for the on-line gambling group, which made him part of a "conspiracy" (of course), to commit an act that was not even illegal. After 6 months in a Costa Rican jail, they put him on a jet and flew him to a corrupt jurisdiction that would prosecute whether a law was broken or not and hold him until he agreed to plead "guilty" to something. The Western District of NC would be his home for the next few years until they broke him.

We had much more freedom in 4200 than I'd been accustomed to in the murderer's pod, and the "Rec" area was at least twice as large (about 20' x 40'), where Michael and I used to walk.

But the pleasant times were short-lived.

One evening the Captain came in and moved Randy and "Chief", leaving Michael Forchemer and me into cell-block 4200.

A few nights later, the Captain came in again during lock-down and had the guard open my door only. Not a good sign. "Woltz! Get your ass out here!" he shouted.

He had a newspaper under his arm. As I got closer to him, I could see that it was one of ours...Despierta, America!

I'd like to say that it didn't "shake me" and that I was like Cool Hand Luke on the way to the "Cooler", but I wasn't. Once upon a time I would have believed that there was such a thing as the First Amendment, and it would protect me. Freedom of speech without retaliation, right?

But by that time, I knew better than to believe in such fairy tales. Americans have no rights when the Feds or the Sheriff decides that you don't.

He held up the beautiful, four-color publication, and said, "I believe this is yours, Mr. Woltz."

He then opened it to the first inside page where it gave the credits.

"Hey! Look! EDITOR- HOWELL W. WOLTZ, TEP! That's you, isn't it?"

"Editor!" he said smiling. "How about that?"

And then the fake smile went away. He closed the newspaper, slapped it against my chest for me to grab, and said, "Pack your shit, Woltz. You're coming with me."

When you're living in a building where an average of one un-convicted citizen a month dies from neglect or abuse, some pretty strange ideas can run through your head. The jail population is, in general, young, tough, and in its healthiest prime. No one could ever get a straight version of how these un-convicted citizens died, either. The local Charlotte paper was always sure to take care of their boy, Sheriff Jim Pendergraph, and cover it up or not even mention the circumstances of the death.

The most recent monthly death had been a young man who had been in the jail before, his medical records were already in the computer, and he'd begged for his medication, to no avail. He was dead the next morning, but the newspaper ran the story of his tragic death in true truckler fashion, never asking a single hard question about how it had happened. In the same edition, they published another glowing page and a half "hero" tribute to the man who was ultimately responsible for the boy's death, Sheriff Jim Pendergraph.

Aside from being in extremely poor taste, and undoubtedly a source of intense resentment for the young man's family, it sealed everyone's opinions about any chance of wrong-doing ever being exposed by the local press.

It also occurred to me walking down the hall with the arrogant captain that I could simply die at their hands, and all that was likely to occur was another adulatory "hero" article about my murderers in the local Charlotte newspaper, alongside a short mention of my death.

But we soon arrived at Pod 6500--the infamous sleep deprivation pod I'd heard about since the jail became my home nearly a year before--and all thoughts were numbed by the first view of the crowded mega-pod. This was where they sent the "problem" inmates and violent young street thugs who hadn't quite made it up the criminal ladder to murder and Pod 6800.

The good news was, I hadn't been beaten with rubber hoses, and I got to keep my newspaper.

The better news was, my fellow "troublemakers", Randy Martin and "Chief" Seeley were already there.

The best news was that Michael Forchemer was close behind me, guilty by association, I suppose.

We had a foursome for "Spades", at least, while suffering together in the freezing conditions and sleep-deprivation program. There were two large tiers of tiny rooms, without toilets, for the longer term residents, and almost as many of us "temporary" residents there for some air conditioned torment, forced to sleep on the floor, out in the open, with the lights on 24 hours a day.

The whole cell block "shared" the filthy toilets and sinks in the corner bathrooms. That was a treat, I must tell you.

Unlike the similarly overcrowded Raleigh jail, however, the guards actually stayed within the cell-block and forced some organization onto the inhabitants as to where their sleeping mats could be put on the floor, and in which areas, all of which were already taken that night. Michael and I were relegated to the little space under the grated stairway leading up to the second tier. It was quickly dubbed "The Harry Potter Suite", in honor of the under staircase dwelling in J.K. Rowling's books.

Harry had it good by comparison.

The temperature, according to a maintenance man's gauge, was 64°F. We were only allowed to put our mats on the floor after 11:30 PM. By the time that was done, it was midnight each night.

We were only allowed to use our thin blankets during this brief four hour repose between midnight and 4 A.M., when the guard would begin yelling for us to put up the mats and our blankets to prepare for the 4:30 a.m. line-up and "feeding".

The rest of the twenty hours each day, we were not allowed to use our blanket against the cold. We also were required to sit upright, or stand for the entire time. No reclining was permitted anywhere for any reason.

We joked about the articles of "torture" of foreign prisoners being held in Guantanamo Bay and our nation's "secret" prisons abroad, and wondered if the guards had been trained in Charlotte. Most of the methods were the same. The foreigners got it no better or worse than an un-convicted citizen did in the hands of the Feds right here in the heartland of what was once the "Land of the Free". It was the same people....the federal government... doing the abusing. Why would anyone expect it to be that different?

It's like Albert Einstein's famous statement, "True madness is expecting the same people, doing the same thing, to yield a different result."

But the phones were the real killer in the sleep-dep pod. As in most of these overcrowded, open-style places, one of the gangs or "crews" would take over a phone and try to charge for its use.

The members of the gang would stay on the phone, in turns, often with no one even on the other end of the line, just to maintain control, or have their local "homies" play them rap tunes to pass the time until a sucker came along that would pay.

One large, black kid named Harris had been my next door neighbor when I was first abducted the year before, and was in the sleep-dep pod as well. He would have one of his "ho's", as he referred to his lady friends, talk "dirty" to him and masturbate in his jail pajamas, openly, behind the large post on which the phone was mounted, out of sight of the guard. Fortunately, even Harris could only carry on so many of those conversations in a day (though phone cleanliness remained an issue in everyone's mind), so he wasn't the major problem.

Another young street dealer, also named "Harris", but no relation to the mad phone-gunner, was the real problem. He would have one of his women make "three-way" calls for the other inmates, in exchange for their food or commissary items. Rather than hang up and allow them privacy, however, Harris would have her listen in on the conversation and eavesdrop. She would then report back to him, who was getting money if they had discussed that, or pass on any information that he could use for "snitching" to the police in order to get a time reduction for himself.

He had quite a game going. When he learned that someone had money coming into their commissary account, he would inform the gangs. They would then either extort the mark to buy them items, or simply rob them once they got their commissary items, and Harris got a "cut" for being the informant.

The men, who were dumb enough to talk about their crimes or sensitive information over the sheriff's monitored phones, were also giving Harris information at the same time via his eavesdropper, unknowingly. He would then befriend them, find out enough about their family and life to sound like he had known them, pump them for information and details, and then rat them out. Not a bad scam.

But he and I had our problems, because I refused to pay. After waiting in line for an hour to use the phone, no thug was going to tell me that it wasn't my turn, or that I had to give them something to use "their" phone. I wouldn't do it, which eventually led to a problem, as others began to refuse as well.

I usually had Randy, "Chief", and Forchemer in line as well behind me, so our little "crew" didn't pay them much mind. Our little foursome usually spent the twenty "stand or sit" hours each day playing Spades, which kept our minds off of the freezing temperature and fatigue. During that time, we became fast friends. "The Old Farts Gang" was overheard more than once in reference to our little group.

It's a funny syndrome, being in jail together. It forges bonds like fighting in a war side by side, or experiencing a tragedy as a group. We watched each other's backs, kept the thieves out of one another's meager belongings, and survived the surroundings, as violent and unpleasant as they were, by sticking together.

Our Harry Potter Suite under the staircase was just outside the cell door of a black man charged with child molestation.

He had supposedly been carrying on relations with his girlfriend's very young daughter while she was off supporting them at work each day.

But his personal crisis had led him to the arms of Jesus, he claimed. In fact, he told Michael Forchemer and me one night, that he had come to the realization, after great introspection and much prayer, that he was Jesus. He was mankind's Savior, in the flesh, back for Round Two. He was the Second Coming, just late and long in that realization.

One gets accustomed to "nuts" in jail, but this one was a particularly noisy one. Jesus would preach to himself day and night, requiring unpleasant interchanges from time to time to get him to shut-up, so we could sleep.

The open-air Harry Potter Suite was anything but soundproof, and we relished our four hours of nocturnal bliss.

Our pedophile neighbor, whom we openly called Jesus by that time, had taken a particular dislike to a Muslim disciple of the Nation of Islam by the name of....yep...Mohammed.

Jesus and Mohammed took to arguing on a regular basis over various fine points of an esoteric nature, and seemed to favor our little space as the venue for their holy debates, which added to the disturbance, robbing us of quiet enjoyment thereof.

We were headed for an unpleasant resolution when I guess the hand of God intervened and the two prophets went at each other instead one morning, hammer and tongs, when the religious discussion took a particularly nasty turn. Both claimed their way to be the "only" way to God and salvation.

This major event, the battle between Jesus and Mohammed, drew quite a crowd. They had a "captive" audience of seventy eight residents that day. The battle of the prophets raged on for some time, with violent blows being landed on the holy men, by the holy men....all for God, of course just like nations do it, until finally the Sheriff's "finest" came boiling in, many with biscuits and donuts still in hand.

We figured they must have come for the entertainment, as Michael and I counted thirty eight of them roll through the door, but not one of them lifted a finger to stop the struggle of the prophets. The captain trailed his stalwarts by some distance, making the total number of uniformed officers watching the altercation, and doing nothing about it, thirty nine.

Finally, two inmates broke it up and dragged them apart before they killed each other, so I cannot report to the reader how the age-old battle over which so many people continue to die so senselessly might have been settled in our little microcosm.

Perhaps we should have let them fight it out since so many seem to think that's what God wants.

Having been brought up a Methodist in little Mt. Airy, I hate to admit it, but Jesus took a pretty good drubbing before the doughnut-boys got the handcuffs on him and hauled the two combatants to the "hole" that day. Perhaps the matter was settled there. We'll never know.

But I had my own worries. At fifty three years of age and weak from inadequate food and sleep for some weeks, I was testier than a spring badger.

Starvation and sleep deprivation, combined with an overcrowded and violent atmosphere is a combustible mix.

As long as our little foursome stayed to ourselves, we were all right, but I was so tired after three weeks of torture that I could hardly think.

My wife and mother came to see me one day during those days and I barely remember their visit. Vernice, my wife, became so concerned at my mistreatment that she began calling the U.S. Marshals to complain, but she might as well have phoned the Kremlin or Tiananmen Square. They'd have cared more.

The crew of Randy, Chief, and Forchemer gave me diversion to keep going, however. Between Randy's exploits (and scandalous letters), Chief's constant humor, and our famous actor/tennis pro/gambler's tales of life in the fast lane, it was as entertaining as sleep deprivation in a "Cooler" can be.

One night, as we sat together staving off starvation with some homemade rice burritos, I looked around at each of them and held my junk-food aloft like a "toast", and quoted the old favorite line from the 1986 Super Bowl beer commercial: "You know guys, it just doesn't get any better than this!"

Forchemer eyed me and said, "You stole my line."

"Stole _your_ line," I said. "That came from a beer ad twenty years ago."

"I know," Michael said. "I was in it. That was _my_ line," and with that, he took the position and look of the handsome, lanky guy he was in 1986 (and still is, so the ladies will know) and repeated the line as he had in the famous TV ads two decades earlier. Sure enough, it was "him".

As an aside, we've kept in touch ever since those days, and I heard from Michael just before the publishing of this book. They put this innocent, pleasant man in solitary confinement, as they had me, for nearly a year to force a "confession" from him for his uncommitted "non-crime".

Such are the Feds. We've pledged to have drinks at some sun-soaked beach bar somewhere far from this wicked place once our respective nightmares with the "federales" are over. That's a promise I look forward to keeping, assuming that we both survive what they're doing to us.

But the close camaraderie of the Old Farts Gang also came to an end. Events came to pass that would put me on a tortuous path, never to return to that room again.

My case was soon to go to trial without me. Rick Graves, the attorney who they had named as a "co-defendant", was to begin picking his jury on April 2nd. It was late March, and Kirk Osborn's plan was to attack my plea agreement as illegal just afterwards, whether Rick Graves was found guilty or not. I was confident of the outcome, even in the corrupt Charlotte judicial district, as a jury of citizens would easily see that no crime had been committed. Even in Charlotte, they still had to prove that something had been done wrong. Without me to help AUSA Martens fabricate something, they wouldn't be able to convict him.

My refusal to lie for Martens had cost me dearly, but I was proud of the decision and would do it again. Even with confidence that a jury of his peers would do the right thing, I was still on pins and needles, however. Today, the corruption by the prosecutors has become so great, that complete strangers are often employed by these devious people to make up stories out of whole cloth in exchange for a time cut.

One such case was going on at that time in Charlotte and the witness to the government's fabrication was with me in the sleep deprivation pod. I suppose they wanted to make sure he was well rested. He was a young man by the name of Bon Stroupe. He and two others had heard the government's "time-cut" snitches practicing their fabricated "scripts" against an old curmudgeon, Mr. Monroe, out on the rec yard, for days on end.

In concert with the Feds, if not at their direction, they had invented a story and crime to pin on old Monroe, for a 10 year time-cut off each of their own lengthy "crack-cocaine" sentences. The old man wouldn't sign a plea to something he hadn't done. Today's Feds don't tolerate that, or brutally punish anyone who persists and does exercise that constitutional right to go to trial. But Monroe refused to lie or sign one and got "life" for the completely fabricated crime.

The only real lawyer left in Charlotte after so many years of corruption (besides Tolly Kennon), was Peter Anderson, who had been a clerk to the senior judge, Graham C. Mullen. Therein lies Pete's protection, in my opinion, or the U.S. Attorney's office would have run him out of town too.

Fortunately for old Monroe, he had been assigned Pete Anderson by the court. Pete actually tracked down Bon Stroupe and others who had heard the government's co-conspirators in their false prosecution making up the stories and practicing them. He brought them back to Charlotte to testify, as the government's complete fabrication had gotten old Monroe a life sentence. He hadn't even known what they were talking about when they read the charges.

I took particular interest in Pete's case as he was also representing my "co-defendant", as they call one's fellow case members, and what they had done to old Monroe was not much different than what they were doing to us. Pete was representing Rick Graves at the upcoming trial, with basically the same scenario, except that the IRS had attempted to fabricate the "crime" in our case rather than some slightly more common snitches. The IRS agents now get a "cut", I've heard, rather than a "time-cut". That's about the only difference I see, and both are against the law, but the practice is common.

I'm sure that the few lawyer friends I have left will be spinning after that statement, so I'll quote the statute and let the reader decide if the prosecutor offering these payments, bribes, and time-cuts are not in violation, of the law.

Title 18 USCS §201(c)(2), clearly states: "Whoever directly or indirectly, gives, offers, or promises anything of value to any person, for or because of the testimony under oath or affirmation given or to be given by such person as a witness upon a trial, hearing, or other proceeding, before any court.... shall be fined under this title or imprisoned for not more than two years, or both."

You can call me silly, but an agent getting three percent of the take in a white-collar case or a crack head getting ten years of his life back sounds like "something of value" to me.

If this law were enforced, however, every one of America's 94 U.S. Attorneys, all of their Assistant U.S. Attorneys, and every District Attorney in the nation would be "fined under this title or imprisoned for not more than two years, or both."

But the U.S. Government and especially the U.S. Attorney's office in the corrupt Western District of North Carolina, don't let little things like that get in the way of their 99.6% conviction rate. No siree. And as Assistant U.S. Attorney Matt Martens told me in one of his little interrogation sessions (without my attorney, which is also against the law), "All of you out there have done 'something'. We just haven't gotten around to you yet." And if they have to break the law to get "all of us", I can tell you from first hand experience that they won't let that stop or deter them for a second.

With the trial to start April 2nd of 2007, I didn't have much time to wait, but the twenty three days of sleep deprivation were taking their toll. My wife's intimate knowledge of the jail's medical practices from her own terrible experience there, paid off. After my incoherent visit, she wrote me what to do.

As she recommended, I put in medical requests to see the doctor specifically. That usually takes a minimum of 3 visits at $10 to the nurse, where the answer to anything is "No" before a real doctor is ever seen, but she somehow shortened that cycle.

I got to see Dr. Wait. He was a pleasant fellow about my age, and could not have been kinder. From my wife's doing or my own poor condition after the maltreatment, I don't know, but he ordered them to get me off the floor and into a "wet" cell where I had my own toilet and could sleep.

His medical directive was timely, as things were about to get even more dangerous. Room #1 was where they locked up the "crazies", and Room #2 was the handicapped cell. They were the only two in the place with toilets.

I got #2, and slept every minute for the next couple of days, except when I was required to be in one of their ridiculous line-up counts or eating, with few exceptions.

But that Saturday in late March of 2007, just before the trial was to begin, I walked out of cell #2 and heard the news blaring, "Famous attorney, Kirk Osborn of Chapel Hill, has had a heart-attack and is in critical condition...", over the television.

I don't know what else they said. I never heard the rest of it. I went stone cold.

Our entire strategy and my freedom rested completely with that fine man, and he was near death.

When my mother and wife had come to visit just a couple of days before, they had given me a report of their meeting with Kirk, and my wife said he had just been in Charlotte with her the day before the visit, meeting with the Feds on our behalf.

I simply couldn't believe what I'd heard.

It was very early, and no one was on the phones, so I was able to reach my wife immediately. She was hysterical and could barely speak through her tears and anguish.

Kirk Osborn had become like a father-figure to her since coming to our rescue in late 2006. He would call her every day to give her hope and let her know that he would soon have me free as well.

Just the day before his heart attack, he had driven from Chapel Hill, North Carolina, all the way to our farm on the Yadkin River, where my wife was living, picked her up (as our son had wrecked the car), and drove her to Mt. Airy to meet with my mother.

He had laid out his plan for this worried lady and assured her that not only had my wife and I committed no crime, but that those that had done this to us would suffer the consequences after the up-coming trial was over, just days hence.

After all the sorry lot we'd hired to defend us....all a waste and more harm than help...I cannot express what this warm and honest human being, J. Kirk Osborn, meant to us.

He was as compassionate and decent as the Freedman/Tisdale/ Hoefling/Mayberry collection had been uncaring and indecent. He was an amazingly skilled attorney and an even more wonderful person.

I went into a deep and dangerous depression, as all hope was gone, and didn't even want to be around my new friends. It was a dark few days, and all I wanted to do was sleep, so I could escape the knowledge that I was doomed.

Kirk Osborn died on Sunday night, March 25th, 2007.

With him died all hope for justice. Our knight in shining armor was fallen and I faced the Dark Lord alone without a Champion.

CHAPTER 33

TRIAL WEEK, APRIL 2007

The plea agreement I had been forced to sign in January of 2007 clearly stated that its basis and reason was to free my wife. "As a condition of this Plea Agreement, the Government has agreed to recommend immediately the release of V. Woltz. This recommendation is made at the request of defendant H.Woltz." It was a hostage exchange, plain and simple. The three young attorneys, Hoefling, Mayberry, and Davey, had done everything possible to keep those words out of the agreement telling me that government would never allow it. It made what was really being done to us too apparent, and Kirk Osborn had predicted they would object to it on AUSA Martens' behalf.

But as Kirk also predicted, AUSA Martens would accept it, thinking that with his three accomplices....my attorneys....as my only defenders, a challenge would never be mounted. They were in his pocket, and just picking mine.

He did not know of Kirk's plan to take over my case and go after him (Martens) as soon as the trial was over, which was my ace in the hole, or so I thought.

Kirk and I had privately decided to do whatever we had to do to get my wife out. She'd almost died once already in the infamous Mecklenburg County jail and after her letter in mid-January saying 'goodbye', I'd taken this action against all of my own principles to save her.

There was no choice. An average of one un-convicted citizen a month was taking a one-way trip to the morgue due to abuse, neglect (or hopelessness), and we wanted her out of there alive before we started the war with Judge Britt and AUSA Martens.

We weren't overly concerned with what the agreement said anyway, as it was temporary at best and could be withdrawn at any time before sentencing, once we proved my actual innocence. The Government's own "evidence" proved that. Kirk had forced the kids from Helms Mulliss Wicker (now McGuire Woods) to put enough specifics into the plea agreement to make it clear, not only that it was extorted and strictly being signed to free a hostage, my wife, but also worded so that government admitted that I had not known of the wrong-ding.

"The Government has advised me, and I stipulate..." which translates to, "government has told me this, I didn't know it, but I'm having to agree with it to get my wife free...", and so on. They tucked the truth on the very last unnumbered page, in the last paragraph, where no one would ever read it, but it was in there, and all Kirk needed. All I admitted to was transferring $7 million in mostly non-cash assets of a trust *on the order of my Regulators*, to a new trustee, the assets of which had never been claimed to be of criminal origin, so the crime was impossible. You can't "conspire" to launder the proceeds of crime where one has never occurred, and your Regulators (government) ordered you to do it, making the transfer anything but a crime. AUSA Martens admitted that he knew I didn't know, and had e-mails between Sam Currin and his new trustee, Walt Hannen, proving it. He also admitted to withholding this evidence, which is against the law, right in front of Attorney David B. Freedman, who did nothing about it. Kirk would make hash of this arrogant young man for it, had he lived to do so.

Government had added its new "money laundering" charge though it was eight months after the law allowed it. 18 U.S.C. §3161(b) requires any related charge to be filed within thirty days of arrest. It also violated their own "non-affinity" agreement that had been executed by them on April 27th, 2006, as well as the contract Freedman and Martens had pledged to me was "memorialized" and said *no new charges of any kind*, so Kirk was sure that was not an obstacle either.

That could all be brought up later, we thought. We would kill AUSA Martens' and Meyers' illegally added charge. In spite of government's last minute trickery, we had gone ahead with the agreement and signed it as getting Vernice out of that place alive was our sole focus. Once the trial of my only alleged "co-conspirator", Attorney Rick Graves, was over, we planned to immediately withdraw the plea as coerced, and have it voided as illegal and a breach of government's own contract (which Tweedledee, Tweededum, and Tweededummest had refused to do).

Kirk was the only attorney who had reviewed the facts and files out of all of them from Freedman to Tisdale to the three little boys from Helms Mulliss & Wicker (now McGuire Woods). He knew Rick Graves' attorney, Pete Anderson, and knew that he would win at the trial in April. I had actually spoken to Pete about it as well on the phone one day when he was on with Bon Stroupe about the Monroe case. There had been no "conspiracy" ever and the transcripts and records proved it. We returned the IRS con-men's money, and wrote them a letter telling them that we did not want their business. No transaction ever took place. End of story. A jury would have to acquit him. All we were worried about were the corrupt characters who had control of the process----Judge Britt and AUSA Martens.

I later learned by suing the McGuire Woods attorneys that they had been informed just days before the plea agreement was being written that the entire IRS "sting" operation had been in violation of U.S. law as it had no authorization from the Tax Division of the U.S. Justice Department, (which is required), and AUSA Martens was in violation of USAM (U.S. Attorney Manual) Title 6 in prosecuting it. There had been no approval of the "sting" operation by The Bahamas, which made it an international crime itself. Going there to attempt to fabricate tax crimes and conspiracies, neither of which are recognized by that nation, was a violation of their laws and constitution, according to no less a personage than Prime Minister Perry Christie himself, confirmed by my investigator.

All of this was known by the HMW/McGuire Woods attorneys *prior to* the discussion of a plea taking place, yet they refused to challenge it or even let me know they knew it. They had made a deal with the prosecutor to deliver me up for thirty pieces of silver, though the entire prosecution had been illegal, vindictive, and itself a serious international crime.

And as for the thirty pieces of silver, it was much, much more than that. I later learned that government now pays these attorneys to coerce their clients into taking a plea. They are paid an enormous sum to sell out their clients in cases such as mine, as a portion of "the savings to the taxpayers" in avoiding a trial.

That bit of enlightenment put much of the incredible misconduct and abject refusal of all of these attorneys to defend me into perspective, but it was far too late for it to be of any assistance.

Had they done what they were ordered to do, or filed for dismissal of the indictment, as every one of them was also ordered to do, the case would have been over. No huge fees. No kick-back bribes from the government.

The HMW/McGuire Woods crew raped my family for over a quarter million dollars and never did a single thing we told them to do. I will one day learn whether or not they were paid a kick-back by government for selling me out, and may heaven help them then.

But I knew none of this at the time, and they were able to keep their knowledge of all these facts and illegalities hidden from me until early 2009 when they were forced by the North Carolina State Bar to release these records which proved their malfeasance and malpractice.

Kirk had told me not to worry, as once Attorney Rick Graves was acquitted, that acted as an acquittal of me as well, automatically, even though I had pleaded guilty.

Kirk didn't feel that it really mattered whether Rick Graves was acquitted or not, as the whole enterprise from inception by Elizabeth Streit at the CFTC and her friends at the IRS had been an illegal prosecution and would have to be thrown out when put before an honest judge without an agenda. But it mattered to me. I had been falsely and vindictively accused of crimes never committed or even considered. Vicariously, through Rick Graves, my sole alleged "co-conspirator", I would be vindicated when he was acquitted by a jury of his peers.

In one day, however, my solid position with the rock of Kirk Osborn as a foundation had become nothing but shifting sands. Government had brutally attacked Tolly Kennon for mounting an adversarial process in the case and were out to destroy him (and did), so I was left only with Caesar's own little trio of centurions as my "defense"----Tweedledee, Tweedledum, and Tweedledummest, which was cause for stark terror. Prison, became possible after all for uncommitted crimes simply because I had no one to defend me or to challenge the criminals in the government and court as Kirk had intended to do. He was already planning his public assault on AUSA Martens and the whole cabal, including his old friend, Judge W. Earl Britt, the day he mysteriously died, which was just the week before Attorney Rick Graves' trial began.

So the trial of Attorney Rick Graves had taken on an even greater meaning and context for me, as Kirk had assured me that under law, his acquittal would act as an acquittal of me, as I was his only alleged "co-conspirator." Everyone else had been a government agent, and agents cannot count as "co-conspirators," and Sam Currin's charge had been dropped as "mere presence" is inadequate to sustain a conviction. Kirk had even mentioned some case law on the matter, "Musgrave" and "Austin-Bagley" and so on.

I tried again to gain access to the law library or get assistance from someone at the Mecklenburg County Jail, to help me find these cases and do a motion to the court, as was my right under law, but Sheriff Pendergraph had denied all access to both. I later learned that this was a violation of the Sixth Amendment and cause for overturn in and of itself. He'd shut the law library and requests for legal assistance were answered, "Ask your family," or some other snippy response. I couldn't ask the three 'Tweedies', as they were in Martens' employ, not mine. I was just paying them, and even Jack Fernandez, the consultant, had faded from view after the death of his "conscience", the great Kirk Osborn. He went from a fighter to a pussycat in a matter of days.

Three-quarters of a million dollars and not a real lawyer among them. But if Rick Graves was to be acquitted, as both his lawyer, Pete Anderson, and our hero, Kirk Osborn, were certain would happen, then I would be automatically acquitted as well...under law.

Even the crooked old curmudgeon they'd hand-picked down in Raleigh, Judge W. Earl Britt, would have to let me go...or so the law said.

I was so excited about seeing Matt Martens get beaten in court by Pete Anderson, that I begged my wife to get a local Charlotte cell phone so I could call her from the jail and keep in touch during the trial. I had to fight to get the phone some days (literally), but we spoke every few hours. She actually took off from her new job and was there every day, I assumed to watch after my interests, but that was not the real reason.

Only later did I learn that Matt Martens and the government had tricked her into testifying at the trial against Rick Graves....with yet another false promise of letting me go or substantially reducing my sentence if she would help them.

She never told me about this, as she knew I would be very angry, but she was doing everything she could to get me home, not knowing that she was actually hurting me, as his acquittal required my release. She made the mistake of trusting them. Had I known that this formidable woman was on Martens' side for that week, I would have been doubly nervous.

Each day she did her best to curb my hopes for a not guilty verdict by telling me all of government's crooked attacks and untrue statements, never revealing that she was in the shadow of their wrong-doing. I can only imagine the suffering that caused her, doing wrong for evil people, based on their false promises to set me free. By helping to make Rick Graves "guilty" she was assuring my conviction as well, but she never knew that, and Kirk was no longer there to tell her. I assumed that he had told her what he planned, but I would learn almost two years later, that he had not. What we were going to do was on a "need to know" basis, and I suppose he figured she was free, so she no longer "needed to know".

The tension built for me, daily, and I could not focus on anything else. My captors moved me three times that week to different cell-blocks, I suppose, just to keep me off-base, having to deal with a new, hostile group of their victims each day, but by that time, I couldn't go anywhere without knowing someone or running into men I'd helped, so I can't claim that was too difficult by then. At least I had a bed and a toilet.

My focus remained on the trial, however. I could not get it off my mind for even a moment. Meditation, which had been my salvation throughout, became impossible. Even the meager food went uneaten.

After a week, the government rested its case, and the jury began its deliberation. By the day we expected the verdict, I had been shuffled all the way back to cell-block 4200, where I'd been before being taken to the sleep-deprivation pod as punishment for being the editor of Despierta America! They'd turned it into something of an immigration unit by then, it seemed.

There were men from Senegal, The Congo, Saudi Arabia, Norway, Nigeria, Mexico, Columbia, Honduras, Turkey, and Lebanon.... a regular United Nations. I figured that my Bahamian address on my paperwork had landed me there, but it was a pleasant distraction to get to speak and practice languages I'd learned over the years traveling the world.

My years in Haiti speaking their <u>patois</u> allowed conversation with several of the African men as well. Wherever the French had occupied a nation in Africa, patois of a similar nature had developed as in Haiti, and was more or less understandable. They understood my "Creole", as we called it in Haiti, and I understood their <u>patois</u> from their homeland, which was quite amazing. The Senegalese was almost identical, meaning that the base African tribal languages must have been the same.

Between Spanish, French, Haitian "Creole" and English, I could communicate with every man in the cell-block, and help them to be understood to the guards, when needed, as well.

I had promised to call my wife the day of the verdict at an appointed time, but that became impossible, even as anxious as I was to hear the news.

A black Haitian man who'd been living in Columbia passed out from hunger while taking a shower. The stalls were right outside of my cell #2, and it sounded like a pistol shot when his head had hit the tile floor.

The female guard ordered everyone to "lock down", but she was not doing anything to help the poor man, so I crawled under the locked stall door to make sure that he was all right. He was not. His skin was cold, and the water was spraying into his open mouth, drowning him, as he was unconscious.

His head was quickly swelling from the severe blow of hitting the tile floor, it appeared, and the guard was still screaming at me to "lock down", rather than worrying about man who was about to die unnecessarily.

"Call medical, NOW!" I screamed back at her. I turned off the water, got him on his side so the water could drain out of his mouth and throat. He did not cough, and was not breathing, so I got him on his back and began pressing his chest and performing CPR to keep the blood flowing, and hopefully get him breathing again.

He finally choked and gurgled. The guard was still screaming at either me or the other men, I don't know, as I was paying her no attention, but finally shouted at her, "Quit yelling and get medical up here, NOW!"

The man was coughing up water and breathing, but was seemingly in shock. I remembered how bird dogs sometimes got in the same state after running in field trials, appearing almost dead. We always kept corn syrup or some sweet liquid to give them in case that happened, as it would revive them. I unlocked the shower door from the inside and ran to my cell to retrieve some "contraband" sugar I'd kept from breakfast, and a cup. I put the sugar in his lip and wet it with water, massaging it into his gums so he would absorb it.

This process took some minutes, and by the time I looked around, there were five or six officers behind me, all in rubber gloves, watching, but doing nothing.

They had a wheelchair, so I said, "Help me get him into the chair and cover him up. He's in shock."

One of them laughed and said, "I ain't touchin' no naked inmate!" Every one of them joined in the laughter. Not one of them moved to help me, so I lifted him up and dragged him out by holding him under his arms and hoisted him into the wheelchair, then covered him as best as I could with his jail pajamas and towel.

"Get a blanket over him immediately. He must be kept warm. Tell them downstairs that he may be in diabetic shock." I put more sugar in his lip and wet it with water from my cup. "He's breathing again, but is still in shock, and may still have some water in his lungs. He's had a bad blow to the head and may also have a concussion."

About that time, the man groaned and coughed. He was reviving. I told him in "Creole" what had happened, and what was going on. He smiled, either at hearing his native tongue from a white man, which had surprised him that morning, or maybe he was just glad to be alive.

The heartless guards had apparently been trained to see and treat un-convicted citizens under their care as sub-human, and took him out the sliding door still giggling and making jokes. I looked at the clock before going into my cell to "lock down". I'd missed the appointed time to call and find out the verdict. The phones wouldn't be turned back on until late that evening.

I was sorely disappointed, but wouldn't have changed a minute of that day. The verdict wouldn't change just because I didn't know what it was for a few more hours, and I felt good about helping the man, especially when I thought, about what would have happened to him if I'd left it in their hands.

At 4 p.m., the guard opened the doors to our cells for the evening meal. I was still wet from helping the man in the shower. She just stared at me and never said a word or offered to get me dry clothes.

It occurred to me that perhaps she was planning to punish me for not locking down on her order. It really wouldn't have mattered to me by that point in time. After nine months in solitary upstairs in the murderer's pod, it wouldn't even seem like punishment to go to the "hole", but I didn't want to miss my phone call.

So I asked her how the man was doing, just to break the ice and get a reading.

"He OK," she said, giving me another long stare, which I could not read, and she turned away from me.

After dinner, she locked us back down, but came to my cell and opened the door. "That was a nice thing you done for that man today. How you know what to do?" she asked.

I didn't think it wise to tell her about the bird dogs, or being an Eagle Scout or try to explain, so I just said, "I've been around. It just came to me."

She made a noise, "Humph!", and closed the door to my cell.

A few minutes before 7 p.m., she let us back out for "shift change" and the fifth alphabetical roll—call of that day, as if one of us could have escaped. We suffered through the same boring "orientation" speech, I had heard 720 times before by the guard coming on duty. Half the pod didn't even speak English, which made it all the more ridiculous. I tuned her out and watched the second hand slowly round the face of the cheap wall clock, waiting to make my call.

We were then locked back down until after 8:00 p.m., when the guard let us out. Men had raced for the few working phones, and I didn't get to one first.

The wait seemed forever, but finally, the young man's time was up. I dialed my wife's new cell phone number and she answered on the last ring before voicemail.

I plunged right in, which is considered poor manners in the Caribbean paradise she's from, and I paid for it. She required polite chit-chat first, and dragged out telling me what had transpired until my time was nearly up, as punishment, I thought then.

But a year later, I learned what it was really about. Government had falsely led her to believe that Rick Graves' conviction would set me free if she would help them get it, while in actuality, only his acquittal would do so. It was a cruel trick by AUSA Martens, as dark and Machiavellian as any I've ever known. He planned to use my wife to keep me convicted of a crime that was never committed, by falsely convicting an innocent man as my "co-conspirator", after extorting a confession to it from me, to make a "conspiracy" where none had ever been. It was sordid. It was Martens. It was out of control government at its very worst.

That night, my wife thought she had 'bad' news for me. That was her hesitance in telling me what had transpired, so she reviewed the whole trial. She was also fearful of letting me know that she had 'aided' them in that terrible enterprise, though she had done so only to try and set me free.

She also felt as though she had let me down, not knowing that Matt Martens had tricked and lied to her again, just as he had on every occasion and at every opportunity throughout the entire case.

"Vernice, I'm almost out of time. Please....just tell me....did the jury find him guilty or not guilty?"

"Howell, it really isn't going to help you. With Kirk dead and no one else willing to go against these people, it...."

"Vernice, please just tell me."

"But I don't want you to get your hopes up, and you know how crooked these people are..."

The automatic operator came on to warn that the phone call was ending.

"Vernice, please!"

There was a long pause, and the seconds ticked away my phone call's remaining moments. Just before the phone went dead, she said, "The jury acquitted him, Howell, but don't get your hopes up, please. They are so corrupt it may not make any difference. They don't go by the law. We've seen that, and....

The phone went dead.

Rick Graves, my only alleged "co—conspirator", had been acquitted by a jury, which under law, is unreviewable. They had decided that he was no conspirator, and there had been no conspiracy. That acted as an automatic acquittal of me as well, under law, as the only remaining person. The conspiracy law requires "two or more".

Even the corrupt old Judge Britt would have to let me go.

For the first night in a week, I went to bed and slept peacefully. I was going home a free man. The nightmare was almost over.

CHAPTER 34

JUSTICE DENIED

But as the reader has probably guessed, my nightmare in the American "justice" system was far from over. In many ways, it was just beginning. As I write this chapter, I'm on the back side of an 87 month sentence for things I never did, on a conviction which is itself a violation of law.

It was not until I got to prison that I was ever allowed into a law library to verify Kirk Osborn's promise that I must be acquitted by law, and I've lived there ever since. He was, of course, correct. That was very much the law and still is all these years later.

The case he had mentioned, was actually United States v. Austin-Bagley Corp., 279 US 863, 73 Led 1002, 49 S.Ct. 479.

It was the seminal case on this issue after America passed its first outrageous expansion of "conspiracy" laws, and the Supreme Court had ruled, "Acquittal of all defendants except one invalidated conviction of latter."

The other case he'd mentioned, was actually United States v. Musgrave, 414 US 1025, 38 LEd2d 316, 94 S.Ct. 450. It was listed in the annotated statute book itself, with the law, and said, "Conviction of only one defendant in conspiracy prosecution under 18 USCS §371 will not be upheld where all other alleged co-conspirators were acquitted." It just doesn't get any plainer than that, yet I'm still in prison. My wife had been right.

The law doesn't matter to these people anymore.

I've quit keeping track of them, but they all say the same thing, "Where only person with whom defendant was alleged to have conspired was acquitted, conviction could not be sustained." Worthington v. United States, 64 F2d 936. "Acquittal of one of two alleged conspirators acquitted other." United States v. Wray, 8 F2d 429. "Conspiracy requires at least two participants, and acquittal of all but one of alleged conspirators should operate as an acquittal of that defendant as well." United States v. Fleming, 504 F2d 1045, and on and on.

318

Not one case or any statute allowed me to be convicted and sentenced, but I was and am, outside of law and constitution and no one will do anything about it. Justice has been denied.

I am serving a seven and a half year sentence for a crime that does not exist, and an illegally added charge to a crime that never happened, and every court and judge of jurisdiction knows it all the way up to the Supreme Court (Case No. 08-8285 and 09-10841, In re Woltz).

Inspector General of the U.S. Department of Justice, Glenn A. Fine, has been aware of it all since 2008. He took no action, however, other than to refer it back to the FBI, who had participated in the criminal activity, and let them decide if they had done anything wrong. They never asked a single question of anyone who could have told them what had happened, and have refused to talk to me, as I can now prove their crimes.

I suppose it should surprise no one who has read this far that in the fall of 2009, the FBI decided that they had done no wrong, without ever asking a single question of any of the victims, or reviewing the now available evidence.

After the Graves trial, I begged the boys at HMW/McGuire Woods to help me, but was ignored. They refused to even file objections to the pre-sentence report, and I finally had to fire them in May of 2007 to stop the outrageous billing, but they kept on charging us anyway!

Months and months after their termination in writing, huge bills were still rolling in for up to $10,000 at a pop, for unrequested and un-rendered services, never detailed or explained.

We had to sell our home to repay my brothers, Jim and Thomas, and my mother, who had advanced the king's ransom to pay these pettifoggers and guaranteed the payment to them. HMW/McGuire Woods took that as a carte blanche for robbery, while never following a single order or performing even one task I ever asked them to do.

As for AUSA Matthew Martens, he was not satisfied with just illegally charging, incarcerating, prosecuting and convicting me with a "shopped" judge, or destroying us financially, he decided to torture me after the fact as well to "punish" me for not lying at his trial against Rick Graves. He made my life a living hell, putting me on "the road" for months, on a virulent form of torture known as "diesel therapy."

Fearful that I might find a real lawyer, he kept me on the move where that was impossible. In May of 2007, when the torture started, I had even been set up for an "escape charge", which is documented and part of the record in the case, but also ignored by those who are intended to guard the citizen from such wrong-doing, as it was their own that did it.

In the middle of the night, an unknown man who was not our guard came to my cell door and opened it. "You're leaving, Woltz," he said. "Pack it up. They're setting you free."

While the law did require them to do that, I knew the system well enough by then to know that they did not do these things at 2:45 a.m. No one was ever discharged after 12 p.m., until the following morning.

My well-earned paranoia went into high-gear, and I scribbled Tolly Kennon's address on 2 pieces of paper with a note of what to do for Ronald Adams, my next door neighbor in cell #3, and Allen Coffey, whom I could see watching and listening to what was going on from upstairs, looking out of his cell door.

I told the stranger I wanted to give them my remaining "commissary" items, since I was leaving, and used that as a pretext to slip each of them a note and tell them to document what they had heard and send it to Tolly in case I was about to join the mysterious "Mecklenburg Dead". (They did so).

The stranger then took me downstairs and told me to dress in my street clothes which they had ready for me...the same ones I'd been wearing the day of my abduction back in April of 2006.

They had also prepared a cashier's check for my commissary account balance, and once I was dressed, they opened the double doors to the street. I could look out to freedom and was told it was mine. I was free to leave, they said.

I have no idea what would have happened if I had walked out those doors that starry spring night back in May of 2007. A fusillade of bullets or a charge of "attempted escape" were the only expectations I had that night. Without any documentation to prove that the court and government had released me, what else could I expect from these people?

Dressed in street clothes, with a money order in my pocket, and a beautiful spring night, it was very tempting, but my radar went on high alert when the night desk officer began encouraging me to do so. "Go on. Door's open. Go ahead. You're free."

That confirmed it. These are not nice people that do these jobs.

"I need to see the release paperwork and get a copy of the court order before I walk out that door," I told him.

"Go on. You're free. You don't need that," the transplanted New Yorker said.

"Not until I get some paperwork," I replied, and sat down.

"Suit yourself," he said, and announced to the 'property" clerk that he was going on break. She promptly announced that she was going to the ladies room "for a while" and disappeared as well.

I was left, in the discharge and property office of the Mecklenburg County Sheriff's Department all alone at 3:30 A.M. Even during the many violent episodes I have experienced in the past four years, I have never been frightened except that one time. Sitting alone in the sheriff's office, knowing that I had been set up to be murdered or charged "escaping" by those who had already broken so many laws to put me there was very disconcerting. Hell, it was terrifying.

It would be done in a way that made me look like a criminal, as well, and under "color of law." I knew that.

After several minutes of this terror, a black sergeant came in and looked around the room, then at me, then at the double doors left wide open to the streets and said, "What are you doing here?"

Before I could answer, he turned and shouted to the empty room, "Where is everybody?" and people immediately began emerging from behind doors and counters.

"We're here Sarge," said the overweight night officer from New York, stepping out from behind a doorway.

"Right here," said the property lady, having only hidden behind her large counter.

"What the hell is going on?" he barked.

No one answered him. He apparently had been left out of the loop on the set-up, and didn't like it, as it would fall on him, I suspected, if something went wrong.

"I'll tell you," I said, and quietly explained the events of the last forty-five minutes and what I thought was going on.

He was livid. He went to the computer, moving the chubby New Yorker aside, pulled up my name and file, and cut loose with a string of curses. He ordered me into a small closet toilet behind the duty desk, and closed the door, with the lights off, (unintentionally, I think).

His tirade went on for some time. I could well understand his anger, because government's "set-up" had to have been done with Sheriff Pendergraph's knowledge and participation, but no one had told the sergeant in charge. He was going to be left to hang if something went wrong, and had clearly not been informed of it. He was the "fall guy" and anything that bounced back or went wrong would have fallen on him and he apparently realized that.

I heard him ask who the man was that had brought me down. None of them knew who he was and he had conveniently disappeared. It was looking like my foreboding was real. As I'd heard in jail, "It ain't paranoia when they're really after you!"

For the next seven hours, I sat in the dark until a day-sergeant came into the little closet and saw me. "What are you doing in here?" he asked me.

I told him the story. It didn't take much imagination to know who was behind such a criminal enterprise, and I suggested that he call AUSA Matthew Martens at the U.S. Attorney's Office if he wanted to know what was going on.

He did, and I could hear him say, "But this man hasn't even been sentenced yet. We can't do that!" There was then silence for several seconds. Then, "Yes sir. Yes sir," followed by a lot of hushed conversation after he hung up the phone.

The suspense didn't last long. I was taken out of the closet and shackled, hands, waist and feet, to be shipped to the ancient U.S.P. Atlanta, where Al Capone did time back in the 1930's. Built on the literal "bones" of a civil war prison camp in 1908, this brutal monument to the worst of our nation is still in service to America's dark and sinister side.

I had come to know the female deputy organizing the human shipment during my long months there and asked her, "How can I be sent to Atlanta U.S.P., when I've yet to be sentenced."

"You can't. You must have been sentenced and be on your way to prison or you wouldn't be on this bus," she answered.

"Would you do us both a favor then and check the computer? You'll see that I have never been sentenced for anything in my life. Then call the U.S. Attorney's Office and ask for Matt Martens, and see why he's doing this."

She looked at me and nodded silently, and went away.

A few minutes later, she came back with a startled look on her face, and said, "I called him and explained that you had never been sentenced and he said to put you on the bus anyway. He was very nasty about it."

"That's him. So you spoke directly to Matt Martens?" I asked.

"Yes," she said, then paused and added, "I'm sorry, Mr. Woltz, I really am. There's nothing I can do about it, or I would."

"I know," I replied. "I just wanted to make sure that he was behind all of this. Thanks."

And with that, I was shipped to America's worst prison which was not expecting me. There was no paperwork, and the officer there just laughed at me and said, "Boy, somebody up in the U.S. Attorney's Office don't like you!" I finally got put in an old dungeon cell to sleep on the floor some time after midnight. It was number 161. I still remember. I saw my first very large sewer rat about ten minutes after the door was locked.

From there I was bussed to Butner and then to the condemned Wilson County Jail in eastern North Carolina. According to the nurse there, Ms. Dewalt, it had been condemned by the county as unfit for human occupancy, but the Feds used it anyway. It was so old, the cells had been built with no lights and none had ever been added after Edison had his bright idea. Four bunks hung from chains in each tiny cell like a medieval chamber with iron bars as in days of old.

From there I was shipped to Louisburg, North Carolina, and stored in a wide-open human warehouse where I ran into Yari Leake, the prisoner who had brokered the "peace" back in the Wake County Jail months before when my commissary had been stolen by the dusty-looking, pock-marked gangster. Some of my Hispanic friends who had been on my side were also there.

I also ran into John Britt, a man I'd met in the Raleigh federal courthouse holding pen from Columbus County. The sheriff down there had raided his home with the DEA, killed his dog, and shot him four times through his own front door with a .45 caliber H&K sub-machine gun. John was also one of Judge W. Earl Britt's victims.

The black-suited thug drug warrior of government then came into his home and shot him a fifth time at point-blank range, lying on the floor of his own home, intending to kill him.

No warrant shown. No warning. No probable cause. Bullets were flying through the trailer house from other government bandits on the outside, and pierced the chair where John's wife had been sitting with their granddaughter before the attack began.

The government thugs left the tough old Lumbee, John Britt, to bleed out for forty-five minutes without ever calling for medical help. He lay there, conscious the whole time, with five massive slugs having pierced his abdomen, chest and one of them having nearly blown his right arm in two. An ambulance was called only because when he wouldn't die, a female member of the assault team threatened to tell on the would-be murderers herself if they didn't call for medical help.

They found no drugs, and John heard them talking about what to do. They'd almost killed a man in his own home for no cause and nothing to show for it. John watched one of the black—suited thugs plant a small plastic bag under his sofa cushion so drugs could be found later, but they belonged to the police, not John Britt.

I filed a §1983 lawsuit for John just as I had for "J.R." in Charlotte, and immediately was pulled out of there and put on the "road" again.

Even under assault by the Feds himself, Tolly Kennon tracked me down and filed two complaints and a report on Martens' "escape" set—up with the court. Two were necessary because they had to go to Judge Britt, who was part of the scheme himself. It was old Britt who had signed the order allowing Martens to send me on this torture tour, and Tolly had to press him to undo the illegal enterprise by putting it in the record, placing himself at risk by doing so.

The next month, I was threatened by the Judge Britt/AUSA Martens cabal with fifteen years in prison if I did not fire Tolly Kennon. They wanted me defenseless.

The date of that threat was July 9th, 2007 and the transcript actually shows the court sending my brother, Jim, back into U.S. Marshal holding to deliver their message. Tolly was with me when Jim passed on the warning from bench and bar.

To this brave man's credit, it was also him (Tolly) who demanded that I let him go to protect myself from the venomous pair of outlaws out in the courtroom.

After that, I begged the consultant, Jack Fernandez, to help me, but his conscience and sense of outrage had departed with Kirk Osborn's soul, or possibly he shared in the thirty pieces of silver with the HMW/McGuire Woods attorneys from Martens. I don't know. But rather than challenge the illegal conviction as Kirk had planned to do, he joined the chorus and said, "You pleaded guilty. You just have to live with that," and refused to do anything to help me.

When I told him to withdraw the plea the week before sentencing, after another major fee was paid him to do my bidding ($85,000), he would not do it, claiming that AUSA Martens had promised him a major reduction in the sentence if I would not withdraw it.

"But I'm innocent. I can't be a sole conspirator, Jack! There's no such thing! I had to be acquitted, by law, when the jury acquitted Rick Graves!"

"You pleaded guilty," he kept repeating, "so you just have to live with it."

Thirty-five Thousand of the Eighty-Five Thousand Dollars had been charged extra for the inclusion of a senior partner in Jack's firm by the name of William Taylor, who was supposed to be a friend of Judge Britt's and would get all of this "worked out". Four days after that conversation, I was sentenced to 87 months anyway, and Attorney William Taylor was a "no-show." So was the extra $35,000.

It never came back.

After this outrageous sentence for a crime that did not exist, I was immediately shuffled off to a private prison in the Dismal Swamp of Tidewater Virginia and sequestered there so an appeal was impossible during the brief 10-day period during which it must be made. Mysteriously, I could not get the phone to work for those days, and I had no money to buy mailing supplies. It worked. I missed the deadline.

When I was finally able to get my brother Jim on the phone and ask him about the appeal, he said that Jack had e-mailed him just before the 10-day period to give notice expired and said that he would need even more money - lots more money - to do that.

When Brother Jim told him to use the $35,000 that was to go to the "no-show" lawyer, Bill Taylor, Jack said that they had applied it to "expenses". He would need more! It was too late to send more money, and Jack knew it.

It would be hard to tell anyone who has not experienced American "justice" and these "criminal" attorneys what sort of despondency this set of circumstances can cause in a person. Trapped in a horrible private prison-for-profit, The Tidewater Regional Jail, (reputedly owned by 3 local Suffolk, VA judges), with no recourse, falsely charged, impossibly convicted and sentenced as a "sole conspirator", and then sequestered up in a swamp prison to prevent appeal of judge and prosecutor's final act of treachery and nowhere to turn

It was then that I realized that I could count on no one but myself. I would have to learn the law and fight my way free alone. Those were bitter months, but it was then that I began the transition to "jailhouse lawyer". Not just filling out "Bivens Action" forms as I had for "J.R." and John Britt, but learning real law and how to file motions. It dawned on me that if I had known that, I would not be on my way to prison. I would be free and back in The Bahamas. It angered me, but also drove me to learn it and help others. Teach others. If the lawyers would no longer protect us from wrongful prosecutions then we would have to learn to do so ourselves. I swore to myself then that as soon as I reached prison, I would live in the law library (which I have done).

The judge-owned private dungeon was a perfect place to start. Almost exclusively, the men were poor, black, and had no means or connections of any kind. The judge-owners were ordering these poor fellows here for months on end, and collecting a bloody fortune from the state. How these judges got away with this was unimaginable until I thought on my own circumstances. They could get away with anything, unfortunately. Judges are above the law, by law.

Many of these poor men did not even know why they were there, or had been parked there for months and months on end by the judges for minor traffic violations or petty offenses, and never tried for them.

This semi-legal leeching of the system and state by these corrupt judges and their "private" prison became one of my targets.

I got examples of motions wherever I could, gleaned case law from every document that had them in it, and got my wife to download a copy of The Speedy Trial Act of 1974 and the Supreme Court case, <u>Zedner v. United States,</u> and send them to me.

In the waning months of 2007, I began a one-man war on the local state and federal courts of the tidewater region, filing motions to dismiss indictments of these men's cases, based on violations of their right to a speedy trial. Hardly a man in there had not been violated by these terrible judges.

Eddie Cross, Michael Brown, Milton Mizell, the famous Nigerian boxer, Imoudu "David" Izegwire, and many others. I remember working on motions most of Christmas night in 2007, with Izegwire at my side. He and I celebrated the season by sitting on the floor, dead tired, and eating a blueberry donut, when the last motion was finished.

Someone in the lower part of the crowded, open cell-block started singing <u>Silent Night</u> very quietly at first, then louder. Soon, a few other voices joined in, and by the end of the first verse the entire unit, Christians, Muslims, atheists, and Native American alike were singing or humming the seasonal song.

It was not a moment I shall ever forget, nor will I ever forget those good men that society's supposed protectors had so unmercifully parked there in their private prison to make a profit on their misery.

The cell-block was silent when the song ended. Each man turned to his own thoughts, memories, and personal sadness at being away from those he loved.

I collapsed on the little cot, too weary to undress, and fell immediately into a deep sleep.

But moments later, I was awakened by my many friends. It was a strange sight. Ten to twelve black men from the streets of D.C. and eastern Virginia who would have never given me the time of day in another setting, were standing around my cot looking down at me as if I were dying, with true looks of brotherly love on their faces.

"What's wrong? I asked.

"They just called you, Professor, (the nickname they had given me). They're taking you out of here," Milton said.

"On Christmas night?" I asked, still half-asleep. "I didn't think they worked on Christmas."

"You filed too many motions, Professor. You're bad for business. They want you out of here," Old Joe said, and in retrospect, he was right. Had I stayed in that corrupt place, I could have emptied it.

They helped me pack my meager belongings, and we said our heartfelt farewells. Mark Davey promised to call my brother and tell him I'd been moved yet again.

And that has been my template ever since. At each "move", I've set up shop and begun educating prisoners on everything I wish I had known, everything I've learned, and teaching them to file their own motions and suits to fight government injustice.

Even once I got to prison, the diesel therapy never stopped. After little more than a year, I was pulled out and put on the road again for nothing but pure torment, and to stop my filing appeals for men there. I lived in the law library from the moment it opened before daylight, and was usually the one to close it down at 8:30-9:00 at night, seven days a week.

I've lost count of the appeals filed, habeas corpus petitions submitted, and cannot remember all of the Speedy Trial dismissals sent in for men being held in jails across America, illegally, just as I had been unlawfully incarcerated in Mecklenburg County.

As Henry David Thoreau wrote 150 years ago, "I've become an enemy of the state," I suppose. I love my country and what it is supposed to be. I sometimes get emotional just reading my battered little Constitution, thinking what our nation could be if we still lived by it, and I detest what our leaders and their henchmen have done to our once—free homeland.

I've been moved now twenty-five times between jails and prisons in less than four years, and lost track of how many cell—blocks within them I've been shuffled through, but that has allowed me to interface with literally thousands of those whom our "justice" system would have the public believe are the "worst" among us.

But they are not. Forty-seven percent are in prison for marijuana, which would have landed our last three presidents in prison, if they had been caught. And even those who are "real" criminals have yet to match the cruelty and inhumanity of those I've met who put them there.

From the murderer's pod in Charlotte, North Carolina, and ancient Atlanta U.S.P. in the east, to the human warehouses in Chickasha, Oklahoma, I've never met a man yet as evil in nature as those who participated in this false prosecution, and who generally inhabit the "justice" system in America.

The few "real" criminals I've met in this system did what they did to survive, to make a living, to support their own addiction, or made a mistake in a moment of debilitation, poor judgment or anger.

Elizabeth Streit of the CFTC, AUSA Matthew Martens of the Justice Department, Scott Schiller of the IRS, and perhaps worst of all, the corrupt judge they found to suborn it all, W. Earl Britt; these men and women do not have the very human reasons or excuses for the terrible offenses they commit on a daily basis.

They're educated, very well-paid, and make conscious choices to do wrong. I'll say it once more. These are the adults that were once the type of kids who enjoyed pulling the wings off butterflies and tormenting small animals, just because their overwhelming power allows them to. They're still doing it, but to humans and just because they can...and because no one is watching them.

But they are doing these things in our names and under the pretense of "law". It must stop.

As Baron Montesquieu wrote in <u>The Spirit of Law</u> back in James Madison's day, "There is no more cruel tyranny than that which is exercised under the cover of law, and with the colors of justice."

Some things have not changed since 1776 when those words were first published and it is now my goal in life to use this experience to fight for change, just as our founding fathers fought the tyrants of their day.

Unfortunately, our tyrants are within our nation today, and not external as in their time. They are in quasi-federal agencies and departments not found in the U.S. Constitution, and precluded by the Tenth Amendment, yet here they are, ruling our lives and taking our liberty.

The tyrants are in the prosecutor's office, which is a place that didn't exist in Madison and Jefferson's day. Judges have become the tyrants of the courts rather than the servants of the jury, as they were meant to be. This country belongs to us, We the People, and WE must take it back from these petty straw man tyrants, who by law and constitution were to be our servants in public duty rather than our masters and rulers in every aspect of our lives.

One in thirty-one American adults are in the corrections system of America today. One in nine has been. You now know how that happened. Justice was denied, not in every case, but I can assure you from inside the belly of the beast, that it certainly was in most of them.

As Senator Jim Webb wrote in April of 2009, when he announced the true number of Americans in the system (1 in every 31 adults) he said, "Either we are the most evil people on earth, or we are doing something very wrong."

There is no doubt which is the answer. We're doing something very wrong.

The question now is…what are We the People going to do about it?

Howell W. Woltz #20758-058

Federal Corrections Institute-Beckley

P. O. Box 350

Beaver, WV 25813

www.howellwoltz.org

Send letters to:

Grey Hawk Press
c/o Arthur P. Strickland
P. O. Box 2866
Roanoke, VA   24001-2866

EPILOGUE

FEDERAL CORRECTIONS INSTITUTE – BECKLEY, WEST VIRGINIA – EARLY 2010

It has taken the better part of three years to get <u>Justice Denied</u> in print. Chapter after chapter (the first eight mailings, to be exact), were diverted by the federal prison clerks who illegally opened my outgoing mail. They never made it to safety. I finally had to smuggle the manuscript out by an inmate whose time was done and he was leaving prison. He took it out with his "property".

The prison officials were illegally attempting to prevent this book from being published.

My wife waited for me for nearly four years, but has decided to move on with her life. We're still dear friends, but the torment, torture and endless months of abuse back in 2006 took their toll. The process employed by prosecutors, agents, defense lawyers and judges today to coerce pleas of guilt, is designed to turn husbands, wives, friends, lovers and relatives against one another and supplant trust with suspicion, truth with lies, and love with hate. You're just emotionally numb by the time they are done with you. That's the system.

I won my appeal under a §2255 petition by summary judgment (Rule 56) back on August 13, 2009 (Case No. 3:08-cv-438), but my old pal, Judge W. Earl Britt, refuses to sign my release. There is no power on earth, from my experience, that can make a federal judge follow the law, do the right thing, or that is willing to remove him. I've tried.

All my efforts to make him recuse himself or have him removed have been derailed by his associate judges on the Fourth Circuit Court of Appeals where he serves as an alternate from time to time. The first three complaints (any of which demanded his removal under law), were handled by his friend, Judge Karen Williams, who acknowledged the bias in her opinion, but ruled in her peer's favor anyway, in violation of Canon 2 of the Judicial Code of Conduct and Supreme Court case law (<u>Berger v. United States</u>, 255 US 22, 41 S.Ct. 230, 65 L Ed 481.

Judge Williams left the bench soon thereafter due to her disability (Alzheimer's disease), but the Court refuses to review the opinion she gave during that period of incapacity, which was itself bizarre and evidence of dysfunction. Worse, it was in violation of law and ethics in protection of a peer.

Her replacement, Judge William B. Traxler, Jr. (a former prosecutor and District Court judge himself), has taken up the protection of Judge W. Earl Britt, outside of decided law, and refuses to remove him as well. I was not even allowed to see the unpublished opinion last year. Thanks only to North Carolina Congresswoman Virginia Foxx, and the Office of the Court Administrator in Washington, was I able to get a copy this year (2010).

Stymied by the lower courts, Justice Ruth Bader Ginsburg allowed me to file a habeas corpus petition to the Supreme Court in December of 2008 (08-8285) under 28 U.S.C. §2241. It was then scheduled for review on January 20, 2009, while she was on medical leave due to pancreatic surgery. Without my champion there, the Robert's Court dismissed it without review.

I sued both David B. Freedman and the "billing-crew" of Helms Mullis Wicker/McGuire Woods, for malpractice and negligence back home in North Carolina. Both the Davie County and Mecklenburg County courts dismissed the respective cases against the attorneys before "discovery" was ever allowed, which is against the law under Rule 56, but they did it anyway to protect them. That again, is the system.

I appealed the illegal dismissal in <u>Woltz v. Freedman</u>, to the North Carolina Court of Appeals last year (2009), but they dismissed it without reason or even advising me as Plaintiff, Freedman as defendant, or the lower court of it, to prevent challenge within the allowed time period.

The dismissal at both lower court and appellate levels were outside the law, the North Carolina Constitution, and the Untied States Constitution, but what's a little corruption and unlawful conduct to protect a fellow "officer of the court" and peer from the disinfectant of sunlight and public scrutiny? That again, is the system.

I've appealed the unlawful decision (and act) to the Supreme Court of North Carolina, and will know soon if the corruption goes that high as well. I'll keep going until access to the court, as required by law and constitution, is allowed me.

The other case against the McGuire Woods "billing crew" is on appeal under Rule 59 in Mecklenburg County. The court there denied me discovery, while allowing McGuire Woods a hearing without notice (violation 1), before a judge who would not give his name (violation 2), and a deposition without notice (violation 3), before dismissing it in (violation 4) of Rule 56. The judge, Gentry Caudill (I later learned from an order he signed), had broken law, rule and Code of Professional Conduct in service to his peers with the first three violations, and I submitted a complaint to the Judicial Commission, which ruled that while they were not condoning his (illegal) conduct, they were not going to taken any action! That again, is the system.

My complaint to the North Carolina Bar was equally outrageous in subterfuge by the supposed "protectors" of the public, after an attorney at McGuire Woods had called to threaten my brother, Jim, to pay their post-termination bills, or they would sue him. In the conversation back in August of 2008, the attorney (who is married to my cousin), claimed that the State Bar had already confirmed it would rule in their favor on my complaint. That was about August 10th, by the way.

The file didn't even reach the State Bar until September 3rd, yet its chairman, James Fox, had already decided how he would rule on it and assured his pals they were "covered".

The rubber stamp committee didn't meet until the end of September, though McGuire Woods had been advised how they would decide before the report was even filed or reviewed, in early August.

When I complained about this chicanery on the part of the Chairman himself, all he did was recuse himself for a "previously undisclosed conflict" and order his underling to dismiss it. Robert A Wicker (as in Helms, Mulliss, Wicker) was a past president, and that's the system.

But I had so much stirred up by then that Judge Britt decided I needed a vacation, so he pulled me out of federal prison on a writ of no purpose, and put me on "diesel therapy" for two tours around the U.S. Twice I was ridden around the country to prevent access to court and law, but after 5 months on the road and my second pass through Georgia (via Oklahoma and New York), I filed a habeas corpus petition on the back of the inmate handbook cover down in some private prison in Ocilla, Georgia, using a golf pencil. They wouldn't let me have paper or pen, and I had to trade by food tray for an envelope and stamp, but it got out to the court up here in Beckley, West Virginia, and 10 days later I was back in prison (via Chickasha, Oklahoma!).

And this appears to be where I might get justice at long last. Out of desperation, I filed yet another appeal with the U.S. District Court in Beckley. It has been taken from the previous judge who was just sitting on it, by Honorable Irene C. Berger. She was recently confirmed by the Senate and is by all reports an honest and ethical judge. That would certainly be a change from what I've dealt with thus far. Perhaps it will get me out of Judge Britt's field of influence at any rate, and an honest and impartial tribunal can take a look at what these folks have done.

Thanks to my dear brother, Jim, who has stuck by me through all of this, we now also have a former federal magistrate judge, Arthur P. Strickland, of Strickland, Diviney & Strelka in Roanoke, Virginia, investigating the whole sordid mess. I think I can say on his behalf that he is appalled. He's upset enough by what he has seen that he has allowed his staff to assist me in getting this book edited and published. Were it not for Art and his efficient legal assistant, Patty Ballard, you would not be reading these words right now.

The beautiful cover, artwork within, and publishing arrangements are to the credit of a dear friend I met in here, Dr. Larry Joel of Louisville, Kentucky, who suffered a wrongful prosecution and conviction of his own. His son, Cody, and his classmates at the Savannah School of Design in Savannah, Georgia, have pitched in and I'm forever grateful to them all. Another former federal prisoner and friend, Steven Cullinane of Salt Lake City, Utah, pitched in with the editing and effort as well. He has served as my critic for some years now.

All I can tell you is that the people Uncle Sam puts in his prisons are a far higher caliber of folks for the most part than those who do the putting.

Art Strickland has also contacted Supreme Court Justice, Sonia Maria Sotomayor, and forwarded my latest Supreme Court appeal to her for review, after the clerks sent it back (twice) for silly reasons like paper size, which I can't comply with from prison (by design), and font size, which this old typewriter doesn't have. It is still under her review as a §2241 motion. I am being held unconstitutionally after winning my appeal last year in August (2009), and so Justice Sotomayor has the power to order my release.

That, again, is the system, but I am hopeful now between Judge Irene Berger and Justice Sotomayor that justice may yet come.

Justice has been denied me at every level; state, circuit, and federal, by design. That's how the United States became the largest and worst in terms of imprisoning its own people in the entire history of mankind. No tyrant, dictator or "evil empire" has ever come close, and it is not by accident, or that we are evil people. It is by design. That is the system, and relief from injustice after it has been done is extraordinarily rare.

As long as corrupt judges cannot be forced to follow law or be removed for breaking it, and prosecutors can falsely charge and convict the citizenry without penalty to themselves for so doing, it will continue to get worse. You can count on it.

That is where <u>We the People</u> need to force change. That is the battleground. We need to get the genie of over powerful and corrupt federal government out of our lives and back in the bottle. We need to elect members of Congress who will abide by the United States Constitution rather than trash it, and discipline its appointees who fail to follow it. Judges such as W. Earl Britt must be removed from the bench and prosecutors such as AUSA Martens penalized for their crimes.

That is my mission. I have become an enemy of the state, to quote old Henry David Thoreau once more. Not an enemy of my nation and its people, whom I love, but an enemy of those who have so wantonly destroyed our liberty and republic, through greed and a lust for power.

And I will not rest until they no longer have a place in government.

CPSIA information can be obtained at www.ICGtesting.com
Printed in the USA
LVOW131626140513

333783LV00002B/308/P